A SUDDEN LIGHT

ALSO BY GARTH STEIN

The Art of Racing in the Rain

How Evan Broke His Head and Other Secrets

Raven Stole the Moon

GARTH STEIN

A SUDDEN LIGHT

**SIMON &
SCHUSTER**

London · New York · Sydney · Toronto · New Delhi

A CBS COMPANY

First published in the USA by Simon & Schuster Inc., 2014
This edition first published in Great Britain by Simon & Schuster UK Ltd, 2014
A CBS COMPANY

1 3 5 7 9 10 8 6 4 2

Simon & Schuster UK Ltd
1st Floor
222 Gray's Inn Road
London WC1X 8HB

www.simonandschuster.co.uk

Simon & Schuster Australia, Sydney
Simon & Schuster India, New Delhi

A CIP catalogue record for this book
is available from the British Library

HB ISBN: 978-0-85720-575-9
TPB ISBN: 978-0-85720-576-6
EBOOK ISBN: 978-0-85720-578-0

Printed and bound by CPI Group (UK) Ltd, Croydon, CR0 4YY

for my dead father

We do not see things the way they are,
we see them as we are.

—ANAÏS NIN

CONTENTS

RIDDELL FAMILY—1990

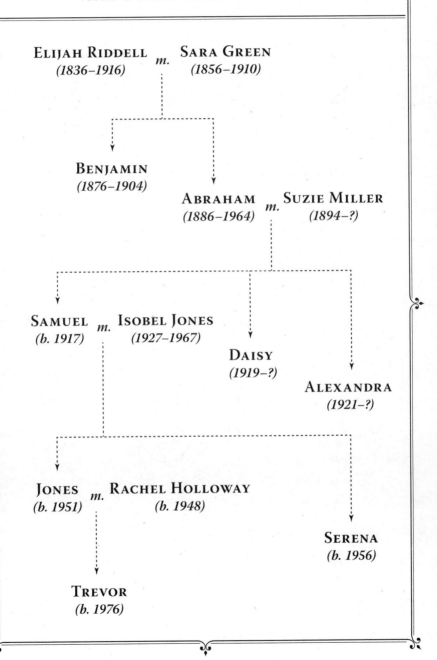

ELIJAH RIDDELL *m.* **SARA GREEN**
(1836–1916) *(1856–1910)*

BENJAMIN
(1876–1904)

ABRAHAM *m.* **SUZIE MILLER**
(1886–1964) *(1894–?)*

SAMUEL *m.* **ISOBEL JONES**
(b. 1917) *(1927–1967)*

DAISY
(1919–?)

ALEXANDRA
(1921–?)

JONES *m.* **RACHEL HOLLOWAY**
(b. 1951) *(b. 1948)*

SERENA
(b. 1956)

TREVOR
(b. 1976)

A SUDDEN LIGHT

THE CURSE

Growing up in rural Connecticut, I had been told the name Riddell meant something to people in the Northwest. My paternal great-great-grandfather was someone of significance, my mother explained to me. Elijah Riddell had accumulated a tremendous fortune in the timber industry, a fortune that was later lost by those who succeeded him. My forefathers had literally changed the face of America—with axes and two-man saws and diesel donkeys to buck the fallen, with mills to pulp the corpses and scatter the ashes, they carved out a place in history for us all. And that place, I was told, was cursed.

My mother, who was born of English peasant stock on the peninsula of Cornwall, made something of herself by following her passion for the written word, eventually writing the dissertation that would earn her a Ph.D. in comparative literature from Harvard University and becoming the first in her family to receive an advanced degree. Though she never did anything of note with her brilliance, she did carry it around with her like a seed bag, sprinkling handfuls of it on what she deemed fertile soil. She spent much time quoting literature to me when I was young, thus sparking my own avid reading habits. So the theme of the Ancient Mariner and his story, as told by the poet and philosopher Samuel Taylor Coleridge—and how the Mariner's story was emblematic of my family's history—was something I had heard often before my fourteenth birthday.

The curse. When one destroys something of beauty and nature—as did the Mariner, who shot the kindly albatross that led his ship out of the perilous Antarctic seas—one will be punished. Cursed. My mother told me this; my father nodded when she did. Punishment will rain down upon the offender and the family of the offender, I was told, until the debt is settled.

The debt owed by my family has been paid, and then some. My mother believes our family's story was settled with that debt—she has always maintained an unyielding faith in the cathartic power of denouement—which is why she has chosen to go for a walk this morning, rather than stay with us to hear me tell our story again. But I disagree with my mother: there is no tidy end to any story, as much as we might hope. Stories continue in all directions to include even the retelling of the stories themselves, as legend is informed by interpretation, and interpretation is informed by time. And so I tell my story to you, as the Mariner told his: he, standing outside the wedding party, snatching at a passing wrist, paralyzing his victim with his gaze; I, standing with my family at the edge of this immortal forest.

I tell this story because telling this story is what I must do.

Twenty-some years ago, before technology changed the world and terrorism struck fear into the hearts of all citizens. Before boys in trench coats stalked and murdered classrooms full of innocent children in schools across this fair land. Before the oceans were thick with oil slicks and the government ceased to govern and Bill Gates set out to love the world to death and hurricanes became powerful enough to stagger entire cities and toxic children were drugged into oblivion to drive up the profits of Big Pharma, and genetically modified foodstuffs were forced upon us without us knowing we needed to care. Before smoking marijuana at gay marriages became passé—before gay people became, eh, just like anyone else, and weed became, eh, just another source of tax revenue. This was even before another famous Bill, the one surnamed Clinton, became famous for his choice of cigars. It seems like ages ago, looking back on it. No smartphones. No On Demand. Nary an iPad in sight.

So long ago. Yes. This story begins in 1990.

On a hot July day in Seattle, a sickly pea green rental car drives from Sea-Tac airport northward on Interstate 5, through the sprawl of neighborhoods hidden by hills, tucked away behind bridges and bodies of water. Its passengers, a father and a son, don't speak to each other. The boy is nearly fourteen, and he is unhappy. Unhappy with being displaced from his childhood home and forced on an unwanted road trip. Unhappy with his mother for not being with him. Unhappy with his father for simply being. So he doesn't speak; he concentrates on Pink Floyd's *The Wall*, which he listens to intently through the headphones of his Walkman.

His father looks over at him frequently, nervously. He seems to crave the boy's approval, which the boy will not give. As they approach the city from the south, the boy glances up and notices the Space Needle, that ubiquitous and baffling Seattle icon. He winces at the irrelevance of the monument—who on earth would build such a thing, and what kind of citizenry would *keep* it?—and lowers his eyes again to his shoes, which are far more interesting to him.

He doesn't notice as they drive through the city, but drive through the city they do. They emerge on a high bridge.

"Don't you want to see this?" the father says, finally, desperately, tapping the boy's shoulder and indicating the glory of Seattle all around them.

The boy lifts his eyes and looks around. Bridges, lakes, bland buildings, radio towers, floatplanes, mountains, trees. He's seen it.

"No," he says and returns his focus to his music. The voices chant at him: *Tear down the wall. Tear down the wall.*

And so my story for you begins.

1

THE NORTH ESTATE

When we exited the freeway at the northern city limit, I remember being disappointed at plunging into typical American suburbia. A House of Fabrics and a Las Margaritas Mexican Restaurant. Cliff's Card Room, Gene's IGA, an ARCO station, a plumbing supplier. It was worse than I could have imagined. We crossed a bleak avenue at an intersection with far too many cars waiting to turn left on a green arrow. But then the street narrowed to two lanes instead of four, and the trees began to lean over the road, blocking the sky. I took note of the transformation. I clicked off my Walkman as my father turned our car onto a still smaller road and guided us down a drive; soon we reached a guard booth with a gate. My father rolled down his window; the door of the wooden booth slid open and a uniformed guard stepped out. He was an old guy and soft, and didn't look like he could stop a full-out assault if someone wanted to lay siege to The North Estate, which he was evidently paid to defend.

"Who are you visiting?" the guard asked cheerfully.

"Not visiting," my father said. "Coming home."

The old guy cocked his head, and then realization swept over his face. "I'll be good goddamned," he said. "Jones Riddell."

"Val," my father said. "I can't believe they still have you working the gate."

"They tried to retire me a few years ago, but I couldn't stand being alone all day so they took me back."

Both men fell silent, and I remember feeling a nearly overwhelming urge to blurt out the blatantly obvious question: *How is sitting in a guard booth by yourself all day not the same as being alone?*

"How long has it been, Jones? A long time."

"Twenty-three years."

"Twenty-three years. Your mother was a fine woman."

"Indeed she was."

"A real tragedy."

Val nodded to himself and then smacked the roof of the car and straightened with a hitch of his pants. He walked to the old wooden gate and pulled a counterweight; the arm arced upward, clearing the path. As we eased by, Val waved. "Welcome home," he called out.

What tragedy? The death of my grandmother was a taboo subject. I'd tried asking about her before and it didn't work; my father wouldn't talk about it. I'd become convinced that my father would never talk about it.

As we drove away from the guard booth, the world changed as if we had been teleported into a medieval forest. We snaked through ravines and past driveways leading to houses I could barely see because they were set so far back and a million trees stood between the houses and the road. Evergreen trees: cedars and spruce, firs and pines. Deciduous trees: oaks and birches, maples and madrona, that peculiar Northwest species with its red peeling bark. Deeper and deeper we drove into the forest; the house markers grew less frequent, the drives became more grand, gates began to block access, jagged stone walls ran alongside the road. As we continued, it felt like we were going further back in time. The winding lane withered into a pockmarked and pothole-riddled gravel path that crunched under our tires like the brittle bones of the dead, and then we got to the end of the main road. To the side of the road was a broken iron gate, laid off its hinges long ago by grounds workers long gone, and I knew we had arrived at our destination because there was nowhere else to go.

We crossed the threshold of the property and continued along the winding driveway, which dipped down into a cool ravine before rising quickly to a crest that revealed a broad clearing on a bluff overlooking Puget Sound. My father pulled the car to a stop on the drive, and I found myself speechless. Not out of protest; no. But because I was stunned into silence by the sight of Riddell House.

My father had told me about it, the place of his father's birth and home to two generations before that. He'd described in vague, sketchy terms the house built by his great-grandfather nearly a century ago. But he'd only outlined the deficits of the house. It was falling down, he told me. It's practically condemned, he said. We're only going there to put it out of its misery, knock it down, sell off the land, and be done with it. But he didn't tell me the whole story, apparently, because Riddell House was not what he'd described. I was expecting a rickety old shack, hardly worth the time to glance at. What I saw was not a shack.

My father climbed out of the car; I followed and stood next to him at the edge of the drive. Across a vast field of dry grass loomed a massive structure made of logs and bricks and stones, crowned with a roof of heavy cedar shakes accented by green copper downspouts and flashing. The house was circumscribed by a veranda on both the first and the second of the three floors. The drive swept past a grand front stairway and looped around to meet up with itself again, while a spur split off and disappeared behind the house. I quickly counted a dozen chimneys, though I was sure there were more; I estimated at least a hundred windows, though I didn't take the time to count. The house appeared squat from our perspective, as if it were hunkering down to the earth. The pillars that encircled it and made up much of its exterior walls were tree trunks. Fully grown, giant trees. Stripped of their limbs and clad in their native bark. Each one, a perfect specimen. The tree pillars stood vertically, side by side—the tallest of them fifty feet, by my estimation, at the roof's peak—a regiment of silent, glaring giants.

Riddell House.

I took a deep breath and inhaled the breeze: shellfish and seaweed and mud. It smelled like low tide when I was a kid and my parents would take me out to Mystic, Connecticut, for the day. Littleneck clams and rock crab and seaweed. The wind blowing, and me, fighting against the flapping paper nest that held my fries in the plastic basket. My father smiling at my mother with soft eyes, and then leaning in to kiss her. My mother kissing back. And me, finally retrieving a fry, and thinking it was the best fry in the world.

The things we remember.

To the west, Puget Sound sprawled out between us and the trees and wilderness of the Kitsap Peninsula and the curtain of mountains beyond that, rising blue into their jagged peaks.

"First objective completed," my father said. "Locate and identify Riddell House."

My relationship with my father at that point in my life wasn't horrible, but it was pretty superficial. It was based on things that weren't, rather than things that were. We didn't simply go to the store or clean the gutters; we executed "missions." We used code words. We went into "stealth mode," or did something "commando-style." His big line was "we're in the acquisition and development phase." Like we had to create an artifice around everything. An ironic layer. We wrapped a protective coating of self-consciousness around the things we did, and, as a result, sincerity was almost entirely lacking. We were going to buy eggs at the store. But not really. We were embarking on Project Ovum, which entailed executing a series of missions that concerned national security. When I was little, I thought it was cool; I didn't think it was cool when I was verging on fourteen. Because I began to realize it wasn't a kid's game for my father; it was how he lived his life.

I stretched and rolled my head around on my shoulders. It felt good to be out of the car and in the hot sun. I watched the breeze sweep across the meadow and bend the long grasses toward me with an invisible hand. The breeze reached me, swirled around, and cooled my neck.

"I don't get it," I said. "It looks fine to me. Why are we tearing it down?"

My father looked at me for a moment.

"It's rotten" was all he said, and he motioned for me to return to the car.

We drove the final stretch of gravel drive that sliced across the field like a gray scar; when the car stopped, a cloud of dust swallowed us whole for a moment. When it cleared, we got out to examine the monolithic house, which, from up close, soared into the sky and blotted out all else. The heft of it was powerful; the trees that made up its walls were immense. Maybe it was the long flight and the long drive; maybe it was feeling like I was on solid ground for the first time after our journey— but I felt almost overcome with emotion. I didn't cry, but I had that precrying feeling, and I wondered at it. I wondered why I felt something so visceral. I felt somehow inspired.

"It's rotten," my father repeated.

Why should my father insist on such a thing? I looked over at him; he shook his head pitifully. I looked back at the house and tried to see it through his eyes: the brick foundation was brittle; mortar between the bricks had flaked away in places and holes penetrated into the darkness. The flower beds were unkempt; ivy snaked up the log pillars, heavy and tenacious, glued to the wood with pale tentacles. We mounted the steps, and I noticed the warped planks of the porch. The windows were composed of small panes of rippled glass, distorted, full of imperfections. Many of the panes were cracked, and some of them had been broken out and replaced by plywood. My father rapped his knuckles on one of the pillars and frowned at the hollowness of the sound. I heard it, too. It sounded dead.

My father picked at the chinking with his fingernail; the dry mortar scraped off, turned to dust, and was gone. We both saw the paint on the window frames, which peeled off in long, jagged strips, and we saw the cracks between the window frames and the cedar shakes. Riddell House was, indeed, rotten.

"Would it pass inspection?" I asked.

"You mean by a person who wasn't in a coma?" my father responded.

He knocked at the door. He tried the latch. He knocked again: nothing.

"I told Serena what time we were getting in."

He reached up and felt along the top of the doorframe; he produced a key.

"Some things never change," he said, and he slipped the key into the lock. The front door opened.

I remember feeling pulled in by the magnetism of the place as I stepped into the entry hall. It was like a time capsule, recently defrosted from the center of a giant glacier. A fully intact world from turn-of-the-century Seattle; a museum. A dusty, faded, moth-eaten museum.

It was a world that smelled of decay, heavy with moist, thick air, which floated in the rooms like an invisible fog. The interior was constructed of fine wood, in contrast to the unmilled trees of the facade. Dark wood with inlays and tight grain and chocolate stain. Oriental rugs in all the rooms and a grandfather clock that was not tick-tocking, its hands poised at six-fifteen. The foyer soared upward into an atrium. A hallway opposite the front door disappeared into the darkness, and a wide staircase climbed up to a second-floor balcony. I stepped into the room to my right and looked around. The furniture was plush and overstuffed; the rugs and walls and ceiling were dark and somber. Iron lions, sitting up on their haunches with their claws bared, guarded a central fireplace. On the wall next to the fireplace hung a painting nearly eight feet tall, depicting a well-dressed man with wild silver hair and a cane. He was looking directly at me, and he held out his hand in such an aggressively welcoming gesture that I was startled.

"Your great-great-grandfather," my father said, standing behind me. "Elijah Riddell."

"Why'd he put a painting of himself in his own house?" I asked.

"That's what rich people do."

"Rich people are weird."

"Maybe she's in the kitchen," my father said, starting off toward the back of the house.

I wanted to stay and explore the rooms, but I was intimidated by it all. The house began to feel alive, almost, and breathing—a thought disturbing enough to make me follow my father toward the kitchen rather than linger by myself.

We walked past a dining room with a table nearly twenty-five feet long, surrounded by dozens of chairs, then a dark room with floor-to-ceiling books and stained-glass windows. Eventually we arrived in the kitchen, which I initially judged to be larger than our entire house in Connecticut. To one side of the kitchen was a cooking area with a large butcher block table worn smooth by decades of chopping, a bread oven, and a giant cast-iron stove beneath an expansive copper exhaust hood. Opposite the stove was a long wooden table with a quirky assortment of wooden chairs, an entertainment area of a sort, with a couple of easy chairs and a small sofa and a new TV on an old TV cart. On another wall was a stone walk-in fireplace outfitted with long hooks, which, my father explained, were used for cooking cauldrons of stew in the old days. He pointed out the rotisserie brackets, too, which were used for sides of lamb and slabs of beef.

"To feed the armies?" I asked, but he ignored my comment.

"This place was built before electricity," my father said. "There was no gas supply. The whole area was wilderness when Elijah built his estate. Everything in this house was coal fired; I'll show you the basement; it's a pretty fascinating place. At some point someone put in a cutting-edge system where they used calcium carbide and water to produce acetylene to power an electrical generator—"

"How do you know all this?" I asked.

"I thought it was cool when I was a kid. I can show you the system. Anyway, they had electricity up here before anyone else did. Long before The North Estate was annexed into the city and they brought up municipal electricity and gas."

"Is that where our inheritance went? Developing a cutting-edge electrical system?"

"You know," he said, "at some point you're going to realize that being a smart-ass isn't as much about being smart as it is about being an ass."

"That's good," I said. "Did you read that in a fortune cookie?"

"Probably."

I smiled for the first time on our ridiculous journey. Part of it was my father's joke. Part of it was my father, himself.

I mean, he looked ridiculous. He looked like Shaggy from *Scooby-Doo!* He was wearing the same old khakis he always wore and a white T-shirt and boating shoes—and he traveled like that! He'd gotten on an airplane and flown across the country looking like that! When my grandmother and grandfather on my mother's side would visit from England, they would wear formal clothes to fly. My grandmother would wear pearls and a fancy dress, and I once asked my grandfather why they did that and he said, "If we crash and die, we want to die in our best clothes." Now *that's* respect for the system.

Jones Riddell—my father—was sporting a wiry beard that was too long and gray, and the mustache covered his upper lip, which drove my mother crazy—but she never said anything. She never made him change. I knew she let him be all the things she disliked so much so she could continue disliking him. The hair on his head was too long and his face was too tan and was getting wrinkled because he spent so much time outside in the sun working on his boats. My mother didn't make him wear sunscreen because she had given up. If I walked out to the road to get the newspaper from the box, my mother made me put on sunscreen, but not my dad. She had given up on him altogether.

We stood awkwardly in the kitchen of the empty house. I glanced out the bay window that faced north to the meadow and saw a woman riding a bicycle, looking like she had been plucked from an old-fashioned movie. She rode an antique-style bicycle, with baskets attached to a platform extending over the rear wheel. The baskets were full of groceries overflowing from paper bags. The woman, who was youthful and lithe, wore a long dress that fluttered coquettishly over her tall boots, and somehow—miraculously—never got caught up in the chain. Her long auburn hair was held by a ribbon tied low near the nape of her neck, and she held her face slightly raised toward the sky, as if to greet the sun. I pointed to her and my father noticed.

"There she is," he said as the woman cruised up the drive.

She spotted our car parked in front of the house and looked to the bay window and must have seen us inside because she smiled and waved. She rode up to the back of the house and disappeared from view; a few seconds later, she entered the kitchen. Her cheeks were flushed and she was out of breath. Her eyes were bright and smiling and, I noticed, locked on my father. She rested one hand below her neck and the other on her hip. Her dress was sleeveless, revealing her toned arms, and it fit tight around her waist, showing off her womanly aspect in a way I had only seen in movies and on TV.

I was quite taken with her. When my father said I was going to meet my aunt, who lived with my grandfather, I assumed she'd be wearing mom-jeans and have jowly arms and sagging elbow skin and a couple of chins. I figured she'd be nice and all, but old-lady nice, with a hairdo that ladies get at the salon, fixed in one place and glued to stay that way for a week without moving. I didn't think my aunt would actually be *hot*.

"Brother Jones," she said, luxuriating in the words. She didn't take notice of me at all. "You've come to save us."

My father was flustered.

"Serena," he said, trying to snap himself out of it. "You look . . ."

"I look?" Serena prompted playfully.

"You look grown-up."

"Oh, please. You can do better than that!"

"You look beautiful."

"That's better," she said with a smile.

She stepped to my father and embraced him in a way that made me uncomfortable. I had always thought of hugs in boxing terms. There's the clinch and then the break. Usually the boxers break on their own, but if they hang on too long, the referee has to separate them. In this case, I realized I would have to be the referee because the clinch was lasting way longer than it should have, so I cleared my throat deliberately. Serena released my father, but as she pulled away, she said, "You really have to shave that awful beard," which I found amusing, not only because it was true but because it was like when one boxer takes a swipe at the other after the referee separates them. You're not allowed to sucker punch your opponent on the break; you have to wait for the ref to signal fight-on.

"You must be Trevor," she said, whirling toward me and swallowing me entirely. There was no other way to describe it. I was paralyzed.

"Give Aunt Serena a kiss," my father said.

Serena smiled at my awkwardness. I couldn't stop staring at the hollow where her throat met her collarbone.

"A handshake will suffice for now," Serena said, holding out her hand. "We'll save our kisses for later, okay?"

"I'll take a kiss," I managed to squeak, and she laughed. She leaned in and gave me a peck on the cheek, and I could smell something good, a whiff of something citrusy and fresh.

"Aren't you sweet?" she said.

"Yes, ma'am," I said.

"I am not a ma'am, and I hope to never be one. I'm Aunt Serena, if you insist on formality, though I wish you wouldn't. Simply Serena will do."

"Yes, Simply Serena," I said, eliciting a grin from her.

"Cheeky monkey," she said, and she looked me over carefully like I was on the sale rack at Macy's. "He has your eyes, Jones. Not in color: the coloring must be from Rachel. But in shape. He's definitely a Riddell."

"He's definitely a Riddell," my father agreed.

"But I'm being selfish! You must be starving. I've never been on an airplane myself, but the movies say how awful the food is. You must let me make you something to eat. Have you had lunch? Even a snack to hold you over until dinner."

Without waiting for an answer, she rushed outside.

"Help her," my father prompted, so I followed her and helped with her shopping bags.

Serena made sandwiches because we hadn't had any lunch: a freshly roasted turkey waited for us in the refrigerator. When we had finished, Serena took us upstairs and showed us our rooms, which were at opposite ends of a long hallway.

"I thought you'd like some privacy," she said to me as she led me down the hallway after we'd left my father in his room at the front of the house. "Plus, it's cooler near the back of the house. I put your father in his old bedroom so it would feel familiar. But it's very hot in the afternoon sun and we don't have air-conditioning. I think you'll be happier here."

She showed me to a room that was empty except for a bed, a dresser, an oscillating fan, a small desk, and a rocking chair; the walls and the floor were bare.

"Your father told me you want to be a writer when you grow up," she said. "That's an admirable profession. I've always admired writers. I moved this desk in for you. Do you need pens or paper?"

"I have my notebooks," I said.

"Oh, nice," she said with a satisfied smile. "It's a little rustic here, but it's very peaceful. Please make yourself at home. I know you're tired after your trip, so I'll leave you alone to take a nap. Dinner will be at seven downstairs. You'll get to meet Grandpa Samuel. Won't that be a treat?"

"Do you have a job?" I asked her.

She seemed startled by the question, and I felt embarrassed for wanting to know more about her.

"Of course I have a job. Someone's got to put food on the table, and Daddy certainly isn't going to do it."

"What do you do?"

"I work for a real estate developer. I'm sure it would seem quite boring to a young man like you: a writer! Steeped in the world of letters! Well, it's important that we all have our goals, though some may be more modest than others."

She left me alone, then, as promised. But I didn't take a nap; naps made me nauseous. And, besides, I wanted to figure out Serena. What adult has never been on an airplane? My family was practically poor—well, we were *actually* poor at the time, but before that we were only practically poor—and I had been on an airplane a bunch of times.

I unpacked my bag into the dresser. I paced around in circles for a while because it was hot and I was tired. Finally, I lay back on the bed, laced my fingers behind my head, stared at the ceiling, and listened to the fan making its whirring noise, tipping back and forth on the floor.

I must have fallen asleep for a moment, because I was startled awake by the sound of someone's voice, or so I thought. Was it my father? There was no one in my room, and the rest of the house was quiet. I got up and looked down the hallway. Nothing. I felt a slight chill; the breeze from the fan brushed my neck and I shivered. I could have sworn I'd heard someone say my name.

And as I closed the door and returned to my bed, I heard a low creaking sound, somewhere deep in the joists of the house, as if the house itself were calling to me.

2

LEAVING NEW HAVEN

I was two days shy of my fourteenth birthday when we arrived at Riddell House in July 1990, but I remember being so sure of things back then. I knew the simple facts. My parents were broke. They'd filed for bankruptcy and lost their house in Connecticut. My father had lost his business—which was part of the reason they went bankrupt in the first place, a cataclysm which caused a great deal of tension in their relationship. I knew that my mother had left my father and me to seek refuge with her family in England. And I knew my father had brought me to a bizarre house in Seattle so I could see my past, my history. I'd never been to Riddell House before; I'd never met my grandfather or my aunt, and my father wanted me to know them. If you're a chicken, at some point your rooster father shows you an egg and says: "That's where you came from." I understood that.

And I also knew that my mother's flight to England and my father's flight to Seattle were more than separate summer vacations. It was the

beginning of their trial separation. Because things had been difficult between my parents for a while. And a couple can only fight with each
other for so long before they cave in each other's souls and collapse.
Even if they once loved each other a lot. Even if they still did.

There were other kids at school in Connecticut whose parents had
gotten divorced. I'd seen it. Kids bragged about the two Christmases
they got. Double the presents. Double the love. But I could see it in their
eyes, even then, when I was a kid. I could see they were bluffing. Hot
Wheels only last so long before the axles get bent and they don't drive
straight. RC cars are only fun until you can't find the controller.

It was a dark time in our lives when the bank foreclosed on our house
and put it up at auction. We went to watch—it must have been a life lesson my parents wanted me to see, but I'm not sure it was a good idea. It
wasn't exciting, like selling a painting or an antique car when they show
it on TV. It was pretty boring. A guy announced a price, someone else
handed him a couple of pieces of paper, and he banged his gavel: our
house was sold to a company in Alabama.

I felt let down. Is that an understatement? I thought my father was
going to save us. I thought we went there so he could trump everyone
with a final bid on our own house. He would raise his hand and the auc-
tioneer would point to him and call for any challengers, of which there
would be none, and our life would be back to normal.

But he didn't save us. We walked away like everyone else did: our
hands stuffed into our empty pockets.

It was very warm, an old-fashioned July heat wave, when we retired
to our motel near the airport in New Haven. It wasn't a horrible motel: it
was clean and had a large parking lot and a pool surrounded by a tall iron
fence. I'd been an only child my whole life, so I knew the drill. I put on
my swim trunks and went to the pool, which didn't entirely suck, even
though some German tourist kids were winging a tennis ball back and
forth in a weird game of chicken ball—three kids, whizzing a saturated
tennis ball around like a missile, skimming it off the water. It was so in-

tense, I was afraid my teeth would get knocked out if the ball hit me. I liked the pool, but I didn't feel safe with the tennis ball flying around like that, so I got out and wrapped myself in extra towels I had taken from the towel cart, and I lay down on a vinyl lounge chair next to my parents, who were in the middle of a tense conversation and so didn't notice me.

"Look at our lives," my mother said to my father. "Everything is gone. You're bitter and angry all the time."

My father said nothing.

"I've been patient, Jones," my mother continued. "I really have been. I've tried to help you. But you have to help yourself. I love you, Jones. On some level, I will always love you. But you have to understand: the moment has been forced to its crisis."

There was a long silence. I was buried in my towels; I don't think they even saw me or knew I was listening. That was how I got most of my information: listening in on conversations not meant for me.

"I feel like an ass when you quote poetry at me," my father said, finally. "Who was that? Coleridge again?"

"Eliot, actually."

My mother shook her head sadly.

"You're not finished with that place," she said. "You've always told me you were finished, but you aren't. You still carry it with you wherever you go."

"It's difficult," he said.

"No. Splitting an atom is difficult. Confronting your past is just something you're meant to do. I've already agreed to let you take Trevor. So take him to where you grew up, to Riddell House. Show him who you are and show him *why* you are. And maybe you'll find yourself there, too. And then . . ."

"And then?"

"And then we'll be better able to see where *we* are."

He nodded, but didn't meet her eyes. She looked at him for a long time until he looked back.

"I hope you know what you're doing," he said as she stood up to leave.

He reached his hand toward her. She hesitated a moment, and then she, too, reached out her hand, but not all the way, just until their fingertips touched. She nodded once, turned, and left.

My father lingered for several minutes, and then he left, too. As he walked away, one of the German kids winged the tennis ball across the pool; it ricocheted off a lounge chair, hit my father in the ribs, and bounced dead at his feet. He paused a moment, then picked up the ball and threw it as hard as he could, harder than I'd ever seen a person throw a ball. It soared out of the pool area, across the parking lot, bounced off a motel balcony railing, and landed in the bushes. And then he walked away.

Later that night, when my mother and I were together in the motel room—my father was in the shower—I asked her again to come with us to Riddell House.

"Oh, Trevor," she said. "You simply don't have the life experience to understand what's going on here."

Maybe I didn't, I remember thinking very clearly. But I understood two things: first, somewhere along the way, my father had gone wrong and my mother stopped loving him; second, I could fix him. I could pull him together. And I believed that, by the end of the summer, if I did my job right, I could deliver my father to my mother as if he were a regular, loving person, like when she first met him.

And then? Well, then it would be up to her to decide where her heart lay. A kid can only do so much.

3

DINNER IS SERVED

I didn't like Riddell House. Every moment it seemed to creak or groan or sigh, like it was alive. Like it was an old tree swaying in the wind, complaining about being pushed about.

I snuck down the stairs—I didn't want to bother my father, in case he was napping. I went out onto the front porch, which was blazingly hot. The sun was smashing the house with its solar rays, and in the glare of a late afternoon haze, I found it difficult to see anything. That's why I didn't notice him until I heard him speak.

"Who are you?" a man asked.

I nearly jumped out of my skin. I raised my hand to shade my eyes and, squinting, looked over to where the voice came from. I saw an old man in a wooden rocking chair. Next to the man, on a side table, was a tray with a couple of glasses and a pitcher of what appeared to be lemonade. The old man looked remarkably like the portrait of Elijah Riddell in the front parlor. He had long stringy white hair, a tired face, and big ears and a big nose. For a second I thought he might *be* Elijah Riddell, but that was impossible. Logic and common sense—and the fact I knew I wasn't in a horror film—told me the man was Grandpa Samuel.

The man I assumed to be my grandfather made a pained face and adjusted himself in his chair. He mopped his brow with a kerchief. He must have been uncomfortably hot, because he was wearing black pants and a black T-shirt, and the sun loves to torture black clothes.

"Who are you?" the man asked again.

"I'm Trevor. You're Samuel, right? My grandfather."

"I suppose I am."

"I'm your son's son. Jones Riddell. I'm his son. Nice to meet you."

I took a few steps toward him, and I noticed the words printed on his T-shirt: GOD was MY COPILOT . . . BUT WE CRASHED IN THE MOUNTAINS AND I HAD TO EAT HIM.

"That's funny," I said.

"What?"

"Your shirt. It's funny."

"Do you know why we named him Jones?"

"It was his mother's maiden name," I replied, thrown off a bit by the non sequitur, but knowing the story and wanting to prove myself. "Your wife, Isobel Jones. And also because it was different. People remember things that are different and she wanted people to remember him."

"Did you know her?" Grandpa Samuel asked.

"No. I'm fourteen. I'll be fourteen the day after tomorrow. She died before I was born."

"She loved him more than anything on this earth," he said, after working his mouth for a bit, lost in thought. "I think he loved her even more than she loved him."

He fell into an old-person silence. Ruminating. Which has always been one of my favorite words. Goats and cows are ruminators: they chew their food and swallow it and then puke it back up into their mouths to chew it some more, and swallow it again, and so on. So if you think about stuff a lot, you're kind of swallowing thoughts and then puking them back up into your mouth to think about them some more. I still like that image, even now.

"I want a shirt like that," I said, finally.

Grandpa Samuel looked down and lifted the front of his shirt as if to read it, then let it go and shrugged.

"Serena buys my clothes."

"Can I have some lemonade?"

He considered my question at length; then he poured a glass and handed it to me. I sat down next to him and we didn't say anything at all. We ruminated. It was very Zen. The sun beat down on us. We drank our lemonade until our glasses were empty, and then he refilled our glasses and we baked in the sun some more. And for a minute I thought that if I were at home—or, rather, if my parents still had a home I could be "at home" in—I would be watching baseball on TV or reading a book, and I would be killing time, but I wouldn't be *ruminating*. And it occurred to me that I might have just met the wisest man on the planet. My grandfather didn't pepper me with questions and then not listen to my answers, like most adults. He didn't entertain me with playful anecdotes. He wasn't concerned with whether or not I was occupying my time in a productive way. He didn't tell me to put on sunscreen. We sat together. Together, we sat. That's all we did for nearly an hour. Until Serena came out onto the porch through the grand double-door front entrance to Riddell House.

I was surprised that I hadn't heard her approach; the house was so creaky, surely I would have heard her walk down the hallway. I looked down and noticed she had removed her boots, which explained the mystery: bare feet make no noise. I meant to look away, but I couldn't. Her feet were perfect. The gentle arc to her arches was graceful and her toes, exquisite. Her toenails were painted an azure blue that was mesmerizing. I tried not to stare, but I obviously failed, for she smiled at me and said, "I always walk about the house au naturel; it's better for one's posture."

"Sure," I said, because I was almost fourteen and I had a boner, and that's what almost-fourteen-year-olds with boners say.

"It's time to wash up for dinner. I see you've met your grandfather. Daddy, were you nice to Trevor?"

"I gave him lemonade," Grandpa Samuel said.

"Did you? Well, isn't that nice of you."

"He likes my shirt."

"Hmm. It's a bit irreverent, don't you think? God and cannibalism in the same thought?"

"I'm not sure it would be cannibalism," I said, hoping to impress Serena with my intellect. "You have to be the same species for it to be called cannibalism. So technically, it wouldn't be considered cannibalism to eat a god. I mean, if there were a god nearby that you could eat."

"Aren't you clever? Clever Trevor."

"Simply Serena," I said without thinking.

"It's okay, you can make fun with me. Don't be shy. Say it louder."

"Simply Serena," I said louder, as she commanded.

"Ha!" Grandpa Samuel shouted and slapped his thigh with a percussive smack. "Simply Serena!" he bellowed and tipped his head back and laughed and laughed.

"How nice that you've bonded with your grandfather at my expense," she said. "Now go wash up, boys," she added after Grandpa Samuel had calmed down.

Grandpa Samuel led the way. When it was my turn to pass through the front door, Serena held it closed a little so I had to stop.

"I know you East Coast people have contempt for us out West," she said with studied sweetness. "You think we're not very bright."

"I don't—"

"Oh, you *do*," she said. "And that's fine with me. Provincialism cuts both ways. But be aware that we uncultured westerners play a little rough sometimes. So, if you get hurt, well, I apologize in advance. I certainly didn't mean it."

She looked at me in a way that scared me a little.

"I'm sorry, Aunt Serena," I said with genuine contrition. "I didn't mean to offend you."

"You didn't, Young Trevor." She beamed at me, and she hugged me to her so I could smell her citrus scent again. "You didn't offend me at all."

Serena. Blue toes and citrus scent and catlike eyes.

The table was piled high with an enormous amount of food, certainly more than four people could eat at one sitting. There was fresh-baked bread that filled the kitchen with a steamy, yeasty smell, and homemade fried chicken, wedges of watermelon, a chopped salad and potato salad, steamed corn on the cob, sugar snap peas, and a pitcher of lemonade with rosemary sprigs in it—one of Serena's specialties.

"Wow," I said.

"Just a little something I threw together."

Grandpa Samuel took his seat. Serena removed a medicine bottle from the cupboard.

"Can you run upstairs and get your father?" she asked me as she took two pills from the container and placed them before Grandpa Samuel. "I told him dinner was ready, but he seems to be lagging."

"Take your medicine," I heard her say as I left the room.

I went upstairs, knocked briefly on my father's door, and then let myself in. My father was sitting on the edge of his bed, curled forward with his face in his hands. He'd changed into clean khakis and he was wearing his boating shoes, because that's all he ever wore unless he wore the one suit he owned, in which case he wore his plain black loafers. But I noticed he was wearing a crisply laundered man-tailored shirt. My mother must have packed that shirt, because my father was a slob and didn't know what a creased sleeve was or why one should have one. He raised his head when I entered the room, and I recoiled comically. My father had shaved his beard. Just like that. Serena made one comment and my father shaved. Which proved my theory that my mother let my father keep his beard so she could feel physically repulsed when she looked at him, and that he never really cared about his beard and would have been happy to shave it off had she said something. My father had no idea he was complicit in his own demise.

He looked years younger without his beard: his skin was pale where the bushy hair had been, yet his cheeks and forehead and ears were tan, creating something of a raccoon effect. Sitting there like that, with his starched white shirt and his hair combed and wet from the shower, he looked like a kid. I felt bad for him. I felt like I'd come to his room to bring him to the grown-up table. Or the gas chamber.

I tried to make a joke out of it, so I said, "Any last words?" and he literally started trembling.

He stood up and took a deep breath, put his arm around my shoulder, and walked us both out into the hall.

"Promise you'll make a lot of jokes at dinner," he said. "Because I feel like I'm going to vomit."

I didn't know anything about my father's relationship with my grandfather. Grandpa Samuel had been so absent from my life up to that point, it was like he was dead. Rarely spoken about. Never spoken to. Not a single photo of him, or anybody else in my father's family, for that matter. It never occurred to me to wonder. But then, my father was a mystery to me as well. We hardly did anything together in those days, and, when we did, we didn't talk a lot. Sometimes he would start to tell me something about his childhood, but then he would stop in the middle of the story, as if he didn't want to remember it. Like he had closed the door on that part of his life and didn't want to open it again.

I helped him down to the kitchen (I really thought his legs would have collapsed if I hadn't been there to help him with the stairs), and Serena and Grandpa Samuel looked up.

"Oh, don't you look nice!" Serena said cheerfully. "I knew there was a face under that tangled mess. Daddy? Look who's here. It's Brother Jones!"

Grandpa Samuel and my father regarded each other cautiously.

"Hello, Dad," my father said.

"Hello, Son," Grandpa Samuel said with a perfunctory nod, not even lifting his eyes.

"I love these warm and fuzzy reunions!" Serena chirped. "Now try not to get all mushy, boys. There's plenty of time to catch up! Sit, Jones. Join us."

We took our seats and food was passed around and nobody said a word. Dead silence. There was gesturing and smiling and nodding, all very polite. There was chewing and swallowing and drinking. Dabbing of napkins to corners of mouths. Otherwise, total silence except for the fan.

Finally, Grandpa Samuel leaned over to me and whispered, "Pass me some of that watermelon." When I handed over the platter, I realized my grandfather didn't have all of his fingers on his left hand. He was missing his entire forefinger, as well as his middle finger above the second knuckle.

"Dickie called to say he got caught up," Serena announced abruptly, indicating the empty place setting I had noticed but was afraid to ask about.

"Who's Dickie?" my father asked.

"My boyfriend, silly," Serena said. "How do you think I survive these lonely nights?"

"I didn't know you had a boyfriend. Is it serious?"

"At my age, Brother Jones, any relationship is serious."

"How old are you?" Grandpa Samuel blurted out, just when I thought he wasn't tracking the conversation.

"That's not a polite question to ask a lady, Daddy. But since you don't remember a thing about my arrival in this world, apparently, I'll tell you. I'm five years younger than Brother Jones, and he is thirty-nine. Can you do the math, Daddy?"

"I can do *math*," Grandpa Samuel said, irritated.

"You have to eat more than watermelon."

I looked over at Grandpa Samuel's plate; it was piled high with watermelon and only watermelon.

"But I *love* watermelon!" Grandpa cried.

I found it difficult to keep from guffawing. Grandpa was like a comic book character. His hands were big and his head was big and his hair was everywhere, and when he said "love," he threw up his arms—and I couldn't help but stare at his missing fingers.

"Do you see?" Serena said to my father and me. "This is what I have to deal with every day. Sometimes he's here, sometimes he isn't. He has to write things down to remember them, and even then—"

"*I love watermelon!*" Grandpa cried, continuing his protest.

Serena made a face at us, showing her exasperation.

"Take some chicken," she said.

"I don't like chicken," he whined. "It has tendons."

"All animals have tendons, Daddy," Serena said. "Tendons and ligaments. Sinews and gut. Fibers and connective tissues. Bones are connective tissue, did you know that, Trevor? I bet you've already learned that in biology class. We think of bones as steel rods in our bodies, but, in fact, they are pliable, entirely flexible organs that serve important functions beyond structural integrity, like producing both red and white blood cells."

We fell silent. All of us seemed stunned by Serena's impromptu lecture on bones. And maybe that was her point. Maybe that was how she dealt with Grandpa Samuel's outbursts about tendons.

"Just as bones must be flexible," she went on, "so we must be flexible in our relationships in order to achieve harmony. We must acknowledge that relationships are dynamic things—always changing—and sometimes they come to an end. You can speak to that, can't you, Brother Jones, with your recent separation from Rachel?"

"It's not actually a separation," he said.

"No? What is it, then? She's in England and you're here. That seems awfully separate to me."

"I mean, *legally* we're not separated," my father said, glancing at me.

"Laws are made to regulate the economy, Brother Jones," Serena said, "not affairs of the heart. Legally or not, you are *separate* from your wife, am I not correct?"

"But they're getting back together," I blurted out, causing Serena to look over at me.

"It's just a break," I confirmed. "It's not forever."

"As I said, relationships are dynamic things," she said with a shrug, suggesting I had proven her point for her. "Please take some chicken, Daddy. You need your protein."

"I don't like chicken—"

"You have to eat something."

"Is this house haunted?" I asked, trying to steer the topic away from tendons.

Serena continued eating for a moment before she replied, "Are you afraid of ghosts?"

"No."

She took more potato salad and then pointed to the platter of fried chicken.

"Chicken," she said to Grandpa Samuel.

"Tendons," he replied, pouting.

"Why do you ask of ghosts, my nephew?"

"Because I heard something. I think I heard a voice."

"A house like this talks to you," Serena said. "It has a lot of things to tell you."

"Like what?"

"Riddell House is nearly a hundred years old," Serena said with a shrug. She picked up her fork and took a bite. "Think of all the people who've walked across this floor. The floor knows them all; I don't. Your grandfather hears dancing at night upstairs in the ballroom. But he suffers from dementia, so no one pays attention to him."

"So Riddell House *is* haunted?"

"It depends on how you define the term 'haunted.'"

"Serena, please stop," my father said.

"Ben is nervous," Grandpa Samuel muttered. He stood up and went to the telephone table, took a pen, and wrote something on a Post-it note. He wrote very deliberately and with much concentration.

"What's he doing?" I whispered to Serena. "Who's Ben?"

"He can't remember anything, so he writes things down on Post-it notes. It's all gibberish; none of it makes sense. They say in the later stages of Alzheimer's disease, your brain resembles a damp sponge. Dwell on that image for a moment or two."

"This is *important*," Grandpa Samuel cried, lifting his face to the ceiling. He finished writing his note and returned to the table.

"Where were we?" Serena asked, rolling her eyes. "Oh, yes. The question of haunting. Jones, haven't you had *the talk* with Trevor?"

"What is *the talk*?" I asked.

"The talk about states of being, states of awareness. We had *the talk* around the dinner table nightly when your father and I were young. Our mother lectured us about it incessantly. I mean, there's so much we *don't* know, how can we consider ourselves to know anything at all? Daddy, I really must insist that you eat some chicken."

Serena picked up a piece of fried chicken with her tongs and placed it on Grandpa Samuel's plate. He recoiled and shoved the thigh off his plate onto the tabletop.

"Is there an entity in this house?" I asked.

"Define 'entity,'" Serena said. "We must use the proper nomenclature. Terminology can be confusing unless we're agreed on the definitions."

"Knock it off, Serena," my father growled. "For real. You're scaring him."

"I think Trevor knows more than you're giving him credit for. He's the one who asked."

Serena stood up and grabbed a box of matches from the counter next to the big, old-fashioned stove. She dropped the box on the table before me and then resumed her seat.

"There are all sorts of hiding places in this house," she said. "When

Riddell House was built there were many things to be afraid of. Not Indians, of course. The Northwest Coast natives were a docile lot, happily trading with each other and white men alike. But there were bandits and thieves who targeted the very rich; they would kidnap and ransom family members when they could. At least that's what Elijah believed, though he was a noted misanthrope, so grains of salt should be taken as necessary. Nevertheless, this house was designed with secret passages and places to hide so Elijah could feel safe—they call them priest holes, a term held over from the Reformation in England, when Catholics would hide their priests from the Protestant establishment. Do you know what they did when they discovered a priest hiding in the walls during the Reformation?"

"What did they do?"

"They hanged him, or they burned him alive. A good hanging has its drama, but there's nothing like the scent of burning flesh lingering in the air to roust a priest or two from his hidey-hole. I'm sure you can imagine."

"*Serena*," my father scolded.

"There's a secret stairway in Riddell House," Serena continued without a pause. "I don't know where. It's a secret, isn't it, Jones? A secret you shared with Mother? I was too young to be allowed in on the secret. There's a hidden stairway, Trevor, and if you find it and strike a match, you will see an apparition in the sudden flash of light. The ghost of Riddell House. But we shouldn't talk about this; it upsets Daddy. Daddy finds talk of spirits very disturbing. You remember the night Daddy took the ax to the stairs, don't you, Brother Jones?"

"I shouldn't have come here," he mumbled, exasperated.

"Perhaps not," Serena agreed. "And yet you're here. You came here with some amount of deliberation. You didn't fall through the floorboards and find yourself at Riddell House. You got on a plane. You checked luggage. You rented a car . . . Daddy, please put your chicken back on your plate and eat it. Eat all of it, tendons included, or else you will weaken, fall, and break your hip. And studies show that once mobility is diminished by a broken hip, life expectancy is greatly decreased."

"I don't like chicken!" Grandpa bellowed. "I don't like chicken! I don't like chicken! I don't like chicken!"

Serena calmly put down her knife and fork.

"This is a very important dinner," she said. "Brother Jones has returned, and he's brought his son along with him. If you cannot be civil, you will excuse yourself."

She didn't say it harshly, but she said it with undeniable clarity.

"I don't like chicken," Grandpa Samuel repeated meekly one last time.

"Then eat vegetables instead. Take some corn, some salad, and some peas."

Grandpa Samuel surveyed the food on the table, his focus darting from bowl to bowl. He seemed overwhelmed by the task set for him.

"May I be excused?" he asked.

"You haven't said a word to Jones."

He worked his jaw and nervously rubbed the stumps of his missing fingers. "At night," he said to me with a whiff of conspiracy, "if you listen carefully, you can hear her dancing."

"That'll be enough of that, Daddy," Serena said sharply. "You know what it does to your blood pressure."

"You can hear footsteps," Grandpa Samuel whispered.

"Daddy!"

He stopped. Serena glared at him, and he didn't dare speak.

"You can hear *who* dancing?" my father asked pointedly.

Grandpa Samuel glanced at Serena; he looked down at his plate.

"It's the rain," he said. "You can hear the rain."

"*Who* can you hear dancing?" my father demanded.

Grandpa Samuel didn't reply. My father looked to Serena, but she ignored him.

"You can read it to him, if you can't remember," Serena said to Grandpa

Samuel after a moment. "Read what you've written. You worked on it so hard."

My grandfather seemed confused; my father, frustrated.

"In your pocket," Serena suggested.

Grandpa Samuel felt his pants pocket. He produced a slip of paper and grew calm. He read the paper to himself. Then he looked at my father.

"I've missed you," he said. He glanced at the paper again. "I regret that it's been so long. I'm happy to see you and to meet Trevor."

He looked down at his paper, and tears filled his eyes but did not overflow.

"Read all of it," Serena said.

"I hope that you can forgive me for my transgressions," Grandpa Samuel read. He quickly folded the paper, returned it to his pocket, and swiped at his eyes with the back of his hand. "My transgressions," he repeated. "It means things I've done wrong."

My father scowled. "Is this for real?" he asked Serena.

"Of course it is."

"May I go to my barn now?" Grandpa Samuel asked. "I'd like to go to my barn."

"You may," Serena replied. "But don't stay late. And turn on the lights so you don't hurt your eyes. Sometimes he forgets to turn on the lights and I find him working in the dark!"

Grandpa Samuel nodded and shuffled out the back door of the kitchen.

"What the hell was that?" my father demanded after Grandpa Samuel had gone.

Serena sighed heavily and got up from the table.

"I'm so sorry," she said, obviously disappointed. "He knows exactly which buttons to push with me. I shouldn't have reacted. I'd hoped our reunion dinner would have been more pleasant."

She gestured to the myriad plates and dishes of food spread across the table.

"A written apology?" my father asked.

"He wanted to apologize to you. He asked me to help him with it. I don't think you fully comprehend the extent of his condition. It's not easy living with him."

She closed her eyes, took a deep breath, and exhaled, swinging her arms in an arc over her head, like a dancer or a yoga instructor.

"Do you like pie?" she asked me with forced cheer. "I have a blackberry cobbler for dessert."

"Yes, please."

"Of course, a cobbler isn't technically a pie," she said, removing a pie tin from the oven and setting it on the counter. "But my cobbler has a biscuit topping I think you'll like. These are last year's berries; it's too early for this year. Tomorrow, I'll show you where they grow and you can keep an eye on them for me. Once they ripen, we have to move quickly or else the birds will get them. Would you like some pie, Brother Jones?"

"No, thanks."

Serena cut a large piece of the cobbler and set it down in front of me. I took a bite and it was crazy good; the filling was bubbling and syrupy and almost too hot.

"Would you like coffee, Jones? More lemonade?"

"Do you have anything harder than lemonade?" he asked darkly.

Serena laughed, opened the lower door of a cabinet, and produced a bottle of brown liquid with a white label. She placed it on the table in front of him, her hand gripping the neck firmly.

"Is this hard enough for you, Brother Jones?"

I snickered at the innuendo. He took the bottle and examined the label; it was Jim Beam.

"It'll do, Sister Serena. It'll do."

Serena took two glasses from the cupboard, and my father poured brown liquid into them while I ate my cobbler and tried not to be noticed. For a moment, Serena and my father sat across from each other, sipping their shots of whiskey and not speaking, and I realized there was a whole world they shared that I had no idea about. None at all.

"I don't like you staring at me," my father said.

"I'm relearning you," Serena replied. "I've realized the memories, the images we keep in our heads, aren't really images at all. They're much more vague. When I think of you, I don't think of your face, I think of your shape. You're faceless in my memory. You move through my memories and I know it's you, but what I picture is without detail."

He shrugged in response.

"If I were a painter," Serena continued, "I would paint people without faces. Or with eyebrows only. Eyebrows and hair and chins. Because that's what we remember. The points. But now that I see you again, I can fill in those details."

"That's an elaborate metaphor," my father said. "Trevor, you should write that down. Clearly, your aunt is the writer you aspire to be."

"Woe be the family of a writer," Serena said. "They will forever bleed in his stories. Isn't that right, Brother Jones?"

"Why do you call him Brother Jones?" I asked.

"It's an artifact from our childhood," Serena said with a chuckle. "It's something we call each other."

"Why?"

"Why?" she echoed wistfully. "Why does the cock crow? Don't ask him; he doesn't know."

Silence again, then Serena said, *"I will return for you."*

My father didn't acknowledge the comment, so I felt I had to. "What does that mean?" I asked.

"It's what your father said when he left. I was eleven years old. Mother had died and Jones was going away. He hugged me tightly in his big, strong, holding arms, and he said: *'I will return for you, Sister Serena. I will return.'* It was poetic; ripped from the pages of a novel. Maybe your memoir, Young Trevor. *I will return for you, Sister Serena.* I've been waiting, and he hasn't returned. Until now."

"Life is complicated," my father said after an uncomfortable pause.

"So I've heard," she said. "And yet some things are not so complex as they initially seem. The fate of this house, for instance."

Again, my father was silent, but he was thinking about something; I could tell.

"What about the fate of this house?" I asked.

"It is both simple and complex at the same time," Serena said. "The goal, of course, is to achieve simplicity; the method may be circuitous."

"Maybe we should table this conversation for the moment," my father said. "I'm not sure Trevor is interested."

"He should be," Serena said. "Trevor, are you interested in your family's legacy? Or would you prefer to turn a deaf ear and leave your fate in the hands of those who may or may not have your best interest in mind?"

"I'm interested," I said.

"You see?" Serena said to my father. "And, anyway, I believe in full disclosure. He's one of the family. I don't think secrets should be kept from children under the pretense it is for their own good. It isn't for their own good; it is for the convenience of the secret keepers. But I suppose that's my own little pet peeve. What do you know already, my nephew?"

"I know we're here because we're broke," I said. "And I know we're here to sell the land. That's all I know."

"It's a start," she said. "I'll tell you the rest as briefly as I can. Elijah, your great-great-grandfather, had two sons, Benjamin and Abraham. Benjamin, tragically, died quite young with no children, leaving Abraham as Elijah's sole heir. When Elijah died, he put this house and property and what was left of his money into a trust for the benefit of Abraham; Abraham could use the house, but it wasn't his. You see, Elijah didn't want Abraham getting control of the property because Abraham wanted to sell it and develop it. Elijah had a vision that when the Riddell family has faded from the earth, this place would be returned to wild and untamed wilderness. He wanted The North Estate to be turned into a park."

"That's weird. Why?"

"He felt it was his moral duty to give back to the earth for all he had taken from it, even if it were but a small, symbolic gesture. Still, laws are laws, and the law of the land is that one can't set up a trust that lasts forever. There's a legal reason for it, called the rule against perpetuities. It's meant to prevent dynasties. Americans hate kings and we hate dynasties. Elijah could stop Abraham from developing the land, but he couldn't stop future heirs from doing what they wanted."

"How do you know all this?" I asked.

"My grandfather Abraham was obsessed with it and made your father and me learn about it. Grandpa Abe wanted more than anything else to develop this land for profit, and Elijah stymied him. Elijah hoped that some future Riddell would uphold his final wish and let this land lie fallow for eternity rather than exploit it. When Grandpa Abe died, the trust was dissolved and the property and holdings were disseminated to Grandpa Samuel to do as he pleased. Thus far, Daddy has adhered to Elijah's final wish and refused to sell the house and land. Since his mental health is rapidly declining—as you can clearly see—it's time to move him into an assisted living facility that can properly care for him. But he won't go because he believes Mother is dancing for him in the ballroom—"

"Wait," my father interrupted. "*That's* who he hears? He hears Mom?"

"No, no, of course not. Mother died a long time ago. He hears the rain on the roof or the mice in the walls. In his dementia, he has conjured the ghost of Mother. It's all in his mind."

My father frowned at her, and she turned her attention back to me.

"It's time for your father and me to take charge of the house and grounds and develop the property so we have the financial wherewithal to care for your grandfather long term, should that be needed. Naturally, as developers, your father and I would also benefit from this transaction."

"Oh," I said, understanding the scheme. "*That's* why we're here."

Serena shrugged obviously.

"Do you know how much this land is worth?" my father blurted. "Millions. Millions upon millions if the subdivision is developed properly. I can't walk away from that. I'll be able to provide for my family, which I haven't been able to do of late, if you haven't noticed our current living situation."

I knew what that meant. It meant he believed my mother would take him back if he had money. I believed it, too. He didn't have to be rich, he just needed enough to buy our house back. Then my mother would love him again. She loved that house, and I did, too. We probably couldn't get our old house back, but we could get one like it.

"You should do it, then," I said to my father. "Do whatever it is that will make Mom love you again. You shaved; that's a good start."

Serena laughed; she leaned over and refilled my father's glass.

"Of course there is the minor obstacle of getting Daddy to grant us power of attorney so we can do what needs to be done," Serena said. "That's your father's job."

"Why don't *you* do it?" I asked her.

"Because I'm the one who stayed behind," she said, smiling at me curiously, as if the answer were obvious to everyone.

She raised her eyebrows, finished what little was left in her glass, and stood up.

"There's a tradition in this house, Trevor," she said. "The one who cooks doesn't clean. Your father started the tradition when Mother first became ill. Before that, she did all the cleaning. Well, before *that*, we had servants, didn't we, Brother Jones? Before Grandpa Abe died and the entire Riddell Empire was dismantled. Remember those days?"

"You had servants?"

"Oh, yes," Serena said. "We had a driver to take us to school in a big black car. And we had a cook and a housekeeper, and there were men who tended the orchard. That was a time, wasn't it, Jones?"

"Is that where our millions of dollars went?"

"No," Serena said, laughing. "Our millions were gone before that. Elijah gave most of his fortune away before he died. Everything except this house. The cynic in me thinks he was trying to buy safe passage for his soul to the afterworld, but I may be unfairly extrapolating. It's an interesting story; maybe one day your father will tell it to you. And then Grandpa Abraham lost his inheritance because some people are losers, and, no matter how they fight it, they will always lose. Your father and I have nothing unless we can sell this house. I ask you, Trevor, where is the justice? Well, no matter. Justice has arrived in the form of Brother Jones, who will fix all things, won't you, dear brother? Oh—"

She went to the telephone table and picked up a thick, blue three-ring binder, which she set down in front of my father.

"Here's some reading material for you, Brother Jones, should you suffer from any insomnia *après voyage*. It's fascinating stuff, and I'm sure you will find it quite compelling. Good night, gentlemen. If you need something, you can find me in the servants' wing, down this hall. Otherwise, I assume you will make yourselves at home."

"Why do you sleep in the servants' wing?" I asked her.

"The inquisitive mind always has another question," she remarked patiently. "It's nice here in the main house now, because it's summer. But it can be so drafty and leaky during the rainy season, which runs from October until June. Daddy and I stay in the servants' wing because it's more comfortable and easier to manage. Anyway, I was able to take today off from work, but tomorrow is a workday for me, so it's time for me to retire."

She yawned sleepily and glided out of the room in a way I could only describe as balletic, taking her beautiful blue toes with her. I looked at my father, who didn't meet my eyes. He swept the binder off the table and set it aside before I could see what was written on the cover.

"Will you tell me the story of Elijah?" I asked.

He poured more Jim Beam, which seemed like a lot. I was concerned Riddell House wasn't the best environment for him.

"Not tonight," he said, downing his shot of whiskey in a gulp.

"When?"

He poured another shot but didn't drink it.

"You must be tired. You can go upstairs; I'll clean this up."

"I'll help you if you tell me. Why did Elijah want this to be a park? And why did Abraham want to develop it so badly?"

"It's natural to want to make money. You can use it to buy food and clothes and cable television—all good things to have."

"So tell me the story."

"I don't know the story," he said with an edge of anger. "I don't know it, and I don't care about it. Now go upstairs and leave me to clean this mess."

I waited for a moment, hoping he would relent. He didn't meet my eyes, but he knew I was still there.

"I'm sorry," he said. "I'm getting a headache. I didn't mean to snap at you."

I left him to clean the kitchen. On my way out, I stopped at the telephone table and swiped the Post-it that had Grandpa Samuel's writing on it. As I walked down the long hallway toward the front door, I read the words he had scratched on the paper: MUIR MTNS CA. The letters were written in caps, and he had gone over each letter several times so they were boldfaced. He must have been pressing down hard when he wrote it because I could feel the indentation on the paper from underneath. But what did it mean? I looked up and met the eyes of Elijah Riddell, who glared at me from the portrait in the parlor. The old man with his white hair and his cane, reaching out his hand as if to pull me into the painting with him.

4

THE MIGHTY ELIJAH

Since 1990, I have devoted much of my free time to researching my family's history, and I have yet to discover an authorized biography of my great-great-grandfather Elijah Riddell. I have no corroborative evidence, but I've constructed a fairly convincing circumstantial case to prove, at least to myself, that Elijah had lieutenants whose job it was to listen for reporters with ambitions—those who might be found sniffing around the mills and yards with questions about Elijah's past in order to advance their own careers. When approached, an author of an accounting of Elijah's personal and business activities would likely be persuaded that continuing with such a project would not suit the best interest of either party, while a cash settlement would be mutually beneficial. The offer, I believe, was made only once. Should it be rebuffed? Well, in those days many tragic accidents happened in the north woods of Minnesota—where Elijah first began to assemble his empire—and often bodies were not recovered until after the spring thaw, and memories rarely lasted through the winter anyway.

This doesn't mean several *unauthorized* biographies weren't written, published on small presses and left to linger in the remote stacks of small-town libraries, or available for fifty cents in the dusty reaches of a St. Paul used bookstore. Over the years, I have come into possession of several of these accountings of Elijah's life, which profile his thoughts and motivations, so that, while much of Elijah's history remains vague, some of it is known. Enough for me to paint a picture of the man, at least.

Judging by the writings I have unearthed, as well as Elijah's private papers, he was a solitary man and a shrewd negotiator. He kept no counsel. He conducted his business in a small building on the site of his first mill in St. Paul, Minnesota, and, from that cold room, he built an empire that was truly impressive, even by American standards. He worked doggedly, never taking a vacation or break, never stopping for illness. He worked six days a week, and, though he observed the Sabbath by conducting no business on Sundays, he worked in his mind every Sunday, making plans and conducting business in his head in order to make up for the lost work on the following Monday, when he would work doubly hard. He lived alone and worked alone, corresponding with his deputies by letter or telegraph. Such was his reclusive nature. But one day, feeling a profound emptiness inside, he stepped out of his shed, looked at the world he had created, and saw that it was empty of people. So he set about to rectify the situation by creating a child.

It was not hard to execute his plan. He had a house built to look like the houses of other wealthy citizens of St. Paul. He had clothes made so he would look like another wealthy citizen. He hosted large parties, to which he invited the other wealthy citizens, and at one of these parties, he selected a woman of satisfactory breeding and intelligence, who was also sturdy enough to withstand the difficult Minnesota winters. Her name was Sara Green. Elijah paid a healthy dowry to her family, married her immediately, and impregnated her. He then packed his things and left for the rich forests of the West Coast. After all, he had an empire to build.

He detailed his departure for the West in a letter to a colleague:

Before I departed, I told my wife I would send for my son when he
was ready. She giggled at me in that flirtatious way I always find annoying, and asked me how I was sure it would be a boy. About certain things, I have no doubt. When my child is born, he will be a boy.
I know this much. His name will be Benjamin, and he will change
this world for the better.

And it was so. Benjamin Riddell was born as his father amassed acres
and acres of Northwest forests.

Elijah returned to St. Paul once a year to check on the status of his
son, Benjamin, who was healthy, strong, terribly intelligent, and precociously wise. Elijah had provided servants and a generous allowance so
mother and son could live quite comfortably in their expensive house.
He never returned to St. Paul for more than a fortnight's stay.

It was ten years later, the records show, in 1886, that Elijah returned
to St. Paul to collect his wife and son, whom he planned to have join
him in Seattle, a town which Elijah deemed acceptable for a woman and
a boy—his previous headquarters of Portland, Oregon, and then Aberdeen, Washington, being too rough-and-tumble, according to him. Sara
Green willfully refused to move westward one inch. In fact, she told him,
rather than move west, she was planning to move east, to New York,
where her family resided. She was tired of the cold and lonely Minnesota life; furthermore, she was tired of her cold and lonely bed. "I was
so incensed by her intimations, I 'warmed her bed' for her on that very
spot," Elijah wrote in his journal. "The following morning, I departed
for Seattle with Benjamin, who chatted without stop as we crossed the
country by train in our private coach."

A year after that, Elijah received a letter from his wife in New York.

She had given birth to their second child, another son, and gave him the name Abraham. Elijah replied by return post that she and Abraham must move to Seattle immediately. She, by return post, flatly refused. And he: a stern warning that if she and her son did not report without delay, she should consider both herself and her son disowned. Thusly, their correspondence ended.

After a few short years in Seattle, Elijah escorted his son Benjamin to Phillips Exeter Academy, where the most promising boys from affluent families were sent. Years later, after Benjamin's death, Elijah recounted their final dinner together. I learned this through his diary, which I found that summer at Riddell House:

> We finished our meal in grand style with a toast of fine port. I told Benjamin I would come for him when he was ready. He looked at me in a striking fashion, with his thick black hair and piercing eyes and a sense of suppleness about him, like a tree bending in the wind so as not to be broken, and I remember thinking he was still a boy, but standing on the precipice of manhood.
>
> "I will be ready, Father," he said.
>
> I nodded and left him in the care of the faculty there. I have always been amused that he did not afford me the chance to seek him out, for he was more able than that. Seven years later, when he had graduated from Yale College a full year before his peers, he delivered himself to my door in Seattle. My longtime manservant, Mr. Thomas, received him.
>
> "Do you have an appointment?" Mr. Thomas asked the forceful young stranger who stood before him on the porch of my city residence on Minor Avenue.
>
> "Tell my father I am ready," Benjamin said.
>
> Mr. Thomas stiffened with recognition.
>
> "Master Benjamin," he said with a deep bow, opening the door wide to reveal me standing in the shadows of the entry hall. "We have been anticipating your arrival."

5

IN THE NIGHT KITCHEN

I remember feeling frustrated and homesick that first night at Riddell House. I had to walk down a long hallway to get to the bathroom, and I resented the fact that Riddell House was so big but had so few bathrooms. I wanted our old house back. It was small, and my bathroom was across the hall, not a football field away. And my parents were within easy reach when I was little and had the occasional nightmare. I missed our house. I missed my mother. I knew I wouldn't be able to fall asleep, so even though it was late and the house was dark, I went downstairs to the kitchen to get a glass of water. I opened the refrigerator door, and in the blue light that spilled across the kitchen floor, I saw someone sitting at the table; my heart jumped before I realized it was my grandfather.

"Serena?" Grandpa Samuel ventured, squinting into the shadows.

"It's me," I said. "You scared me."

"Where's Serena?"

"I don't know. She must be sleeping."

"She usually makes my medicine."

I closed the refrigerator door, and the room returned to darkness. I turned on the lights, revealing Grandpa Samuel, who sat at the table wearing pale sleepy-blue old-fashioned pajamas, with long sleeves and buttons up the front. He reached across and rubbed the stumps of his missing fingers, which was something I noticed that he did a lot, a nervous tic. When he was stressed, he massaged his stumps. I wondered if he felt his fingers still. Phantom digits.

"You don't know how to make it yourself?" I asked.

"Serena makes my medicine."

"What kind of medicine?"

"Sleeping medicine. She makes it for me when I can't sleep. Will you make it for me?"

"Where is it?"

"She keeps it in the cupboard, there," he said, indicating with his hand. "There's a bottle of medicine in there. She puts some milk in it so it doesn't taste bad."

I opened the indicated cupboard door, but there was no medicine that I could see.

"What does it look like?" I asked.

"I don't know. I don't see her do it. It's in a bottle with a white label."

I saw only one bottle in the cupboard: the whiskey Serena and my father were drinking earlier. But it did have a white label.

"This?" I asked, pulling out the bottle of Jim Beam.

"Yes, that's it."

"It's whiskey."

"It's medicine," he said. "It helps me sleep."

"I'll bet," I said. I wasn't sure if it was clever or cruel of Serena to give Grandpa Samuel whiskey to get him to fall asleep. Either way, to misrepresent the booze as medicine was dubious. Still, I felt I had to abide by the customs of Riddell House, so I set the bottle on the counter and retrieved a glass from a second cupboard.

"Mix one part medicine with two parts milk," Grandpa Samuel instructed. "That's what Serena does. Sometimes she warms it up for me, but I don't need it warm."

"I'll make it cold, then," I said. "I don't know how to light the burner."

I mixed the drink as instructed and set the glass down before him. Then I poured myself some lemonade and sat across the table. I wanted to ask Grandpa Samuel about the ghost. I wanted to ask him about his fingers. So many questions. But we were doing the Zen thing, so I held off.

"Can you hear her dancing?" Grandpa Samuel finally asked, breaking the trance.

"Who?"

"Isobel. Can you hear her? Serena says she can't hear her, but I think she can. Her steps are very soft because she was such a good dancer."

"Isobel was?"

"When I met her, she was going to dance in the ballet. Not the kind with pink skirts, but *modern* dancing. Oh, she was beautiful, and when she danced, everyone sat up. No one could take their eyes off her. I told her I had a ballroom in my house and asked her if she wanted to see it and she laughed. She had a very long neck and a perfectly shaped face, and when she smiled, her whole face laughed. She said that was the best pickup line she'd ever heard, but then I showed it to her."

"A ballroom?"

"On the third floor. You don't believe me?"

"I haven't been up there."

"I brought her home and showed her the ballroom and she danced for me. I played records on a portable phonograph I had. I wanted to get a console, but my father refused to allow it, so I got the portable Crosley instead. I had jazz records I played for her, and she danced."

He drifted into reminiscence, but I wanted to hear more.

"What did she dance to?" I asked.

"She kissed me. Oh, Isobel. You kissed me and I told you I would do anything for you, but I couldn't do it. In the end, I couldn't do what you wanted."

He looked so sad and lost as he sipped his medicine. But I didn't want him to stop talking; I was thirsty for clues about my past and about my father.

"How did she die?" I asked, because my father had never told me. I knew that she died when my father was sixteen, but that's all I knew.

Grandpa Samuel looked at me through his liquid eyes and said in a hushed whisper: "Listen!"

I listened, and I could hear footsteps, like Grandpa Samuel said, coming from somewhere in the house. I was about to say something, but he hushed me, and then said, "Sometimes, if you're lucky, you can hear music, too."

I listened carefully. I practically stopped breathing, that's how quiet I was. And I heard music. Jazz. A saxophone playing.

"I hear it," I said.

"You do? Serena says she can't hear it. She says I'm crazy. But do *you* hear it?"

"I do."

I heard it all. Footsteps. Music playing very softly, far away. It was exhilarating.

"Is it a ghost?" I whispered.

"It's her," Grandpa Samuel said. "She comes and dances for me."

And then the music ended and the footsteps stopped.

"What happened between you and Dad?" I asked Grandpa Samuel.

He looked at me with his milky eyes.

"Can I have some more medicine?" he asked.

"Not until you tell me. Something happened, because he hasn't been back here for twenty-three years, and he never talks about you or Serena or Isobel. Something happened. What was it?"

"Serena gives me more medicine," he said.

"Serena isn't here," I replied willfully.

"You're just like him," he hissed in a harsh whisper, his eyes fixed on me. "*Spiteful.*"

I stared at my grandfather for a moment, feeling stung by his words. I had no animosity toward him, and I wasn't sure why he would speak to me so harshly. But then I remembered Serena's talk of his dementia. I imagined a brain looking like a wet sponge.

"That's okay, then," I said, standing. I picked up the bottle of whiskey and uncapped it.

"One part medicine—"

"Two parts milk. I've got it."

I gave Grandpa Samuel the drink, then I put away the milk and the whiskey.

"Do you want me to leave the light on?"

"Turn it off," Grandpa Samuel said, so I did.

"It's my house," he said from the shadows at the dark end of the table. "You can't have it."

I was struck by the definitiveness of his declaration.

"I don't want it," I said.

"I can stay as long as I want, and you can't make me leave."

I didn't understand my grandfather's last remark, and worked to puzzle it out as I climbed the stairs to my room. When I got to the landing on the second floor, I heard a ticking sound coming from the third floor. I cautiously continued up to the landing; the air was humid and smelled of must. A long hallway, decorated with ornate wood panels and burgundy floral wallpaper, disappeared into the shadowy darkness; to my left was a small reception area with double doors opposite. The ballroom. I stood very still and listened: the house moaned, as I'd already grown to recognize, and I heard ticking from behind the doors. I crossed the reception area and into the dark vestibule both nervous and excited by what I might find. I opened one of the ballroom doors and peeked inside: it was a long low room with a bare wooden floor and a stage on the far side. A chandelier hung from the ceiling, and light sconces adorned the walls, but all the lights were dark. In the moonlight, I could see the cobwebs gathered on the fixtures, as well as in the corners of the room, and I could see a coating of dust on everything. I could also see footsteps in the dust on the dance floor. I glanced around in search of the ticking. On the floor next to the stage was an old portable record player in a leather, hard-sided case: the phonograph Grandpa Samuel had told me about. I crossed over to it and saw the cause of the ticking: the turntable was running; a record spun on the platter, though it had finished playing, so the needle ticked against the paper label.

I switched it off, and I sensed a stirring in the room behind me. As I turned around, I noticed someone else was in the ballroom, and I felt a tingling in my spine. It must have been my father or Serena, I thought, because I'd left Grandpa in the kitchen.

"Hello?" I asked as I took a couple of tentative steps forward. But the figure did not reply. "I see you," I said, and a pang of fear cut through me, because if it were my father or Serena, they would have said something. I took a couple more steps, and I could see the person shift slightly in the shadows.

"This isn't funny," I said, my voice unsteady. "I'm turning on the lights."

I bolted across the dance floor and hit the switches by the doors; the lights sprang to life, but when I turned around, the room was empty.

Whoever it was—and I *knew* someone had been there—had vanished. I was alone in the ballroom, and I was afraid.

6

THE TALK

I woke up late the next morning. After my encounter with the danc-ing figure in the ballroom, I wasn't able to fall asleep until light started sneaking into my room. I couldn't get the visions out of my head of rec-ord players playing on their own, footsteps at night, a spirit in a secret stairway who is revealed by striking a match. The voice I thought I'd heard say my name. Something weird was going on. And since we clearly weren't going to abandon Riddell House based on my experiences, I had to get to the bottom of it.

I went downstairs in search of my father. In the kitchen, I found a note from Serena encouraging me, once again, to make myself at home, though I didn't feel I would ever, really, feel at home in Riddell House. I didn't even know what time it was, since I had misplaced my watch somewhere between chasing a dancing ghost and waking up in the morning, and there was no clock in the kitchen. I skipped breakfast and went outside.

My father wasn't in the meadow, so I ventured into the courtyard behind the house. The front of Riddell House faced westward to Puget Sound and the Olympic Mountains, and had a majestic, sweeping facade; the rear of Riddell House was something different: a formal garden, which must have been impressive at one time, had deteriorated into something better suited to a haunted house. Broken stone paths were overgrown with clover. An impressive fountain, cleaved from a great slab of marble and standing taller than me, was stained with rust and appeared to have been a dedicated rainwater collector for decades. The box ferns were shaggy and overgrown, the flower beds were covered with moss and sword ferns, and the roses had grown so long and leggy they couldn't keep themselves up but tipped their heads over to rest on the hard ground.

Behind the garden, down a path of pebbles and weeds, was a crumbling swimming pool; a foot of black and green sludge percolated in the deep end like tar. The tile walls, which surely were once beautifully patterned, were cracked and broken. The pool house had been long abandoned, and the door yawned open to the darkness inside. To the east of the pool was a patio with fluted urns sitting upon a sturdy balustrade that opened to a broad staircase stepping down to a clay tennis court with no net and broken standards and a cracked and brittle surface.

My father was still nowhere to be seen.

I circled around again to the meadow and spotted him out by the bluff. He glanced back at me when he heard my approaching footsteps, but other than that, he didn't move, standing on the edge of the cliff looking down.

It was dramatic on the precipice. The drop was almost two hundred feet. The beach below was rocky and full of driftwood, entire trees bleached by the salt and the sun. At the base of the cliff were two sets of railroad tracks on a rocky berm that snaked off along the shoreline both north and south, bending as the landform undulated against the water.

"Elijah Riddell built those tracks," my father said as I approached.

"I thought he was timber money," I said, already feeling the sway of vertigo. It wasn't that I didn't like heights, it was that I didn't like falling from those heights and dying.

"Timber and railroad companies were intertwined. It was a very insider world. You must have learned about Teddy Roosevelt and trust-busting and all that in American history. The government gave land grants to the railroads, the railroads made deals with the timber barons to harvest the trees, the timber barons sold off mining rights to the precious metal concerns—"

"Precious metals?" I asked. "Here?"

"Broaden your scope. The Northwest used to be considered anything west of Chicago. They found a lot of silver in the panhandle of Idaho. Sapphires in Montana. But the big money was in copper."

"Why not gold?"

"The telegraph. Suddenly everyone needed copper wire. And it's horrible stuff to mine. It abuses the body."

"Ah," I said, impressed by my father's knowledge of the arcane.

"Anyway, Elijah was in all of it. He had a piece of everything. Your great-great-grandfather supplied all those railroad ties down there, every single one of them. Have you heard the horns from the trains when they pass?"

"No."

"Now that I've pointed it out, you will. When the trains pass, they always blast their horns in salute to Elijah Riddell."

"Really? He died a long time ago."

"That's the thing about tradition," he said. "People don't really need to know how it got there; they do it anyway."

"Sounds like religion."

We paused for a moment, and I didn't break the spell. For my entire life, I'd wanted to bond with my father; that we were finally doing it on the edge of a cliff seemed somehow foreboding, but it was a step in the right direction.

"I lost my wedding ring," my father said after a time, feeling the ring finger on his left hand. "Is that some kind of a sign? The crumbling of my marriage?"

"Did you look under your dresser?" I asked.

"I looked everywhere. It's gone."

I thought for a moment. My watch was missing. Could they be connected?

"Grandpa Samuel hears Isobel dancing at night. In the ballroom."

My father responded only by nodding his head.

"She's dead," I added. "She can't really dance."

"Grandpa Samuel hears things," my father said. "It's part of his dementia."

"Sure," I agreed. "But . . . I heard it, too. And I don't have dementia."

"When did you hear it?"

"Last night. And I saw someone in the ballroom, but I'm not sure I really did. Maybe it was nobody."

"But you're not sure."

"And I can't find my watch. I put it on my dresser last night. Now it's gone."

"So you're suggesting . . . ?"

I stared him down, and then I ticked off the mysteries on my fingers.

"A lost wedding ring, a missing watch, a spirit in a hidden stairway, dancing footsteps, and a man in the wall calling my name. At least, I think. Maybe it was a dream. You brought me to Weirdville so we could tear down the house. But we can't tear down the house because the man who owns the house thinks his dead wife still lives here. Dad. I think it's time for us to have the talk."

"The talk."

"The one you had every night around the dinner table when you were my age. States of being. Spirits. Ghosts. The nomenclature. It's time."

"Ah, yes," my father said, nodding deliberately and scratching the ground with his foot. "So, Trevor. I have to confess something. My mother was a flake."

"Crazy?"

"A New Age flake. She was a flower child. She sat in a pyramid to gather energy."

"A *pyramid*?"

"It was a frame," he said. "Made of metal. A pyramid, I don't know, four feet or so tall, and, you know, yay big. She sat inside it. See, you don't understand. Look, the belief is that our journey in our earthly bodies is just that—part of our journey. We come here for a while to hang out and touch things and eat things and listen to music and, you know, jack off—"

"Come on, Dad."

"You know," he said, "make love. Indulge in the physicality of our world. So—and this is how my mother would tell it, and she wasn't a trained psychic or anything, she was 'in-tune'—she said that after we die and our soul enters the nonphysical dimension, we can interact with the physical world if we focus on it, and we can come back and visit whenever we want. We can always drop by and say hello. And sometimes a person will see one of these visits. Well, that's not really a ghost. That's a spirit. That's like a flyby. Football players get this a lot. 'I felt my dead father was with me,' they say when they score a touchdown. Well, their dead father *was* with them. But then, there's another kind of thing."

"A ghost," I said.

"A ghost. Exactly. A ghost is a soul that's stuck. Someone who didn't finish something or has some lingering need and is stuck in this world. My mother would say: A spirit can come and go anytime she wishes, but a ghost is stuck, because a ghost *doesn't see the door.*"

"The door," I repeated.

"To the nonphysical dimension," he said. "That's why our nomenclature has to be correct. Does Riddell House have spirits, or does it have ghosts? There is a difference. But don't take it all seriously. My mother sat under pyramids, and she used a pendulum to decide whether or not she should give her kids cough medicine, or to see if I could eat strawberries without breaking out in hives."

"What?"

"Pendulum testing. Don't worry about that part."

"You don't believe it," I said.

"No. No, I don't think so."

"And you don't believe in ghosts."

"No," he said. "I don't think so."

"But you did when you were my age?"

He looked at me long and hard.

"Yes, I did," he said. "If you want me to be perfectly honest."

I wanted him to be perfectly honest, so I held his look as long as I could.

"Why did you lose your faith?" I asked.

He looked away, dug at the ground again, shrugged dramatically.

"Why does the cock crow?" he said. "Don't ask him, he doesn't know."

I rolled my eyes at my father's ridiculous aphorism, a repetition of what Serena had said the previous night.

"My mother used to say that," he said, swiping back at my contempt, and then he started back to Riddell House.

"Who *does* know?" I asked after him. "If the cock doesn't?"

"We have a mission," he said plainly. "We're here to get Grandpa into a home, sell this place to an experienced residential developer in a lucrative real estate transaction, and get out. In and out commando-style."

"So you can get back together with Mom," I confirmed.

"So I have a *chance* of getting back together with Mom," he clarified. "So let's keep our eyes on the prize, buddy. Your cooperation in this endeavor will be greatly appreciated. Thanks in advance for your understanding."

He headed off across the meadow.

Frustrated by my father's Vulcan-like air of disinterest, I called after him: "Hey, Dad, repeat after me: 'Primary objective: getting back together with my wife—'"

He kept walking.

"'So my son doesn't hate me for the rest of his life,'" I finished.

He stopped dead in his tracks, hesitated a moment, and then turned to face me.

"There's a long line of people who will hate me for the rest of their lives," he said. "I will do everything I possibly can—everything in all of my power—to make sure you are not in that line, Trevor. I hope you know that."

I shrugged.

"Well," he said. "As your mother would say, the proof is in the pudding. We'll see if I earn it, okay? I admire you for your persistence. I suppose, if I had approached my father in the same way, things might have turned out differently."

"What about what *your* mother would say?" I asked. "The pendulum thing she did—curing your colds and checking you for strawberry allergies. Did it work?"

He thought for a moment.

"Yes," he said. "I suppose it did."

I nodded significantly.

"No further questions," I said. "The witness may step down."

7

THE BOOK OF JONES

In 1967, my grandmother Isobel Jones Riddell died, after which my father, Jones Riddell, was sent away to a boarding school in Connecticut. He did not return home to Riddell House for twenty-three years. The boarding school was not far from where I grew up, before my parents lost everything and we became, for all intents and purposes, homeless. I knew the school. It was called Mount Sovern Academy, and it had a reputation for taking students who didn't fit into a "traditional academic environment." In other words, they took the fringe and the dregs and stored them until they were eighteen and legally allowed to terrorize society without the need of a guardian. The antisocial, the asocial, the pathological, the violent, the drug-induced hysterical, the cruel, and the good old-fashioned whack-bot crazies. Basically, when the judge said, "It's either Mount Sovern or a penal colony off the coast of Venezuela," the smart kids chose Venezuela. The rest were dumped at Mount Sovern.

My father attended Mount Sovern for two years, graduated, and joined the workforce. There was a local boatbuilder nearby who had a kind heart and paid him minimum wage. My father proved his worth sweeping floors for a few months, and, soon, he was brought into the fold. He was taught the trade of traditional wooden boat building. Apparently, he was pretty good at it. When he met my mother, he had already achieved a good measure of success, but she inspired him to go even farther. I was too young to remember any of this, but the story goes that, when I was a little kid, word of my father's gift with wood had spread across the Atlantic seaboard, and the volume of work thrust upon him earned him enough money that he could afford to buy a little farmhouse that reminded my mother of her childhood in England. We had a modest apple orchard and a creek on the far edge of the property, which edged up to a little forest where I roamed and played and learned to climb a tree. And then, after my father had set out on his own and established his own business, in a generous act of civic responsibility, he offered an internship to Mount Sovern Academy so that a student could learn the craft of wooden boat building.

The program was quite successful; the first student went on to apprentice as a carpenter and, later, get his union certification.

"Rah, rah, rah!" the community cheered.

The school asked my father if he would do it again. The next term, he took two kids. Also very successful. The school wondered if my father would offer a summer program for kids who really couldn't go home because if they went home they would probably fall victim to the overwhelming temptation to slit open the throats of their sleeping parents.

My father said, "Sure thing!"

Eight kids lived at Mount Sovern that summer and were bused to my father's workshop every day. He taught them how to sail. They went hiking together sometimes, swimming; they played Wiffle ball. (All things my father never had time to do with me.) They built a boat together. A beautiful skiff with lapstraking. Everyone was impressed. A local community patron paid way too much money for the boat at a fund-raising auction. And, after the last day of camp, one of the kids snuck out of Mount Sovern after midnight, walked eight miles or so to my father's boat workshop, and burned the building down to the ground. Entirely. Literally nothing left but wisps of smoke.

How's that for a story?

Insurance covered the loss. The school apologized profusely for the security lapse—after all, how do you promote goodwill with the locals if your delinquent residential students are running around the neighborhood burning down businesses? And the kid was sent straight to the penal colony off the coast of Venezuela. But something happened to my father after that event. He changed. He became fixated on helping the kids at Mount Sovern Academy. He never told me why. But I might suggest that, as a graduate of Mount Sovern, my father had found his salvation in wooden boat building; perhaps he wanted to pass on this redemptive trade to others. If he could save a kid by teaching him how to do something constructive with wood, wouldn't that be enough? After all, our family had made a fortune by destroying the forests. Shouldn't someone benefit by creating something positive from the fallen corpses?

My father dutifully rebuilt his workshop, but he stopped taking orders for new boats. From then on, he pretty much only ran semester-long workshops for Mount Sovern boys. In each semester, and at a camp over the summer, they built a skiff. They'd build one, and then auction it off to raise money. Build one, sell one. Build one, sell one.

Each time they finished a boat, a local patron would step up and pay too much for it and my father would get enough money to pay his bills. But babies and puppies are only cute for a little while. Then they become what they're going to be for the rest of their lives: people and dogs. And people will overpay for a baby or a puppy. They won't overpay for an old dog.

I don't have a business degree. I've never even run a lemonade stand. I know nothing about economics. But even I know: *Selling three skiffs a year will lead to bankruptcy!*

Surely, I exaggerate. I was a kid when this was going on; I saw only my own limited perspective. I have no doubt there was more subtlety to the decline of my father's business. Poorly negotiated leases, a slumping economy, the skyrocketing cost of exotic hardwoods from Indonesia, his insistence on building boats from scratch and not dabbling in restoration or repairs. But when a business is on the rocks, it only takes a couple of careless missteps to dash it to bits. And so, it was dashed.

I have no doubt this sequence of events is why I spent all of my time as a child reading books. (My mother kept so many books in our little farmhouse, stacked on everything, piled everywhere—they were impossible to avoid!) With a book—presuming it's a *good* book—you can depend upon an outcome that adheres to the necessities of drama. The question will be answered. It has to be. The answer may not be happy; we can't guarantee a comedy. Sometimes tragedy strikes. But there will be a *conclusion*. Of that we can be sure. That's the whole point of a book.

But in real life, there is no guarantee that any question will ever be answered. Real life is messy because we don't know where it's going to go. And, really, there's no end in sight. Except death. And it wasn't clear to me back when I was fourteen, considering my initial experiences in Riddell House, that death was the end it had always been made out to be.

It still isn't clear to me now.

8

INNOCENCE LOST

Before dinner that evening—only our second day at Riddell House, but it felt like so much had happened since we'd arrived—I ventured out to the porch in search of Grandpa Samuel, who, I hoped, would be having his lemonade in the sun. I wanted to question him. Glean insight from his half answers. I wasn't even sure what he could possibly tell me, but I had to find some way to help my father become whole again so he could get back together with my mother.

I was hugely disappointed to find that my father had already taken my place on the blazing veranda. He was sitting on my chair. He was drinking my lemonade. He was talking to my grandfather.

"Oh, hey," my father said cheerfully. I couldn't help but notice the blue binder open on his lap.

"Oh, hey," I echoed.

He looked up at me with the expectant look of the impatient, like he wanted me to ask him a question and be gone, or else just be gone. But

I didn't go and he didn't stop looking, his neck twisted around the way a dog looks at you when you say, "Biscuit?"

"I came for my lemonade," I said.

"Ah!"

My father relaxed because I had made a socially appropriate request and, apparently, I had no agenda other than to acquire a glass of rosemary lemonade. I poured myself a glass and noticed that Grandpa Samuel had a sour look on his face and his jaw was set. His eyes were narrowed and fixed on the railing before him. And then, as if on cue, a black sedan emerged from the other side of the ridge and headed down the gravel drive toward the house. I sipped my lemonade and waited. The car drew closer and then was upon us. It stopped and was consumed by the cloud that followed cars that crossed the meadow.

"What's going on?" I asked.

My father forced a smile.

"Why don't you run inside and see if Aunt Serena needs some help with dinner," he said.

"No, thanks," I replied, and I sipped my lemonade, which was always perfectly cold and tart enough to make a satisfying pucker.

An older man got out of the sedan. He was carrying a well-worn satchel with a Swiss Army badge on it. I noticed the details. ("Good writers see everything," my mother has always told me. "Not simply the clothes a person is wearing, but *why he is wearing them*.") This man wore a dark suit that buckled at the shoulder, indicating he had bought it when he was thinner. He wore a wide necktie, which appeared to have been knotted in 1974, a giant fist of silk bound tightly, as if tied by Midas himself. He walked around the back of the car, and I saw his shoes, which were old and worn, the rubber gone and the leather of the heels going. The scalp beneath his thinning hair was tanned. He had traveled far for little compensation, this man, and he was tired. He just wanted to go home. But there was a job to do—there was always one more job to do—and it was his job to do it.

"He's here," my father said to Grandpa Samuel. "We're going to sign the papers now, okay?"

"Okay, okay, okay," Grandpa Samuel grumbled. "We're going to sign the papers."

"Just sign them, okay? And I promise, you'll be taken care of."

"Who will take care of me?" Grandpa Samuel snapped. "You?"

My father held the binder toward him as if to offer proof, but Grandpa Samuel waved it away dismissively. My father gestured for the stranger to join us on the porch, which he did. My father pulled a manila folder from the back of the binder and handed it to the stranger, who opened it and looked at the pages contained within.

"Okeydokes," he said. "I'll need a driver's license."

"He doesn't drive," my father said. "There's a passport in there."

"Does he travel internationally?" the man asked with a smile. His version of a joke.

"No," my father responded flatly. "He got it for this purpose."

"A state ID card would have sufficed. Less effort on your part."

"Will the passport work?" my father asked testily.

The man's bushy eyebrows rose, and, thusly chastened, he inspected the contents of the folder. Nodding, he extracted a black notebook from his satchel, opened it, and began entering data from the passport. Then he looked at Grandpa Samuel.

"Do you know what you're signing?" he asked.

"Yes, we do," my father interjected.

The man shook his head, still looking at Grandpa Samuel.

"Do *you* know what you're signing?"

Grandpa Samuel nodded.

"It's a power of attorney," the man said. "It's significant."

"I'll be taken care of," Grandpa Samuel said almost angrily. "Everything will be taken care of."

"In a manner of speaking," the man replied skeptically. He turned to my father. "Does Mr. Riddell know what he's signing?"

"The gutter is broken," Grandpa Samuel said. "The window is swollen shut. The roof leaks. We have worms in the walls. The pool is broken. The pipes are clogged. The foundation is cracked. It will all be taken care of."

The stranger arched his eyebrows again. When he did his jaw dropped, creating hollows in his cheeks. An odd look.

"He knows," my father said. "I explained it all to him. I'm not sure why he's doing this."

"I can't notarize something if he's not aware of the impact—"

"Please notarize it," my father said. "That's why you're here. That's why Dickie sent you. My father knows what he's signing; notarize it and let's get on with things."

The man sucked his teeth and I could see a little crescent of tongue pinched between his uppers and his lowers. He held the papers out toward Grandpa Samuel.

"Do you know what you're signing?" he asked again, so patient and so even with his tone.

Grandpa Samuel looked at the papers hazily, as if he were trying to focus.

"Because he told me to," he whispered, pointing a finger at my father.

"It's a power of attorney," the notary said. "It means that you're signing over your decision-making ability to your son. Do you understand what that means? It means he can act on your behalf without consulting you. Do you agree to that?"

Grandpa Samuel wiped his chin, and I read his T-shirt: SOMETIMES I WONDER, "WHY IS THAT FRISBEE GETTING BIGGER?" THEN IT HITS ME . . .

"My son told me to sign it," he said. "Because I do what he says because he knows better. He's always known better."

"Come on, Samuel," my father protested.

"If you listen closely, you can hear her dancing," Grandpa Samuel whispered to the man.

"Who?" the man asked.

Grandpa Samuel looked up at my father.

"*I* was supposed to be the one," he said. "But it was you."

The notary squinted at Grandpa Samuel and groaned skeptically. He looked from Grandpa Samuel to my father several times. Then he handed the folder back to my father and put his black book in his satchel.

"I'm not satisfied," the notary said. "I don't believe he understands the implications of this document. I'm afraid I can't notarize it for you."

My father took an intimidating step toward the man.

"Are you *kidding* me?" he snapped. "When I go bankrupt, notaries are everywhere, willing to notarize anything. Anything that takes my money away from me, my business, my house. No questions about that. But now? Now a notary has a *conscience*? You're joking, right?"

"Good day, Mr. Riddell," the notary public said, shouldering his bag and heading to his car.

"You're kidding me!" my father shouted at him. "Today is the day a notary public gives a damn about who's signing what? Are you serious?"

When he reached the trunk of his car, the man wheeled around and glared at my father.

"This is my job, Mr. Riddell," he said. "I take it seriously. Your father doesn't understand the ramifications of that document. My job is to testify that all parties understand the contents of the documents and are not signing under duress. If you've had other experiences with other notaries, well, that's something I can't control. I can only control myself, Mr. Riddell. I will stand by my belief that your father should not be signing a document like that unless he understands the ramifications. I refuse to be bullied by you."

The man opened the driver's door.

"How do I get him to sign it, then?" my father shouted. "He's ill. He's *demented*! He may *never* understand."

"You go to court," the notary replied over the roof of the car. "You have him declared incompetent—non compos mentis. Doctors will testify. The judge will designate you custodian. *Then* you will have that power. I will not notarize a power of attorney without knowing that all parties understand what's going on. Good day to you, sir."

"Good day to you, sir?" my father muttered to himself as the man drove away. *"Bad* day to you! A *very bad* day to you, sir!"

I could tell that what was going on was serious, but I had to work hard to stifle a laugh at my father's curses. The car drove away, and my father looked after it angrily. He slapped the manila folder against his thigh and shook his head. He glared at Grandpa Samuel.

"I guess fucking with me is what you do best, isn't it, Dad?"

"Why did you do it?" Grandpa Samuel replied with a hiss.

"Someone in this house had to be a man," my father said. "And it clearly wasn't going to be you."

He snatched the big blue binder from the chair and went inside, slamming the door after himself.

Grandpa Samuel relaxed a bit. He sniffed once and picked up his lemonade. He rocked back and forth and, looking out to the sound, took a sip. He retreated to his Zen world and lost track of me entirely. Or maybe not. Maybe he'd retreated into the hedge maze of his dementia. I wasn't sure.

I went inside after my father, down the hallway to the kitchen, but before I entered the room I stopped. I listened from the threshold. My father was talking with Serena. I did not reveal myself but instead listened in.

"Oh, Jones, what were you thinking?" Serena said, exasperated. "If it were *that* easy, don't you think I would have done it already?"

My father didn't say anything. I heard movement. Serena moving around in the kitchen, preparing dinner.

"I brought you here so you could work your Jones magic," she continued, making tsking sounds and sighing with disapproval. I could easily picture her. Removing a dish from the oven and kicking the door with her foot so it slammed shut with a great whump. Blowing at a wisp of hair that dangled in her face. Chopping a carrot on the chopping block with great insistence. *Tack, tack, tack, tack, tack.*

"What did you expect?" I heard her say.

"Why can't we just have him declared non compos mentis?"

"That's not as simple as it sounds. Doctors get involved—*many* of them! Batteries of tests, analyses, competency hearings, judges, review boards. Just think of the time, not to mention the money! No, we must do it this way. But you can't act rashly; you must be deliberate about the goals you wish to achieve, and then you must set intermediate goals and so forth, in order to *build* your victory convincingly. Thoroughly. You must lay the *groundwork.* Surely, you can't expect to achieve your objectives without laying the groundwork."

"The *groundwork!*" my father scoffed.

"The groundwork, Brother Jones," she scolded. "The *groundwork!*"

More chopping. An onion this time. A zipping sound—or maybe something like sandpaper: a tearing, abrasive sound—before the snap of the blade on the block. Yes, that was it. An onion. Little sprinkles of caustic juices spraying invisibly into the air and wafting into her eyes to make her cry. She sniffed and made another cut. *Shuuut-tuck!*

"You need to reconcile with him," she said. "You need to forgive him and allow him to forgive you—"

"Forgive *me?*"

"None of us is without guilt, Brother Jones. Except, perhaps, me. But that's only because I was so young, I hadn't yet lost my innocence."

"Then why don't *you* do it?" my father lashed out. And I knew that was where she wanted him to go, because there was a dramatic pause, during which, I was sure, she wiped the blade of her knife and carefully set it down.

"Because I'm here," Serena replied in an even tone. "Because I'm the one who stayed behind. Because I'm the one who dresses him and bathes him and feeds him. I take care of him when he's sick, and I allow him to treat me meanly when he's not. Because he *needs* me, and because needing me makes him hate himself and his own limitations, which makes him treat me with contempt. So I am his enemy. I am the lightning rod of his hatred."

"That's an awful lot of words," my father said. "A wall. A tsunami of words."

Serena sighed with disappointment.

"Is this how you treat Rachel?" she asked. "With such dismissiveness? I can see why she would leave you."

A pause followed, which included more shuffling, and I wasn't sure what was going on; the sounds were vague and confusing to me. Then Serena said, "Before dinner?" and I realized my father was helping himself to the medicine.

"I hate this place," he said, and I heard the cap unscrew. I heard the liquid pour. "I hate my father. I hate everything about this world. Let's forget the whole deal. I'll join the Peace Corps and spend the rest of my life handing out mosquito nets in Africa, Trevor will go off to live with Rachel in England, and Dad can sit on the front porch with a drool pan, staring into the sun. Who cares."

"Oh, please!" Serena cried. "You're such a waffle! After spending all this time on the outside, you should be honed razor sharp, Jones! You should be an axhead, looking to strike! If anything, we owe it to the world to wipe this place off the face of the planet. It's our duty to obliterate the brutal history of our forefathers, who raped and pillaged this country for profit. I have no doubt Elijah would be proud of us for trying to *do* something with this land. We're trying to make something of ourselves, Jones, unlike the other Riddell underachievers who've wandered these halls, like Daddy, like Grandpa Abe, shuffling and muttering to themselves. We are not going to let our fate be determined by them; we will not be victims. We will determine our fate for *ourselves*. Now buck up, boy. Get to work! You have to convince Daddy this plan is for the good of the family."

I liked that line: "You're such a waffle." Was that what my father was? A waffle? A pancake with grand aspirations? A weak person who flopped back and forth as if saturated with maple syrup? Someone who always chose the path of least resistance?

They'd stopped speaking, and I sensed they were onto me. I heard Serena's footsteps so lightly on the wood floor. I wondered if she was walking toward the hallway—maybe she'd heard me and was sneaking up on me—I looked for the quickest exit and spotted the door to the servants' stairway. I ducked across the hallway, opened the door silently, slipped inside, and closed the door as fast as I could without making a sound. With my heart pounding, I took the stairs quickly and quietly, up and into the darkness out of sight, and then I stopped and tried not to breathe. The door opened below me. I measured my breaths so I wouldn't be heard.

"I know it's you," she said boldly, though she couldn't see me and wasn't sure I was really there. Her voice reeked of doubt. "I know you've been listening. You're good, but you're not *that* good. Don't think I don't know everything you do here, because I know *everything*."

She paused, and, still, I didn't move.

"Dinner is in thirty minutes," she said, finally. "Be prompt."

The door closed and I was free to breathe again.

– 9 –

THE MOUNTAINS OF CALIFORNIA

When the ringing phone woke me up the next morning, I was swallowed by a wave of melancholy. It was our third day at Riddell House, and I felt as if a great chasm had opened up between our world and the world outside of The North Estate.

I went downstairs. The house was empty. The phone rang with a relentless tempo, and the ringer was so loud that the space between rings was filled entirely with the echo of those rings. I found the black phone on the telephone table in the kitchen. I lifted the receiver midring and held the device to my ear. I heard a click and hissing, and I forgot to say anything.

"Is anyone there?" I heard through the earpiece. It was a tiny voice. A woman. "Hello? Is anyone there?" I heard sounds of confusion and rustling, and then, dimly, perhaps words said to someone else in the room: "The ringing has stopped. Maybe I've been disconnected."

It was my mother. Through a magic portal, she had found me. She had reached halfway around the world—or maybe she went *through* it. Maybe the telephone cable linked us directly through the center of the earth; like with a tin-can phone, we were connected by a taut umbilical cord.

"Mom?" I croaked in my morning voice.

"Trevor!" she exclaimed. "Trevor, is it you?"

"It's me," I said, feeling my melancholy lift so quickly I was almost giddy.

"Can you hear me? You're very dim; be sure to speak up."

"I can hear you."

"It's your birthday!" she shouted. "My baby! Fourteen years old! How does it feel?"

"The same."

"Not at all different?"

"No different," I said. "But I'm glad you called."

"I wouldn't have missed it for the world. I wish I could be there with you to help you celebrate, but I'm afraid this phone call will have to do."

She told me about her world in a flurry: her father had a cold; her mother's fish and chips were too greasy; her sisters still resented her; her brother pulled her hair when he passed behind her chair. I tried to think of something I could offer her, but nothing seemed appropriate. I wanted to be upbeat and match her enthusiasm, but all I could think of to tell her about were my misgivings, my concerns, my lingering questions about Riddell House. And I definitely didn't want to tell her about my fear that I would be forced to spend the rest of my life with her in Penzance while my father handed out mosquito nets in Africa.

"What about your aunt and your grandfather?" she asked. "I've never met them. What are they like?"

"Well, Serena. She's . . . weird."

"Can you be more specific?"

I thought about it for a moment. "Not really. It's just a feeling."

She laughed. "Okay. How about Samuel?"

"He's weird, too. But in a different way."

"I see."

"Say, what do you think of this?" I asked, struck by a thought: my mother was an expert at crossword puzzles. "Grandpa scribbles things down all the time. Ideas that come to him or something. Serena says they're gibberish; she says he does it because he has Alzheimer's. But he wrote this Post-it note at dinner. It said, 'muir.' M-U-I-R, and then M-T-N-S space C-A. I can't figure it out. What does it mean?"

"John Muir," she said immediately. "M-U-I-R?"

"Yes."

"Right. John Muir was a famous Scotsman. He did great work in the field of environmentalism; he essentially began the conservation movement. *The Mountains of California* was one of his books. M-T-N-S space C-A. Maybe your grandfather read it years ago and thought of something he wanted to look at again so he jotted down a note to himself."

"Maybe," I said, wheels spinning in my head. "How did you do that? How did you just know?"

"Well, I haven't read *much* John Muir, but I've read *about* him. It's one of those facts that sticks in your head."

"Sticks in *your* head."

"Yes, well. And how's Dad?"

I didn't know what to say. How's Dad? How should I answer? It occurred to me that my mother wasn't only calling with birthday wishes. That was her gambit, of course. But she was also calling to check up on my father. I saw an opening.

"Dad's doing really well," I said, in a brazen attempt to sound cheerful. "I mean, despite missing you."

"He misses me?"

"Are you kidding?" I boasted. I felt the need to create a myth. Get her hooked, then get my father hooked. A parent trap. "It's crazy; he talks about you all the time. And he shaved his beard."

"Did he?"

"He's got a face, you know," I said, and I was pleased to hear my mother's laugh. "And it's pretty thin. I guess I can see why you were attracted to him. You know, a long time ago. Back in the beginning."

"He was very charming as well as being good looking," she said.

"Overall, he seems healthier," I assured her. "I think it's the air or something. And he seems happy, too. I mean, as happy as he could be under the circumstances. You know, because of his business and all, and you not being around."

"That's terrific, Trevor. Thanks for telling me. I was worried that going back to Riddell House would dredge up some pretty painful things that might push him in the opposite direction."

"No way," I said, getting carried away. "He and Serena get along great. And he and Grandpa Samuel are like best friends. I practically expect them to go outside and toss a baseball back and forth. You know, like it was thirty years ago."

There was a long pause, and I realized I might have overplayed my hand. Toss a baseball? What was I thinking?

"Your father never had a good relationship with Grandpa Samuel," she said. "Even thirty years ago."

Crap. Just because my father hadn't told me about the animosity between Grandpa Samuel and him didn't mean he hadn't told my mother.

"I mean, they *seem* happy together," I offered.

"Is that so?" my mother wondered after a moment. "I'm glad to hear it, if it's true. Is Dad around? I'd like to check in, if he has a moment."

I panicked. Of course she would like to check in. But where was my father? Where was *anybody*?

"Um. Let me see if I can find him."

"It's all right—"

I set down the phone and quickly ran down the hallway to the front door, looking in the rooms I passed. I ran up the stairs and checked my father's bedroom. Nothing.

"Dad?" I called out down the hallway. Desperate, I ran up to the ballroom. Empty. Back down the stairs to the first floor, I hurried along the corridor to the south wing, calling out for my father. But my father was nowhere to be found. I returned to the phone, breathless.

"I don't think he's in the house," I said to my mother, panting.

"I'll call another time, then—"

"Maybe he's in the barn. Hold on."

I ran out of the kitchen and noticed that the car was gone, which did not bode well. I cut the corner of the meadow and sprinted down the hill to the barn. I threw open the door.

"Dad!"

Grandpa Samuel looked up from his workbench. "Son!"

"No, Grandpa. It's me, Trevor. Do you know where Dad is?"

He stared at me blankly.

"Never mind."

I ran back up the hill, angry with my father. This was his chance. She had called. She was showing an interest. She wanted to talk to her husband. She *cared*. But he wasn't there. An opportunity missed.

I picked up the phone from the table.

"I can't find him," I told her, dejected.

The only response I got was a dial tone. She had hung up. My eyes burned with tears as I placed the handset in the cradle.

The library was impressive. Dark mahogany everywhere, and a ladder that climbed about ten feet to a catwalk for the second tier of books. A giant table stood in the middle of the room, rooted and oaken, surrounded by heavy chairs with brass studs affixing the leather upholstery to the wood, and adorned with beautiful brass lamps with green glass shades.

I could smell the must of a million decaying pages, books that had been unopened for years. Decades. So many books pushed so tightly together. They just wanted to be opened and read! I walked the perimeter and looked at the spines. Anderson, Andrews, Andreyev. Burroughs, Burton, Butler. They were alphabetized, separated by fiction and nonfiction. In fact, the nonfiction titles were grouped in such a way . . . The Dewey decimal system, but without the decimals. This library had been carefully curated and cared for at one time.

It was not hard to find the natural sciences. It was easy to find Muir, John, in the natural sciences.

Everyone knew who John Muir was. Even my mother, who was from England. He was the founder of the Sierra Club. The creator of the national park movement. The guy who ruled Yosemite in the name of white Europeans everywhere. He wrote a lot of books. They were lined up right there on the shelf. *Travels in Alaska, The Yosemite, Our National Parks.* And a slender edition entitled *The Mountains of California.*

I slipped the book from the shelf. It was clothbound with gilded edges and an image of leaves embossed in gold on the cover. I blew the dust off and cracked the cover. First edition, first printing, 1894. It was signed on the title page: "To Harry Lindsey, a great lover of the mountains, John Muir." I flipped to the overleaf and found an additional inscription: "Harry, I hope this keeps you warm this winter, when I cannot be there to warm you myself. I hold you in my heart, though I cannot hold you in my arms. You are forever mine as I am forever yours. Love, Ben."

A ribbon trailed from the binding to use as a bookmark, like they had in old books. I flipped to the marked page. I found an essay entitled "A Wind-storm in the Forests." It began, "The mountain winds, like the dew and rain, sunshine and snow, are measured and bestowed with love on the forests to develop their strength and beauty. . . ." I wanted to read it. As I settled back in a club chair and flicked on a reading light, a yellowed envelope slipped out of the back cover of the book. It was addressed in black handwriting, curly script in India ink that had been ghosted where the ink had shrunk away from the paper fibers: "Harry Lindsey, Esq., in the care of Riddell Timber Mill, Aberdeen, Washington." The "from" address simply read, "B. Riddell, Seattle." I opened the envelope and removed the enclosed letter. The creases were so crisp and the letter so unblemished, it seemed as if it had never been read at all. Or maybe just once.

January 17, 1902

My dear Harry,

I can only assume my letters and packages are getting to you, or will get to you eventually when you check in with the mill, so I am not worried. I had a chance to meet Muir last month and so cajoled him into inscribing this volume to you. He's quite a quirky fellow and objected strenuously, but I prevailed. When pledging money for his cause didn't work, I pledged him my father's senators, which was more than agreeable to him. So we have turned old Elijah to the cause of conservation! Bully on him!

The essay on the windstorm—which I have marked for you— is quite remarkable. He knows of which he writes, this Muir. You can't bluff that, can you, Harry? I'm sure those stunted little firs in Yosemite are nothing compared to what you and I have climbed together on the coast. But perhaps I say that only because I am feeling trapped by this earth. Alice is always around, and I am constantly forced into the stiffest clothes and made to sit like a Turkish bear, not allowed to doze at a dinner party when the conversation is so tedious I have to pinch myself to stay awake. Oh, Harry. Harry! Simply writing your name makes me feel better and allows me to feel comfort in knowing you are there for me. How I long for a journey with you into the mountains and to set a camp by a river, just the two of us. A trout to roast, or a rabbit we have snared. A hot fire and a bottle of whiskey and the night around us.

The season will begin in April. I have already told my father I will return to the coast to supervise the harvest, and then we will see each other again. I have been making great progress with our plan.

My father has desecrated this land so; I will make amends for him. You and I, together, will work to restore this land to its pristine state, not from a position of weakness and protest, but from a position of power. The deal is moving forward, and as long as I am able to stand a bow tie tight around my neck, I will prevail. I will be meeting Roosevelt in two weeks, and his man Pinchot. They will expect to meet someone who is like the others they have met: terrible, avaricious men. When they shake my hand, they will know the truth of it. They will know they have an ally who is richer than all the rest of them.

I will not be able to return before April, however; as much as I had hoped to ride down to see you for a few days, I'm afraid things are too busy here, and I must stand by Alice's side always to ensure her complicity. But know, Harry—always know!—when I dream at night, I dream of you.

> Until we meet again, I am,
>
> Faithfully yours, Ben

I folded the letter and placed it back into the volume. Was it the letter that Grandpa Samuel remembered? Did he want to remind himself to read it again? (And yet it looked practically unread—as if it hadn't been touched for decades.)

I'd heard of Ben. Serena said he was Elijah's first son, who died tragically young. The only other time I'd heard his name was when Grandpa Samuel jumped up from the table at dinner on our first night and wrote the note: MUIR MTNS CA. "Ben is nervous," Grandpa Samuel had said. And his note led me to this discovery.

Alice and Roosevelt and "his man Pinchot." And Harry Lindsey, the subject of Ben's dreams.

People didn't really talk much about homosexuality when I was fourteen. At least not in Connecticut, where I had grown up. Except for the kids at school, of course, when they wanted to pick on someone. I remember being embarrassed and confused by what I had read: Did this letter mean my great-granduncle was gay? And what was it even like to be gay in the early 1900s?

I closed the book with the letter still inside and replaced it on the shelf.

I headed up to my room, but, as I passed the front parlor, I stopped. I hesitated, then went inside. I stood before the giant portrait of Elijah and gazed into his powerful eyes and at his hand that reached out into the room as if it might pull me into another dimension. Next to the big portrait of Elijah was another oil painting, much smaller but large enough, with a small plate on the frame that read: BENJAMIN RIDDELL. It was a portrait of a young man with wavy black hair and nearly black eyes, smiling out of one side of his mouth as if he knew a secret.

10

BEN'S WORLD

I came to learn much later that the life of my great-granduncle Benjamin Riddell was steeped in contradiction. The heir to a timber fortune, he wanted nothing more than to be one with the trees. Enthusiastic and able, he held an idea of "proper work" that differed greatly from his father's. Ben understood the need to attend to business dealings and negotiations; overseeing the daily operations of such a vast conglomeration of companies demanded an endless string of meetings and tedious conversations during which people talked around their true intentions. He understood the need. He simply didn't think *he* needed to be the one doing these things. He was much more comfortable hiking around the forests of the Olympic Peninsula and the inland forests owned by Riddell Timber, experiencing the *nature* of the trees. And so he contrived to spend a great deal of time on the coast, surveying tracts of land designated for harvest.

Ben didn't keep a diary, as far as I know, but he did write field notes, which he sent back to his father. These notes carried a tone of wonderment and fascination, and a belief that all things are connected in ways we can barely fathom, as if he were trying to convince Elijah of something. I know that Ben spent much of his time at Yale studying the work of the Transcendentalists—Ralph Waldo Emerson, Henry David Thoreau, Margaret Fuller—and he was quite taken by the poems of Walt Whitman as well as the early writings of John Muir. This was a fashionable thing of the times: the young elite pondering nature and our connection with it.

The first forestry school in the United States was the Biltmore School of Forestry, established in 1898 under the patronage of George Vanderbilt. It was followed quickly by forestry schools at Cornell and Yale Universities, backed largely by very wealthy families, such as the Riddells. For those who made their fortunes through the exploitation of forests, the management of those forests made practical business sense. For those who saw the health of the forests as a reflection of the health of the human soul, conservation was equally important.

But Ben's enlightenment came at a great price. He couldn't reconcile the philosophies of the Transcendentalists and the new breed of conservationism with his father's mission, which, as far as he could tell, was to destroy nature for profit. Ben's relationship with his father was complex to say the least. Ben had faith that his father was a good man and loved the forest as much as he did, yet while Ben felt compelled to save nature, Elijah felt compelled to consume it. Ben's struggle to reconcile their differences was the central conflict of his life.

"The rain has been incessant. It feeds my soul. I feel that it washes over my body, and a part of me drips into the soil with the rain, and a part of me becomes the soil and is drank into the roots of these trees and I have become one with them."

That note was written by Ben on a ledger page that estimated 700,000 board feet would be harvested from a certain tract and sent to San Francisco to build the young city.

"All good wood," another note said. "Finest quality possible. A person living in a house built with these trees will prosper and remain in good health, for the wood will keep him well."

Curious, indeed, is the idea that a good tree will produce lumber that will make a house that is good, a house that will nurture its tenants. A house that does not merely serve as shelter from a passing storm but actually and *actively* promotes the good health of those who reside within its energetic realm. That the life and personality and soul of a tree continue, even beyond its felling, milling, drying, and utilization. These were the tenets of Ben's philosophy, with which he felt he could save his father's soul.

It only makes sense that like-minded spirits tend to find each other. Which explains why Elijah found himself attracted to J. J. Jordan, the railroad tycoon, and together they discovered more efficient ways to shake money from the trees. It explains also why Ben found himself attracted to a young cutter on the coast by the name of Harry Lindsey. For it seems that being intimate with the forest wasn't the only reason Ben spent so much time on the coast; there was intimacy of a more carnal nature being explored as well.

The passions that inspire two young, idealistic men when they are alone in the woods do not need to be subjected to the approval or disapproval of others. But they do make the landscape a bit more complicated when decisions about love and business intersect, as was the case in this situation. For Elijah Riddell and J. J. Jordan had conspired that the best way for them to grow their empires was to form a merger. Not only of their companies but of their children as well. The timber industry of the late nineteenth century was notorious for such couplings. And so it was decided that Benjamin Riddell would marry the lovely and sophisticated Alice Jordan.

Riddell and Jordan shook on the arrangement over a cordial and a fine cigar. The deal was done.

Still, Benjamin Riddell had entirely different feelings on the matter.

11

BIRTHDAY DINNER

I anxiously awaited my father's return. I hadn't seen him all day and I wanted to tell him of my mother's phone call—that she had asked after him and cared about him and wanted to talk to him. I went downstairs at dinnertime, figuring the time change in my head. He couldn't call her back now—it was the middle of the night in England—but he could call her first thing in the morning.

"Is my dad here?" I asked Serena.

She was busily making dinner, still dressed for work, though with bare feet.

"I'm afraid not," she said. "And I don't know when to expect him, so I hope you don't mind if we start without him."

I shrugged and took my seat, relying on an air of indifference to mask my disappointment. Grandpa Samuel was already sitting docilely at the table. Serena took the medicine bottle and put three tablets in front of him. When she saw that I had noticed the transaction, she said: "His Alzheimer's medication."

She shuttled plates of food to the table.

"Can I help?" I asked.

"You sit, Birthday Boy," she said with deliberate cheer. "I have it under control."

She presented the last of the food, a wooden bowl of salad, and took her seat.

"Do you have a car?" I asked as we served ourselves.

"We do have a car," she replied. "It's behind the barn. Why do you ask?"

"I never see you drive it. How do you get to work?"

"I ride my bicycle to the bus stop and then take the bus. Aren't you the curious one?"

"Even in the winter?"

"Winters are quite mild in Seattle, and no one minds a little rain. That's why God invented fenders for bicycles, to keep ladies like me dry."

We ate deliberately and silently. I felt that everything was slipping apart. My parents were no closer to reconciling, and my father was more remote than ever. I was trapped in the world of Serena and Grandpa Samuel. And nobody cared. Even on my birthday.

"It is not my place to apologize for your father," Serena began, "but I understand that you must be disappointed that he's missing your birthday dinner."

"Whatever," I said. Which was a lie. It really *did* bother me. It bothered me a lot. I thought my father was a jerk for being absent on my birthday. But I didn't think it would help to tell Serena that.

"Really? Surely it's incumbent upon a parent to recognize the birthday of his or her child."

"My mom called me this morning," I said quickly, and I immediately regretted saying it. I had wanted to keep that information from Serena as a secret I shared with my mother. And here I was, pandering for my aunt's approval.

"Did she?" Serena asked, looking impressed. "You and your mother must have a very special relationship. I'm sure you love her very much."

"Sure," I said.

"'Sure.' 'Whatever,'" Serena mocked. "It's cute when you speak like a teenager, but I know better, Trevor. I know you have many more feelings and emotions tucked away in that heart of yours, and you have abundant words to describe them. Tell me, how do you feel about this separation of theirs, be it temporary or not?"

"Why do you keep calling it a separation?" I asked, bristling. "They're getting back together."

"Are they? Perhaps they will, but perhaps not altogether happily. Would you prefer they be together and unhappy, or apart and happy?"

"Neither."

"Umm. You're holding out for door number three. An idealist!"

"What's wrong with being an idealist?" I asked.

"Nothing at all," Serena replied. "I suppose my interest in hearing your thoughts is more selfishly motivated than I have revealed. I was eleven when my mother died, and so I know what it's like to feel lost and confused by the unraveling of a family. I thought perhaps in you I had found a comrade with whom I could commiserate. We are kindred spirits to some degree, aren't we, Trevor? You and I aren't afraid to speak our minds, are we?"

I scowled; I didn't want to dwell in Serena's world any longer.

"Can I ask you a question?"

"You don't need my permission to ask a question," she said.

"Who was Benjamin Riddell?"

Grandpa Samuel looked up from his plate; Serena seemed startled by the question. She cleared her throat and put down her fork. She folded her hands together and looked down at the meal laid out on the table. Pork chops and applesauce and iceberg lettuce salad with cherry tomatoes, slices of red onions, and mushrooms, which I picked out because I didn't like mushrooms. And lemonade. There was always lemonade.

"Daddy?" Serena said after a few moments. "I believe young Trevor's question is directed toward you."

I noticed her voice was slightly strained, and she didn't make eye contact when she spoke.

"Ask him again, Trevor," she said.

"I'm wondering about Benjamin Riddell. And Harry."

"I don't know," Grandpa Samuel replied unsteadily.

"Yes, you do, Daddy."

"I don't."

"Tell Trevor what you know."

"The only thing I know is what my father told me," Grandpa Samuel snapped at Serena. "And he was a liar. He lied about everything! Don't you see? He lied about it all!"

"I'm sorry," I said.

"Don't be sorry," Serena said. "Grandpa Samuel is quite sick. Alzheimer's disease. They won't diagnose it when he's alive, though. They call it senile dementia; that's the clinical diagnosis. They won't call it Alzheimer's until he dies and they perform an autopsy and examine what's left of his brain, which, of course, we will happily donate to science; they say it will look as if a mouse has chewed holes in it. Terrible."

"You think I'm crazy!"

"No, Daddy, I think you're demented: that's an important distinction. Try to remember it."

"I'm not crazy," he whined.

"No, Daddy, you're not crazy. You're demented." She took a bite of her pork chop. "Go ahead and eat; there are no tendons in this."

Grandpa Samuel studied his food; he took up his knife and fork, but he didn't eat.

"Ben was my father's brother," he said under his breath. "He gave away everything we had. He ruined our lives."

"He ruined our lives," Serena repeated—not to me but to the table. And not loudly, but very clearly. *He ruined our lives.* "You remember,

Daddy. Benjamin Riddell ruined our lives. He convinced his father that to save his soul he had to give everything away. All of his money, all of his land. Even this house. And old Elijah, well, that's what he said he wanted, isn't it, Daddy? To give Riddell House to the trees. What a thought! Only someone as demented as you would take such an idea literally. Only you would cling to such a thing."

"I don't want to leave," Grandpa Samuel whispered.

"I know, Daddy. We all know. You don't want to leave, and so we're stuck."

Grandpa Samuel rubbed the stumps of his missing fingers, and I really didn't know who to believe at all.

We cut and chewed our food. And we waited for my father to return home.

Grandpa Samuel and I were doing the dishes when my father entered through the back door, looking a little embarrassed. He apologized that his meeting had run late and he'd missed dinner, even though he smelled like alcohol and cigarettes, and I knew he was drunk. It was a pattern that had begun with my parents' financial troubles in Connecticut—my father going missing for the evening hours and coming home drunk. Maybe I wanted to move to England after all.

"We were waiting for you," Serena said.

She went to the refrigerator and removed a chocolate cake. We took our seats and Serena set out plates and she lit a single candle on the cake. The three of them sang a warbling, tuneless version of the happy birthday song. I wished the whole thing were already over.

Serena rummaged through a kitchen drawer in search of something.

"Ack," she muttered. "I can never find things where I left them. Why is it when I put things back where they belong, they end up someplace else?"

She slammed the drawer shut and picked up a dinner knife.

"I'm afraid my cake server seems to have sprouted legs and walked off," she announced. "So we'll have to make do."

The cake server gone. Another disappearance.

She sliced the cake with the knife and made an obvious effort out of getting the pieces onto the plates. As she struggled, my father placed two small packages on the table and pushed them toward me.

"Happy birthday," he said.

I thought about not taking them. About rejecting them and saying, "What I'd really like for my birthday is a father who gives a shit." But I didn't. I took the gifts and I knew what they were already by the shapes of the boxes, one as long as my hand, narrow and rectangular, and the other broad and flat and the shape of a book. I opened them. Sure enough, a fountain pen, black with gold details. It was pretty, but he didn't give me any ink, so it was useless. The other was a leather-bound journal.

"So you can become a famous writer and write about this fucked-up family," my father said.

There was no irony to his comment—just self-pity—so I wasn't moved.

"Thanks," I said.

A strange look swept over Grandpa Samuel's face, and he sat upright quickly, cocking his head from side to side.

"What's that smell?" he asked loudly.

"It's nothing, Daddy," Serena said.

"It's a bad smell," Grandpa Samuel said. "What is it?"

"Brother Jones was in a bar," Serena says. "He smells of cigarettes. The man next to him must have been smoking. Isn't that right, Brother?"

"*I* was smoking," my father said.

"Isobel hated cigarettes," Grandpa Samuel declared.

"You were *with* someone who was smoking," Serena said deliberately. "You picked up the smell in your clothing. You detest cigarette smoking, Brother Jones, you know that. You would never do anything against Mother's wishes."

"That must have been it," my father grumbled, rising from the table. "I'll go change."

He walked out of the room.

"You can use your new fountain pen to sign books at your readings," Serena suggested after he had gone. "Perhaps you will move to Seattle and become inspired by the rain and darkness that typify our oppressive winters."

I shrugged.

"Daddy and I got you a present, too," she said, handing me a small, thin, book-like package.

I jokingly held it to my ear and gave it a shake.

"A book?"

"Open it," she said. "Gently."

I tore back the tissue paper wrapping.

"We don't have the kind of money to buy you designer fountain pens, I'm afraid. This is a book from our library. But I had it appraised by a seller of rare books in Pioneer Square, and he confirmed that it is quite valuable."

I held a thin booklet that looked fragile. *Daisy Miller: A Study*, written by Henry James.

"It was first published in 1878 in England. Later, James revised it for the American market, but, you know, it's always best to read the original text of an author—before the forces of marketing and social acceptability gain sway. What you are holding is a first edition, first printing of the original novella."

I looked down at the small booklet, which seemed to have grown heavier with this history.

"It must be worth a lot," I said.

"It is," Serena confirmed. "Elijah was not a big reader, as far as we know. But he liked to collect things. And since cost was not an issue for him—before he began to disassemble his empire—he collected many treasures such as this. You may peruse the library for these gems. And when I say 'peruse,' I use it in the true sense of 'study thoroughly,' not the common misuse, which is to confuse it with 'browse.'"

"What will I find?" I asked, piqued.

"Well, I wouldn't want to spoil the discovery process, but I'm happy to tease you with the idea that a first edition of a famous book about a white whale and the captain who pursued him graces the shelves of Elijah's library."

I stared at her for a very long time, while she smiled at me smugly. I had never read *Moby-Dick*, but my mother had, and she'd told me about it, and she revered it. In that moment, I missed my mother terribly. Her love of books. The way her face relaxed into a smile when she stumbled upon me unexpectedly as I read a book on the living room couch or on the porch or standing in the kitchen, book in hand, because I was so compelled by what I was reading that I couldn't stop even to pour a glass of juice.

"My mother would love to be here," I said.

"Yes," Serena agreed. "But she isn't. And so this book is merely a symbol of our gift to you, Trevor. To *you*. Not to your mother. Your grandfather and I are giving you the collection of Elijah Riddell. The books are yours so you can use them in the way they were meant to be used: to be read. After all, an unread book is nothing more than a colorful doorstop, isn't it? All of Elijah's books are now yours. Isn't that right, Daddy?"

Grandpa Samuel, who had slouched into his chair during the whole conversation, raised his eyebrows.

"All of them," he muttered.

"You're giving a valuable collection to your only grandson!" Serena chirped loudly. "I think more enthusiasm is in order."

"All of them!" Grandpa Samuel shouted, raising his hands above his head in triumph.

I was stunned by the gift. Who knew what else might be in the library? Famous books. Rare books. Books of great value.

And yet my mind buzzed with a question: Why wouldn't Serena have sold this stuff off over the years? She always complained about money, yet there were incredibly valuable things in the house. It didn't make sense.

"Thank you, Aunt Serena," I said.

"No kiss?" she asked.

I hesitated, wondering how serious Serena was about a kiss; I found her very difficult to read sometimes. After a moment, I got up and gave her a kiss on her cheek, and she grabbed me and hugged me tightly for a few seconds before releasing me.

"You're practically a man, and I missed all of your childhood," she said. "I should have been there when you were a baby to give you a bath, to change your diaper, to hold you when you were afraid or upset. Touch is so terribly important to relationships."

"Simply Serena!" Grandpa Samuel howled.

And my opinion of Grandpa Samuel was again influenced by his behavior. Before, I thought he was forgetful but otherwise coherent. Now he seemed difficult and unpredictable. Erratic. Possibly unstable.

"Yes, Daddy. Simply Serena wanted to hug Clever Trevor because touch is so important to the human experience. Touch heals. Touch conveys love. Without touch, babies would never be made. Why do they call some shamans hands-on healers? Because the connection between one person and another is so important. It can breathe life into the dead."

She turned and spoke directly to me.

"When Mother was dying, your father sat with her for hours, holding her hands or stroking her hair. He wanted her to feel his healing touch."

"I remember—" Grandpa Samuel started.

"You don't remember anything, Daddy," Serena cut him off. "You were too drunk. You were a drunkard back then, and you remember nothing of the horrors we were forced to endure."

He looked at Serena sadly. He furrowed his brow like he really did remember, like he wanted to tell us what he remembered, but Serena's glare was cold, so cold, that his attempt was thwarted. He nodded his head.

"I don't remember," he said compliantly.

"You were too drunk and you forced Brother Jones to take care of Mother and me and you, didn't you?"

"Yes, I did."

"Brother Jones gave up everything he had. All of his plans. The track team, and his acting. He dropped classes so he could take care of us. We owe him a debt of gratitude. We need to show him that we remember the sacrifices he made for the family. And we need to acknowledge that what you did to him in return was wrong. Don't forget it, Daddy."

"I won't."

"He used to run," she said rapturously. "His legs were so long and he was so powerful, and he would glide. I would watch him at his track practices after school; I would sit in the bleachers and watch. And I would see the other boys. They plodded and they clumped on the cinders. They were football players and wrestlers looking for something to do in the off-season. They had bunchy muscles and no grace about them at all. But Jones! Long and lean. When he ran, he *ran*!"

"I remember," Grandpa Samuel said.

"But then Mother got sick. And you kept drinking. You drank even more, so you wouldn't remember."

"I remember."

"Not all of it, Daddy. You don't remember all of it."

She stopped talking and we fell into a coma of silence, Grandpa Samuel and I staring dumbly at our plates. She had put us into a trance.

"Touch is a powerful thing," she said.

My father returned to the kitchen wearing clean, odorless clothes. He took his seat.

"What were you talking about?" he asked.

"We were remembering Mother," Serena replied.

"She's here," Grandpa Samuel added. "She dances for me."

Everyone froze in place until Serena pointedly put down her fork. My father squinted at Grandpa Samuel.

"Is she here?" my father asked. "Is she *really* here?"

"She's here," Grandpa Samuel repeated.

"Nonsense," Serena interjected.

"Is she *really* here, Dad?"

"I've heard her, too," I offered.

Serena looked incredulously at us all.

"It's the rain," she said. "He only hears the rain. That's all."

"The rain," Grandpa Samuel echoed.

But my father was caught up in the emotion. The idea of his dead mother dancing in the ballroom. I could see it on his face. He hadn't lost his faith, he had just pushed it down and hidden it from view. I saw the glimmer in his eye. He *wanted* his mother's ghost to be in Riddell House.

Serena got up and went to him. She sat next to him on the bench and put her arms around his shoulders, and he folded into her, his head tipped against hers, and she held him and rocked him back and forth, and I saw that my father was crying. She rocked him and stroked his hair and he was sobbing.

"Shh," she said, soothing him. "Let me heal you."

I saw it all clearly. How my father desperately wanted to see his mother. How Grandpa Samuel held his belief so strongly. How Serena controlled the narrative of the family. Telling Grandpa Samuel what he should remember and what he shouldn't.

I saw how she controlled my father, too. How she picked at the scab just enough to get her nail under the edge, enough to lift until she felt it tear and saw a drop of blood form underneath, but then how she pushed down so it didn't bleed more. I used to do that when I was a kid and I skinned my knee or my elbow. Pick just enough to feel some pain, but then apply pressure. Because my mother used to tell me that if you tear off the scab entirely, you get a scar.

I thought briefly of telling my father about my mother's phone call, but I held myself back. I had come to Riddell House with a mission to reunite my parents. My strategy was to fix my father by helping him to fix his broken life. It was a simple plan, because I thought his problems were just about money. But then I saw that it wasn't as simple as that. Watching Serena hold my father made me realize that my father was a lot more damaged than I'd thought. And until I could get him repaired, it was probably best that he not talk to my mother at all.

— 12 —

ROOSEVELT AND
HIS MAN PINCHOT

What did we do before Google? Before Wi-Fi? Before cable modems? Before cell phone towers on every building?

Before that?

We did what we had to do because we were resourceful. We had initiative. And we understood that the process is fundamental to the result: a poor process produces a poor product.

And now? Now we let someone else worry about the messy details. We delegate that responsibility.

And so we delegate our privacy. And so we delegate our liberty. And so we forsake the control of our own destinies.

Well, we can't complain, can we? We checked the box. We accepted the Terms and Conditions without reading them, didn't we? So we have only ourselves to blame.

But I was a child of a different era. Remember, in 1990, there were

places called libraries, and they had people called librarians, who could
help us with our research, if we chose to take advantage of such.

I figured it out. The next day—Day Four of our Adventure—I had my
father drive me up to Greenwood Avenue so I could take the number
5 Phinney bus downtown. From the abandoned JCPenney's on Second
Avenue and Pike, I walked the few blocks to the Seattle Public Library.
I found a helpful librarian. I asked questions. The librarian sent me in
various directions, and I did my research.

"Roosevelt and his man Pinchot," as Ben had written in his letter. Oh!
It's all about national parks and forestry and conservation. Teddy Roosevelt was the president who started the whole national parks concept,
taking millions of acres and setting them aside for the common man,
land that would normally fall into the hands of the rich timber barons,
like Elijah Riddell, my great-great-grandfather. Gifford Pinchot, whose
timber-baron family made their fortune clear-cutting nearly the entire
Adirondack Mountains, was the first chief of the United States Forest
Service. Together, Roosevelt and Pinchot worked as crusaders to preserve the beauty of a world which had existed long before them and yet
which was being rapidly destroyed in the name of progress. Both men
came from terribly rich families, but they took a position of advocating
for all people, not just the rich. They believed that some things were too
good for one person to own.

Gifford Pinchot was an interesting fellow. He married a dead girl.
His fiancée, Laura Houghteling, died before they wed, so he went ahead
and married her after she was dead, and then they lived together for a
long time like that, one of them dead and one alive. You think I'm joking. I'm not. It was the heyday of Spiritualism. Everyone accepted the
presence of ghosts and spirits as a normal part of their experiences. So
no one thought it was all that strange for their friend Giff to take long
walks with the ghost of his wife. Or set a plate for her at the dinner table.
Or consult with her on issues of great importance. And, anyway, he was
fabulously wealthy, so he didn't care what people thought. And his best

friend was the president of the United States, and, together, they went Robin Hood on the trusts and syndicates and took all the land and gave it to the people.

The other fabulously wealthy people (my great-great-grandfather included) couldn't do anything but get mad and stomp around and try to figure out ways to get them thrown out of office. Which happened, eventually. But the damage to the concerns of timber barons—the creation of National Parks!—had already been done.

Once I felt I had an understanding of the context, I went to work on the specifics, which took me to the microfiche readers and newspaper archives. I quickly learned that early daily newspapers in Seattle were different than modern papers. They didn't have a lot of photos, first of all, just column after column of poorly written reportage. And they had biases which were not well disguised. *The Seattle Republican* made fun of politicians they didn't like, calling one of them an "oaf" and a "walrus." *The Seattle Star* was a little goofy and spent a lot of time on the police blotter, which was filled with reports of drunken people stabbing each other. *The Seattle Daily Times* tried to act serious and responsible, but I wasn't sure they pulled it off very well.

I found quite a bit of material on Elijah Riddell and different mills opening and closing, and a big land deal that got pushed through, much to the dismay of the *Seattle Daily Times* reporter: THE END OF THE FOREST? the headline wondered. I also found a few stories on Roosevelt's visit and his meetings with Elijah.

And then I found something in the *Republican*:

FORMER RIDDELL EMPLOYEE FEARS FOR LIFE

An erstwhile carpenter for Riddell Timber, who shall remain nameless to protect his innocence, has come forward to this reporter's office with proof positive that activities of a diabolical and indiscreet nature have taken place over the course of many months at the construction site of The North Estate, Elijah Riddell's famously extravagant, fifty-plus-room "cottage" in the woods north of Seattle.

While few details were provided, said carpenter reports he was terminated after witnessing an undignified act being performed between "someone who looked to be Benjamin Riddell," son of timber baron Elijah Riddell, and an unknown worker. The carpenter could not confirm the identity of either person involved, though he swears both parties were men. However, the carpenter is sure he saw what he saw, and, after seeing, was immediately sacked without cause or recompense. The carpenter claims that others have fallen upon similar situations and were told to keep their mouths shut. The carpenter now fears for his life, as retribution is clearly a possibility. The police department has made no arrests for indecency, and they say none will be forthcoming, considering it happened—if it happened at all—at The North Estate, which is outside of their jurisdiction.

I knew what "indecency" was code for: homosexual activities. So it was true. Ben was gay. Which was kind of weird, I remember thinking. I was fourteen, after all, and it was 1990, and there was a lot of talk about AIDS and everything. And I knew what being gay was, but I didn't know how you ended up gay or not gay. I mean, I didn't know at the time if it was inherited or just a lifestyle choice. Or if it was a tendency, and if you thought about it a lot, maybe you became *more* gay, but if you didn't think about it at all, you became *less* gay.

I was confused about it enough to ask a librarian to help me. I screwed up my courage and found an older—possibly gay—librarian, and I asked him: "Were there a lot of gay people in Seattle in the early nineteen hundreds?"

He perked right up, as if historical gay Seattle were his specialty.

"Seattle has always been a gay city," he said. "There was a tremendous gay scene in the thirties in Pioneer Square, which was nicknamed

Fairyville. Little-known fact: King County was named after Vice President William Rufus King, who just so happened to be—"

"Not after Martin Luther King?" I interrupted.

"No. It was named long before Martin Luther King was born. The mid-eighteen hundreds. King County was named after William Rufus King, known as Miss Nancy to his friends. He was President James Buchanan's gay lover."

I raised my eyebrows in surprise.

"Gays are everywhere," he said. "Throughout time."

"So, it was common?" I asked. "You know, the gay thing?"

"The gay thing is *always* common. It's just a matter of how it's accepted by the culture of the time."

I felt uncomfortable talking about the subject, but the librarian seemed pretty knowledgeable, and he was nice, and I needed to know more. So I pushed on.

"So if I were a gay man in 1903," I ventured, "and if I were in my twenties and my father were a really rich and powerful guy . . . what would that look like?"

"Nineteen oh three? Rich guy? Seattle?"

"Timber baron. Really rich."

"Your father would have considered it a youthful dalliance," my librarian said. "He would have waited until you 'grew out of it,' and he probably would have arranged a marriage for you with a manly woman, who was likely a lesbian. You would have wanted to keep your money and power, so you would have agreed. You would have had your boyfriends on the side, your wife would have had her girlfriends. You would have gone to important social events together as if you were breeders. And almost everyone would have been happy."

"What's a breeder?" I asked. "And who *wouldn't* have been happy?"

"Your *father*," he said obviously. "He wanted heirs but wasn't getting any. Breeders are straight people. The whole point of having a child is to keep the bloodline going. It's the *only* point, really. I mean, unless you enjoy mopping up poop and vomit and having angry teenagers scream in your face and force you to pay for college. Why did your father have *you*? I mean, the fictional 'you' of 1903. I'm not asking why *your* father had you. The father of the 1903 gay guy you've invented. Did *he* have a wife?"

I thought about it a moment.

"I don't know," I said.

The librarian nodded at me and then scrunched his face and shrugged.

"Do you have a parent here or something?" he asked. "You're asking a lot of questions that maybe you should be asking your parents. Sexual identity is more of a family matter than a library matter."

"I'm not gay," I said, catching his drift: he thought I was talking about myself.

"It's nothing to be afraid of," he said. "I mean, it is what it is. So it's better to embrace the 'is,' because people can tear themselves up about it. That happened a lot in 1903. It just wasn't out there like it is now, so gay people did terrible things to themselves to make themselves more 'normal.' But what is normal? I know a counselor you could talk to. He talks to teenagers about, you know, sexual identity issues. It's totally low impact, and it's not like he converts people or is looking for recruits. Do you have a parent here?"

"I'm cool," I said, realizing we had morphed from gay history into gay counseling. "Thanks for your help."

I went back to my microfiche reader and kept looking. Sure enough, about a year after the article insinuating indecency, I found another article. It was in *The Seattle Daily Times*, and it touted the engagement between Benjamin Riddell and Alice Jordan, eldest daughter of James J. Jordan, the railroad tycoon. Their engagement party, by invitation only, was scheduled for Saturday, September 17, 1904, and was to be held at The North Estate. All the leaders of Seattle would be in attendance, the article boasted.

Oddly, I found Benjamin Riddell's death notice published in the Sunday edition, September 18, 1904, referring to his date of passing as September 11, 1904. The notice reported that Benjamin "was an adventurer and a lover of Nature. His explorations took him deep into the forests and into the tallest of trees." Benjamin Riddell, "an enlightened and kind-hearted spirit," would be truly missed.

A month later, October 12, again in *The Seattle Daily Times*, the headline read: FORTUNES OF RIDDELL DOUBLE IN SIZE. And there was a long article about the merger between Riddell Timber and Northern Pacific Railroad, which had been whispered about for years and had finally been consummated. The consolidation of these industries "assures that Seattle will be the dominant city on the West Coast," and the "living gold of the Pacific forests will continue to fill Elijah Riddell's coffers." It was noted that the deal went through in the wake of the "terrible accidental death of Benjamin Riddell, who was being primed to succeed his father at the helm of Riddell Timber," and who had made it clear to everyone he spoke with that he would have carried with him "an agenda of conservation and a spirit of cooperation in working with President Roosevelt and his forestry lieutenant, Gifford Pinchot, with the intention of gifting millions of acres of pristine timberland to the United States government in exchange for a 'considered and deliberate' harvesting plan, thus preserving land for public use as well as reasonable private exploitation." The article ended with a sardonic rejoinder: "We can only hope that the ghost of Benjamin Riddell lingers at The North Estate to ensure the spirit of conservation wins out over the spirit of decimation and deforestation, which is Elijah Riddell's preferred method of wealth accumulation."

What an odd way to end a newspaper article, I thought. And, as I considered the meaning, my stomach growled. I looked up at the clock and realized I was starving and it was already late in the afternoon. I made my way back to the bus stop on Second Avenue and bought a chili dog from a hot dog stand to hold me over. I rode the number 5 Phinney back north; the bus let me off two blocks from the gate to The North Estate. I waved at Val as I passed, and then I made the long walk down the twisting road and back to Riddell House.

13

THE DISCOVERY

When I came down for dinner that night, I found my father sitting in the gentlemen's parlor with a tumbler of whiskey. I joined him in the dark room.

"What did you discover today?" he asked.

"I'm not sure yet," I replied. "I'm still confused about why Elijah changed. What made him switch from being a timber baron to being a conservationist?"

"Grandpa Abe said it was because Elijah was afraid of going to hell and facing all the people whose deaths he caused."

"I *might* buy that."

"Timber is the most dangerous industry in the world," my father said. "The statistics, even today, are staggering. The number of deaths . . . And in brutal ways, being crushed to death by a tree that twists wrong, or losing an arm and bleeding out, or getting hit by a widow-maker."

"What's that?"

"A dead limb that gets hung up in the tree. When you start to chop down a tree, it'll come loose. And they can be huge. Grandpa Abe didn't spend much time in the field, but when he was younger, Elijah sent him to inspect cutting sites. And he said he once saw a guy drinking a cup of coffee and a widow-maker came down so fast, by the time he heard it, it was too late. A big branch crushed his skull, drove it right into the ground. Grandpa Abe said the man's arms and legs kept on moving. Twitching. He said it was like when you step on a spider and its legs keep squiggling around."

"That's disgusting, Dad," I said.

"I've got more. The topper who was a hundred fifty feet up. He took a swipe with his ax and the whole tree beneath him crumbled. It had some kind of fungus, you know? It was rotten, but he didn't inspect the base properly. A hundred fifty feet up. Straight down. Thud."

"Nice."

"And you'd think at least it's a pleasant outdoor job, clear-cutting trees. But no. In those days, the conditions were horrible. They made them work long hours, and they'd be in camps without running water or toilets for months at a time. Disease and vermin were rampant. And when they let them go into town, all the men got drunk and went to the brothels, which were full of STDs. There was this guy in Aberdeen, Billy Gohl, the Ghoul of Grays Harbor. He murdered hundreds of men in his bar. He had a trapdoor he dropped the bodies through to a boat under the dock, and then he'd go through their pockets for money and dump the bodies in the bay. And Elijah Riddell—and all the other timber barons; he wasn't alone—did nothing to stop any of it. They didn't improve working conditions until they were forced to by the government. They didn't compensate the families of the men who died on the job. They didn't help the towns with law enforcement. They just sat around in their fancy houses in Seattle and Olympia and Tacoma, smoking cigars and sipping brandy and eating elaborate meals prepared by world-class chefs. So I guess, if Grandpa Abe was right and Elijah saw the light, he'd have to do some pretty serious penance if he wanted to avoid punching his ticket for hell."

"Huh," I said. "That's weird."

"What is?"

"I'm related to them. It seems like a whole different world."

He and I both looked at the portrait of Elijah, our patriarch, towering over us in the parlor.

After dessert, Grandpa Samuel asked if he could go down to the barn to work. Serena gave her permission under the condition that he not do any more sanding. "You've already had your bath," she said. "I won't give you another, and you know how you itch if you go to sleep filthy."

I asked if I could go along to keep him company, but really, I wanted to go because I wanted to know what exactly it was that he *did* in the barn. Grandpa Samuel was excited by the prospect.

"I like company," he said. "No one ever visits me in the barn, unless Serena brings me lunch. She doesn't do that very often."

"That's a very generous offer," Serena said to me. "I'm sure Grandpa Samuel would love some company, and it would give your father and me a chance to catch up a bit on the old days."

We walked down to the barn together. It was evening, and the breeze off the water stirred the warm air. The sun had slid behind the jagged maw of the Olympic Mountains. I could taste salt in the air; I could smell the grass. Faintly, a freight train sounded its horn in the distance.

"Are they really saluting Elijah Riddell?" I asked when I heard it.

"That's what my father told me," Grandpa Samuel said. "I don't know if anyone remembers."

"Remembers what?" I asked after a few steps.

"My grandfather died before I was born," he said, "so I don't know. But he made this place. Seattle and Shelton and Aberdeen. He built the

Northwest. And then he gave it all back. Everything except what my father had taken for himself."

"Why did he do it? Why did he give it all back?"

"I don't know," he said, and we continued walking a bit before he added, "Isobel knew."

"What did Isobel know?"

"If you feel you don't have enough, you hold on to things," he said. "But if you feel you have enough, you let go of things."

"How much is enough?" I asked after a few paces.

"I don't know," he admitted with a shrug, and we arrived at the barn.

It was quite large, as far as barns go—Riddellesque, one might say—with massive sliding doors on one end that looked to be rusted shut by the weather and the years. The boards that made up the barn's walls were easily a foot wide, abraded by decades of rain and wind, but still in remarkably good shape considering the age and unfinished nature of the building. Centered along the broad side of the barn was a small door, flanked by long, low windows. Grandpa Samuel led me to the door and inside; he flipped a light switch, and fluorescent work lights flickered to life, revealing a dusty, disheveled woodshop.

I peered around cautiously. The plank floor was feathered with a bed of wood chips and sawdust years in the making. Stationed throughout the barn were giant machines, old and constructed of heavy steel. I knew these tools, as I had spent much time in my father's workshop over the years, but these specimens were much older: a band saw and a lathe and a planer and a drill press. More than that, even. A table saw and an oil drum rigged with some kind of contraption I couldn't fathom.

"Wood steamer," Grandpa Samuel explained.

There was a workbench that spanned the entire back wall and, above it, a wall of tools on pegboard. The opposite wall was adorned with as many shelves as would fit, stocked with bottles and cans and jars, dozens of old coffee cans sporting tape labels to identify their contents. Dust-filled spiderwebs occupied every possible corner of the barn, no doubt limiting the amount of nutrition the spiders would earn from them, as they surely were visible even to the blindest fly. The entire room held a fragrance that was composed of so many elements, and yet was so distinctive. The scent of different woods—cedar and cherry and oak and more—of wood oils, of glue, of varnish, and the slightly acrid odor of wood burned on the saw or the drill press. The smells of sweat and spilled coffee. The smell of ozone emitted from the bushings of an electric motor trying too hard, spinning too fast, burning itself to death if only to please its master.

"What do you do here?" I asked.

He shrugged.

"Wood," he said.

I found a large stack of various types of wood and, next to it, a pile of chair legs or something. I didn't know what. Spindles for a banister, or table legs. Dozens of them, all slightly different. Some raw, some oiled, some finished with a glistening varnish. I picked one up.

"You repair things?" I asked, examining the piece.

"Sometimes."

Dozens of chair legs. Or more like studies of chair legs. Maybe a chair leg factory.

"You make chair legs," I said. "Do you sell them?"

"I like using the lathe," Grandpa confirmed. "But Serena said I can't get dirty tonight."

He opened a can of linseed oil and started painting it on a spindle that was being held in a vise on the workbench.

I sat on a stool adjacent to him and watched. He was very intent with the oil, painting it on in long, even strokes. More Zen of Grandpa. He worked on wood for the sake of woodworking. It was the process, not the product.

"Is that what happened to your fingers?" I asked impulsively, and immediately regretted it. But sometimes a question had to get asked. "The band saw?"

Grandpa didn't respond. He continued applying his oil. After a few moments, he spoke.

"I fell when I was a boy," he said. "I fell through a window."

"Ouch." I winced, and he looked up at me.

"It's all I remember."

He held my gaze for a moment, and I wondered if he was telling me something deeper.

"Clever Trevor," he said. "Why do they call you that?"

"They don't. Serena does, but no one ever has before."

"Because you're clever."

He took a deep breath and closed his eyes. He stretched out his left hand, palm flat and facing me, and he held his hand toward me so I could see the scars of his missing fingers.

"You can touch them," he said.

So I did. I reached across the table and took my grandfather's hand. The skin was old and worn. The flesh was thick. But I ran my fingers over his palm and finger stumps and it wasn't weird or anything. It wasn't creepy at all, though it may have read like that to someone who wasn't there. He stood with his eyes closed, letting me feel his missing fingers, and I felt them, too, in a way. I felt what Grandpa Samuel's fingers used to feel.

"Touch," he said, and he lowered his hand and opened his eyes. He turned away and went about his work, leaving me to myself.

I wandered around the shop, examining the tools, the endlessly different planes that had caught my eye in my father's shop in the marina. I wasn't invited there often. My father never tried to recruit me into the ranks of woodworkers or boatbuilders. He didn't deny me, but he didn't invite me into his world, either. And I always wondered why. Why didn't my father want me to follow in his footsteps? Most fathers did. At school, the boys who had lawyers for fathers wanted to be lawyers. Those whose fathers farmed the land grew up learning how to farm. But not me. Even though I always loved visiting my father's workshop in the marina, discovering things of interest. The spokeshave was my favorite tool, for no other reason than that I imagined shaving little wooden spokes to make wheels. I loved the Japanese saws as well, and different mallets and augers. I was drawn to the tactile nature of it, the sensory experience. I saw how my father's arms were so strong from the physicality of it. And yet, my father seemed to cede me to my mother. To her world of books and academia and learning. Which was nice, and I was good at it. But deep down, I always yearned to learn to use my hands.

I walked in on my father once, in his workshop, when I was a kid. I had started riding my bike to school, and I was pretty proud of myself, so sometimes I would go by the shop on my way home. When I walked in the room, I saw my father alone, sitting in a chair and leaning over, his head resting on his arms, which were folded across strips of wood laid out across sawhorses. He was asleep. At least I thought he was asleep. He wasn't. When he heard me standing there shuffling my feet, he opened his eyes.

"What are you doing?" I asked him.

"I'm listening," he said.

"What do you hear?"

"I hear hundreds of years of life. I hear wind and rain and fire and beetles. I hear the seasons changing and birds and squirrels. I hear the life of the trees this wood came from. Try it."

So I pulled up a chair and sat next to my father and put my head down. I couldn't hear anything except an outboard motor running in the engine shop next door. I raised my head, disappointed.

"I can't hear anything," I said.

"Everything has life," he said. "Everything has a history. The trick is allowing yourself to hear it. Maybe one day you will."

I nodded and acted like I understood what my father was saying, though I didn't have a clue. And I'd never heard him talk like that before; I had never thought of my father as a spiritual person. But after a few days at Riddell House, I was beginning to understand what he had meant. And I also was beginning to understand that, if he grew up with a spiritual mother and a nonspiritual father, he might have been conflicted in the same way Ben was. How do we reconcile the differences between what we see and what we know?

On the far side of the barn, opposite the big doors, was a loft with a ladder leading up to it. Grandpa Samuel was busy sorting through a Folgers coffee can in search of something, so I climbed the ladder up to the loft. The work lights spilled across the loft floor, but it was still nearly dark. I noticed a dangling string; when I pulled it, a bare lightbulb came to life.

There wasn't much to see except spiderwebs and, shoved to the back of the space, a half dozen old footlockers. Vintage lockers with wood bumpers and leather straps and RIDDELL, THE NORTH ESTATE, SEATTLE, USA, stenciled on the sides. Tucked behind one of the lockers was a canvas bag. I unbuckled the strap and looked inside. It was filled with metal spikes and leather straps, coils of rope and a length of chain. Intriguing, but meaningless to me. I tried to open the footlocker closest to me, but it was locked. They were all locked. And the locks were serious iron things. Internal locks, not padlocks. A screwdriver and a hammer wouldn't open them. I climbed down the ladder. Grandpa Samuel was still looking through the same Folgers coffee can, sifting through it for something he couldn't seem to find.

"What are you looking for?" I asked him.

"A screw," he replied. "I need a screw."

I leaned over and peered into the can. There wasn't a single screw in it.

"Those are keys," I said. "You have the wrong can."

He stopped and considered the problem; then he handed me the coffee can and went to get another can from the shelf, a can that perhaps had screws in it. And I had to wonder: he'd been standing there for five minutes looking for a screw in a can of keys; I was hoping to find keys that might open the lockers. . . . Something clicked in my head.

"Did you ever read *The Mountains of California*?" I asked him. "By John Muir."

Grandpa Samuel looked up from his new coffee can: Chock Full O'Nuts.

"I don't think so," he replied.

"Did you ever find a letter Benjamin wrote to Harry about working on the coast?"

He stopped and thought at length.

"I don't think so," he repeated and turned his attention back to the Chock Full O'Nuts can.

"Ben is nervous," Grandpa Samuel had said that night at dinner. Maybe it wasn't a note to himself he had written on the Post-it. Maybe it was a note to *me*. And maybe it wasn't from him but from someone else *using* him. I felt sure that it wasn't a coincidence. Just like it wasn't a coincidence that the Crosley record player was playing in the ballroom or the wall said my name. A ghost—or a spirit—was trying to reach me. I felt a little shiver as I looked around the barn and wondered who.

I took the coffee can up to the loft and sorted through the keys. The trunk keys seemed pretty distinctive, so it wasn't hard to find a few of them. I tried them on one of the trunk locks. None of them worked, so I moved to a second trunk and tried again. Success. I opened the lid, but there was nothing inside but dust. I left the key in the lock so I'd know which one it belonged to and tried a third trunk: blankets.

The fourth trunk was a little more interesting. It was full of clothes— sweaters and jeans, mostly. Man-size. I pushed them aside, hoping I wouldn't disturb a spider as big as my head. Beneath the clothes were papers gathered in old folders. School papers. I looked through them. They belonged to my father. Essays and math tests. A few paperback books with notes in the margins. Camus and Fitzgerald. A small hardcover book titled *A Magician Among the Spirits*, by Harry Houdini. A play script with highlighted lines: Mr. Paravicini in *The Mousetrap* by Agatha Christie. (I didn't know my father acted, but Serena had mentioned it.)

I slid my hand down the side of the locker to feel what was at the bottom. I discovered an orange and blue track cleat with rusted spikes. (More evidence.) And an old Magic 8 Ball, which read REPLY HAZY TRY AGAIN when I turned it over. I dug around some more until I found a sweater wrapped around a hard object. I unwrapped it and discovered a carving of a hand grasping a globe. It was dark wood and highly polished. Everything about the hand was exaggerated, slightly larger, slightly thickened, like the hand from Michelangelo's *David* that I had seen in photos, veins and tendons showing under the skin. The globe held by the hand was the earth. The continents were all in their proper place. Very deliberate. The sculpture appeared to have been hacked off something else. I could tell because the bottom of the piece was not stained and, in fact, was rough and choppy. And there was another thing that I found unusual: when I held it, I could feel it. It was like my father and the planks of wood in his shop. I could feel its life, its journey: a strong sense of relief at having been discovered. But to believe that, one would have to believe inanimate objects have spiritual energy. One would have to have faith.

I bundled the carving up again and wondered how I could sneak it out of the barn without Grandpa Samuel noticing. I wasn't convinced he would notice much of anything, to be honest, but still. I took off my sweatshirt and wrapped it around the sculpture and tucked it under my arm.

"What are you doing up there?" he called from below.

I moved to the edge of the loft.

"Looking around," I said.

"Be careful," he warned and wandered off again.

I descended the ladder with my bundle. There was no danger of Grandpa Samuel busting open my smuggling operation—he was agitated and unfocused, wandering around muttering to himself—and, even if I were discovered, would it matter? It was a hunk of wood, though it felt more substantial than that. Grandpa Samuel took a dowel to the lathe and switched the machine on. Then he muttered something and switched it off. He took a plank to the table saw and switched the saw on. Then he switched it off. Clearly, he was struggling with his mandate not to create sawdust.

"I'm going back to the house," I said.

He didn't acknowledge me, so I left and headed back up the hill.

My father and Serena were still in the kitchen talking, so I slipped around the house and went in the front door. The foyer was dark.

As I started up the stairs, I heard my father call to me. "Trevor," he said, and I figured I was busted, so I stopped and wondered if my father would notice the bulge in my shirt and ask what it was. I waited for him to come down the hall, but he didn't appear.

"Trevor," my father said again, like he was standing right behind me. But he wasn't right behind me. I stepped down the couple of stairs and stood in the middle of the foyer. "Trevor." I looked down the hallway and saw the light in the kitchen and I could hear them talking. My father and Serena were in the kitchen.

"Trevor," the voice said again, right into my ear. I whipped around: no one. My heart was beating fast, but it wasn't only out of fear. I felt something else as well: a need to know who or what was trying to reach me.

14

TREE CLIMBING

I knew I was dreaming. I was fully aware that I was asleep in my sticky room, entangled in the bedsheet, and yet I was caught up in a dream that seemed so familiar and welcoming, I didn't dare struggle against my sleep for fear of destroying it . . .

I am in a deep forest with trees so thick at the base—as big as a house— and a canopy of branches so dense, barely a speckle of light hits the forest floor. I'm with someone. I know this person: it's Harry. The two of us hike across the terrain, which heaves and rolls like waves at sea. The spongy ground is covered with moss and needles. We climb over roots as tall as ourselves. It is dark and cool and the birds sing. We arrive at the base of a tree at least forty feet in girth, its thick bark old and gnarled. I look up at the branches, which begin far above my head. Harry smiles at me.

I open my canvas satchel and remove my leather gloves, my climbing gaffs, and a length of chain. They are strangely familiar to me, as if I use them all the time. As if I know exactly what to do. We carry no axes, no saws. No, we are not here to cut this tree down. We are here to climb it.

And then we are ready. Harry asks the tree to protect us. And then we climb.

I hold the ends of my flip line, which encircles the massive trunk. With a whipping motion, I snake the chain up a foot or so and pull it tight. I dig in with my spikes and up I go. Higher and higher. I pause to rest and I look down. Harry is not far below me; the ground is much farther. It must be a hundred feet up to the first branch, maybe more. When I reach that branch, I pull myself up and climb onto it. It's three feet in circumference, easily. I balance on it without effort or concern, and I remove my spikes. I tuck them into my bag along with the rope, and then I remove my boots and socks and gloves.

"What are you waiting for?" Harry asks, still holding on to his flip line, poised below the branch.

I look up into the crown of the tree and see the branches jutting from all sides, reaching out and weaving together with needle-covered spars, but near the trunk there is space, and I can see exactly how we will work from branch to branch, up into the tree. I reach up from where I stand and take hold of a higher branch with one hand, and, with a small hop, I grab on with my other hand so I am dangling. I push off the trunk with my feet and walk myself up to where I can sling my hip over, and then I am sitting on the branch above. I spy another branch to grab on to and I continue my ascent. I know Harry is following me; I don't have to look for him.

Higher we go, and higher still into the tree's bosom. The rush of adrenaline is so intense it is explosive. Nothing but our own muscles and strength keeping us alive. Rubbing pitch on our hands to grip through the sweat. The need to focus on one thing—the next branch—until the branches swallow us, and, soon, we can't even see the forest floor. The higher we go, the denser the branches grow, until, perhaps three-quarters of the way to the top of the tree, we find that it is like being in a room made of branches. There is no fear here, as almost nothing can be seen except brown branches covered with gray moss and lichens, and green and brown needles of the tree. So many branches are within easy grasp; the thicket is so dense, I believe that, if I fall, I will become tangled in the branches themselves. As if the tree would save me from my death.

Higher. I lose myself completely in the task. Where I stop and the tree begins is unclear to me; I have become a part of the tree. Up past the crown, into the very top, where the spread begins to taper and other tree-tops can be seen below us as we climb. Higher! Until only a few feet remain and the trunk narrows (as the trunk of a Douglas fir does, so close to the top), and is impossibly thin and sways with the weight of Harry and me without any consideration of the wind, which, when it blows, makes us sway that much more. Then the terrifying reality hits me: the tree that we have climbed is the tallest in all of the world, or at least of all the trees I can see in the world, which are many, as the sky is clear and the forest spreads out endlessly below. All around me, I can see the tops of other trees poking above the canopy, so thick and lush, like a cloud of pine needles. Two hundred feet—two hundred fifty—three hundred—more!—into the spire of a great living being. Above the canopy are birds and clouds and sun and heat and wind and a feeling that, if I were a giant, I could walk across the treetops. I could step out and walk for miles on the blanket of the forest. The rest of humanity, which is hidden so far below, is ignorant of all that Harry and I can do and see.

We stay there for a long time, feeling the sun and wind on our faces, existing as one with the tree and with each other. We don't speak a word; there is nothing to say. The magnificence of that perch is singular and needs no words to mark it. I am transformed by the experience, swallowed by nature and digested and have become a part of nature. We linger in this feeling, which could last forever. And yet it cannot.

Reluctantly, we make our descent. And then we are on the ground again, which feels so wonderful and solid beneath our feet. Exhaustion sets upon me suddenly, and I swoon. I open my eyes and I am by a camp-fire, our unsaddled horses nearby, chomping the grasses. A rabbit roasting on a spit above the leaping flames. And Harry carving at something, a block of wood; he holds a chisel and carves intently.

"What will it be?" I ask.

"The earth," Harry says, looking up at me. "A globe. And a hand will hold it."

"Whose hand is it? Is it yours?"

"No," Harry says, breaking into a broad smile. "It's yours."

I close my eyes and try to remember: the trembling of my muscles racked with fatigue, my body limp, its energy fully spent; the feel and the scent of the earth, the soil in my hands, the taste of water on my lips; the depth of my sleep, filled with visions of soaring through the air, flying over the trees and mountains in the warm sun—such dreams!

15

AWAKE THE SLEEPING GIANT

I woke up and it was night. My room was silent, and my heart, my soul were drenched with my dream, my vision. I was Ben. The spirit who occupied my thoughts now dreamed through me, and I saw those dreams. Ben showed them to me. Or maybe I showed them to Ben. Maybe Ben couldn't see the things he missed so much. The things he loved. The trees, and Harry. If ghosts can't dream, by my dreaming for him, perhaps Ben was allowed to see again.

The alarm clock read 2:03 A.M. The door to my room was ajar; it hadn't been ajar when I went to sleep.

I slipped out of bed and poked my head out into the hallway. Dark and silent. I closed the door and got back in bed.

The hand. The hand. I found the hand in the trunk, and then I heard the voice. Cause and effect. I found the hand and then I had the dream. The hand was tucked away safely beneath my bed, and yet it seemed to exude an aura; it was magnetic; it drew my thoughts.

Staring at the ceiling, listening to my fan, I heard a click. I turned toward the door and watched it open ever so slowly. I knew that any logical person would explain away this door-opening phenomenon. The logical person would say I hadn't latched the door completely, and the hinges had recently been oiled and were slippery. He would say the door hung in a way that made it tend to swing open. He would refer to the barometric pressure, the discrepancy between high and low pressures in the room and the hallway. The moisture content of the air, which was saturated by my own wet carbon breath. Humidity causes wood to expand, anyone knows that, or it adds weight enough to create a pendulum effect. There were so many ways to explain it. And yet.

I got out of bed and closed the door again. I tugged on the doorknob to ensure it was indeed latched. I returned to my bed, but I didn't lie down. I sat on the edge and waited; I didn't have to wait long. Soon the knob turned. The latch clicked. The door opened.

A chill ran down my spine. With my heart pounding, I rose from the bed and looked out into the hallway once again. I couldn't see anything, but I heard a click from the end of the hall and the creak of a hinge and the settling of weight on a floorboard. Someone wanted me to follow.

I made my way down the long, dark hallway, the old runner bristling under my feet, until I reached the servants' stairs. The narrow spiral staircase twisted downward into an inky blackness, the totality of which made me afraid to continue on. But I heard a sound at the bottom of the stairs and I knew I had to follow the phantom.

It was so dark in the stairway, I couldn't see my hand in front of my face. But I could feel the handrail, so I was okay. I continued down to the first floor, where the door was ajar and some light seeped in from the hallway. From there, I listened for the sighs. I listened for the groans and creaks and I followed them down one hallway and then another, around corners, through doors, until I was in a part of the house I had never been. In fact, it seemed few people had been in that part of the house in recent years. Decades, even. The runner in the corridor was dusty and faded, and the wallpaper on the walls above the wood paneling was peeling at its seams. And then I got to a stretch of hallway that seemed to have nothing in it. No doors at all, though I did notice an anomaly: part of the wall seemed to have a seam.

I approached the seam, and saw it was a hidden door with the same wallpaper and paneling as the corridor, so, unless you knew to look, you wouldn't see it. I opened it to reveal an empty linen closet with a dangling chain. I pulled the chain, and a light came on, but the closet shelves were empty. I noticed a small ring flush with the back wall, just about waist height. I flicked at it with my finger and it popped up. I lifted it and twisted and it clicked. It was a teeny door latch. I pulled, and the back wall of the closet swung toward me with a great, yawning, vacuous sound, as if I were opening a tomb.

I peered inside and saw a brief chamber, then a narrow staircase that spiraled up into the darkness.

I remembered Serena's words: *There's a secret stairway, Trevor, and if you find it and strike a match, you will see an apparition. The ghost of Riddell House.*

I clearly couldn't go any further without light, so I retraced my path back through the corridors until I arrived in the main hall, and then I hurried to the kitchen. Fortunately, Grandpa Samuel wasn't sitting at the table with his medicine. I grabbed the box of matches from the stove and, as quickly as I could go without making noise, rushed back to the linen closet.

I started up the stairs. As soon as I rounded the first few steps, the light from the room below dropped out. I struck a match against the side of the box, and it flared to life. I climbed the stairs until the match was nearly out. I took out another match and lit it from the first, and I kept going until, in the tenuous light, I saw a narrow landing at the top of the stairs. As I curled around the stairs to the landing, I stopped short, frozen, because in the dim flicker I saw a man looking at me. And, in that moment, the flame burned to my fingers and I dropped the match. I licked my burnt fingertips, quickly grabbed a new match, and lit it.

The man was gone.

For a flash. For a moment. I had seen someone I recognized from the painting in the parlor: I had seen Ben.

My heart thudded in my chest. I blew out the match before it burned me again, and then I stood perfectly still in the blackness, listening to my own breathing. I sensed that Ben was with me, and, soon, I noticed something peculiar. My breath had fallen out of sync with itself. Or rather, what I heard as my breath was really two distinct breaths, slightly out of phase. It was a subtle shift, but I knew it. Two of us breathed in the darkness. I was standing in the dark, breathing alongside of a ghost. It was almost so frightening as to be assuring, as if my fear had gone so far over the edge, it had circled around again to calm.

I lit another match, and, from what I could see, the small room was empty. I felt sure there was more to this ghost chamber, but I wouldn't be able to figure it out until I had more light. I needed to try again when I was better prepared.

I blew out the match, returned the matchbox to the kitchen, and went back to bed. As I tossed and turned, trying unsuccessfully to fall asleep with my mind filled with the image of Ben lit by a match, I heard the click again. My door slowly opened.

"Seriously?" I said out loud, but Ben didn't respond.

I looked at the clock. It was 2:30, and I was wide awake. And then a thought occurred to me: the middle of the night in Seattle is morning in England.

Again, I snuck downstairs and into the kitchen. I took the phone and huddled on the couch by the bay window. I called my mother.

"What's wrong?" she said immediately.

"Nothing."

"What are you doing up at this hour?"

"I miss you," I said, which was true, but not the real truth.

"I miss you, too. I love you and I miss you. But go get your sleep and we can talk when it's a proper time for you."

I wanted to do what she asked, but I couldn't hang up the phone just yet.

"I saw a ghost," I said.

"A ghost?" she asked incredulously, and then she laughed. "What kind of ghost?"

"The kind of ghost who lives in a secret room behind a secret door in a linen closet in a part of the house people don't really use, and if you light a match, you see him. Serena said Dad used to see him when he was a kid."

"I think Serena is pulling your leg."

"Dad never told you? He never said he and his mother used to light the match to see the ghost?"

"No," she said. "Your father has never talked much about his mother. I know that she was into spiritual things, but I suspect that was because she knew she was dying and she was looking for something to give her hope. I've never heard of this ghost. And you should be asleep. Go to bed now."

"I can't sleep," I said. "He opens my door."

"Maybe the latch isn't set properly. Tell Dad. He's good with things like that; he can fix it for you."

"Mom, there's no way I can fall asleep. This house is creaky and dark and haunted."

"So read yourself to sleep, like you've always done. You said there's a library with books. Go find a good book to read. Did you ever find that John Muir book you were looking for? *The Mountains of California*?"

"Yes."

"Well? Did you read it?"

"No."

"Why on earth not? You read everything. I'm surprised."

I didn't think it would be smart to tell her that I'd found Ben's love letter to Harry in the book, and that's what I had read instead. She probably wouldn't have believed that, either.

"Fetch that book and read some of it," she said. "John Muir was a wonderful writer. I've picked up one of his books at the library for my-self. I think you'll like him."

"Okay."

"And for heaven's sake, go to sleep. I love you, my baby."

I hung up and returned the phone to the stand. I started off to the library, but, before I did, I checked in the kitchen drawers and the pantry. I didn't want to light up the whole house and thought maybe I'd find a flashlight. I did: under the sink. I took it to the library, retrieved the Muir book, and retreated to my room. I left my door open, since I knew he would just open it again if I closed it. I clicked on my flashlight and opened the book to the bookmarked essay, "A Wind-storm in the Forests."

I immediately fell into Muir's words; the way he described nature and the world around him was captivating. The essay told the story of John Muir finding a valley of beautiful trees and then, upon seeing an approaching weather front, climbing to the top of a tree and clinging to it to ride out the raucous storm, which whipped him back and forth in the wind and the rain. When the storm passed, he climbed back down to the ground and felt transformed by the experience. The sun shone on the tree branches so gloriously, it seemed to be saying, "My peace I give unto you."

Reading the essay didn't make me sleepy, as my mother had hoped, but it did give me an unusual sense of contentment. I read straight through until I got to the final words: "Never before did these noble woods appear so fresh, so joyous, so immortal."

So fresh. So joyous. So immortal.

The words echoed in my head. No—they echoed in my heart, in my soul—and then I felt sleep draw over me. I set the book aside, turned off my flashlight, and closed my eyes. As I fell into a dark sleep, I kept hearing the words: *My peace I give unto you.*

16

CHAMBER OF SECRETS

Looking back on that summer, I wonder why it wasn't obvious to me. There was a reason my father had jumped the gun on getting the power of attorney signed and had called the notary too soon. He wanted to fail. He could have executed the plan properly—if he had laid the groundwork, as Serena had said. But he hadn't. Because if he had, the problem would have been solved, and then we would have gone on our merry way, our pockets stuffed full of cash. We would have headed for the white cliffs of Dover, scooped up my mother, and lived happily ever after.

But my father didn't want to solve the problem that easily—or, at least, he didn't want to solve the problem we all saw. There was something deeper he was getting at. I didn't know what it was. I'm pretty sure Serena didn't know, either. I'm not even sure my father knew. But it was there. I could feel it rumbling under the surface of everything we did. Riddell House was no longer dead. The old trees that held up the walls and the roof were stirring. They were waking from a long slumber, and their sap was flowing once again.

I woke early the next morning, and, though I hadn't gotten much sleep, I felt refreshed. I ate my breakfast quickly and hovered around the kitchen, waiting for Serena to go to work and for my father to go off and do whatever he did during the days, which was still a mystery to me. When they had cleared out, I returned to the linen closet and checked around carefully to ensure that I hadn't been followed by Grandpa Samuel. I opened the false wall in the back of the closet, turned off the light, and slipped behind the shelves, closing the door after myself and making sure it held fast before I turned on the flashlight I had retrieved from under the kitchen sink. Up the narrow spiral staircase I went, winding around until I reached the landing at the top, where I had seen Ben's apparition. It wasn't really a room. More of a short corridor. Though it was difficult with only a flashlight, I examined the walls as best I could. They were smooth, and the space had no doors or openings. Maybe it was a dead end. Just a small chamber to hide in or something, like Serena said. Hide your priests here.

I decided to examine the walls by feel, not by sight, so I turned off my flashlight and tucked it under my belt. In the blackness, I placed my hands on the wall at shoulder height and slid them along as I traced the perimeter of the space, feeling for some clue. On my second pass of the area (which I paced off and judged to be twelve feet long at most and five feet wide), I held my hands at waist level, and, when I reached the short wall opposite the staircase, I felt a piece of the wall move. I pulled out my flashlight and shone it on the spot. There was a bit of wall, about two inches by five inches, that was flush and almost invisible because of the grain pattern but was loose and hinged on the top, so, when I pushed on it, it flapped open. I slipped my fingers into the hole and felt a latch. I pulled the latch, and the entire wall swung away from me. Humid, musty air flowed into the landing from beyond. I aimed my flashlight past the threshold of the hidden door, but the light couldn't penetrate the thick air, heavy with the dust I had already disturbed. The corridor appeared to continue another ten feet or so to a narrow, steep staircase—really, more of a ladder—that climbed upward again.

I stepped into the corridor. The walls were made of unfinished wood. Douglas fir, I thought confidently, as if I had inherited a shred of intrinsic tree sense from my ancestors. (I came from a long history of timber giants, after all.) The wood had a tight, sturdy grain and a distinctive fragrance, still, even after a century. There were no handrails, so I was careful to mount the stairs without touching the walls. I knew it was probably silly, but I wanted to preserve the integrity of this secret place. It was like going into King Tut's chamber for the first time. At the top of the stairs was another door, but this one opened with a regular doorknob. I guessed whoever built this place figured if you'd made it that far, you must know what you're doing.

The room at the top of the stairs had a window and was dim but not dark. I turned off my flashlight to preserve the battery. As my eyes adjusted to the light, a somber, manly room came into focus. A rich crimson and tobacco rug stretched nearly wall to wall. Those walls were about twenty feet apart, I judged—though I didn't pace it off—and each wall was composed of a dark oak floor-to-ceiling bookshelf. The shelves were filled with leather-bound editions. If this place were some kind of a safe room to protect people from kidnapping bandits, as Serena suggested, the occupants would have had plenty of reading material. Across from a small dormer window was a modestly sized fireplace—at least when judged against the other fireplaces in Riddell House—constructed with smoky brown tiles cast with reliefs of nature scenes. A high-backed velvet sofa, an ornately carved coffee table, and two dark leather club chairs were gathered nearby. A writing desk and chair stood near the window. Several light fixtures adorned the walls. The lamps had kerosene reservoirs; the room, built before electricity, apparently had never been discovered to electrify.

It felt like something of a violation for me to be in that place. I examined the ceiling, which had dark beams crisscrossing at three-foot intervals with an elaborate wood carving set within each square of the grid. Scenes of trees, of loggers, of men working, and of horses hauling. Scenes of men climbing high into the branches, clinging to the top. I remembered my dream, which seemed more like a vision now. A visitation. I thought of John Muir and his essay, and I wondered what this place was. A place to hide? A sanctuary of some sort? A place to worship. A place to be safe. Not from bandits, but from the rest of the world.

The dormer window was too high for me to see out of, and I thought that was something of the point, because beneath it was a wooden step stool; clearly, no one could see into the room from the meadow. I climbed up on the stool, which enabled me to look out over the sill, and it was all there: the meadow, the bluff, Puget Sound. A beautiful view. But the one thing I noticed most of all was a single tree, perfectly centered in the window frame. It was taller than all the other trees around it. Considerably so. It stood out from every other tree I could see. I wondered how old it was, what secrets it knew.

I turned back to the room and let my eyes adjust. On the wall opposite the fireplace was a second door. I opened it and turned on my flashlight to see what was inside. A storage closet. The shelves were filled with boxes of blankets, tins of meat and sardines, stacks of tins with HARD BREAD stamped on them, bottles of wine and bottles of water, really old matches, some survival gear: a shovel, a hatchet, and a knife. The only other thing was a sturdy case—not a footlocker, not nearly as large, but built in the same fashion. I opened it and saw it was filled with notebooks. None of them had titles stamped on their spines, so I removed one. A journal. I opened another: a sketchbook with drawings of a house in it. Riddell House. There were other books, too, which appeared to be accounting ledgers. I removed another book and opened it. It was the diary of Elijah Riddell.

Tuesday, September 13, 1904
I begin this diary to address events of a mysterious nature, which
have occurred since Ben's death two days ago. I must record these

events for fear of forgetting them, or worse—convincing myself that they never happened at all.

To begin, we must go back a step to Sunday afternoon, when I found a letter left for me in my study.

"Dear Father," the letter read. "I had hoped to depart with Harry yesterday. Alice had promised to look after business affairs in my absence. She is quite bright and intelligent—though her father may doubt her—and she is very capable of managing the companies. As such, she willingly granted my wish: to spend my life with my true love, which is not her but Harry. But she knew that already.

"To my dismay, an accident occurred last night, and Harry is dead; I have buried him on Observatory Hill. My heart is broken, Father, and I cannot stay here. I must go in search of him, for I know he is waiting for me; I will find him.

"With much love, I remain forever your faithful son, Benjamin."

It was six-fifteen yesterday morning when I was awakened by Mr. Thomas, who told me a groundskeeper had found a body. The body was Ben's. He was dead.

I was exhausted by evening, having felt so many emotions at the death of my son. It is impossible to describe, so I will not. Mr. Thomas brought soup and brandy to me in my study, and, after eating and drinking, I must have fallen asleep at my desk. I remember having vivid dreams. In these dreams, strange things happened. I climbed trees with my deceased son. I spoke with him, as well. Benjamin. He spoke to me. And while I couldn't discern his words, I felt anxious at his presence, and my sleep was disturbed.

When I opened my eyes, I was surprised to find a pen in my hand and surprised, further, to find a card on my desk with writing on it . . . writing in my own hand! Could I have written it in my sleep? It seemed impossible, and yet . . .

"I will stay here with you, Father," the card said. "Bury me on Observatory Hill, next to Harry. You have never understood our love,

but do this for me, as it will show me that you understand we are all connected. If you do this, I will stay with you to look after The North Estate until it is returned to the forest. When it is, your redemption will be complete. My peace I give unto you, Ben."

This morning, as I sat in my study gazing out the window at the trees which fluttered in the breeze, I saw him standing by the curtains. My Ben! He was with me. I know it is true, and this diary will serve to prove it to myself, else I convince myself my visions are the products of an addled mind.

I was fascinated by this entry. Harry died somehow, just as he and Ben were going to elope, and Ben died the next day. It must have been terrible. But what I found most intriguing was Elijah writing a note in his sleep. A note from Ben, after Elijah had such vivid dreams. It was Ben, the ghost, who had written the note, clearly, channeled through his sleeping father, as he used Grandpa Samuel to write for him.

I turned the page and read the next entry.

Saturday, September 17, 1904

We buried Ben today. A cold fog lingered near the ground in the morning, lifting later. It didn't rain. (It wouldn't dare rain on the day my son was buried.) The turnout for the funeral was impressive. Thomas counted four hundred at least. Food was served to all, per custom. A feast with much port tapped—only the finest. Why should I hoard it? For what gathering would it be better suited? I briefly considered having an altar erected and a lamb sacrificed, as I thought Ben might get a laugh out of that. Thomas suggested such a gesture might play wrong in the press. I briefly considered having a newspaper editor or two sacrificed at an altar so I could eat their hearts. Again, Thomas's better reason prevailed.

I don't think our guests will leave soon. As of now, they are encamped on the meadow—many have traveled from Portland and

Aberdeen—and some of his classmates from back East have come as well—a testament to Ben's nature.

I shall miss him. I already do.

I keep his card in my pocket—his last note to me. It was written by me, which I don't understand, but do understand as well. I slip my hand into my pocket and finger it at times. The sharp corners poke into my fingertip, and I can make it hurt if I like.

We buried Ben next to Harry—on Observatory Hill, as Ben wished. I hope that they will find, in death, a peace together they were unable to find in life.

I found the diary too hard to resist, so even though I could hear footsteps through the wall, and I could hear people calling for me, I read two more short entries.

Monday, September 19, 1904

The guests are still here. Sixty of them at least. I have told Thomas to slaughter a fresh lamb each day they stay—we are on our third.

Truth be told, I don't want them to leave. Their campfires, which burn day and night in the dampness, are beacons for Ben. I walk among the mourners each evening, embracing the bereaved, and talking to them. I feel Ben is with me on these walks, and he likes what he sees.

Wednesday, September 21, 1904

They are all gone. Thomas and I are alone now, and the house shudders with emptiness.

I closed the book and listened. Serena and my father were calling for me, but I was safe from them inside Elijah's sanctuary. I didn't know what time it was, because I still hadn't found my watch.

I returned the diary to the box, closed the closet door, and descended the stairs quickly but carefully, unlatched the door and closed it behind myself. I didn't want to be discovered, so I didn't turn on my flashlight but went down the spiral stairs in the dark instead. I slipped out of the false linen closet and into the hall.

Just when I thought I was clear, Serena called out from behind me.

"Where have you been?"

"Around," I said, trying to act calm.

"Why are you in the south wing?" she asked. "No one uses the south wing. Are you looking for something?"

"I was just . . . interested. I was looking around. That's all."

She scrutinized me for a moment.

"I came home early so we could all go to dinner on the waterfront," she said finally. "Fresh cracked crab. Are you ready?"

It was dinnertime already? I'd spent the whole day in the secret room? I realized how hungry I was.

"I should put on a nicer shirt," I said, since I was wearing only a T-shirt.

"If you like. But then you'll be Seattle Formal. If you're wearing pants that go down to your ankles, shoes that cover your toes, and a shirt that covers your forearms, you're in formal attire in Seattle."

I laughed with relief; Serena suspected nothing.

"I'll just wash my hands."

"Do hurry," she said. "It gets crowded downtown on a day like today, and I don't like Grandpa going to bed late."

"I'll hurry, Simply Serena."

"Like the wind, Clever Trevor. Like the wind."

17

THE RETURN OF THE HAND

We returned to Riddell House after dinner, and the sky was still light with the evening sun. Our small group dispersed, and I decided to make the hike up Observatory Hill, a place I was determined to visit. I wanted to see the graves. When I reached the top, panting from the hike, I found a small patch of weeds in an enclosure formed by a low, dilapidated picket fence. Within the enclosure were five tombstones. I stepped over the fence and into the mini-graveyard to examine the stones. Harry Lindsey, Benjamin Riddell, Elijah Riddell, Abraham Riddell, Isobel Jones Riddell. The dates on Harry Lindsey's tombstone were January 2, 1883–September 10, 1904. The dates on Benjamin's tombstone were May 12, 1876–September 11, 1904.

The epitaph on Benjamin's tombstone was difficult to read, as the limestone had been eroded by the wind and rain, but I brushed the lichens from the stone with my thumb and blew away the dust so I could see.

MY PEACE I GIVE UNTO YOU—JOHN MUIR

From *The Mountains of California*. And from the card that Ben had written to Elijah after he died.

I returned to my room and opened the windows, hoping for a breeze. With the lights off, I aimed the fan at my head and lay down on the bed, cradling the carved wooden hand to my chest; I felt a visceral need to hold it close. Ben. Harry. Elijah. They were just shadows from my family's past, but they were becoming so real to me. And then the images came harder. They came before the dark shade of sleep had been pulled down. Branches whipping against my face, and the breathlessness of falling. I fought against it. I didn't want Ben's dream, though Ben fought so hard to give it to me. Lying back and seeing the sky, the clouds, and falling. Endlessly falling, the hollow feeling of my stomach in my mouth, of despair. I struggled. I resisted. I battled. Until I woke up with a start, sweating and shaken. Still, I held the hand.

The room was dark. The house was quiet. I went to the door and opened it tentatively. The hallway was silent. Not a creature stirring. I glanced at the clock. Just after nine. I wandered down the long hall and to my father's room, which was empty. Down the stairs and back to the kitchen. I found my father sitting at the table, watching television quietly. A baseball game. My father didn't even like baseball.

He looked up when he heard me enter.

"Oh, hey," he said. "You feel okay? You look like you've seen a ghost."

I blinked at him.

"What have you got there?" he asked, noticing the hand, which I still cradled in my arms.

I had forgotten I was holding it. I lifted it and held it out for my father to see. My father beckoned. I approached and set the carving down on the table.

"Where did you find it?"

He didn't reach out for it; he just stared at it. I grew uncomfortable but said nothing.

"Where did you find it?" he asked again.

"In the barn," I said. "There are a bunch of footlockers in the loft. I found it in one of them."

"What else was in the footlocker?"

"Clothes and stuff. Old school papers."

"*My* old school papers?" he asked, but he clearly already knew the answer. Still, he did not take his eyes off the hand, as if he were afraid it might vanish if he stopped looking at it.

"Yes."

A balloon of silence expanded in the room. It started small, and with every breath it got bigger and bigger until the silence practically squeezed my father and me against the walls with its explosive potential.

"Do you know what my father said to me after my mother died?" he asked eventually, and the air eased out of the balloon so gently. "He came into my room, handed me a suitcase, and he said, 'They're coming for you in the morning; you can take one bag.'"

He looked up at me for the first time since the wooden hand had been set on the table.

"I've wondered what happened to the things that didn't fit into that suitcase," he said.

"They're in a locker in the barn."

"Why are you looking for things?"

"Because I'm a truth seeker," I replied.

"A truth seeker," my father echoed.

He gave me the hand, and then he led me down to the barn through the night air with the crickets creaking and the frogs singing so loudly in the darkness it was almost disturbing. The moon was perfect and there were so many stars.

Grandpa Samuel wasn't in the barn. My father dug around the long workbench with all the vises and devices attached to it and all the tools hanging above it, everything covered with sawdust and some things more worn and rusted than others. He unearthed a box of small wooden dowels and filled his pocket with a handful of them. He gathered a hand drill and scavenged a drawer for bits until he found one that matched the diameter of the dowels. He grabbed some coarse sandpaper, a bottle of wood glue, and two wood clamps, and we headed back to the house.

"What are we doing?" I asked, once we were back outside.

"You know, Trevor, sometimes you have to set the universe right."

"I know. I've been trying. It hasn't been working very well."

"I guess we both have to try harder."

Back in the foyer, my father used the rough-grit sandpaper to take the sheen off the top of the newel at the bottom of the main staircase. As soon as I saw him working, it all clicked for me. I *knew* there was something missing. I knew the newel looked truncated in some way, but years of being oiled by hands rubbing against it, and maybe even some cosmetic sanding, concealed the scar. My father got the newel roughed up enough that when he set the carved hand and globe atop, it fit almost perfectly; the wrist appeared to grow from the banister and hold up the earth for all to see. Like Atlas, almost. Like God, maybe.

My father pulled a pencil from the stash of stuff he'd grabbed in the barn, and he made some marks. He used the hand drill to bore holes into the hand and the newel post. When he was done, he used wood glue and clamps to secure the hand to the newel and banister.

"Do you feel it?" he asked, as he admired the restored hand.

"Feel what?" I asked in reply.

"The power. The energy."

"What does the energy do?"

"Maybe it will bring her back," he said.

"Bring *who* back?"

"My mother."

I was right: there was a lot to be resolved by my father before we would be able to move forward with any real future plans to get our family back together. We could develop the land and make money all we wanted, but it wouldn't solve the real problem that was gnawing at my father.

We remained silent for a moment, and then footsteps approached. Serena entered the foyer.

"What are you two up to?" she asked.

She followed our eyes to the hand.

"Brother Jones! I declare! What have you done?"

"I've put it back," he said.

"But why? It will make Daddy crazy."

"He's already crazy."

"He's *demented*," she clarified. "*This* will make him crazy."

"I don't care," my father said, still staring at the hand. "I did it for Mom."

Serena sidled up behind him and touched his arm lightly. Touch. Until he looked at her.

"Tell me you're not getting sentimental on me, Brother Jones," she said. "Tell me this won't change our plans."

"I'm setting things right," he said firmly.

"And when they're right, you'll get Daddy to sign the papers, yes?"

"Yes."

She leaned into him and kissed his cheek.

"I knew you would come to save me," she said softly. "I never once lost faith."

She drifted down the hall in her flowing dress with her bare feet not touching the ground, gliding, her nails painted blue, her toes she used to tease me, slipping off her shoes in the kitchen when she sat to rest after a hard afternoon of cooking, sitting and pressing her thumbs into the balls of her feet to release the tension and I would watch her do it and I would see the blue nails and get a hard-on. She did it for too long and she did it too obviously and she took too much pleasure from it, and then she would stop abruptly and hide her feet under the table and say to me, "Run along now and wash up," so I would go upstairs and lose myself in the images of Serena's small waist and big boobs and blue toenails, her citrus scent that I could smell as if she were in the room with me. She was so hot and she was playing with me—but I somehow wanted to be played with. So I didn't shy away from it at all; I felt the stiffness rising and I resisted the urge to adjust. And I despised myself for my base urges.

"My mother said this hand belongs to the spirit of the house," my father said after Serena was gone.

"Who took it away?" I asked, refocusing on my father as the citrusy scent dissipated.

"Grandpa Samuel. He took the ax to it."

"But why?"

"People destroy things they don't understand," he said. "Those things make them feel inadequate and insecure. So they destroy. But now it's back. I'm back. And he can't hide anymore."

"Hide what?" I asked. "What's he hiding from?"

"The truth, Trevor. Do you know what he said to me before he sent me away?"

"'You can take one bag'?"

"Before that," he said after scrutinizing me for assholery or snideness, of which there was no evidence. "He said: 'Go away from here. You're no good to me anymore.' He might as well have killed me."

"Why did he say it, though?" I asked.

"Because of what happened," my father said.

"What happened?"

"I don't want to talk about it."

I'd heard that before.

"Isn't that why you brought me here?" I asked. "To learn to talk about it?"

"What do you mean?"

"That's why you brought me here instead of letting me go with Mom, isn't it? So I could look for things. So I could find things."

My father nodded to himself silently. "I'm not sure."

"I heard you," I confessed. "You were fighting about it. She wanted me to go to England with her, but you said you needed me to go with you. You said you didn't know why, but you felt it so powerfully, you couldn't deny it. If she didn't let you take me here, you would probably die. And with that kind of a threat, what was she supposed to do?"

"Is that how it happened?" he asked. "I don't remember."

"I remember," I said. "That's how it happened. Just because you don't know the reason doesn't mean there isn't one."

"Then I hope you know what you're doing," he said softly, and he climbed the stairs for his room.

I didn't know what I was doing. I was going by instinct; I was following my intuition. I'd read enough fairy tales to know that, if my heart was true, I'd be able to do the right thing for all of us; I could save us all. And I'd read enough Kafka to know that, if I did it wrong, it might lead to the end of all things.

18

SERENA'S VISIT

Later that night, I was writing down my thoughts about the wooden hand as well as why my father felt it was so necessary for me to accompany him on this trip, when I heard a soft knocking at my door. Serena opened the door without waiting for a reply.

"May I come in?" she asked, poking her head into the room and then stepping inside.

She was wearing a nightdress of thin, white cotton, held up by two narrow straps. It left her shoulders exposed, and her ankles and toes. She perched on the end of my bed. She had washed the makeup from her face, and her skin was scrubbed and vibrant. The oscillating fan that chirped like a bird as it turned left, but not when it turned right, blew a strand of auburn hair across her face. She tucked the hair behind her ear and smiled at me.

"Do you have a moment?" she asked.

No, I thought. I have no moments, because time has stopped with Aunt Serena.

"Sure."

"I think it's sweet that you're bonding with your grandfather. I can see that he's taken to you, and it's important that he has this personal connection. But before you become too emotionally involved, I think it's only fair to clarify what I've already mentioned to you: Grandpa Samuel is ill, and his prognosis is death."

"Isn't everyone's prognosis death?" I asked after a moment.

"Hmm," she agreed, smiling and nodding. "Clever. But your grandfather is going to die *soon*, and in a terrible way. He will lose sight of his immediate history first, and then his past. He won't know who you are, and he may say mean things to you. You should know that."

"I know it," I said. "It's Alzheimer's."

"You're able to see him in a new light now, having met him for the first time. You see him freshly. You don't know his past, his history. You haven't seen what your father and I have seen. And so your little episode with the wooden hand tonight . . . Well, you don't understand the implications. You don't have a full understanding of the context."

"What is the context, then?" I asked quickly. I was already understanding Serena's ways. Her twisted dialectic.

"That's what I'm here to tell you," she said, again pushing the hair back from her face. "If you can spare a few moments."

"Sure," I said, closing my journal and setting it down on the nightstand.

She adjusted herself at the end of my bed, scooting back so she could lean against the wall, so her legs were straight before her and her blue toenails stared at me.

"Are you listening?" she asked, waving her hand in front of me.

"I'm listening."

"Grandpa Samuel wasn't always as sweet as he is now; don't be deceived by his easygoing nature. That's his medication at work. Years ago, he was an angry, cruel man. Bitter and spiteful. After Grandpa Abe died and we realized how far in debt he really was, Grandpa Samuel fell into the bottle, as my mother would say. He became a heavy drinker, and it was not pleasant. He was angry all the time, flying into rage at the slightest provocation. He spent long hours in the barn, doing whatever it was he did there. I don't know why Mother became ill then. I'm sure doctors would have an explanation for it, because that's what they are paid to do—explain things within the context of their belief system. But, as the saying goes: If your only tool is a hammer, everything looks like a nail."

"I'm not sure I get that," I said.

"Science bludgeons us with formulae and theories, but do the practitioners of science know more than anyone else? They say what they believe with great force—and they are sure to ridicule anyone who may hold an alternate opinion—but isn't that a familiar defensive posture, which has been seen before in religions like Christianity, Judaism, and Islam?"

"You're saying that science is a religion?" I asked.

"I'm saying that sometimes there are triggers for disease that may be rooted in the metaphysical realm, and, when something like that occurs, medical science tends to dismiss the connection because it does not exist within the pages of their medical tomes. But let's not get bogged down in such a debate this evening. My point—which is of some import to you, I believe—is that if one were to look for the source of Mother's illness scientifically, one might say she had an entirely idiopathic disease and there is no accounting for its origin. But if one were to take a more holistic view, one might conjecture that Isobel grew ill because she took on the suffering of her husband, whom she loved very much."

"What was she sick with?"

"Oh, ALS. Lou Gehrig's disease. I'd assumed you knew—"

"No," I said. "And how do you make yourself sick with Lou Gehrig's disease?"

"She didn't make herself sick," Serena said patiently. "She allowed herself to become ill because she refused to resolve a psychic rift within her. Are you following me? You seem brighter than most, and that is the

2

only reason I am confiding in you so. Mother's need to save Daddy was so great that his decline and her desire to save him collided, like two oppositely bound freight trains on the same track. Eventually the truth will out."

"I see."

"Grandpa Samuel suffered mightily at the demise of the Empire. Your grandmother took on his suffering. Additionally, she protected your father and me. She held us. She shielded us from Daddy's anger and rage and sickness. She kept us healthy and loving. And she always told us to thank those who were protecting us. It wasn't only her, she told us. But the house. The Estate. Mother believed a spirit watched over the house and us, and that spirit's energy was focused in the carved hand. She had us touch the hand—the one you and your father reinstalled this evening—each night before we went upstairs to bed. The three of us would pause before the hand. We would touch it and feel its warmth, and while we uttered no words, in our hearts we prayed for the hand to protect us.

"As you can imagine, the system became symbiotic: the angrier Daddy grew, the more we depended upon the hand; the more we depended upon the hand, the angrier Daddy grew. We were together in our faith; he was left out. And so it went until the system erupted. One night, Daddy could take no more. He was at his end, and surely his next step would have been to drink himself to death, which likely would have happened that very night, had he found no other outlet for his rage—I have a secret belief that, in an alternate universe, Daddy died that night of acute alcohol poisoning; a coward's way to die, but effective nonetheless. But Daddy has always been more selfish than that; rather than take himself out, he destroyed the easiest target he could find. He fetched an ax from the barn, and, with great blows that shook the house, he chopped the hand from the newel in the foyer.

"We heard the blows from the kitchen, and we ran in to investigate the commotion. He had a crazed look on his face, like he was possessed by the devil himself, as he swung the mighty ax—he swung his ax like a true logger would—until the hand broke free and flew into the air. Of course, Daddy was as drunk as a skunk, so, when the hand flew, so did he, spinning backward, falling and cracking his head open on the floor. The ax flew out of his hands and landed at our little bare feet, stabbing into the floor before us—you can see the scar of it to this day, if you don't believe me. A terrible shudder echoed through the house. If you think we weren't fearful for our lives, Trevor, you are sorely mistaken."

She paused for a moment and smoothed her dress, brushed back her hair. I was completely absorbed in her story and sat staring at her.

"Daddy gathered himself and the severed wooden hand and left the house," she continued after an appropriately dramatic pause. "Blood was trickling down the back of his neck from where he had hit his head. He left the ax, we don't know why, and Brother Jones eventually took it downstairs into the basement so we wouldn't have to see it again. We didn't see Daddy for days after that. We went about our business, because that is what people do. But we all felt—Mother, Brother Jones, and I—that our hearts had been cleaved from our chests with the cleaving of the hand."

"So what happened?" I asked.

"When Daddy finally returned, we accepted him into the family as if nothing had happened, because that's what Mother asked of us."

"But why? Why would she ask you to do that if he was so mean?"

"Mother felt it was her duty to save him. It was her duty to *cure* him. That's when her illness grew. And it grew quickly."

"She took on his illness."

"Her illness had been brewing, obviously," Serena said. "But she had hidden her pain. After the hand was taken away, the illness spread very quickly. Soon she was bedridden. Soon after that, she was dead."

"That's terrible," I whispered. "For her to die like that."

"It was her path," Serena told me. "It's not for us to judge. No one knows why it was her path. One might argue that it was what she could do to save him; after she died, Daddy stopped drinking entirely. Since that day, he has refused to touch a drop."

I cocked my head at that, knowing about the "medicine." Serena stopped speaking and raised her eyebrows, inviting my question, but I thought better of asking it.

"Just thinking," I said.

"Of course. Even sober, Daddy saw his own guilt reflected in the eyes of his children—your father and me—and he couldn't stand living with his shame. Your father was sixteen, I was only eleven. That was how Grandpa Samuel justified sending your father away. Brother Jones was old enough to go out on his own, he said. I was still young; I was a child. I didn't come to the realization that he kept me with him because he needed a servant until much later—until I was already enslaved. And while Daddy still felt his shame about Mother's death, at least he could resent me for my presence, which he always has."

"Why didn't you leave?" I asked.

"I've tried, Trevor. Believe me, I've tried. But I am my mother's daughter, and so, on some level, I want to make him well, too. To honor her, I suppose. And I've stayed because I've always had faith that Brother Jones would return to save me, as he promised me he would."

After a long moment, she sighed and clapped her hands against her thighs. She scooted herself forward on the bed and stood up.

"It is a dark history we share, my nephew," she said, looking down upon me. She leaned over and kissed my forehead. "The hand has been returned, which is your doing, I know. Because the blood that flows through me, as well flows through you. So I know everything you do. You and I are Riddells, Clever Trevor, and nothing can separate us. No one knows what Daddy's reaction will be to the returning of the hand; perhaps he won't even notice. But you should be aware, as you pursue your investigations, that waking a sleeping giant is not always the best way of achieving one's goals. Which leads me to wonder if you know what your goals are, Trevor. Do you?"

She looked at me again, at length, to let me settle on the question and begin to contemplate the answer.

"But I suppose that's a topic for another conversation," she said breezily. "Good night, my dear. Sleep tight."

She turned off the overhead light as she left the room. I tossed and turned but could not get comfortable. My mind was churning. Yes, I knew my goals. Of course I knew my goals. I wanted a father and a mother and at least a shot at having some kind of happiness in my life.

19

THE SEARCHERS

When I was a boy, my mother told me that my father had a feel for wood. That was why he was so good at building wooden boats, she told me. Wood was in his blood. He was descended from a long line of loggers and timbermen, and so he knew the inner thoughts of trees.

I believed her because I believed everything my mother said was true. But what did that mean to a seven-year-old kid? *Your father has a feel for wood?* When I imagined "loggers and timbermen," I thought of plaid flannel shirts and bushy beards. But that wasn't the Riddell family at all. It turns out I was descended from a long line of businessmen and deal makers and profiteers. Not a flannel shirt among them, except for Ben.

But that night at Riddell House, when my father returned the carved hand to the newel where it was supposed to be, he did it in a way that was at once reverential and deliberate and confident. My father *knew* something. I could see it in his eyes. He knew what was right about the world he was in. He knew what was supposed to happen, and I wasn't sure I'd ever seen my father with that look when he wasn't holding a piece of wood. So I was pretty sure my mother had told me the truth: wood *was* in my father's blood.

I wasn't sure what was in my own blood when I was fourteen. I hoped I was like my father, and that there was something—not wood, but something else; words, maybe; stories—something I could touch and, when I touched it, it was different than when other people touched it. I wanted very badly to have an affinity for something that would become transcendent when I held it in my hands. I don't know that I've ever found that thing; sometimes I suspect I have, but then I doubt myself. Perhaps I'm looking for it still.

Perhaps that's what life is about—the search for such a connection. The search for magic. The search for the inexplicable. Not in order to explain it, or contain it. Simply in order to feel it. Because in that recognition of the sublime, we see for a moment the entire universe in the palm of our hand. And in that moment, we touch the face of God.

Walking down the hallway toward the foyer, I came upon Grandpa Samuel standing before the wooden hand. He looked perplexed, but not agitated or distressed. I stopped midstep and silently watched my grandfather.

He stood for several minutes, not moving at all. And then he reached out and touched the carving with one hand, then with both hands. He ran his hands over the dark, smooth wood: the fingers, the wrist, the globe.

He dropped his hands to his sides and turned to me. His T-shirt said: FREE NELSON MANDELA.

"Who are you?" Grandpa Samuel asked calmly. "Why are you here?"

"I'm Trevor. Your grandson. I'm here because it's the only place we have to go."

Grandpa Samuel nodded, then turned and left the house through the front door.

After he had gone, I scanned the floor and I spotted it. The deep gouge of an ax. The scar. Darkened from the years, but unmistakably the scar about which Serena had spoken.

They say that, to a hummingbird, people seem like stone sculptures. The metabolism of hummingbirds is so fast that time is different for them. Their wings move too quickly to be seen by us; surely our hulking presence must make us look like trees to them: massive and rooted. So maybe hummingbirds are to humans as humans are to trees. We think of trees as static creatures, but they live for thousands of years, and so their scale of time is different than ours. Or, I should correct myself. *Some* trees live for thousands of years. Only a few, really. Many die of natural causes: landslides, fires, disease. The vast majority are chopped down by people and pulverized in gnarly chewing machines, their remains bound with formaldehyde-based glues and pressed into chipboards that will be used to build nurseries so our children can grow up in a toxic, outgassing environment and develop horrible health problems as they age, yet will be unable to sue anyone for damages because, well, there simply aren't enough studies to prove anything conclusively.

Riddell House and its eternal groaning. The old house sighed and groaned and shifted as if it were constantly moving, shrugging itself toward the bluff like an old man, mumbling and complaining with each step. I noticed it especially at night. Sometimes I lay awake and thought I could hear the house sinking into the ground—or the ground swallowing the house. I wasn't sure which.

The night after the wooden hand had been restored to the newel in the foyer, however, it wasn't the house that made noise but one of its inhabitants. I heard footsteps in the hallway and on the stairs at nearly 4:00 A.M., so I went upstairs to the ballroom. I found my father standing in the middle of the dance floor wearing only pajama bottoms. He didn't notice me.

He was waiting for her to dance for him, like she danced for Grandpa Samuel. It was clear to me. We hadn't come to sell off the place, or to reconcile with Grandpa Samuel. But to see if Isobel might still be there. And the footsteps Grandpa heard were the evidence my father needed to believe she was here. So he waited.

I didn't want to call attention to his quest. While I wasn't entirely convinced it was the act of a healthy mind, I suspected that deep down there was some spiritual healing that would be provided by my father's search for Isobel's soul. Or at least spiritual hope. And all journeys begin with hope; how they resolve is another matter.

Without a sound, I left my father there to wait. Instead of going back to bed, I returned to the linen closet. I opened the door. Inside the threshold of the closet was a kerosene lantern I had found in the barn— Grandpa Samuel had helped me clean the lantern, fill it with fuel, and find a new wick. I lit the lantern with the matches from the kitchen and climbed the stairs. I opened the entry door and ascended to the secret room. I took Elijah's diary from the closet, made myself comfortable in a club chair, and I spent the rest of the night reading. The only sounds were the turning of pages and the hissing of the kerosene lantern that provided my light.

Monday, October 10, 1904

My house is empty save Mr. Thomas. I never imagined I would miss my son so much: his anger and his passion, his rage against injustice and his indomitable will to right all wrongs. His playful and joking spirit, even after a rousing debate that bordered on brawl. Perhaps I took him for granted. I suppose I did.

The Jordan deal is done finally. It wasn't pity but love that finished it. I have no doubt JJ would have washed his hands of the deal and walked away from it had it been up to him. But his daughter, he said, insisted the deal go through even though her part of the bargain was no longer on the table: Ben's hand in marriage. She said it was what Ben wanted. She said we owed it to him—all of us owed it to him. And so now I have gained a fortune. I am wealthy beyond my imagination. And I am alone.

I have paid for my fortune with the life of my son. So now, with whom do I share it?

Alice is right—we all owe Ben for what we have.

When I asked Ben to help me build The North Estate, he told me he would only do so if I understood that none of us owns this place, this world—we simply look after it for a time. If I truly understood, he said, I would not object to his demand. I did not understand then, but I agreed for expedience's sake. Now that he is gone, I feel I do understand his meaning: the forest is eternal; we are merely passers-through.

And so I resolve to do as he asked: when I am gone, The North Estate will be returned to the forest.

20

THE COTTAGE

I awakened in the secret room when it was still early, and it took me a moment to remember where I was. My neck was stiff from sleeping in the chair and the lantern had burned through its fuel, so the room was dim with filtered dawn light. I stood up and stretched. I didn't remember falling asleep. I just remembered reading and reading and then being awake. I rubbed my eyes and glanced around the room and was startled by a man standing in the corner.

"What the hell?" I whispered, totally freaked out.

He stood in the darkness, completely still like maybe he thought he was invisible or something. But I could clearly see him. He wore a long coat and a hat with the brim pulled down so I couldn't see his face for the shadows. He was tall and of slight build. For a moment, I almost convinced myself he was a trick of my eyes, nothing more than an elaborate shadow, but then he moved his hand and I saw he was real.

"How did you get in here?" I asked. "Who are you?"

I took a step toward him, and the shadow of his coat fluttered. I took another step, and then, as if stirred by a breeze, he dissipated like smoke.

I held my breath for several moments, just standing there looking at the corner, wondering if it was true, if I had really seen the ghost.

Shaken by my encounter, I left the secret room and went downstairs to my bedroom. After changing my clothes and brushing my teeth, I noticed a pamphlet on my desk that hadn't been there previously. At least I didn't remember seeing it. I looked closer. It was a brochure for Cunard Line cruises. I assumed Serena must have left it there by mistake, so I took it with me and went down to the kitchen.

The house was desolate, which was something I hadn't grown accustomed to yet; it was such a big house, it was easy for people to get lost in it, like a hedge maze. The kitchen was empty, and I stood in front of the phone. I pulled my mother's telephone number from my pocket. It was afternoon in England. I wanted to talk to her; I wanted to tell her everything that was going on so she could fix it. I wanted to tell her about the ghost so she could explain it. She could tell me that I wasn't losing my mind and I had nothing to fear. I lifted the receiver.

"Who on earth are you calling at this hour?" Serena said, startling me to the point that I dropped the receiver on the table and had to quickly scoop it up.

"I didn't see you," I said.

She was sitting in the bay window with a mug of coffee and a book.

"I'm right here," she said. "I didn't mean to frighten you."

I cradled the receiver in my hands.

"Go ahead and make your call. I simply was curious, but I suppose it's not my business. Feel free."

"There's no privacy here," I mumbled, replacing the receiver on the phone and sitting heavily at the kitchen table. "It's like a prison."

"Welcome to my world, Clever Trevor. Would you like some coffee?"

"My mom doesn't let me drink coffee."

Serena smiled. She went to the cupboard, retrieved a mug, and filled it with coffee. She took it to the freezer, removed a carton of ice cream, scooped a spoonful into the mug, and set it before me with a firm clunk.

"I'm not your mom."

I picked up the mug and took a sip. It was good. Cold and creamy, but also hot and bitter. I loved this drink, this nectar. And Serena delivering it to me, looking as beautiful as she always did, in her lightweight dress, her modest makeup, her blue toes—she always looked so put together. For a moment, I forgot about the ghost and my mother.

"So tell me, nephew of mine," Serena said, sitting at the long table and propping up her chin with her elbow. "What is it you're up to? You didn't sleep in your room last night. Should I be concerned?"

"How do you know?"

"I know everything that goes on in Riddell House."

I took another sip of Serena's potion. It was delightfully good. Was she magic? I was under her spell.

"Information is our commodity, Trevor," she reminded me. "It's how we build relationships."

"I slept in a bedroom upstairs," I lied.

"Why?"

I took a long drink of my ice-cream-enhanced coffee and looked up at her.

"Why does the cock crow?" I asked. "Don't ask him, he doesn't know."

Her eyes narrowed and she was still for a moment; then she stood up quickly and snatched the mug from my hand before I could avoid her.

"Cocks don't drink coffee," she said. "Only good little boys who please their aunts. You can go now."

Serena emptied the drink into the sink and ran the water to wash it down the drain; the elixir was gone. I felt deeply hurt by this betrayal, how Serena gave things and took them back so capriciously; I was always off balance. She rinsed the mug and put it in the dishwasher, and then she noticed me with an exaggerated gesture.

"You can *go* now," she repeated. She shook her head and scoffed, and then returned to her perch in the bay window and took up the book she had been reading.

I hesitated before leaving. I felt both sad and angry at the same time, and that confused me. After a moment, I produced the cruise brochure from my back pocket and placed it on the table. "You left this in my room."

Serena looked up questioningly. She beckoned with an outstretched hand and took the brochure when I brought it to her.

"Where did you get this?"

"In my room," I said. "You must have left it when you came in last night."

"Nonsense."

"It was there on my desk."

"Be careful where you're snooping," Serena warned. "Little boys have been known to lose their fingers around here."

She tucked the brochure away, and I scrutinized her for a moment, trying to glean the nature of her comment.

"Where's my dad?" I finally asked.

"I have no idea. I hope he's off convincing your grandfather to sign that document, but I doubt it. I suppose he's chasing butterflies. Or maybe he's running along the railroad tracks like he used to do."

I left Serena in the kitchen and jogged down the hill to the barn. Or maybe I fled. I felt unsettled that I couldn't call my mother; I needed to make contact with someone who didn't have an agenda. Grandpa Samuel wasn't in the barn. I glanced around to see if he was outside somewhere, and I noticed, on the other side of the orchard, a man working on the yard. He was hacking at something.

I made my way down the far side of the barn to the orchard and wove through the tangle of neglected apple trees, which were tall and leggy and didn't look as if they produced much fruit. As I got closer to the man, I realized it was my father. And he was wielding a machete.

He was wearing his usual work clothes: khakis, boating shoes, and a white T-shirt. But he was almost unrecognizable in his demeanor as he swung the long blade at a mountain of blackberry vines, easily ten feet tall. Relentlessly he attacked the ropes of green brambles, wincing when the vines grabbed his blade and held it tight until he could jerk it free and a vine would jump out at him and tear at his flesh with its razor-like thorns. He worked and worked, and I watched for several minutes until he took a break.

"What are you doing?" I asked.

"Oh, hey," he replied, not having realized I was there. He took a drink from a bottle of water.

"Is there a purpose? Or are you just wanting to kill something?"

"There's a fire pit under all this," he said. "It's big. Made of stones, with benches and everything. When I was a kid, we used to have fires every weekend, unless it was raining too hard. My mom loved it; it brought us all together, she said. It united us. I liked it in the winter when it was really cold. To be able to sit by the fire so your face is hot but your back is cold. I don't know. There's something . . ."

He faded off, and I realized he hadn't looked at me at all when he was talking; he was sizing up the blackberry bushes the whole time, as if the bushes had stolen something from him and he was determined to get it back.

"So you thought you would dig it out," I said.

"Yeah, well. I've got to do something around here or I'm going to go out of my mind. And, anyway, I thought maybe you'd like to have a fire. You know, you can see a little of what my childhood was like."

I was amazed by the very concept. My father could have been in a witness relocation program for all I knew about his history, and here we had it within our reach!

"You want me to help?" I asked.

"No. I mean, unless you want to. Look at my arms."

He held them out for me to examine, and his forearms were covered with long bloody scratches.

"You should wear a long-sleeve shirt," I said.

"I'm on a mission. Can't stop now. Have you explored the woods at all? You should go exploring."

"I found the graveyard."

"There's an old cottage in the woods near the ravine," he said. "The caretakers stayed there when they were building Riddell House. My parents lived there before I was born. And further on, down by the creek, there's an old waterwheel they used for grinding grain. Go wander around. Nothing can hurt you here."

I left him in the orchard and hiked back up to the meadow feeling somewhat successful at making a connection with my father, as brief as it was. I crossed the meadow and walked into the woods, following a broken path to the edge of a ravine, which was home to a swiftly running creek about thirty feet below me. I noticed another path diverging into the woods, and peered down it as far as I could. I was wondering if I should take it when I heard a rustling in the distance—footsteps, perhaps—so I followed the path toward the sound, excited that Ben might be leading me somewhere. The path veered away from the ravine and into thicker woods, eventually leading me to a small, shady clearing and a shingled cottage with a tall peaked roof and little porch out front, looking suspiciously like a place Hansel and Gretel had visited. The cottage felt familiar to me, and not at all empty.

I opened the front door and took stock of the room. There had been no vandals over the years, it seemed, but rodents and spiders had taken over. A kitchen table and a wood-burning stove were tucked into the kitchen area, while a couple of sofas with stuffing ripped out by animals formed a sitting area. Gritty dirt covered the floors.

Upstairs, I found four small bedrooms, each simply furnished with a small bed and a dresser, similar to the generic bedroom setup of Riddell House. Otherwise, they were bare of any personal or identifiable belongings. As I started down the stairs, I heard a deliberate creak from behind me. I turned around and noticed a narrow door at the end of the landing.

I opened it. Tight stairs climbed up into the attic. I considered climbing them, but I had no light and it was awfully dark up there. I returned to the kitchen and looked under the sink because that's where people keep their flashlights, though I assumed I wouldn't find one—or at least not a working one. What I did find, however, was a yellow and white box of plumbers' candles. And, of course, I was always armed with a book of matches because of my encounter with Ben on the landing of the secret stairs. . . .

There was little to see in the attic by the light of a few flickering candles. Spiderwebs, mostly, and bird nests and mouse droppings. A couple of wooden boxes. I looked inside one of the boxes and discovered several handwritten diaries. I carried the box down the stairs and out onto the porch. I removed one of the diaries and opened it. I had found the journals of Harry Lindsey.

I couldn't wait. I flipped to a random entry and began to read.

June 23, 1901

    The climb seemed to have exhausted us both, physically and emotionally; the next morning we didn't climb again as Ben suggested we might, but we lazed about, resting our weary muscles. That afternoon we went hunting with a small-bore rifle, and we bagged several squirrels, who seemed not the brightest creatures on the planet, as they lost all inhibitions and approached us if we stood still long enough; we practically could have killed them with our hands.

    In the evening, we ate well, and we drank well as Ben's horse, Molly, had been burdened with an ample supply of wine and a jug of whiskey, too. As we enjoyed our fire in the dark forest, Ben pulled out his pipe, as was his custom. I had gotten so used to him and his habits; I knew him so well though we'd met only a dozen weeks ago.

    "You've told me about your mother and father and how you were orphaned," he said, working his pipe in his lips. "I suppose it's only fair for me to tell you about mine."

"I think that's fair," I agreed.

He stood up and found the whiskey bottle in a saddlebag, sloshed some into our mugs, and then he hovered over the campfire.

"When I was born, my mother refused to move west with my father. I lived with her in St. Paul until my father deemed I was old enough to learn the ways of the world. Then I was sent to schools to be educated."

"What schools were those?" I asked.

"Phillips Exeter Academy, then Yale College. Places of great culture, with stone buildings and libraries filled with books and young men eager to learn. It was fairly good fun, but too much talking about things and not enough doing of things."

"That's where they taught you to read the books you've given me?" I asked. "Ralph Waldo Emerson and Henry David Thoreau."

"These schools filled my head with wonderful ideas about the spirit and the soul and about nature, Harry. About our connectedness. And then they sent me home to my father so he could teach me how to destroy my spirit and my soul and nature. And not only mine. He taught me how to destroy all spirit and all souls and all of nature. And my father taught me that if I practiced it well and got very good at it, I could become incredibly rich and own everything and control all people and make laws that suited me so that I could make more money still."

"That doesn't sound like a good use of your education."

"It is an irreconcilable contradiction that lives in me every day. But I live with it, don't I? I mean, I'm still living."

"But unhappily, it seems," I said.

"Some days I feel like it will crush me," Ben said with a bitter laugh. "I think it will be my end, and I'd rather not die that way. I'd much rather die falling from a tree! But you must think me mad."

"Not at all."

"My father is building a majestic estate," he went on, "the manor house of which will feature giant trees standing tall, side by side. It

will look like it has grown out of the forest itself, thus paying tribute to the source of my father's wealth. Dozens of ancient trees must be found, cut, halved lengthwise, and brought to the construction site. My father wants me to select these trees personally."

"But have you studied architecture or engineering?" I asked, feeling apprehensive at the idea of Ben's departure. "Can you design and build such a thing?"

"I'm not the architect," Ben admitted. "My father has paid for nothing but the best in that regard: a certain Bernard Asher out of Chicago. Still, he knows that I understand the forest better than any of his foremen. I am to choose the timbers that will be the pillars of his new estate. Also, he intends for me to provide him with a legacy, as I am to inherit this estate."

"A legacy?" I asked.

"Children," he said.

"I see," I said, feeling a pang of envy at the mention of his illusory family.

"Can you imagine cutting down the tree we climbed yesterday, Harry?" Ben asked me sharply. "Can you think to chop down that tree so a man can use its carcass as siding for his house? Can you?"

"Never."

"That's what he wants me to do. That's what he's called me to Seattle to do."

"He's called you to Seattle?"

Ben shook his head sadly and laughed into his cup of whiskey.

"Why do you think I came back out to camp in the middle of our hiatus?" he asked.

"You said you'd finished your business," I said.

"Yes, well, I suppose I lied about that."

"So why did you come?"

"I wanted to know if we were really soul mates, Harry. I wanted to climb a tree, and I wanted to climb it with you."

The inky woods around us were peppered with flashing animal eyes. Ben scuttled the fire until it was embers breathing at us.

"Why don't you tell him you won't go?" I asked. "Why don't you refuse? Is it because of your inheritance?"

"Don't be ridiculous. I hope you don't think me so base as that."

"Why, then?"

"So I can right the wrongs of my father and others like him," he said. "So I can undo some of the damage he's done. If I were to run from his wealth and power for my own preservation, it would be an incredibly selfish act, Harry, you see that, don't you? A man has a moral responsibility to correct an injustice, not to run and hide from it and pretend it doesn't exist. Who else could guide my father's companies in the proper direction but me? I can change the world, Harry. Not just for me, or for you and me and people I know, but for all people. It's my duty. My obligation. Some things simply must be done, no matter the personal sacrifice."

I considered the difficulty of his position, how much easier it would be for him to abdicate, and yet how he had resolved to take the more difficult road.

"When will you leave?" I asked.

"I can get you on a team up north, if you'd like to come along."

"I don't want to go," I said, thinking of my life in the past few days, the past many weeks. I felt like I had found something, my place. My soul mate. "And I don't want you to go, either."

Ben laughed.

"That's very thoughtful of you, but I don't know what I have to do with it."

"You have everything to do with it," I said.

Ben was silent for a moment as he examined the inside of his enamel mug.

"I can put my father off for a while," he said. "It will make him very angry; people don't say no to Elijah Riddell."

"What would Thoreau tell you to do?" I asked, baiting him with his own ideas, for I knew what Thoreau would tell him to do, having been in the same position, the heir to a fortune made from pencils.

"You're very clever, Harry," Ben said with a laugh.

"But am I clever enough?" I asked, and I could feel my heart pumping. I felt excited by the nature of our conversation because it seemed to veer closer to what I had desired for months but was afraid to pursue.

"Clever enough for what?"

"For you," I said boldly, for I felt like I was climbing a tree without gaffs and a flip line now. I was high up in a tree, and, while I knew the danger, I felt safe enough to continue. I looked up at Ben, whose face glowed orange in the flame, and I was touched in some strange way, compelled by an overpowering feeling in my chest, one that I had never known, having never before fallen in love. I was confused, because I had been told that God punished those who defiled their nature, that love like I felt for Ben was an abomination; they told me this in church when my mother used to take me and when my father and I were on the road and went to services so we could attend the picnic afterward and help ourselves to the free food. I went to Ben and pushed my face against his chest; he didn't withdraw. I took his head in my hands and began to kiss him, but he pulled away.

"Am I an abomination in your eyes?" I asked.

"You don't have to believe what others told you," Ben said.

"But they said—"

"One's nature comes from within, not from without. The abomination occurs in subverting one's instinct in favor of a rigid code written by others. Trying to force yourself into a role that confounds your spirit will always break you."

I took hold of his head and kissed him again, and this time he accepted the kiss and I held it, though it was rough and tasted of salt, because it felt good and I was afraid to let go; finally, I pulled away *and stepped back, ashamed, for what if he didn't want that at all? What if I had misjudged him entirely?*

"The trees don't judge us, Harry," he said. "Out here, we can do whatever we want."

"What do you want?" I asked harshly, suddenly challenging him. "Make it clear."

Ben hesitated for a moment, and then he reached out, grabbed my jacket, and pulled me to him; he kissed me hard, so that our teeth smashed together with a sharp click.

"That," Ben said, "and more."

"Then do it," I goaded him. "Do it, then!"

Ben kissed me again, almost violently, and he didn't let go until I jerked free and laughed defiantly. "Like that," Ben said, clenching his fists. "Do it, then!" I taunted. And Ben rushed at me so quickly, hooked under my arm in a wrestling move, and threw me to the ground next to the smoldering fire. We struggled wordlessly, a dangerous fight; we pulled at each other's clothes and looked for an advantage, twisted each other's arms in locks and holds until the other winced in pain. A thigh slipped between legs, leverage gained, opponent flipped, pressed down, face forced hard into the forest floor, tasting dirt and laughing, panting breath in an ear, hearts flailing in effort, hands aching, muscles straining until exhaustion approached, and then, like wolves fighting for a pack, a neck offered to gleaming teeth, eyes locked with eyes, sweat and sinewy muscles entangled, the greater beast dominated and the conquered showed his supplication, and mercy was granted; the grip was released and the greater man embraced the vanquished.

Ben stoked the fire back to life, added fuel, rolled out a blanket near enough so the warmth would be a comfort, but not so near that it would be too hot. He gently coaxed me onto the bedroll. I was exhausted, and he lay down next to me and covered us both with a woolen blanket that scratched our naked skin, but not enough for us

*to do anything about, because the discomfort in some way acknowl-
edged our nakedness and our boldness and effort. And the trees,
which had witnessed everything, said nothing.*

*"The estate my father is building is in the most beautiful place on
earth, I promise you," he said, his voice deep and hypnotic. "The forest
is so thick and green, and a bluff drops two hundred feet to the water,
and the west-facing view with the mountains and the sunset is so
magnificent it will make you cry. Harry, it will be our place. The deal
I've made with my father means he can ask me no questions about
how I manage the estate. He thinks it will be for my future family, but
it will be for us. It will be our haven."*

*"It sounds beautiful, but I want to stay here a little bit longer," I
said, staring lazily into the flames, the fire hot.*

*"I'll stay, too," Ben agreed, nodding to himself. "I think I'll stay a
bit more, too. And then, maybe I can convince you to join me at The
North Estate."*

21

NIGHT DANCING

I suppose if I had been at school or with my friends or something, I would have felt more self-conscious about my gay great-granduncle and his affair with Harry. Of course, people aren't allowed to use homosexuality as an insult anymore. Professional athletes get fined for it, politicians are forced to apologize publicly. The difference between 1990 and the present day is quite remarkable in this regard. When I was growing up, it was commonplace to toss around tags like "gay" or "fag" to put down one's friends and enemies. Kids who weren't good at sports were accused of being gay. Kids who studied too much were faggots. It was a universal depiction of unmanly behavior, and nothing was more insulting to an adolescent boy than having his manhood challenged. So considering the school yard culture of 1990 and my tender age of fourteen, I'm a little surprised I didn't balk at reading a diary entry depicting gay sex. But I didn't. For some reason—maybe because of the isolation of Riddell House?—having a gay great-granduncle didn't bother me at all. In fact, I felt protective of Ben and Harry. I still do.

I went to sleep that night feeling close to Ben and Harry and to the trees they climbed and the wild forest by the coast where they lived, though I had never been there myself. I felt caught up in their relationship, their love, their plight; it was as if they were still alive, grappling with their issues in a timeless state, and I was there with them.

A sound in the darkness woke me out of my sleep. I opened my eyes but didn't stir. I could hear music. I slipped out of bed and opened my door without a creak. I trod softly down the hall until I reached the back stairs, and then I went down instead of up. When I reached the ground floor, I opened the door a crack and saw what I thought I'd see: Grandpa Samuel at the kitchen table with a glass of medicine. Isobel always came to dance when he couldn't sleep. Or vice versa.

I snuck upstairs to the third floor, which was more creaky, so my work was more difficult; it demanded patience. The transfer of weight was the key, as was a belief in weightlessness. It was to have no momentum. It was to be a tree, to grow without notice, but to grow. It was to be still, but always moving. I crept down the hall with the music playing, the footsteps dancing. It took me days. Weeks. I felt as if it took me years to move the fifty feet from the servants' stairway to the doors to the ballroom, but I did it without disturbing a breath of air; the house had grown around me.

I reached the threshold and peered around the edge of the door and saw the record player and someone dancing like a ghost in the shadows. A woman, her dark dress flowing around her as she spun so elegantly across the ballroom floor. I slipped inside the room silently. The waning moon offered some light, but I couldn't make out details. The music played and she danced and I saw my grandmother Isobel. It was her. The house was haunted by more ghosts than I thought. Benjamin, I knew— the man with the hat. But now? She spun and leapt as if in a ballet. Her muted footsteps echoed through the house down to her beloved

Samuel, two floors below. It was really her. I reached for the light button. I pushed it and it clicked; the lights did not light.

She stopped, alerted by the click. She breezed toward me with fluttering hands. I was frightened by her sudden approach, and I turned away. When I turned back, she had vanished.

I ran down the front stairs as quickly as I could. I didn't worry about sound. I ran to my room and grabbed my flashlight. I sprinted back up the stairs to the ballroom and aimed my flashlight around the room. Nothing. The record player ticked at me, so I switched it off. I continued scanning the ballroom.

Against one wall was a row of doors. I opened one. A storage closet filled with chairs and banquet tables. I opened another. More storage, boxes of things, glasses, maybe. I opened a third. It was nearly empty, but smelled of recently disturbed air. Against the back wall, I saw something—a flash of light through a small hole. I made my way to the back of the storage room and shone my light. A finger hole. I slipped my finger into it and pulled. It took effort, but a small hatch door pulled free and came off in my hands.

On the backside of the hatch were two handles. I stuck my head into the newly discovered space. It was some kind of a shaft that plunged downward through the core of the house. It wasn't big—three feet square, maybe. I could see ladder rungs attached to the wall opposite me. I shone my flashlight downward, but it couldn't penetrate far into the darkness.

I considered investigating, but I'd need equipment. A better flashlight, for sure, or a headlight would be better. Definitely some rope. And a wooden stake, some garlic, and a Bible. Because I had no idea what exactly I'd find down there, though I was determined to find it.

22

TELL ME ABOUT YOUR MOTHER

I wanted to get the equipment for my investigation as soon as I woke up the next day, but I saw my father hacking and slashing at the blackberries across the orchard, and I knew he needed to work things out, so I didn't bother him right away. I was pretty sure it was our one-week anniversary at Riddell House, but, to be honest, it was hard to track time there. The days were long, and they blended together into a soup of experience that took effort to sort out in my head. I had come to understand the feeling of isolation Serena and Grandpa Samuel had lived with for so long. My father felt it, too, I knew; it was a natural reaction to pick up a machete and start slashing.

When it was close to lunchtime, I couldn't wait any longer, so I walked down the hill and interrupted my father's brutal battle with the vines.

"I need to get some stuff at the store," I said. "Can you take me to town?"

"Ah, yes," he said, wiping his sweaty brow with the disgusting T-shirt he had removed and tossed in the dead grass. He guzzled water. He was naked from the waist up, and his leathery, lean torso was sweaty and speck-led with dirt. "A mission to replenish supplies. Running low on staples. Orange juice, fruit, Ritz crackers. We must restock the canteen. Let's go."

We walked back up the hill to the house, and I waited in the kitchen while he got a fresh shirt. When he came back downstairs, I mentioned the ballroom light issue I had discovered the previous night.

"Did you try the fuse box?" he asked.

"Where is it?"

He led me outside the kitchen door to the porte cochere. He lifted an old, hinged cover and revealed rows of glass cylinders and a tangle of brown, filthy wires going in all directions.

"Why is the fuse box outside?" I asked. "Isn't that dangerous? I mean, some ax murderer with night-vision goggles could turn off the power and then hunt you down in the dark and you couldn't do anything to stop him."

"That's the way they did it in the old days," he said. "I guess no one foresaw the danger of night-vision goggles falling into the wrong hands. Or maybe no one foresaw the invention of night-vision goggles at all."

He poked around the fuses. A diagram explained which fuse con-trolled which circuit, but it was hardly legible.

"Ah, this must be it," he said, screwing in one of the glass fuses. "It was loose. Probably lost the connection."

"Probably," I agreed, but the wheels in my head were spinning. Why would the fuse be loose?

We didn't really go into town. Not into Seattle, at least. We drove to a strip mall shopping complex a few minutes away from The North Es-tate. The complex was anchored by a supermarket and an old Sears de-partment store that looked like it had been there for a hundred years. A Chinese-Thai combo restaurant was sandwiched between a Radio Shack and a Laundromat, and my father suggested we get lunch before we went shopping, so we went in. Almost everything in Seattle—at least the nar-row slice I had seen of it—was weird, and the Chinese-Thai restaurant was no exception. It was a shell of a place with no redeeming aesthetic qualities: old Formica tables and plasticky chairs and bright fluorescent lighting. A page of the menu said: Vietnamese Specialty Soups. The people who seemed to own the restaurant didn't really speak English; they just hung out at the empty tables like it was a living room—there were aunts and uncles and little kids—and a TV was playing a VHS tape of old news in an Asian language. The only word I could understand was George Bush, which, apparently, has no translation. So even though my father and I were in a suburban Seattle strip mall, it didn't feel like it. We ordered off the Vietnamese side of the menu, even though Vietnamese food wasn't advertised on the neon sign outside. We only spoke with one guy, and the only thing we said to him was "Two number fourteens," and a few minutes later the guy shuffled out with bowls of soup. I tentatively sipped the broth and found that it was amazingly good: the smell and the steam and the taste. It took all five senses to taste it completely, and part of why it tasted so good, I thought, was that we were eating it in this strange place.

"All this stuff is new," my father said, waving his soup spoon at the parking lot outside the window. "The Sears was here, but none of the other stores. There used to be an Ernst Hardware and a Pay 'n Pak over there . . . But I guess I haven't been here in a while."

I added garlic chili sauce to my soup. I added jalapeños and Thai basil. I added lime. I added bean sprouts. I wanted to add everything I could.

"I feel like I hardly see you anymore," my father said as we ate.

"Same here," I agreed.

"What have you been up to? Seeking the truth?"

"Always. I spend my life in the relentless pursuit of truth. Speaking of which . . ."

"Yes?"

"Why did you start building boats? You've never told me. Was it because the boatbuilding place was near the school? That's what Mom said."

"*Because it was there?* That's why she said I did it?"

"More or less," I said.

"Hmm," he said. "No. I went and found it. It wasn't so close that I tripped and fell through the front door. I searched for it and I found it. I wanted to do something with wood that was constructive, you know? I wanted to *build* something. When I was a kid and Grandpa Abe was still alive, all he talked about was destroy, destroy, cut down, clear-cut, sell off, develop, make money, money, money. At some point, my mother took me aside and said, 'You don't like that kind of talk, do you?' I said no. And she said, 'You are your own person. You can create your own future. You don't have to live for him. He's already made a mess of his life; he doesn't get to make a mess of yours.'"

My father worked on his soup for a minute.

"So I thought if I could build something beautiful out of wood," he said, "something *useful* and also beautiful—I thought somehow that would equalize things. I don't know. I guess it's karma. But that's my mother's talk. I don't really believe in that."

I shrugged, but I didn't believe him. I thought he did believe in it. All of it.

"I still don't understand why Grandpa Samuel sent you away to school after your mom died," I said, leaning over the bowl to meet a chopsticks-load of noodles. Relentless pursuit.

"Things were hard for Grandpa. He had Serena to take care of."

"Serena said *you* were taking care of her."

My father shrugged again as he picked at his soup.

"If you were sixteen or whatever," I pressed, "and you were taking care of Serena, why would Grandpa send you away? Wouldn't it make more sense for him to keep you around? It would be less work for him."

"It's complicated," he said.

"It doesn't sound complicated," I countered. "It sounds like you're leaving something out."

"Like what?"

I stopped eating and squinted at him.

"Grandma Isobel was sick, and then she died," I said impatiently. "Grandpa Samuel sent you away after that, and you won't talk about any of it with me. Serena said your mother had Lou Gehrig's disease. What exactly is that? I mean, I've heard of it, but . . ."

My father licked his lips and sighed. He set down his spoon and chopsticks, picked up his napkin.

"ALS," he said. "It's a degenerative nerve disease. It destroys everything in your body but your brain, so you're completely aware of what's happening—you feel all the pain, you see your body shutting down piece by piece, entombing you in a worthless shell—but there's nothing you can do to stop it. There's no cure; there's no treatment. You just have to wait until enough of you shuts down that you die."

I didn't know what to say.

"Eventually you can't move," he continued. "You can barely breathe. You can't swallow. But you can see, and you can feel, and you can think, and you can know. At some point you can't clear your lungs of phlegm anymore. Your lungs slowly fill with liquid, and you drown."

He looked into his soup.

"My mother was terrified of drowning."

I, too, looked into my soup. I filled my spoon with broth and lifted it to my lips. I drank the broth.

"I can't imagine Mom ever dying at all, especially not when I'm sixteen," I said. "So for your mom to die like that. It's really sad."

We both looked up. My father met my eyes for the first time, and I saw a sadness in him.

"Divorce isn't quite as tragic as death," he said.

He had never used the D-word before. Its use at that moment struck me with another wave of sadness.

"They're kind of the same," I said, clinging to my point. "Divorce and death."

"No, they aren't."

"The ending of something," I said, pushing ahead with my thesis. "Your mother left you. Now Mom is leaving you."

"I'm here to get Grandpa to sell the house so we can have some cash."

"I don't think that's why you're here," I blurted out almost involuntarily. And I said it loud enough that the Vietnamese people who ran the restaurant all stopped to look at us. My father set down his eating utensils again and got a cold look on his face. (When he was holding a piece of wood, his face was soft; when he was mad at me, his face was so hard.)

"You're here for Isobel," I said in a loud whisper. "You came to find her."

"Is that so?" he asked flatly.

"You think she's still here. I saw you waiting for her in the ballroom. Two nights ago."

He was ice. He was carved stone. If he hadn't blinked, I would have thought he had been frozen by Medusa.

"I don't believe in ghosts," he said.

"You do," I said. "I *know* you do. You haven't lost your faith; you're just trying to shove it down. I'm sure of it."

"Why are you sure?"

"Because I've seen a lot of things in the past few days. A *lot* of things. And one of the things I saw was your mother dancing in the ballroom."

He said nothing.

"She was dancing last night," I went on. "I swear, she was so close I could have touched her. I saw her, Dad. And I don't think you want Grandpa to sign over the house until you see her, too."

He hesitated half a second at most, and then his hand flashed across the table and smacked my face. Not hard, but loud and startling. The older Vietnamese man turned down the volume on the TV. They were concerned, wondering if they needed to intervene.

I felt the sting, but I didn't stop.

"You're waiting for her," I said. "That's why you're here. You're waiting for her in the ballroom."

He averted his eyes, stood, and went to the counter. He paid in cash, returned to the table, and dropped two dollars.

"Let's go," he said, grinding his molars until his jaw muscles bulged.

I looked at my soup. There was more goodness in my bowl. Steak and brisket and onion slices. Noodles and Thai basil and cilantro and broth. I didn't know what strange spices flavored it, but I could dive into that broth and swim for a very long time.

I was angry with my father for slapping me. Angry for his not seeing the truth that I saw. But maybe he wasn't ready yet. Maybe I needed more information to convince him. I stood up dutifully and followed him outside; we crossed the parking lot toward the supermarket. I stopped when we reached the sidewalk, and it took my father two steps to realize I wasn't next to him.

"I need some money," I said, holding out my hand.

He turned and looked at me, yet he didn't ask the normal parental question—"Why?" Instead, he took out his wallet and handed me a twenty. I didn't retract my hand when the bill hit it; I left it out there to extort more. He gave me another twenty. I folded the bills and placed them in my pocket and I turned away.

"Where are you going?" he asked.

"I have some business to take care of," I said. "I'll meet you at the car."

He considered a moment, then shrugged and headed for the supermarket.

I went to Sears. I found the camping department and purchased a heavy-duty flashlight and a headlamp—the kind rock climbers and spelunkers use. I bought what fit into my budget; it didn't have the fancy flashing feature or the amber night-vision option so my eyes wouldn't dilate if I had to go outside the tent to pee at night. When we met up at the car, my father didn't ask me what I'd gotten; we didn't speak at all.

When we got back to the house, I didn't help him with the groceries. I didn't wait for his apology, which I knew would come. I went straight to the ballroom, strapped on my headlamp, batteried-up my flashlight, and made my way to the hidden shaft.

23

THE BASEMENT

I didn't have a wooden stake, but I did have a head of garlic in my pocket that I had stolen from the kitchen. The flashlight I bought came with one of those cheap carabiners, clearly labeled "not for climbing," so I used it to hang the flashlight from my belt loop. I reached into the shaft and grabbed hold of a rung with both my hands, then I slung one foot out into the void and found a purchase. I hesitated; it wasn't too late for me to back out. There was nothing below me. Less than nothing. I clicked on my headlamp; its feeble light was swallowed by the darkness, and I regretted not having extorted more money from my father to buy the fifty-nine-dollar version. I took a breath, swung my other leg over the threshold, and placed it on a rung. I reached out, lifted the hatch into place, and pulled it shut, leaving me in total blackness except for my headlamp. I clicked on the flashlight hanging from my belt, and downward I went.

The shaft was musty and hot and sweet smelling. The walls, which were constructed of smooth wood, were covered with something slick and unappealing. Every few feet, I turned my head to shine the light around. It didn't matter if the thing that went down the shaft the previous night was a ghost or a person, something went down there; I was sure there was another exit. About twenty feet down, I noticed a lip on the wall behind me. It seemed like a hatch door similar to the one I had entered through, but, when I pushed on it, it didn't open, so I continued on. As I descended, rung by rung, the air grew more stale and more foul smelling. When I looked up, I saw nothing. The walls around me were blank. Below, more nothing.

I was sweating with fear, but I was good at hiding it from myself; I blamed the humidity. I looked between my legs as I descended, and my flashlight glinted on something below me. A gear or something. A few feet further down, I looked again; I saw a floor with a pulley bolted to it. A big pulley, eight or ten inches in diameter, lying on its side. I realized I was in a dumbwaiter shaft. The dumbwaiter wasn't operable, obviously; there was no cable attached to the pulley to make it run. I didn't know if it had ever worked. The hatch in the ballroom wasn't what you'd think of as a dumbwaiter door—one of those horizontal double doors like you see in the movies—so it may never have been put into commission. But that's what it was. A dumbwaiter shaft.

I reached the compartment roof and tapped my toe on it. I tested it with some weight. I couldn't imagine it was sitting at the bottom of the shaft, but it was hard to judge how far down I'd climbed. The dumbwaiter seemed solid enough, so I set my other foot on it and gave it most of my weight. I held on to the rungs to be safe, and then bounced up and down a bit to get a feel for my security. With a loud bang, the compartment let go beneath me. My own plunging weight tore my hands from the rungs; I toppled backward and fell.

Down into the darkness. I only had time to picture the gruesomeness of my demise as I was soon to be impaled by rusted steel bolts and rods and bleed to death in a dumbwaiter shaft, my bones broken and shattered. But then I heard a horrible screeching sound and felt an intense braking sensation. I did not slam into the bottom of the shaft in an explosion of splintered wood and flesh. With a great groan of metal fatigue, the dumbwaiter compartment simply stopped.

Somewhere in the fall I had lost my headlamp. I unhooked the flashlight from my belt loop and aimed it upward. The light flickered through the fine dust kicked up by my fall. And still, I marveled, I was not dead. Those Riddell House designers—God bless their souls—they had put a braking device in their dumbwaiter, a narrowing of the shaft or something. I wasn't dead!

I was on my back and contorted in a grotesque way in the narrow shaft. I tried my best to look around and right myself, but everything hurt. I noticed a mechanism on the wall near my head—a latch—so I reached behind and blindly grabbed at it. Two horizontal doors slid open magically like a mouth. I climbed out and onto the floor outside the shaft. It was quite dark, but not impossibly so, and my flashlight offered something. I glanced around as I got to my feet. I was in the basement.

I found a light switch in the room. It twisted like an old kitchen timer, and a naked bulb sparked to life above my head, casting a dim brown glow. I didn't know when electricity was put in the place, but it had never been updated. There were wires and porcelain knobs everywhere, and they looked dangerous. The room was maybe thirty by forty feet and remarkably empty and clean. I saw a door, and I used it to reach another room, a bit smaller, but clearly designed with an agenda: meat hooks were suspended from the ceiling, and there was a drain and spigot in the center of the room. Along two sides were long butcher block tables. Business had been conducted there, obviously: I found a rack of old carving knives, cleavers, tenderizing hammers, and handsaws, to which my healthy imagination added the sound effects of saw cutting through bone. I aimed my flashlight at steps that led to something resembling cellar doors to the outside. I tried the doors; they didn't open.

I continued through the basement, making my way to another room with a workbench and tools and a wall of supplies in neat wooden boxes. The handyman's workroom. And there, leaning in the corner behind a tool chest, I noticed an ax. I approached it warily, although I didn't suppose it would leap up and attack me by itself. I touched its worn wooden handle, dark with the stains of many hands, and its intimidating blade, which showed the grain of a sharpening wheel on it. Was it the ax that Grandpa Samuel had used to cleave the hand from the newel?

The next room housed a gigantic iron boiler, its arms sprawling from it like those of an octopus, connecting with a central steam shaft that ran the length of a dark corridor, which must have been eighty feet long, or who even knew how to estimate in the darkness? Adjacent to the boiler room was a smaller room with a coal-fired furnace, opposite which was a coal chute about six feet wide, and a smooth concrete slab that angled up to more cellar doors; yet those, too, were locked from the outside. I wondered if I would ever be able to find my way out.

But I knew I would, because there's always another room.

If I made horror movies, I would make one in a basement like that. Dozens of little rooms, all with stone floors and thick brick walls. Cold, like a catacomb. Ceilings of irregular heights, heavy pipes randomly crossing through passageways, an unexpected step down that jammed my heel and snapped my teeth shut, a five-way intersection, and occasionally the grunt of an animal that could have been a rat. Or maybe it was a Minotaur. That place had all the makings of hell. Including the rickety staircase that led out but had collapsed into a pile of rotten wood. Part of it was still intact, but when I pulled at it, it groaned and gave way and crumbled with a sickening clatter. I looked up, and, oh, that door was so far away! I saw the crack of light far above my head and I heard voices and I smelled something good. I smelled cookies, which I knew Serena was cooking while gliding about the kitchen with her blue toes. I shouted for help, but no one answered; no one came.

When I realized that the only exits to the outside were securely blocked, and the only staircase I'd found to the inside of the house was inaccessible, I started to panic, but I worked to keep calm. I could always go back the way I came. I swept the area with my flashlight and noticed something shiny winking at me. I cautiously approached the dark corner, which was partially obscured by old wooden crates. I shoved the crates aside, and when I flashed my light in the brick corner near the floor, something glinted.

I worked my way into the corner and crouched down. Near the floor was a cubbyhole of sorts. Not very big at all, maybe the size of my hand. It was hard for me to squeeze past the wooden crates, which seemed to multiply as I made my way toward the cove as if they had some need to protect it. Still, I wanted to see, so I reached past the crates with my arm at full extension. I got my hand to the lip of the pocket in the wall, and I stretched farther, turning my face away so I could reach a bit more, and I felt something cold and hard. A ring? I was able to tip it on edge and slip my finger into it and retrieve it. I brought it to my face and held the light to it. It was my father's wedding ring.

Excited by the discovery, I worked to shove the clustered crates aside. I pulled them apart to make space so I could get closer to the trove. I dug my hand into the space and found something else: Serena's cake server. And another thing: my missing watch. And another: a silver locket on a chain. I held my flashlight up to the locket and fingered it open. It contained two small, faded photographs of children. A boy and a girl. Jones and Serena.

Someone had been hiding these things here. But who?

I thought I heard a thump from close behind me and turned quickly, flashing my light around the room. I was startled enough that I dropped the locket. I quickly stood and prepared myself for battle, though I had no idea what against. I pocketed my father's wedding ring and my watch; I didn't worry about the other things. It was time for me to get out of there.

The dumbwaiter. I could climb the ladder in the shaft up to the ballroom. I rushed back through the rooms. Through the intersection, past the long corridor. Up the step, around the corner. I was almost there, and I picked up the pace in anticipation of finding the empty room with the dumbwaiter, and around another corner and—pow!—I cracked my head on an iron pipe so hard, my legs buckled. My flashlight dropped with a clatter and went out as I collapsed on the floor of the basement. I didn't even know if I could see straight because it was so dark. My head was rocked with pain, hard and throbbing, and my jaw hurt and my eye sockets ached and there was a ringing in my ears.

I'd been hit that hard once before, I remember thinking at that moment. In fourth grade, I got hit square in the face with a football—a perfect spiral thrown by Kenny, whose last name escaped me. I remember wanting so badly to remember Kenny's last name. But in my wooziness, everything else came back to me about the fourth grade—all of the details. He'd launched a long ball, but I wasn't looking, and then someone called out, "Ball!" and I turned to see an immaculately spiraling orb, so pretty, arcing toward me with the inevitability of a meteor; it hit me on the bridge of my nose and knocked me backward four feet. Blood was everywhere. When I staggered into the class, my shirt covered with blood, my teacher was mad that she had to take me to the nurse's office instead of giving the class the spelling test. She gave wicked hard spelling tests that everyone would fail and she would yell at them for not studying, but I aced her tests every time because I read a lot of books and didn't even really have to study, even though I did, and I knew that if you study for a spelling test even a little, you can ace it.

She took me to the nurse's office and did that sigh-groan thing disappointed adults do, shaking her head.

"There's no point in giving it now," she said to me about the evil spelling test she had so looked forward to administering.

We were alone for a minute, waiting for the nurse to call my mother so she could come pick me up from school and take me to the hospital for X-rays to make sure my skull hadn't cracked open.

"You can still give it to them," I said of the test, trying to make my teacher, Mrs. Minorchio, feel better.

"They'll all fail," she said. "Like they always do. Their failure isn't the point. I pick words I think will trip *you* up. One day I will defeat you."

I furrowed my brow at her as I held a blood-soaked rag to my face.

"You shouldn't be in this grade," she said. "You shouldn't be in this school. For all I know, you shouldn't be on this *planet*."

I remember her saying that and I remember not really knowing what she meant. But after that they started pulling me out of class for tests they didn't tell me were tests. I had to go talk to "specialists" for a while, and they asked me questions and I answered them. Then they said I was going to go to a different school. I didn't want to go, but my mother wanted me to. She liked the idea of me being too smart for that school because it reminded her of her childhood and the opportunities she wasn't offered. So I said okay, but at the last minute my mother changed her mind because she wanted me to grow up with my friends and not as someone who got pushed ahead in the special program.

I remember all of that. I remember feeling relieved and thankful that my mother had saved me. And then? Sprawled out on the basement floor of Riddell House, I didn't even know what my future was. Was I being pulled away from my friends to be sent to some boarding school like my father? Was I being pulled away from my friends to move to England? All I knew was that I felt really resentful. I could have been in college by then if I had realized it was all so transient. I could have been pushed ahead and molded by special programs and been through with all the educational nonsense by then. I'd thought my mother was offering me permanence over the sublime. I'd thought she and I were together with our decision, choosing the safe over the daring and unknown. I trusted her. She struggled so hard with the problem and finally came to her decision, so of course I agreed with her because I hated to see her struggle.

The pain was subsiding, the ringing in my ears fading. But there was no light.

I wondered if the basement of Riddell House would be where I died, and wouldn't that be funny? My lack of life experience flashing before my eyes.

But then I saw light. A crack at first, which opened into a rectangle of blazing brightness. A man stood before me. I was still on the floor holding my head. He knelt down and touched my head, and I felt better.

"Dad?" I asked, because I didn't know who it was. And how would my father have found me anyway?

The man stroked my hair gently, and it made me feel so much better that I closed my eyes and a groan escaped from me involuntarily. The man helped me to my feet and to the steps, up and out. I collapsed on the grass, woozy and dizzy. The man grasped my hand and held it tight, and reached out and lightly touched my forehead, but it didn't hurt at all.

"Grandpa?" I asked, because with the bright white light behind the man, I still couldn't see.

"Trevor," the man whispered.

It was a voice I recognized. I'd heard it before. I strained to focus. I wanted to see, but my eyes were crossed, almost. That was some blow. I couldn't make out the man's face; it was all shadow. I was frustrated because I wanted to see.

"You've come to save us," the man whispered.

And then I couldn't stand it. I *knew* that voice. I'd heard it before, but I couldn't see; my vision was so cloudy—I gritted my teeth and strained against the grogginess that engulfed me. The man stood tall, and then I understood. As much as I tried to see him, I would never see the man clearly. He would always be a shadow, a blur.

"Ben," I said.

When I said it, he seemed to relax, and so did I. He looked up to the sky and took a deep breath.

"How beautiful," he whispered so faintly I could barely hear.

"It's you," I said.

Ben smiled and then vanished in the breeze.

I gathered myself and made my way into the kitchen a bit unsteadily. My father was sitting at the table with his new best friend, the blue binder, and a thought occurred to me, perhaps the result of the blow to my head: Exactly how much did Serena have to do with the blue binder? She said she worked for a real estate developer. And my father had told the notary that Dickie had summoned him. And Dickie was Serena's boyfriend but was never at the house. I felt there was something going on that I didn't quite see. But it hurt my head to think that hard, so I gave up on it.

Meanwhile, Serena was flitting about the kitchen, removing sheets of cookies from the oven with a mitted hand. A baseball game was on the television. The Mariners. What day was it? Saturday?

"Well," Serena chimed cheerily, "look what the cat dragged in!"

She turned to me with her Cheshire grin, which fell flat immediately when she saw the knot growing on my forehead.

"What happened?" she asked with great concern, flying toward me.

"I hit my head."

She touched my forehead; it burned.

"How?"

"In the basement."

"What were you doing in the basement?"

"Exploring."

She shook her head disapprovingly.

"Sit."

I sat, and she brought me a tea towel soaked with cold water and wrapped around some ice cubes.

"What happened?" my father asked.

"I was looking around in the basement, and I ran into a pipe."

"Does he have a concussion?" my father asked Serena.

She rolled her eyes and sighed. She came to me and sat at my side. She took my hands in hers.

"Look at me."

We locked eyes, and she scrutinized me this way and that, studying my pupils. Then she held up a finger and moved it side to side, up and down. I tracked it with my eyes.

"It's not a concussion," she said. "And if it is, it's so mild, the doctor would only tell him not to run around for a few days. So don't run around."

"Did you used to be a nurse or something?" I asked.

"I've been a nurse for twenty-three years, Trevor," she said pointedly. "I was born into it, you could say. I'm hoping to retire soon, however. Please heal quickly so I can go on my way. Are you hungry? Would you like dinner?"

I was hungry. I was starving. She made me a turkey sandwich that might have been the best turkey sandwich I'd ever tasted; maybe the blow to my head had accentuated my sense of taste. As I ate, my father slipped out of the room with the binder, and then Serena sat across from me at the kitchen table, propped her chin on her fist, and stared at me.

"What are you looking at?" I asked, feeling self-conscious.

"What were you looking for in the basement, I wonder."

"Just . . . around."

"No," she said. "I know you. You're goal driven. You're up to something. What is it?"

I decided it was time to confide in Serena. I had enough information to make a case, and maybe change the fate of Riddell House. I slipped my hand into my pocket, removed my father's wedding ring, and placed it on the table between us.

"My dad lost his wedding ring. I found it in the basement."

Serena regarded the ring at length. "I don't suppose it might have fallen off his finger on the chance he'd ventured down there?"

"I don't think he's gone down there, number one. And it wasn't lying on the floor or anything. It was hidden away in a little cubbyhole. Like someone had put it there on purpose."

"I see."

"I didn't do it. My dad didn't do it. Did *you* do it?" I asked.

"Not I."

"That leaves Grandpa Samuel. Or . . ."

"Or?"

"Or the ghost I saw down there."

Serena sat back in her chair and smiled broadly.

"Ah, here we have it," she said. "The ghost of Riddell House. You've been ghost hunting. Of course!"

"But I've seen him," I said. "He's here."

"And who is *he*?"

"Benjamin Riddell."

"And why would Benjamin Riddell be haunting Riddell House?"

"I think it has to do with the development," I said. "He wants the land returned to nature and not developed."

"Yes, yes, Trevor. We know all that. That's why Elijah set up the trust that prevented Abraham from developing the land. But Elijah could only stop Abraham, not any future heirs. So now it's up to Grandpa Samuel to decide—"

"But that's what Ben really wanted. So he's stuck. He can't leave—"

"Well, then, he will continue to be stuck," Serena said sharply. She stood up and cleared my empty plate. "What are we most concerned with? You do want your mother and father to be together again. That is correct, isn't it?"

"Yes."

"The development is the perfect solution to all of our problems. It's the *only* solution, really. Dickie has done an excellent job setting up a very good deal for everyone. So it disappoints a ghost or two. Will we put that ahead of our needs, Trevor? Are you willing to set aside your own happiness, not to mention the happiness of your parents, me, Grandpa Samuel, and your future children for generations and generations just to placate a silly ghost—and one who doesn't bother with much haunting, by the way. We're not rising to the level of that poltergeist movie: no one is sucking you into the TV set, as far as I can see. So, really, Trevor. Let's set all this aside and have no more talk about ghosts; it will give you nightmares. Run along now and play. Or read a book. Or write in that journal of yours; I see you writing in it regularly. But write about something positive. Write about the future. Don't write about the past; it's dreary and depressing and has nothing to do with our potential."

She turned away from me and resumed her kitchen duties, but I didn't leave.

"Dickie is a real estate developer, isn't he?" I asked.

"Yes, he is," she replied, paying me no mind.

"You said *you* work for a real estate developer. Do you work for Dickie?"

She groaned and shook her head, turning to face me.

"I work *with* Dickie, not *for* him. Are there any other questions, Detective? Or can I get back to my cooking?"

I was unsatisfied by her response, but I felt pushing her further wouldn't benefit me, so I left her in the kitchen and went upstairs. I was distrustful of Serena, but my head hurt and I wanted to lie down with my music and my headache. On the way, I stopped in the bathroom. I glanced at myself in the mirror as I washed my hands and noticed the purplish bruise on my forehead. I leaned in toward the mirror to check my eyes and thought my pupils looked a little dilated, but I couldn't tell for sure. I was exhausted from the day and retreated to my room. Before I slipped off my jeans, I emptied my pockets: my father's wedding ring and my watch. I'd forgotten to tell Serena about the watch, though that likely wouldn't have made a difference.

I climbed into bed, put on my headphones, and turned on some Bob Marley. I reached for one of Harry's journals, which I had stowed under my pillow, and I read.

November 12, 1901

November was soon upon us, and preparations were being made to return to town for the winter; the days had grown too short and too rainy for logging, and it was time to shut down the harvest until March. The men, grimy and long bearded, walked through camp with vacant gazes. They were going off to other jobs—at a mill or fishing or longshoreman work—but none of them really wanted to leave; the adjustment to the other life was difficult. They anticipated the emptiness they would feel when their hands no longer held an ax, the longing for the smell of pine sap and burning wood, the hunger for cured slab bacon and johnnycakes and gritty, burnt coffee.

"What will you do over the winter?" Ben asked me late one evening, and I felt stung. Not because I imagined he would make plans for me, but because I hadn't thought to make plans for myself. I had been so contented with Ben and our ways, it never occurred to me that it would end.

"I don't know," I said. "What will you do?"

"Oh, I have to go back to Seattle again and ingratiate myself to my father. Do the social things I'm supposed to do. Be a Good Son."

"Of course," I said.

"I wonder," Ben mused, "if a man is accountable for the sins of his father."

I said nothing, but wondered along with Ben, as we stared into the flames that crackled in the fire pit.

"Thoreau says that the sleepers on which the rails are laid are the bodies of men," Ben continued, "and that the train is carried on the broken spirits of those who built the tracks. My father has supplied

the bodies and the spirits for all the railways in this great land of ours. That's a devastating sum."

Ben was fond of challenging me so: giving me a reading assignment and then testing my fluency with the concepts.

"But Thoreau admits that the men who give up their liberty for work, readily do so," I protested.

"Because they have no alternative," Ben cried, engaging in the debate. "We can feel justified by saying it's their own choice, but choice without alternative is only a sleight of hand; it is a magician's force-play, during which you believe you have free will, but your fate has already been decided: the magician already knows which card you will pick!"

"And so exploitation is your father's offense?" I asked.

"Disregard for the human spirit is his offense," Ben said. "Disregard for the universal spirit. Sometimes I wonder if I was brought here to pay for my father's sins. Or, perhaps, I was brought here to offer him salvation. Perhaps it is through me that he will see the truth that has eluded him thus far."

"If anyone can accomplish the task," I said, "I'm sure it will be you."

24

AUTOMATIC WRITING

It felt as if someone had nudged me awake, but no one was there. I looked over at the glowing LCD clock, which read 02:33. I was terribly thirsty. I went downstairs, using the front stairs because I didn't care if I woke anyone up. It didn't surprise me that Grandpa Samuel was sitting at the kitchen table, and I wondered for a moment if I was going to get Zen Grandpa or Crazy Grandpa.

"You should be asleep," I said as I turned on the hood light so as not to startle him too badly.

He didn't acknowledge me. He was hunched over the table, writing something on a Post-it note pad. He wrote quickly and deliberately, shielding his work with his opposite forearm, his head down. I didn't believe it was my place to interrupt him.

I put ice in a glass and filled it with water from the sink because, to be honest, I was getting sick of the lemonade. The water tasted horrible; it was metallic and made my tongue feel funny. So I poured out most of the water and filled the rest of the glass with lemonade, producing a lemonade-flavored water-drink, diluted enough to take out its sweetness, but with enough flavor to cover the taste of rust. I sat across from Grandpa Samuel and held the icy glass to my forehead between sips, and I imagined myself in an old black-and-white movie in which a guy holds a sweaty glass to his forehead in the heat.

Post-it after Post-it. He scrawled letters, words, sentences at a furious pace and with great effort. After writing a note, he peeled it from the pad and placed it on a pile of other notes. Note after note, until he had a stack of a few dozen Post-it notes. Until he ran out of steam.

He put down his pen and looked up at me.

"You should be asleep," I said.

"Serena usually makes me my medicine."

And after she makes you your medicine, you hear dancing, I thought but didn't say. I wondered briefly if Serena was doing a *Psycho* on Grandpa Samuel. Dressing up and pretending she was his dead wife. I winced. At this point, I trusted no one.

"I'll make it," I said.

I took a saucepan from the hanging rack and spilled some milk into it. I fired the stove. I was going to make it for real this time. While it was heating up, I stood over it, watching for bubbles because my father had taught me how to scald milk, a lost art, thanks to Louis Pasteur.

"Two parts milk—"

"One part medicine," I said. "I know."

"The medicine keeps me awake."

"The medicine makes you sleep," I corrected.

"*This* medicine makes me sleep," he agreed. "The other medicine—the pills—they make it so I can't sleep."

When the bubbles came, I turned off the heat and poured the warmed milk into a tall glass. I filled the rest of the glass with medicine and set it before Grandpa Samuel; then I sat down across from him. He cupped his hands around his glass, closed his eyes, and smiled.

"You warmed it for me," he said. "Sometimes Serena warms it, but not usually. I like it warm."

He took a sip, and I could hear him swallow loudly. My forehead throbbed a bit, but I'd been sleeping, so I felt rested. I reached for the pile of Post-it notes.

"Can I look at what you've been working on?" I asked.

"What have I been working on?" Grandpa Samuel wondered in reply.

"Your notes."

I took them and assessed the pile. It was pretty clear that they were in reverse order, top to bottom. I started to lay them out. Each one had a few words on it, but some had more. Some were small printing and intense; others were only one or two words. I quickly realized that they were not random scribbling. The more I unstuck them and laid them out, the larger the story grew, until the table was covered with Post-it notes.

"Can I borrow your pen?" I asked him.

I numbered each note in the upper-right-hand corner, so I could keep track. I had forty-seven canary-colored Post-it notes laid out. I studied them from above, helicopter view.

"What made you write this?" I asked.

"Write what?"

"Your notes."

"I don't think so," he said, shaking his head and sipping his medicine.

I remembered the note about John Muir. *The Mountains of California*. It seemed to come from nowhere. Even Grandpa Samuel didn't know what it meant. And Serena said Grandpa Samuel did that all the time: jotted down nonsensical notes. Maybe they weren't nonsensical. Maybe they just hadn't been deciphered properly.

"You told me you hated Ben," I said. "Remember that? When I asked about him before, you said he gave away the Riddell fortune or something."

Grandpa Samuel took a long drink of his medicine.

"I ran into him today in the basement," I continued. "Well, I ran into a pipe. But he came to help me. Does he ever help you?"

"Oh, yes."

"When does he help you?"

"He keeps me company," Grandpa Samuel said. "He sits with me when I can't sleep and he tells me stories, and he keeps me company in the barn when I'm working."

"What kind of stories does he tell?"

"He would climb the tallest trees. Not to cut them down, just to climb them. They'd use gaffs to get into the canopy, and then they would climb barefooted and bare-handed, up to the very top. No ropes or anything. It was very dangerous, but also very exciting."

"They?" I asked.

"Harry," he said. "Ben and Harry. They climbed together."

"You said bad things about Ben," I reminded him. "But I didn't believe them."

"Was Serena here?" Grandpa Samuel asked.

"Yes. It was the three of us. It was on my birthday."

"Whenever I talk about Ben, Serena reminds me that I hate him," he said. "Serena tells me the real truth."

"That he ruined our lives," I said.

"Yes. He ruined our lives."

"But he didn't, did he?"

Grandpa Samuel leaned in toward me conspiratorially. He glanced this way and that, and then he said: "He was just here. Didn't you see him?"

I shook my head because I was thinking too many things. Some of the notes were out of order. I rearranged them and studied them for syntax, and then I leaned back to see the big picture again.

"Serena usually gives me more medicine," he said.

I looked up and saw that his glass was almost empty.

"And then she sends me to bed," he added.

"I'll give you some more."

"Will you heat it up? It's better when it's warm."

"But then you have to go to bed," I said.

When the milk was ready, I poured it into a glass and added medicine. I handed the warm glass to him.

"He gets nervous when Serena talks about the house," Grandpa Samuel whispered to me.

"Who does? Ben?"

Grandpa Samuel nodded. "I don't think he likes what she's doing."

I helped him up and started him toward the kitchen door, but then I thought of something.

"Have you seen Isobel since she died?" I asked. "I know you've heard her, but have you ever *seen* her?"

"I hear her dancing. Serena says it's the rain. You hear the dancing, don't you?"

"I do."

Grandpa Samuel smiled sheepishly and went off to his room; I turned my attention to the puzzle on the table. The Post-its, written out, were a letter. And it was addressed to me. The note at the bottom of the pile—which was the first one Grandpa Samuel had written—said: "Dear Trevor." I ran upstairs to get my notebook; when I returned, I transcribed the series of messages. Some of them made no sense. Some weren't even words, but doodles or markings. I did my best to make sense of the ideas:

Dear Trevor,

They say a child—a baby—doesn't understand that his mother is distinct from him. A baby believes that he is connected to his mother on a fundamental level and that she is a part of him, an extension of her body as he pulls her hair and tugs on her breasts. Though he doesn't understand how to control her, neither does he understand how to control his own fingers and toes, and so the mystery does not concern him. In his innocence, the baby understands the truth of this universe: we are all connected to all things.

Fundamental

a part of him

An Extension

As he grows, others impress upon him [best guess—hard to decipher] the limitations of being human. He is not connected to his mother at all, they say, and she might leave him at any moment. In fact, they say, she most definitely will. None of us are connected, they tell him. It is the sad truth of our existence.

They say: "We live alone, and so, we die."

They tell him and they tell him and they tell him until he finally believes.

And why?

In exchange for all we have been provided in our temporal lives, all the advantages and skills and clever tricks packed into our bodies and minds, we have had to sublimate our inherent understanding; the truth is masked from us, to be returned when we have rejoined the larger aspect of nature. Only then will we remember. Until then, we will wonder where we end and others begin. We will feel a desperate need to connect with others because we do not see our connectedness, we only see our lack. We are the sad creatures of Aristophanes' imagination: born with four arms, four legs, two heads, and then split in half, jumbled about, and condemned to spending the rest of our lives in search of our other halves. We will spend our lives in a furious quest to satisfy a thirst that is a phantom of our own imagination. It is not a thirst but a curse.

We are all connected. The living to the nonliving, as the nonliving to the living. All things in all directions in all times. It is only in the physical dimension that we have limitations. (The membrane between us is thinner than you think.)

Of no significance . . . [I have no idea what this means. I think he was trying to say something that didn't get through the static of Grandpa Samuel's mind.]

We must honor the [unintelligible—my guess, based on context, is "connections," possibly "commitments"]. For the things we do have a consequence, whether or not we see it. Because we close our eyes to our obligations does not mean we are not obligated.

Deliver The North Estate to the place from which it came. Return this place to Nature. I know that is what you have come here to do. When it is done, I will go on to my future and you will go on to yours. Until then, I will stay.

May the Pacific live [unintelligible. Maybe "ever in you." Maybe "upward in you."]

Ben

I saw this scrawling of notes on the table and was amazed that Grandpa Samuel could have created it. I didn't believe it was part of his imagination. No. He was acting as a conduit. Ben was speaking through Grandpa Samuel. *The Mountains of California.* All the other Post-it notes Serena said Grandpa Samuel had written. They didn't quite make sense, and Grandpa Samuel didn't know why he'd written them. They were all communications from Ben.

I was so excited, I picked up the phone and dialed England. Three in the morning was the only time I could have a private call, and I needed to tell my mom about this.

"Do you have a father?" she asked when she heard my voice. "Is anyone responsible for you?"

"I'll sleep late tomorrow, I promise," I said. "Night is the best time in this house. At night, Grandpa channels my great-granduncle Benjamin."

"Is that so?"

"And he hears Isobel, dancing in the ballroom. I heard her—I *saw* her, too. And the record player was playing on its own."

"Slow down, Trevor—"

"Grandpa just wrote me a long letter on Post-it notes. But it wasn't from him. It was signed Ben. Grandpa didn't even know he'd written it."

"What do you mean?" she asked. "Was he in a trance or something?"

"Yeah. He was scribbling and scribbling and then he finished. I asked him what he'd written, and he said he hadn't written anything."

"Automatic writing," she said.

"What's that?"

"It was popular in the days of Spiritualism. Around the turn of the twentieth century, people believed in many things like this. They had séances, read tarot cards, conjured spirits. Respectable people. Presidents, even. People hoped their loved ones could speak to them again, and mediums could provide this service, or at least pretend to. The mediums would claim to channel a spirit, and the spirit would write through them. It was called automatic writing. Didn't you have a Ouija board when you were little?"

"Yeah, I remember that."

"It's a parlor game. Silly stuff."

I considered her logic.

"Gifford Pinchot married his dead wife," I said.

"What?"

"Just because people say it isn't true, does that mean it really isn't true?"

"I don't follow."

"Dad lost his wedding ring," I said. "I lost my watch. Serena lost her pie thing. I found them all in the basement, in a little cubby. *And* I found an old locket, too, with pictures of Dad and Serena when they were little. I think it belonged to Isobel."

"People drop things."

"And I saw a ghost. I saw Ben. He helped me after I hit my head."

"You hit your head?"

"On a pipe in the basement. But I'm okay."

"Do you need to get it looked at?"

"Serena says I'm okay. She used to be a nurse."

"Did she? I didn't know that."

"I don't know, actually," I said. "It's hard to tell when she's lying and when she's telling the truth."

"Trevor," she said, exasperated. "I'm very concerned about this. These middle-of-the-night phone calls. Your safety in that house. These ghosts you're fabricating—"

"I'm not fabricating."

"Do you need me to come out there? Do you need me to come save you?"

Those words. That phrase. "You've come to save us." That's what Serena said to my father when we first arrived. My mother echoing her words stopped me dead. I realized she didn't get what I was saying. She was trying to fix me; she wasn't trying to understand me.

"I don't need to be saved," I said. "Dad brought me here because I'm the one who's supposed to be doing the saving."

A long silence hissed on the phone.

"Trevor," my mother finally said, "your father loved his mother very, very much. When she died, it crushed him. And then when your grandfather sent your father away, it broke your father's spirit entirely. Your father doesn't talk about what happened, you know that. But he told me once that his mother promised she would reach out to him after she died, if it were possible. We know that's not possible, Trevor. But maybe your father and Serena have told you some stories, and maybe you're getting swept up into something, some sort of mass hysteria of Riddell House. Don't be swept up. You're the smartest boy I've ever met. Use your intelligence to prevent yourself from being drawn into this world of spirit fantasy. Will you do that for me?"

It was my turn to pause.

"You don't believe me," I said.

"I don't believe you're lying," she replied. "I believe you believe it. But that doesn't make it true."

I didn't know what to say. I was so disappointed.

"I should go to sleep," I said.

"You should. I love you, Trevor. More than you can possibly imagine."

I hung up the phone, gathered Grandpa's Post-it notes, and went upstairs, unable to put my mother's skepticism out of my mind. I felt the rift between us had grown with our conversation.

As I climbed the stairs, I pondered the letter from Ben, especially the question of when my mother and I first grew apart. The things Ben wrote about children and their mothers sounded almost biblical. At what point did I realize that my mother's breasts were not my own? At what point did I understand that my inability to control her wasn't because of my own incompetence, but because she was a different person than I? Was that my moment of original sin? Was it the same moment I realized that I could die, and that death meant I would cease to exist entirely? Not that I would still be here, just invisible, which is what I figured all kids thought about death. But that I would be absent in a more substantive way. And was that belief an artificial construct of my culture? Was the pre-self-conscious child actually the *correct* child? Was it really like Ben explained: the membrane is thinner than we think; all things are connected in all directions in all time?

We are all connected—I believed it then and believe it still now—at least in an energetic sense. And who's to say this energy is not real? We can't see gravity, either, yet we don't deny it. We can't see magnetism, yet we don't question its forcefulness. So why, then, when people—spiritual people—talk about a force or a substance that binds us all, that unites us all—when these people talk about souls—why do we dismiss them as charlatans?

The more I considered those ideas that night, the more I was swayed by fatigue, and I felt my eyes needed to close. I turned off the lights and climbed into bed and pulled up my sheets. As I swooned into the depth of sleep, I heard the door to my room open and then close. I heard foot-steps across the floor, and then I heard someone settle his weight onto the desk chair. I tried to lift my head, but I couldn't. I tried to open my eyes, but they wouldn't open. So I relaxed. Because Ben was in the room with me, watching over me. And Ben would protect me.

25

THE DILEMMA

I awoke the next morning, feverish with a need to know more about Ben and Harry. I understood who they were and why they loved each other so much, but I needed to understand why The North Estate was so important to Ben. Why of all places did he want *this* place returned to the forest? Why not any of millions of other acres owned by his father? I understood the idealism. I understood that his gesture was symbolic, as Serena said. But symbolic of what? Simply of the destruction his father had wreaked on the environment? Or was there something deeper?

Before I even got out of bed, I picked up one of Harry's journals . . .

April 21, 1904

Ben and I had been called to his father's city house on Minor Avenue in Seattle, in a neighborhood where only the richest families lived. It was a grand mansion, with columns and flutes and decorative moldings in the Greek revival style so common among Seattle's

transplanted wealthy citizens. The finer details of the house's archi-
tecture were lost on me, I admit, since I have no education in such
things; so while the scene was nearly overwhelming, I fixated on
something else entirely. Like a child, I was most impressed by the fire:
gaslights—seemingly everywhere—glowing so brightly that the house
looked like it was aflame inside. I was mesmerized by the dancing
flames.

We were three for dinner. Dish after dish was served, a bisque made
with Dungeness crab, followed by salmon gravlax on toast points, fol-
lowed by a chunky duck pâté, a salad, and then a loin of lamb with
braised fiddlehead ferns and blackberry compote. The food was rich
and decadent, and new bottles of wine were opened with each new
flavor, so that I could barely look at the food when it came, won-
dering how much I would have to eat to seem convincing, while Ben
pushed away a plate entirely untouched for every plate he scraped
clean, and he drained every glass of its wine. In contrast, Elijah deli-
cately sampled all food in moderation, sipped his wine, and dabbed
the corners of his mouth with his napkin. And no one said a word;
a silent tension lingered in the air. When the meal was finished, we
adjourned to the gentlemen's lounge for digestifs; Elijah lit a cigar and
cleared his throat.

"I think Mr. Lindsey should get some experience at the mill," Eli-
jah announced, not looking at Ben or me. "He's a bright boy and we
should consider moving him into administration so as not to squan-
der his natural intelligence. He's learned enough in the field—God
knows, the field can only teach so much! It's time to bring him into
the fold. Of course, his salary will be commensurate with that of our
other managers, so he should do quite well for himself. And at such a
young age, with no family to look after. Good for you, lad!"

He sipped his drink, a grappa imported from Italy, Mr. Thomas
noted upon pouring.

"What do you think, Harry?" Ben asked sardonically, his leg looped

over the arm of a club chair, swilling a glass of rye in a tumbler. "The old man appears to have made you quite an offer."

I stumbled, uncomfortable with the dynamic; the undercurrents were thick. But I said nothing.

"You need to know more in order to come to a well-informed decision, don't you, Harry?" Ben suggested to me while smirking at his father. "There are pertinent details which need considering if you are to arrive at the naturally intelligent decision."

"Yes, I think," I agreed. "I'm not sure I'm suited to mill work."

"Tell us more, then, Elijah Riddell!" Ben chirped. "Which mill are you thinking? Surely the Columbia City mill is too small to take on an inexperienced manager for this purpose. And I daresay, you would never tinker with Tacoma—O'Brien has that place running top-notch, the clever Mick! Same with Everett and Shelton, too. I suspect you're thinking of putting Harry down in Oregon City! Tell me I'm wrong, old man!"

"You are not wrong, Ben," Elijah admitted, looking irritated.

"And I suppose there's a need for him immediately?" Ben asked.

"In fact, there is."

"Because, if I'm not wrong, I believe our good friend Johnny McDermott retired quite suddenly last week."

"You are well abreast of the workings of our companies, Ben," Elijah said levelly. "I am impressed that you take such an interest."

"I am my father's son," Ben observed, standing and refilling his glass.

"Indeed." Elijah turned to me. "Here is my offer. You will be associate manager for six months, and made full manager after that. If you stay at the mill for two years, you will become elevated to general manager. After five years, we will bring you up to headquarters in Seattle for grooming as a regional manager, with Southeast Alaska in our sights. The financials are quite good, performance bonuses included, housing allowance, et cetera. You'll make more money in your first six months than you've made in your previous . . . how old are you?"

"Twenty," I said.

"Twenty," Elijah echoed, shaking his head sadly. "That's my offer. What will you do?"

I was chagrined by the proceeding. I realized immediately that Elijah Riddell was using me as a pawn, but I couldn't foresee how the game would play out.

"Thank you for your generous offer," I said after a moment. "I'm not sure how I should respond."

Ben laughed and took a large swallow of whiskey.

"You should tell him to go to hell," he said. "You should say, 'Mr. Riddell, no disrespect intended, but please go to hell.' And tomorrow, you should send him a thank-you note for your meal. (It's only proper, as it was quite delicious.)"

"I'd rather continue working on Riddell House," I said to Elijah, ignoring Ben's caustic advice. "If it's all the same."

"It's not all the same," Elijah said sharply. "I will sack you; then you will have nothing. Where will you go then?"

"You won't sack him," Ben snapped, his temper rising. "He doesn't want to go to Oregon City. He doesn't want to be a manager or a general manager or a regional manager. He wants to stay here with me in Seattle."

"I am thinking of his future," Elijah said with a resigned sigh.

"No you aren't. You aren't thinking of Harry at all. You are thinking of you. You're thinking of Alice, of whom you are so fond. You are thinking about the one hundred dollars you had to pay that poor sap carpenter—the one who opened a door he shouldn't have opened and exposed himself to the 'indecencies' that take place at The North Estate—to keep his mouth shut, all the time wondering how low you could drive the bargain and still ensure his complicity. And where is he now? Somewhere in Minnesota, I suppose, tapping maples for syrup."

"You do take an interest in the business when it concerns you," Elijah said.

"I am in charge of The North Estate as part of our bargain," Ben said. *"I decide who works on the house and who doesn't!"* He paused, then added dramatically: *"You gave me your word."*

"I did give you my word," Elijah agreed. *"And you gave me yours. But you don't seem to be holding up your end quite so well."*

"I'll go see her tonight. I'll go see her right now!"

"Not that part. The part about ending this nonsense. The part about putting aside your youthful adventures and turning your attention to more adult things."

"Adult things!" Ben scoffed. *"What do you think of that, Harry? You must be quite honored to be so diminished by the great Elijah Riddell!"*

"I think I don't know why I'm here for this," I said. *"I haven't said a word."*

"A very wise boy," Elijah said. *"Another reason to send him to Oregon City."*

"You won't send him anywhere," Ben warned. *"I'll make the decisions on this matter."*

"Your decisions are all wrong!" Elijah shouted. *"You insist on having this boy of yours in full public view, even after you've become engaged to Alice. And you've conducted yourself with such indiscretion—I've spent how much time and money fixing this already? Your dalliances on the coast and in the woods and at the house. It must end, Ben. He must go to Oregon City, or he must disappear entirely. Those are the choices."*

"Who are you to make this demand about my life?"

"I am your patriarch!" Elijah commanded, summoning up some strange voice, some spirit that filled his voice with power and depth. *"I am the creator of all things! Everything you have, your entire world, including your very life's breath, has been created by me! I am your God, and I say he must go! He must leave the garden, Benjamin Riddell, and he must leave it now!"*

The words of Elijah echoed through the house, and the power of his voice surprised me, for I felt as if he were God himself, banishing me from Eden. I had half a mind to slink out of the room and head eastward in shame. Ben felt the impact of Elijah's words as well, for he did not speak immediately. Elijah said no more, but stood still, panting, his face red, his finger raised. And I realized that only my intervention would quell this argument.

"I don't know what you were trying to prove when you carried on like that in front of workers in the house," I said to Ben, because I followed Elijah's reference to the carpenter who had walked in on Ben and me one afternoon, when we were engaged in activities of an indecent nature. "I already told you I was done with you."

The words sounded so strange to me, even as I said them. But I had to say them because I knew that Ben was using me against his father, and I knew also that he was using me against himself. Rather than openly confess his homosexuality to his father, Ben used me as a painful splinter in his palm, something he could push on to remind himself that he was alive, that his passion was real. So he could feel the pain freshly. He was torn between two worlds, and I could see that our forbidden relationship and the antagonism it caused with Elijah was distracting Ben from his true mission. He shouldn't have been fighting about me! He should have been fighting with his father about the forests, about conservation, about the working conditions of loggers—things he truly believed in, and things that mattered!

But what I understood, Ben did not. He turned toward me slowly and shook his head, dumbfounded.

"Do you stand behind that? Are you done with me?" he asked in such a way, with such a hurt tone that I felt something break between us.

"You have obligations," I said, plunging ahead. "Commitments. You have a world to change, and it is not for me to interfere with your

work. There's so much you want to accomplish, and I'm in your way. I'll take the job in Oregon City."

"But, Harry—"

He tried to embrace me, but I rebuffed him.

"Harry!" he cried in dismay, and I knew that he felt the breaking, too.

Elijah turned to me swiftly and said, "Ben's only using you to bring me down, as all ungrateful sons do. He doesn't care about you at all."

"You bastard," Ben spat, and in a flash of rage I saw him change. His entire body reconfigured. His shoulders, his arms, his haunches. He coiled, and then he sprang at Elijah, the old man. Ben had his claws out, his fingers ready to tear at the flesh and rip his father apart. Elijah cowered, held up his arms to defend himself; so quickly it was happening, and Ben was so large compared to his father, I feared for Elijah's life, so I leapt forward to intervene.

I intercepted Ben midway to his target. I took him down with my shoulder under his ribs, because I knew he would have killed his father in that moment, he would have torn him to shreds. The two of us toppled to the ground as Ben raged and Elijah stood watching us.

Ben struggled to get up, to get at his father, but I held him. I had wrestled with Ben enough to know his tendencies, so I could thwart his attempts to rise each time he tried. And my moves frustrated him so, he raged harder and harder against me until, in one final effort, he slammed me to the floor, driving his elbow into my left shoulder with so much force a loud pop sounded and a white pain filled my vision and all my nerves cried out and my muscles went limp; my shoulder was dislocated.

Everything stopped in the wake of the grotesque sound, so loud and so obvious, the room itself cringed, as if it were alive. Ben sat back on his knees. Elijah lowered his arms. And I writhed on the floor in pain. But it was more than that. Something had gone terribly wrong.

"What have you done?" Elijah cried.

Ben put his hands on me, he touched my shoulder, but the pain was so brilliant I couldn't keep still, I pushed with my feet and flailed on the floor, and when he touched me I cried out and swung at him with the fist of my good arm, connecting with his jaw. Out of the corner of my eye, I saw Mr. Thomas enter the room in haste. He stopped short.

"Oh my!" he said.

"Send for the doctor," Elijah ordered, and Mr. Thomas quickly left. Ben had stopped trying to help me; he sat on his knees, hunched over, holding his jaw.

"What have you done?" Elijah repeated.

"I've broken him," Ben said soberly. He stood up and swiftly left the room.

I don't know how long it was before I settled into my pain, before I was able to breathe through it and coexist with it. Mr. Thomas returned. He and Elijah lifted me to my feet and led me into the kitchen and had me sit on a bench next to the stove.

I was alone then, for a time, indulging in my pain, for the physical aspect was only so much. There was also the pain of having Ben treat me the way he did. My mind drifted to our first weeks on the Coast and how there was nothing in our world but us, and then this. As if our physical bodies were in our way, our physical existence impeded our real connection.

"Fair warning," a voice said softly from somewhere far off, "it's going to hurt more before it hurts less."

I opened my eyes, and he was there before me. He had returned for me. My vision darkened with pain as he lifted my limp arm and folded it across my body, then gently up and, with a pop, the joint came together. "Better?" the voice asked. Oh yes, better. So much better. I wanted to thank him for fixing me, I wanted him to hold me. But when I opened my eyes, no one was there. Ben was already gone.

When the doctor arrived an hour later, I was nearly asleep on a bench in the kitchen, my head tipped precariously against the corner of the stove.

"I thought you said it was dislocated," I vaguely heard the doctor grumble, his coat still on, his bag in hand.

"It was," the voice of Elijah said, mystified. "He must have reset it himself."

"Impossible," the doctor said sharply. "Or nearly so."

"Maybe it was a ghost," I heard Mr. Thomas offer.

The doctor growled with dissatisfaction and clomped noisily out of the kitchen and back to his warm house on First Hill. Mr. Thomas and Elijah roused me enough to get me to the maid's room on the ground floor, where I could sleep in one of the small beds kept for the help. As they laid me back on the hard mattress, I opened my eyes and looked at them both.

"It was Ben," I told them. "He came back for me."

But they didn't hear me, for they were already gone.

April 25, 1904

I returned to The North Estate the following day with my arm in a sling. The main house was woefully behind schedule and still a skeleton in parts, though the cottage, my home with Ben, was a comforting oasis. It was our haven, as Ben had promised me. A place of spectacular beauty and peace. It was my home.

Ben stayed away for several days, and when he finally returned, he seemed to have grown smaller. He seemed tired. I was sitting at the table in the cottage eating venison stew the cook had prepared, reading some Sherlock Holmes, which was my guilty pleasure and not the sort of reading Ben would like to have me do—he was so insistent on my philosophical development, sometimes I wondered if he had lost the ability to experience guilty pleasures entirely.

"I've ruined it, haven't I?" Ben said when he opened the door and saw me at the table.

"I'm not sure 'ruined' is the word," I replied, not angrily in any way, but certainly reserved. "You've changed it."

Ben nodded, understanding my meaning. He didn't enter the room, he didn't remove his coat or his boots.

"I wonder if you'll ever forgive me for hurting you like that."

"I'm sure you've suffered more than I have for these few days," I said.

"I've suffered," Ben agreed. "I don't know why."

"Because you acted against your nature," I said.

"And what is my nature, Harry? Since you are the keeper of wisdom."

"I don't know," I said. "But trying to force yourself into a role that confounds your spirit will always break you. You taught me that, and I will always remember it."

"But I contain multitudes," Ben said. "So why is it difficult?"

"We don't really contradict ourselves," I said, trying to put meaning to Whitman's words. "We simply don't see the connections, and so we think we're contradicting ourselves. I'm sure, from a distance, we would appear to be one, without contradiction. Though, from our own vantage point, we are nothing but contradiction."

"I don't feel that way," he said. "I feel like I'm a distortion, a Siamese twin. I have one heart, but two of everything else."

"Then listen to your one heart, and it will tell you where to go," I said.

"Are you really done with me, Harry?"

"I'm sorry for saying that," I said. "I knew it was the only thing that would satisfy your father. And maybe it would be the best for you, as none of us can live in two worlds simultaneously."

"It hurt me," he said.

"I know, and I'm sorry. But I've been seeing things differently, like I'm high in a tree looking down on what's happening. I know you're struggling within yourself, but I see you as perfect, and I love you for it."

"But there's a distance. You're in the tree and I'm on the ground and there is a great distance between us."

Ben seemed so sad. I understood his internal battle—at what cost progress? At what cost happiness? I wished there was something I could do to help him, but there was not, other than be with him and support him in whatever path he chose to take.

"I know our life is a compromise," he said. "I cannot give you what you would like: a public commitment. I have family and business obligations that prevent it. But I promise you, Harry. This place we are building. This will always be our place. I will commit to that with everything I am. And when we are gone from here, this most beautiful place on earth, the eternal forest will return to take our place."

26

DICKIE DANCES

Before dinner that evening, Serena was charged up. She was on fire. She put my father and me to work washing the fancy china from the formal dining room, where we would be dining. After that, my father and I were set to polishing the silver. She had Grandpa Samuel sweeping the porch and washing windows with vinegar and newspaper.

Serena, for her part, baked and cooked and chopped and whisked— her mixing bowl clasped tightly to her breadbasket and her wrist snapping around so quickly it was only a blur. She paused to take her relaxation breaths frequently, a quasi plié with her fingers arching at the ends of her gracefully bowed arms as she inhaled and then bent over to stretch. I was impressed with her flexibility, but then, one would assume maximum flexibility from a seductress of her caliber, I guessed. We were having fresh bread and homemade aioli, orange and fennel salad, an olive spread thing, and a dish of thinly sliced raw beef, which was called carpaccio. She'd found the recipe in a copy of *Bon Appétit*, I deduced from the frequently consulted magazine lying on the counter. I'd never eaten raw beef, but Serena assured me I would love it; it was a summery dish, she said.

All of this commotion was because Richard, a.k.a. Dickie, was coming to dinner.

Dickie was Serena's alleged boyfriend. I thought of him as "alleged" because he had yet to make an appearance at Riddell House, and how close can you be to your boyfriend if he never stops by the house? I quizzed Serena about him, but she was less than forthcoming with details. I knew that Dickie was in real estate, and that Serena supposedly worked *with* him but not *for* him, but I didn't know how they met or how long they'd been dating. I gleaned, through a process of deduction in which I factored nonresponses, as well as likely falsified answers and plausibly correct answers, that Dickie was responsible for the telephone-directory-size blue binder my father had been toting around since we'd arrived. Proposal for the Development of . . .

Which meant Dickie was part of the deal, which was good, because Dickie would help facilitate the reunion of my parents, insofar as exploiting the land for profit would result in everybody being happy again. But it was also bad, because the deal ran contrary to the desires of a ghost who seemed to have singled me out for direct communication and implementation of a different agenda. And, to be honest, I wasn't sure I wanted to carry on a conversation with a ghost, especially if the ghost was telling me to do something that would dash my father's plans and, no doubt, snuff out any hope I had of getting my parents back together. So it was with a certain measured caution that I anticipated meeting Dickie. Because I really wasn't sure how Dickie would take to the latest development in the Proposal for the Development of . . . saga.

Dickie arrived, and he was a very large man. He had an incredible amount of flesh slathered over his six-foot-three frame, and all of it was packed into a lightweight suit he'd clearly bought forty pounds ago. His flesh was literally pressing out at the seams of his clothing, and I could see the stitching of his shirt through his jacket; I could see the seams of his briefs through his slacks. Dickie's largeness made me fear for Serena; I remember wondering if he might squash her when they had sex.

Dickie entered the kitchen with beads of sweat on his brow, and, when he sat down, I felt small and insignificant, as if Dickie could crush me with one of his ham hock hands.

"Trevor, this is Dickie," Serena announced. "And now I must get myself together. I've been cooking all afternoon."

She glided out of the room the way she did, her lovely blue toes touching the ground only to steer her. And then Dickie looked at me.

"How old are you?" he asked with an impressive baritone that resonated in my diaphragm.

"Fourteen," I replied. "Just."

"Call me Richard, then," Dickie said. "You won't be able to call me Dickie with a straight face, will you?"

"Dickie," I said with poker in my eyes.

"You smiled."

"I didn't."

"You're pretty good," he said. "Just one corner, but I saw it. More of a smirk."

"Dickie," I said again, and Dickie stared at me until I grinned. "Richard," I said, and I didn't smile.

"See?"

"But what happens when *she* calls you Dickie?"

"Collateral damage," he said. "You know what that means?"

"Unintended civilian deaths in a military strike."

"If you laugh when *she* says it," Richard said, "I can't complain. But if you laugh when *you* say it, I want to smack the grin off your face, and I have some difficulty with my impulse control. So call me Richard. You know how to open a bottle of wine?"

He handed me a wine tote with six bottles of red wine in it. I took one of the bottles, found a corkscrew in the drawer, and channeled my father—wine corking I'd seen as a child—and uncorked the bottle with a certain deftness that impressed even me.

Richard poured himself a glass. He swirled the wine by holding the base of the glass between his fingers and moving his hand quickly in tight circles. He lifted the glass and examined the wine in the light. He sipped.

"You're not drinking?" he asked.

"Oh, I'm drinking," I said. "I'm just—it's a little early for me."

"It's five o'clock somewhere," Richard said. "Get a glass."

I got myself a glass, and Richard poured a little wine into it. He showed me how to put my fingers around the base and swirl.

"You want to aerate the wine," Richard said. "It's a bit young. You want to open it up. You decant old wines for the sludge. You decant young wines for the aeration."

He lifted his glass and examined it at eye level. I mimicked his moves.

"See the legs?" Richard asked. "The wine that lingers on the sides of the glass. That gives you an indication of the alcohol content."

I studied my glass, looking for legs.

"When you drink, you slurp," he said. "You want that extra aeration. It releases the aroma, which, of course, is how we taste. If you plug your nose, you don't taste very much at all. Right? If you have a cold."

"The olfactory senses work in conjunction with the taste buds," I confirmed. Science. "It's symbiotic."

"You know of which I speak. Now take a slurp and tell me what you think."

I slurped. It tasted like wine.

Not that I'd had a lot of wine. A couple times I'd had it. When my father got drunk at Thanksgiving and poured me a few tablespoons in a jelly jar glass and my mother scowled at him. That was pretty much it. He said I shouldn't be taught to think alcohol was taboo or I'd start binge drinking in college.

Still, I wasn't sure my palate was very sophisticated when it came to wine. To me, it tasted red.

"Impressive," I said.

"Parker gave it a ninety-three," Richard boasted. "That's big. Twenty-one bucks a bottle at Pete's. I got the case discount. Ten percent off. That's what they do at Pete's: they give the case discount for half a case. That's how you get loyal customers, Trevor. Can I call you Trevor?"

"My friends call me Clever," I said.

"Do they? All right, Clever. It's about customer loyalty. It's about the personal relationship. It's about shaking a man's hand and looking him in the eye and giving him your word. These lawyers. They're everywhere. They're like locusts. My contract with a guy like you, Clever? My contract is here: in my handshake, in my eyes, in my heart."

"That's solid," I said.

"Solid."

I took another sip of red juice. I slurped to aerate and noticed the approving smile on Richard's face.

"Richard," I said.

"What?"

"Just practicing."

"I know why they call you Clever," he said, leaning back, taking a sip of wine, and admiring the garnet color as he held the glass to the window so he could examine the clarity; I imitated his moves. "You know what your aunt said to me? She said, 'Clever is the kid I would have had, if I'd had a kid.'"

I thought about it a minute, but not too long. Because it was a compliment, but it also reminded me that I was fourteen and not twenty-three. I would forever be a kid to Serena's adultness.

"You don't want kids?" I asked. "I mean, with Serena?"

"I have kids," he said. "They're incompetent losers; everything I worked hard to give them is wasted. I spend more money in car insurance and in alimony to that she-wolf mother of theirs than I spent on their education. Adult children are always looking for the first opportunity to force you into a retirement community in Arizona. And, believe me, they're praying you'll die quickly so they can have the money you worked hard for but won't give them."

I thought about what Richard had said.

"That really depresses me."

"It's not what I said, it's the tannins in the wine that depress you," he said with a dismissive wave of his hand. "They suppress your proprioceptors. You feel depressed, even though you aren't."

"I'm pretty sure I am."

"Tequila is a good antidote. Maybe you're too young for tequila. More wine helps; it takes the edge off the despair."

He poured a little more wine into my glass. And I liked this guy; he treated me like I was just another person and not like I was still wet behind my ears.

"Let's take a walk," he said.

We took our wineglasses outside and strolled across the meadow, which was beautiful with its tall dead grass and purple and white wildflowers and its grasshoppers with their creaky legs. When I was little, I liked to catch grasshoppers and play with them. When I was fourteen, I wouldn't even touch one; it freaked me out to hold a life in my fingers like that. Maybe I thought that was a part of original sin, too; our banishment from Eden; we no longer feel a connection with insects.

As we strolled across the meadow, I noticed that I could see the very top of a tree that was set back deeply in the woods, but the tree still was much more prominent than the others. I remembered seeing it from the dormer window in the secret room. I glanced back at the house and then to the barn; I was triangulating. I wanted to find that tree.

"Riddell House stands on two hundred four acres," Richard said, sweeping his hand across the horizon. "That's sizable acreage for a single-family dwelling. When Elijah built this place, there weren't any other houses for miles. It had all been clear-cut and nobody wanted it. Elijah had his city house and what he called his north estate—right here—where he entertained the high society of Seattle. It wasn't until later that the other rich people started to build around Riddell House, hoping some of Elijah's stature would rub off on them. They used the moniker The North Estate for the gated community. It's all about marketing."

"So all those other houses came later?"

"They did. Construction on Riddell House began in the eighteen nineties; The North Estate was developed in the teens and twenties mostly. The developers paid Elijah to let them suggest the properties were connected, but Riddell House is not a part of The North Estate covenant, and therefore this property is not subject to The North Estate zoning restrictions and lot-size rules, et cetera, et cetera. I'm sure you can extrapolate."

"Extrapolate?"

"Follow the dots. Even when there aren't any dots to follow."

"Oh, yeah," I said.

"There are no covenants or zoning restrictions on this piece of land," Richard said. "It's like we're an Indian reservation. We're sort of above all laws here. In compensation for being first and all. *First Nations.* We get some benefits that aren't afforded to others."

"But we weren't the first," I pointed out. "The Indians were first. Elijah took this land from the Indians."

"It's a metaphor," Richard said. "You can only pick at it so much before it starts to unravel."

We reached the bluff. I glanced over the edge and shied away. I didn't like heights then, and I don't like them now. I moved away from the edge until I felt safe.

"How do you know all this?" I asked Richard to distract myself from my certain demise at the bottom of the cliff. Had he brought me here for a reason? Was he going to kill me? Push me over? "All this history about The North Estate."

"Research, Clever. Research."

"You're a historian?"

"Good question. Yes, I am a historian in a sense. I sell history. I sell *houses*."

He said no more, and while I could kind of track his concept, I wanted him to explain it, so I said, "I'm fascinated by that idea, Richard. I wonder if you wouldn't mind unpacking it for me."

I was thinking about Mrs. Friedman, my eighth-grade English teacher, who used that phrase. "Let's unpack this poem," she would say.

"I would love to unpack it for you, Clever," Richard said. "Houses, even if they're new, have a history. A history of their creators. And, in the case of an old house, the history of its previous owners. Did you know—in the old days more frequently; I'm not sure how much of it you see anymore—the artisans who worked on building a house left pieces of themselves within the walls?"

"How so?"

"A deck of playing cards, or a photograph, or a trinket. When they built walls of lath and plaster, it took real skilled workers. Not like today, when you throw a few drywall screws into a piece of Sheetrock and there you go. When they had to do *real* work, the craftsmen felt that the house held part of their spirit. They wanted to imbue the house with soul. My job, when I'm selling a house, is to understand that my client isn't buying a bunch of anonymous rooms glued together in a more or less convenient configuration. My client is buying the *history* of that house as well."

"I see," I said. "Those artisans. The ones who imbue a house with a soul. Is that a permanent condition? I mean, spirits and stuff."

"There is a history of such occurrences. But you know how difficult it is to prove. As soon as you turn on a camera—"

He made a *poof* sound and threw up his free hand like a magician revealing that the coin has vanished.

"Do you know what a smudge is?" he asked.

"Like a smear?"

"Not a smear. A *smudge*. You take a bundle of dried herbs—sage is

the most common—you take a bundle of it and you light it so it smol-
ders. Then you wave it in the rooms of the house as you walk through."

"What does that do?"

"It clears out the dark energy. It's something you should do when you
move into a new house. Gets rid of the bad mojo, if there is any."

"Bad mojo?"

"Sometimes you have to clear out more than mojo," he said. "There
are people who deal with this stuff all the time. Lights being switched on
and off without explanation. Voices."

"Record players mysteriously turned on," I said.

He looked up at me quizzically, but I didn't elaborate. I wondered if
Richard had heard voices in Riddell House.

"There are people you can call to purge a house of a lingering soul."

"Do souls linger?" I asked.

"You'd be surprised," he said, raising an eyebrow.

"Have you purged the souls at Riddell House?"

Richard looked at me seriously.

"Some souls don't want to be purged," he said.

"What do you do then?"

"You level the place and start over. That's what you do. You bring in
bulldozers."

"What if the souls still stay?" I asked. I could feel my pulse quicken.
Maybe Dickie was the right guy to tackle my particular dilemma. "What
if they hang around after that? What if the souls are on a mission or
something, and they refuse to leave until they finish that mission?"

"At that point, it's not your problem," Richard said. "You've done all
you could. Then it's the problem of the people who buy the new place.
No one said you have to be perfect, they just said you have to give it an
honest effort."

That didn't sound like a very hopeful or convincing answer to me.

"How many times have you sold a house like that?" I asked.

"A rebuild after a teardown? Not very common. But I'm hopeful.

A certain computer technology company went public a few years ago. We're on the verge of an economic explosion of immense real estate significance. Pretty soon there are going to be a lot of really rich people in Seattle looking to buy really expensive building lots for their new mansions. I think you see where I'm going with this."

"But I mean, with a lingering soul?" I persisted.

"Oh, yeah. Usually the smudge clears everything up. I had to bring somebody into a house once, you know, a professional. But that was a special situation involving a murder-suicide in the kitchen. It was pretty brutal. I don't really want to get into it."

"So you don't have a lot of experience with a place like this," I said.

"A redevelopment like *this*?" Richard practically shouted in mock surprise. "I have a *ton* of experience with places like this. Why do you think Serena came to me?"

"Um, I don't know . . . You work together, right?"

"Work together?"

"You know, she works *with* you. In your office, right?"

"Oh, yeah," he said guardedly. "Of course."

"Is she in the same department as you? Is it a big company? What's it like to work with someone you're dating?"

"Ah, hmm. It's a big enough company that we don't see a lot of each other," he said. "We sort of have our own things going on, you know, to maintain a sense of professionalism in the workplace."

"Right," I said, but I noticed him sneak a nervous glance at me.

"The bottom line is, you're in good hands with me, friend," he said, smiling boldly. "This project is right in my wheelhouse."

He tipped back his glass and emptied it.

"Let's head back to the house. I seem to be out of wine."

We left the bluff and started across the meadow.

"Have you thought about taking on a mentor?" Richard asked as we walked together.

"A mentor?"

"You know, a guy who helps with—"

"I know what a mentor is," I said.

"Have you thought of finding one? You seem to be in need of direction."

"I *am* in need of direction, Richard."

He nodded significantly, and I knew he was talking about himself.

"Will you be my mentor, Richard?" I asked.

"I could do it," he said. "I think I'm a good fit for you. A balance of real-life experience and the more esoteric, you know . . . things."

"Concepts?"

" 'Cogitations' is the word I was looking for, I think."

"I'm willing to give it a try," I said. "I think we're vibing."

"I would need certain commitments," Richard said after a moment.

"Like what?"

"Truth, honesty, integrity," he said. "And loyalty. Above and beyond truth, honesty, and integrity, I would demand loyalty. Loyalty above all. You'd have to swear an oath."

The grasses were so tall in the meadow. It made me think of the antithesis of wild grasses: mowed lawns. Was it better to cultivate our lawns, or let them grow wild?

"I'm afraid I can't do that, Richard," I said. "I could never put loyalty above truth, honesty, and integrity. That's not the way I work."

Richard nodded to himself.

"Serena said you wouldn't."

"But you thought you'd try anyway?"

"Look for the soft spot, Clever," he said. "You know how it works. Always look for the soft spot."

"Serena put you up to this?"

Richard stopped and placed his meaty paw on my shoulder.

"Serena is worried about you, Clever. We can't have any defectors in this family. We all have to work together toward the greater good. You understand that, don't you?"

"Were you sent to have a talk with me?"

Richard shrugged more or less: yes.

"I'm not the soft spot," I said.

"So it seems. Forget the mentorship. We're still friends, right? And friends take care of friends."

"I can't commit, Richard. But I'll take it under advisement."

"As smart as you are," he said, "I have to caution you against standing in the way of progress. Things may appear one way to the untrained eye, but I assure you that there is much going on behind the scenes, and it would be good for you to take that into account before you start stirring a pot of someone else's stew."

I thought about it for a minute.

"I'm pretty sure that's a mixed metaphor," I said. "I stand cautioned. But don't demand loyalty over truth. Don't ever do that."

Richard chuckled and turned toward the house.

"Serena needs our help," he said. "It's almost time for dinner, and, as I'm sure you know, she is very punctual about dinner."

Dinner was served in the dining room with formal place settings—lacy linens on the table and crisply ironed cloth napkins and real silver silverware that had to be worth pretty good money. We gathered near one end of the table since the table was absurdly large; thirty people could fit around it at least. Grandpa Samuel explained that when Elijah, and later Abraham, had dinner parties, the whole table would be full of people. The most important people in Seattle. The Stimsons and the Bloedels and the Henrys. They all came to show their respect for Elijah Riddell. I could tell Grandpa Samuel was making most of it up. There's no way he could have been there for it. But I didn't say anything because it was fun to listen. He had a melodic voice when he started telling stories; it was almost like he was singing.

No one else paid much attention. My father and I were sitting on opposite sides of the table, and Serena was practically sitting in Richard's lap; when she wasn't busing food back and forth with my father, she was cooing in Richard's ear. I thought their behavior was inappropriate—not because I didn't like Richard, or because I lusted after Serena. I guess I just didn't understand Serena's attraction to him.

"What about the big deal with Pacific Northern Railroad?" I asked as Grandpa Samuel talked about Elijah's erstwhile immense wealth. He stopped short. "The big merger," I repeated, having learned about it at the library.

Serena groaned loudly and excused herself with pointed impatience.

"That was a long time ago," Grandpa Samuel said.

"In the old days. The early nineteen hundreds."

He looked at me for a long time. Serena was off hiding in the kitchen, so she wasn't there to interrupt. Richard and my father kept quiet, but they were watching and listening, I knew.

"Did you know Elijah?" Grandpa Samuel asked.

"This happened nearly a hundred years ago," I said. "I went to the library. They have all the old newspapers on microfiche."

Grandpa Samuel stroked his sandpaper face; I could hear his fingers scrape against his whiskers.

"Tell me about Elijah," he said.

"He wanted to make a deal for the railroad," I began, and then I glanced at my father, who was also transfixed. "And he wanted his son to marry the daughter of James Jerome Jordan, the railroad tycoon. Her name was Alice. It was an arranged marriage that was going to seal the deal. But his son was gay and had a boyfriend. Don't you people know this? I just got here. You all should know."

But they didn't know. They looked at me blankly.

"Richard," I said. "You're the historian. You know the history of this house."

"I don't know this part of it," he said.

"Benjamin loved Harry—"

"Harry," Grandpa Samuel echoed.

"Harry Lindsey," I confirmed. "His gravestone is up on Observatory Hill next to Ben's. They climbed trees together on the coast. Ben was supposed to marry Alice so the deal would go through, but then Harry died. The next day, Ben died."

"How did they die?" Richard asked.

"I don't know yet. But they died one day apart, and they're buried next to each other."

"How do you know what you *do* know?" my father asked.

"I told you, I went to the library and read old newspapers."

"All of this was in the newspapers?"

"No," I admitted, wondering how far I should go. "I found some old journals, and an old diary."

They looked at each other with what I thought was confusion on their faces. But then I realized it wasn't confusion. It was concern bordering on agitation.

"You found journals?" my father asked. "Where?"

"Serena has never mentioned a diary," Richard added, looking especially consternated.

"I'm not at liberty to disclose my sources," I said quickly. "And anyway, that's not the point. The point is, the clues are everywhere, but no one wants to admit it. There are ghosts in this house. Dad, you saw someone in the staircase when you were a kid—a spirit."

"The power of suggestion," he parried.

"Grandpa. You said Ben sits with you."

"No, no," Grandpa Samuel said, casting a furrowed brow toward Richard. "I didn't say that."

"You said Ben sits with you in the barn. He tells you stories about Harry."

"No, no," he insisted. "I didn't say that."

Grandpa Samuel kept glancing at Richard, and I saw the tension there, so I turned to Richard.

"Dickie," I said without a smirk. "You told me all about houses and their histories and lingering spirits and smudges."

"I've seen too many episodes of *In Search Of . . . ,*" Richard said. "And don't call me Dickie."

They wouldn't admit anything. They were afraid that admitting they believed the unbelievable would derail their plans for Riddell House. I realized I probably shouldn't tell them any more of what I knew until I knew more myself. It was too early to show my hand when all the cards hadn't been dealt.

"I want to stress the need for us all to be on the same page here," Richard said after a lengthy pause. "The sled doesn't move forward unless all the dogs are pulling together."

"You've heard the footsteps," I said to my father, making a final attempt.

"You've heard the footsteps?" Grandpa Samuel asked quickly.

My father glanced at me, but then averted his eyes.

"No," he said. "I haven't heard any footsteps."

"But you're here to find Isobel?" I asked.

"Grandpa Samuel has title to the house," my father said, still not looking at me. "He needs to sign the papers."

"Or we'll have him declared incompetent by the court," Richard added. "Which is a much longer and more arduous process."

After another silence, Grandpa Samuel spoke. With his head bowed and to nobody in particular, he said: "Grandpa Samuel has Alzheimer's syndrome."

"Disease," Richard corrected. "It's a disease, not a syndrome. It's important to use the correct nomenclature."

Serena entered then, with a tray of ice cream sundaes and after-dinner drinks, and set the tray on the table.

"Dickie!" she cried. "Your favorite dessert!"

I looked at the other men at the table and saw that everything we had discussed had vanished, swept under the expensive, old Oriental carpets. We had spoken of things, but those things would not be spoken of again. We ate our dessert glumly, silently, staring at our plates, Serena shaking her head to herself because she really didn't understand what was going on.

When enough had been consumed, Serena stood up from the table.

"Let's go dancing," she suggested with great enthusiasm. And we moved to the ballroom.

The chandelier threw a twinkling light against the ceiling, and old sconces dripped yellow light down the walls. Serena reached behind the curtain on the small stage and turned on stage lights, which I hadn't noticed before. Lights like you'd see in a theater, but smaller, clamped onto a metal pipe attached to the ceiling. Downstage center was the old phonograph.

"Mother taught us how to dance, didn't she, Brother Jones?" Serena said, slipping a record from its sleeve and setting it on the platter. "As I have taught Dickie."

She started the record, and Grandpa Samuel, my father, and I watched as Richard approached her and bowed. Serena curtsied. The music was vaguely Baroque, though I hardly considered myself qualified to identify it more precisely. It sounded like the music my mother would put on the radio station on Thursdays when she cleaned the house. I would hear it if I was sick, maybe, or on a school break. I remembered those days of blaring music and my mother cleaning furiously. There were horns, the pace was not slow, but not especially quick. Whatever the music was, I would forever associate it with the smell of Murphy's Oil Soap.

Richard held his arms open, and Serena stepped into him and took his hands and they began. Their dance was clunky and awkward. Serena held her chin high and kept her face blank; she didn't look at Richard at all. Richard slouched and his moves lacked any precision. He seemed lost much of the time; I could see Serena squeeze his left hand on occasion, giving him a hint on which way to go. The music staggered on until it finally ended; Serena bowed elegantly to her audience; Richard slumped, relieved. We all applauded. The next song began, but Serena lifted the needle before it gained momentum. She took the kerchief from Richard's suit pocket and dabbed his forehead with it.

"My, but you do perspire," she said.

She turned her attention to my father.

"Brother Jones," she said mischievously. "Won't you ask me to dance?"

My father saluted her with a wave of his hand and approached. With one hand behind his back and his head bowed, he offered his free hand to her.

"Sister Serena," he said. "May I have the honor?"

He looked over at me and nodded toward the record player. The record was still spinning and the arm was raised. I lined up the needle over the dark groove as best I could and lowered it with the lever. The music began.

I had only seen my father dance once in my life, at an outdoor wedding my parents had taken me to in Connecticut. It was fall, and the kerosene heaters inside the tent roared to fend off the cold evening outside. My parents were fighting. Not angry fighting, but they were at each other. Sniping. Things had started to unravel with my father's business and there was a lot of tension in the air. The bride was the daughter of a rich guy for whom my father had built a hull in the past, and I think my mother was angry at that very concept: when my father built hulls, we had a future and we had security—and those things were going to be taken from us because he wasn't building hulls anymore.

The groom made a speech, and everyone cheered and toasted, and the band started playing. My father motioned to my mother as the guests moved to the dance floor. But my mother ignored him; she looked away and picked up her wineglass, snubbing my father. I remember my father nodding to himself and picking up his own wineglass and that was that. But then he glanced at me and smiled, as if he'd just remembered

I was there. He took a napkin from the table and spread it out on the grass at my mother's feet. He knelt before her and took her hand. He said something I couldn't hear, and then he let his forehead fall against her knee. She looked down at him for a long time and then she slipped her hand from his and touched his head lightly. He looked up and she nodded. And then they danced. I watched them from the table, and they looked so *together*. Time had stopped. There was no fighting; there were no problems. There was just dancing. And I remember thinking how much I loved my parents. A lot of kids in school didn't even *like* their parents, but I loved mine. And I had faith that they would always be together.

With Serena in the ballroom that night—the second time I saw my father dance—I could see where he learned to dance like he had with my mother. My father and Serena were dancing as one. They looked bone-less, arms and legs working together as they danced around in circles, and then he spun her and then he dipped her and she pointed her toe and arched her back and he scooped her around so quickly, but never with a moment of doubt or hesitation. He was assured. His body was erect and tight. He was in charge and Serena responded to his every command like they had been rehearsing it for years. They were ready for competition.

When the song was over they stopped. Grandpa Samuel applauded loudly, and I lifted the needle. Serena and my father bowed to each other. And Richard said, "I can dance like that," in a self-deprecating way, and Serena took his kerchief to mop her own brow, and she smirked at him.

"No one dances like Brother Jones," she said loudly enough for everyone—but mostly for Richard—to hear, and he felt bad, I could see it in his face. He looked deflated.

Serena approached me, and lust sparked in my chest. She was so sexy, sometimes I thought my head might explode. I was ashamed of my feelings: I felt a flutter in my stomach when she looked at me, and my mouth got cottony and I heard my own words through her ears and

I knew I sounded like a moron. And now. There were beads of perspiration on her chest, and her dress was beautiful, and even though she was wearing shoes and I couldn't see her toes, I still knew they were there. And she smiled down at me, since, with her heels, she was taller than I was.

"Mother taught us to dance," she said to the room. "Mother was a dancer, wasn't she, Daddy? She was the most beautiful dancer ever. Before she got sick, she would dance for us."

"It was a time!" Grandpa Samuel bellowed, surprising us all.

"Before she got so sick she couldn't dance any longer, she taught Brother Jones and me to dance so we could dance for her. It was her hope that she would live on in our dancing. We would carry her up the stairs—Grandpa Samuel and your father would carry her; I was just a girl—and she would sit in a chair by the wall over there. What happened to that chair, I wonder. It was there for years! We must have put it somewhere; we don't throw anything away in this house. Your father and I would dance for her all night. Wouldn't we, Brother Jones?"

"We would," my father said, and I thought I noticed a slight change in him. When he and Serena had started dancing, he was confident and cheerful. Happy, even. But with the talk about Isobel, his demeanor darkened. Not much. But he became melancholy.

"It was a time," Grandpa Samuel repeated more softly.

"Tell me, does Rachel dance?" Serena asked, looking at my father directly.

"A little," he replied.

"A *little*? I'm disappointed that you didn't marry a dancing partner. Think of all the pleasure you have denied both her and yourself over the years. But then, maybe your omission was deliberate. Maybe you've been saving yourself for me."

She held her focus on my father for several moments. I was annoyed with my father for downplaying his dancing with my mother, and I was annoyed with Serena for her sense of possessiveness over my father, but in that instant she turned to me and smiled, and my thoughts stopped entirely.

"You're next," she said. "It's not difficult; follow me."

Suddenly, she took my hands. Suddenly, we were on the ballroom floor. The music began. She leaned in and put her lips to my ear. "You are a soft doll," she whispered. "I am a girl who wants to play with you." And she swept me one direction and then the next and it *was* easy. As long as I didn't set weight on my feet, as long as my arms were firm but pliable. As long as I realized that when she squeezed my hand, we were going one way, and when she squeezed my shoulder, we were going the other. When I got nervous, when I didn't know which direction I was supposed to go next and my arms and legs got tight, she hummed into my ear and I immediately felt like liquid and I conformed to her body and she moved me about with such assurance.

Her eyes half-closed, she didn't see me. Her cheek pressed against mine, she didn't hear me. I was owned by her. She had enchanted me and she would do with me what she would and I wanted her to do it. I saw her dance with my father, the way they danced, and I wanted to look like that. I kept my chin raised, I kept my mind and face blank. I gave myself to her and she danced with me as if we had always danced, as if we would always dance together. As if we were forever one.

The dance was over and she curtsied; I bowed. The others applauded our effort, and, as we parted, she leaned in and kissed my cheek.

"You're better than your father," she whispered. "And he is nonpareil."

I felt flushed and victorious, even though I had no idea back then what "nonpareil" meant. Richard went downstairs for lemonade. Serena danced with Grandpa Samuel and made my father dance with me, which was awkward, but I wanted to dance, so I did it. I had never danced before, so I had never known how much I loved to dance. I loved the feeling of gliding across the floor with someone guiding me without words but with unspoken gestures. My father's shirt was rough and he smelled like a man; I preferred to dance with Serena. But she was teasing me, so

I knew she would hold herself distant, if only to prove that she could. She wanted me to remember our moment, I knew. That was how she did things. My awareness of what she was doing only made me ache for her more.

Richard returned with a tray of glasses, a pitcher of lemonade, and a bottle of vodka. We took a break and he poured us drinks; I was slightly disappointed when he didn't pour vodka into my lemonade, but I was only a kid, after all, so I understood. Grandpa Samuel began to talk about Isobel. How she could dance. How he met her after his father had donated so much money to the university, after they had named buildings after his father, and though he had already received a superlative education in the nation's most elite colleges, Grandpa Samuel still liked wandering about the university campus, sitting in on classes and learning things, smoking cigarettes and drinking coffee and thinking great thoughts. No one ever bothered him during his self-directed postgraduate education. People knew who he was. Other students talked about him, but they rarely talked *to* him. He read the books that were assigned for the classes he sat in on. While he didn't participate in class discussions, he turned in assigned essays with the other students, and the essays would be returned to him without grades, but with notes and comments. And that's how he spent his twenties, because he had little else to do. The army wouldn't take him because of his missing fingers, so he was passed over by World War II. His father wouldn't hire him because Abraham thought of his son as an incompetent dolt. What else was there to do but smoke cigarettes, drink coffee, and learn things? He was the grandson of Elijah Riddell, after all. The son of Abraham Riddell. He didn't need anything but that.

"And then he met Mother," Serena said.

"It was a time," Grandpa whispered almost inaudibly.

"What happened then?" I asked.

"She wanted to dance in New York, didn't she, Daddy? So Daddy and

Mother moved to New York City. Mother was a wonderful dancer, but in New York . . . well, only the best of the best need apply. And while influence takes many forms, Grandpa Abe wouldn't make that donation, would he, Daddy? Grandpa Abe wouldn't make the financial investment necessary to secure Mother's acceptance to an academy and ensure her position in a company of note."

"Why not?" I asked.

"The subjective nature of truth once again rears its ugly head," Serena replied. "Daddy thought it was because Grandpa Abe disapproved of Mother specifically, and the arts in general. We learned later that Grandpa Abe really didn't have any money left that wasn't borrowed, and so there was no money to give. Nevertheless, the result is what people live with, not the cause. After a year of frustration, they moved back here. But they moved back as a married couple, and then Grandpa Abe couldn't deny Mother, could he?"

"We got married in Tarrytown," Grandpa Samuel said. "We took a train. The justice of the peace married us and then we walked out to see the river."

"It was a beautiful fall day," Serena said.

"It was a time."

We all fell into our own thoughts, which were different because we were all different people. But I knew we all pictured our own versions of Grandpa Samuel and Isobel, freshly married, walking along the banks of the Hudson River.

"When they moved back here," Serena said, "Grandpa Abe was furious. He gave Daddy a job counting logs, if you can believe that, and he made Daddy and Mother live in the cottage. Have you seen the cottage?"

I thought a moment and it occurred to me that I *had* seen the cottage. In fact, I'd been inside.

"They lived there?"

"They did. For a long time. They weren't allowed in the main house. Not until Mother told Grandpa Abe she was pregnant with your father."

"I don't get it," I said. "Why was Grandpa Abe so mean?"

"He wasn't mean, Trevor," Serena said. "He was filled with hatred. That's different. Just because you're filled with hatred doesn't mean you're mean."

"No?" I wondered.

"No. If he had been mean, he would have driven them apart. He would have sent Grandpa Samuel off to work in the forests of Montana or Oregon, somewhere where Mother couldn't have followed him. He would have made her wait for him for years, until her youth faltered. He would have intercepted their letters to feed their growing doubt. He would have used all of his influence to destroy their love. If he had been mean, Trevor, he would have crushed their hearts but left them alive to forever feel the pain he had inflicted, the remnants of their broken hearts clenched tightly in their bloody fists."

When she finished, silence rushed in to fill the void of her words.

"Are you a writer?" I asked after a time.

"Undiscovered!" she chirped. She stood up quickly. "That's enough of our break, I think!"

A new album had to be found, new music. Serena put on a smoky jazz record, slower paced, not nearly as crazy as the polka music, or whatever it was she was using to kill the rest of us. A woman was singing, and she had a mesmerizing voice, low and throaty.

I noticed my father shift slightly when he heard the music, growing more tense than he'd been.

Serena turned to him and held out her hand, but he didn't take it. He stared at her and shook his head slowly.

"I can't do this," he said. "I can't do it. It's not right."

But Serena didn't yield. Ten paces apart, they were in a standoff I didn't understand.

"I'm ready for another go," Richard piped in, but Serena held up her hand to stop him.

"It's okay to have feelings, Brother Jones," she said. "It's okay to remember."

She went to him and took his hands and began to dance with him. He danced, but it wasn't the same as before.

"I don't get it," I whispered to Grandpa Samuel. "Who's singing?"

"Billie Holiday," he replied. "Isobel's favorite."

Oh, I realized. They were delving into highly charged territory.

They danced, just the two of them, as the song ended and another began. And then another. Grandpa Samuel was fixated on them with a look of adulation, as if he couldn't imagine a more wonderful scene. Richard kept checking his watch. Finally, after the third dance, Richard stood up and cleared his throat. Serena and my father stopped dancing, though the music kept playing. My father looked over at Richard, but Serena kept her eyes on her dance partner.

"I have an early meeting," Richard announced.

"When will I see you again, my love?" Serena asked, still not looking at him.

"I'd like to come by tomorrow to have that meeting with Brother Jones."

"I'm sure that will be fine," Serena replied, her eyes still fixed on my father, which I found kind of weird. "Drive safely," she said.

Richard winced, perhaps wondering if he should continue the conversation; however, he thought better of it and simply said, "Good night, my love," and left.

Still, Serena and my father didn't move. It was like they were made of wax. We heard Richard descend the stairs, and the front door open and close. He was gone.

The music stopped. The record was over and the platter spun without making any music.

"Put on another," Serena said to my father.

He walked toward the record player, but stopped before he reached it.

"I can't do it anymore," he said. "You're not Mom. She's not here."

She said nothing for a moment. Then she spoke: "Clever Trevor."

"Yes, Simply Serena?"

"Be a darling and put Grandpa Samuel to bed for me, will you? He knows what to do, but he'll try to get away without doing it. Make him brush his teeth and use the toilet. Get him a glass of water from the kitchenette. And make him put on his pajamas; if you don't tell him to do it, he'll climb into bed with his clothes on and then he'll wake up in the middle of the night, crying and confused. Can you do that for me, Trevor?"

"Yes, I can."

"Be firm, Trevor," she said. "But be gentle also. People will respond to you if they understand the strength of your resolve but they believe you will be gentle with them."

"Yes, Aunt Serena."

I led Grandpa Samuel out of the ballroom; as we left, I looked back. Serena had gone to my father. She had pulled his head onto her shoulder. He appeared to be sobbing.

Grandpa Samuel's room was small and smelled like an old person. The lone window had no curtain to open or close, but a thick blanket had been nailed over it. I wondered why, in a house with so many bedrooms, some of them quite opulent, Grandpa Samuel lived in a teeny room in the back. It was almost like a cell. There was a sink in the corner and a medicine chest. Nothing was put away; clean clothes were folded and stacked on the dresser and the easy chair. The closet door was open, and the closet was crammed with old tweed sport coats.

"Brush your teeth," I said, and he did.

"Put on your pajamas," I said, and he did.

"Go pee," I said, and he nodded. He walked over to the small sink in the corner and turned on the faucet; he pulled out his old-man dick and started peeing in the sink. I didn't want to startle him so I didn't say anything until he had finished.

"Couldn't you have done that in the toilet?" I asked.

"It wakes up Serena," he said. "I use the sink. That doesn't wake her up."

I didn't explain to him that Serena wasn't there to wake up. She was upstairs, slow-dancing with her brother.

Grandpa Samuel climbed into his bed, which was almost a kid bed. A single bed that made him look big. He pulled the covers up to his chin and looked at me. With his hair all splayed out on his pillow like that, he almost looked cute.

"I love you," he said out of the blue, and it surprised me that he would say it. I wondered if he knew who I was.

"I'm Trevor," I said. "Your grandson."

"Clever!" he beamed.

So he did know.

I turned off the light and left him to sleep. The servants' quarters, where Grandpa Samuel and, presumably, Serena lived, had six bedroom doors adjoining a common living area, which wasn't big but included a kitchenette and a large table, two sofas and a bunch of chairs. I guessed the servants made themselves dinner there in the old days. The kitchenette was messy and obviously well used, and, when I glanced at it, I realized I had forgotten Grandpa Samuel's water. I opened the cupboards looking for a glass, which I found, but only after finding a cabinet stocked with about fifty cans of tomato soup and dozens of boxes of saltine crackers. I opened the small undercounter refrigerator to look for a bottle of water, but it held only cans of Folgers coffee and cartons of half-and-half. I remember thinking Riddell House was endlessly weird. I filled the glass from the sink and took it in to Grandpa Samuel, who was already asleep; I set the glass on the table behind his head.

As I reached the ballroom on the third floor I heard music, but I didn't hear footsteps. I rounded the corner and reached the doorway, and I saw them. They were dancing, but barely. They were holding each other close, leaning from side to side in time to the music, so slowly. My father's head was tipped down, and they swayed this way and that while Billie Holiday sang to them a sad, dark song.

Serena looked over at me as they danced. She shook her head slightly, and I backed out of the room.

Strange fruit, Billie Holiday sang. Strange fruit.

27

THE FALLEN

I tried to sleep after our evening of dancing in the ballroom, but I had a rough time. It was strange to see my father weepy and vulnerable like that, holding on to Serena so tightly. Looking back on it now, I think the simplest explanation for what went on in the ballroom that night was a brother and a sister consoling each other over the death of their mother—something they hadn't been able to do previously, because my father had been sent away. But while my father's slow dancing with Serena seemed to be about a re-creation of his times with his mother, Serena's motives were questionable.

As I lay in bed, I considered the possibility I was imagining what was going on at Riddell House. Serena and my father slow dancing, the ghost of Benjamin, Isobel's footsteps at night, my demented grandfather. Maybe they were all figments of my imagination—the Great Deceiver showing off his pyrotechnical skills. Maybe *I* was a figment of my imagination. Was it possible? If so—if I'd been swallowed by my own insanity—some rare form of adolescence-triggered schizophrenia—I remember hoping with some desperation that someone would come looking for me. I hoped someone would rescue me from my despair as I wandered the hollow corridors of my mind.

And if no one could save me—if I was too far gone—I hoped someone would at least validate my existence. I hoped someone would tell people that I'd put up a good fight. I'd tried really hard to make sense of the world. But I had only myself and what I could glean from my experiences to rely on, and that wasn't nearly enough.

I wasn't ready for what was to come. But then, I guess if my mother had been there—if she had been able to call me at that moment to talk for a few minutes—she probably would have said, in her matter-of-fact way: "Who *is* ready?"

Still, someone had to explain my father's wedding ring. That was not a figment of my imagination. It was real. I slid open the drawer of my night table to look at the ring one more time before I fell into a fitful sleep.

He runs through the woods at full speed, branches whipping against his arms, his feet finding their own way along the uneven path as if they have eyes, as if they have a sense of where it is they are to take him. He is swollen with a euphoria the likes of which he has never known. A sense of freedom and happiness and forgiveness and acceptance and love.

He needs to tell Harry what Alice said, how she responded to his request. She understood. (Finally, someone in this world understood!) And she wouldn't stand in his way. She was as enlightened as he thought she was, but he hadn't had faith. Not until Harry convinced him to trust her. "If she truly loves you," Harry said, "she won't want to see you unhappy." And Harry was right!

He sprints faster and feels the effort in his muscles, his lungs breath-

ing hard, gulping air, but with confidence and power, not for lack, not for fear. He is a living machine that digests its fuel and outputs its energy as a part of nature. He is a natural, honest man living a natural, honest life.

Harry isn't in the cottage—but where? Ben must find him.

He sees the note on the table: A nice day for a climb.

He smiles. Indeed, it is a nice day for a climb. And since Harry's shoulder has healed enough for him to climb again, he has been climbing nearly every day!

He runs out of the cottage, down another path and deeper into the thicket until he comes to the tree—the tallest for miles and miles. The entire area from Mukilteo to Seattle had been clear-cut years ago; only The North Estate was saved. And this tree is the grandest of them all. At the base of the tree he looks up into the branches. Harry is there. Climbing up or down, Ben doesn't know.

"Harry!" Ben shouts at the figure so far above him, a hundred fifty feet or more, tangled in the branches. "Harry!"

The figure stops and looks down between his legs.

"Join me!" comes the return call.

"Come down!" Ben yells. "I have news!"

"News?"

"Come down!"

And so the figure descends. Ben can feel his blood as it courses through his veins, that's how attuned he is to his own body. Because he is free.

"Hurry!"

Harry descends quickly. He is barefoot and bare-handed, a rope coiled over his shoulder and neck to use as a flip line.

"What is it?" Harry asks, still on his descent.

"She's set us free, Harry! She's set us free! I don't have to marry her!"

Harry stops to look down at Ben.

"What of your father's impending deal?"

"She said not to worry. She would take care of it. She would talk to her

father. Don't you see, Harry? You told me to be true to myself. I was honest with her, and she understood, Harry. She understood!"

"Ha, ha!" *Harry laughs boldly.* "So you see!"

"I see!"

Harry hurries down the tree. Faster. Like a spider, he zips down from limb to limb, lithe and nimble.

"Be careful!" *Ben warns, but Harry laughs and moves even faster; he is almost to the lowest branch.*

And then it happens, as if they both knew it would. Harry misses a grip on a branch and he slips.

"Harry!" *Ben cries.*

Harry lunges out and grabs hold of the lowest branch as his legs flail dangerously below him. He dangles from the branch by his hands.

"Phew!" *he calls out with a laugh.* "That was close!"

"Are you all right?" *Ben calls to him.*

"Yes."

"Climb up, then. You're giving me a fright."

Harry pulls himself up and throws his left arm over the branch. He prepares to swing his leg up and over when they both hear a loud pop. Harry cries out, loses his grip again, and drops down so he is hanging by his hands.

"What is it?" *Ben calls.*

"My shoulder. It's out again."

And with that, Harry's left arm comes free from the branch and falls to his side. He holds on with only one hand.

Ben is filled with dread. Harry's shoulder. The one Ben dislocated.

"Can you hold on?" *he calls to Harry, but he already knows the answer.* "Hold on. I'll get my gear from the barn. I'll come up to get you."

"Don't go, Ben."

"Why not? Hold on for two minutes and I'll be back. You can do it."

"I can't—"

"Harry, just try."

"No," Harry says. "Ben. I don't want to be alone when I die."

"Harry, don't be absurd, just hang on for one minute—"

Harry's grip slackens. He can't hold on any longer. He falls.

Almost in slow motion, he drops toward the ground, not flailing, not crying out. Drifting, almost. Floating down so gently, as if angels are supporting him, cradling him.

He hits with a sickening thud and Ben cries out. Harry, his love, lies broken on the ground at Ben's feet, legs twisted beneath him, arms splayed, one of them a distortion, too far from his body. Ben falls to his knees.

Harry's eyes are open and are bright red with burst blood vessels. Blood trickles from his mouth and ears, and from his nose, bubbles of blood form as he tries to suck air into his lungs.

Harry!

Ben touches his face gently. Harry, what have you done? He leans over and kisses Harry and comes away with blood on his lips. Harry's blood.

Harry sucks in a final breath, and then his body is racked with a spasm. The air escapes with a wheeze, his body relaxes, and his eyes become vacant because his soul has left. Harry is dead.

Ben screws his face tight in agony. Tears spring from his eyes and fly from his cheeks as if they are afraid of him. He lifts his face to the sky and howls, unleashing a sound that frightens the birds and deer and freezes all who can hear the echoes, which go on for miles. He lifts Harry to his chest and clings to him, crying, unable to bear the anguish until he finds the energy to raise his face and howls again, and again.

In flashes, I see the rest. Ben carries Harry's corpse to the barn and lays him out on the workbench. The barn is full of woodworking tools used by the artisans who built Riddell House, and Ben sets to work building a coffin. All night he builds, and in the morning he is finished. He places Harry in the coffin and uses a two-wheeled cart to haul the coffin up Observatory Hill, where he digs a grave. Before he is finished, the rain comes. The hole begins to fill with water and mud, but Ben perseveres, because nothing will stop him. I wish I could help him, as he fights against the crumbling walls of the earth, frustrated, distraught. And somehow, I know that I can. I believe that I can. And so I take up a shovel, climb into the hole, and join him.

Ben stops digging momentarily, looks up at me, nods in acknowledgment.

Together, we dig Harry's grave.

28

THAT MAN'S FATHER
IS MY FATHER'S SON

I stopped in the foyer at the bottom of the stairs. I touched Harry's carved wooden hand. I looked over my shoulder; the morning sun hadn't moved around to the front of the house yet. But the hand was warm, as if warmed by the sun. I knew that the hand truly held the energy of the house and created its own warmth.

I thought about it again, but things were foggy: When did I start having Ben's dreams? How long had we been there? I started having the dreams after I found the hand in the barn. But when did I first see Isobel dance? When did I find the shaft and meet Ben in the basement? After the hand had been returned to the newel. When Grandpa Samuel took away the hand years ago, Ben struggled to be heard, and the family fractured. Isobel was right: the hand was the source of power of the Riddell House. Benjamin could now be heard, even if only by me.

We'd been there more than a week. Of that I was sure.

The haunting image of digging Harry's grave with Ben overwhelmed me with sadness. I felt the need to do something physical to clear my mind, so I joined Grandpa Samuel in the barn. He'd taught me to use the lathe so that's what I would do. I would tool a chair leg. I tightened a piece of squared-off two-by-four between the headstock and the tailstock. I set the tool rest, took up my chisel, and started the spindle spinning. Making slow, careful passes, I cut into the wood as I moved the chisel along the tool rest, pass after pass, until it was close to cylindrical. I stopped the lathe and eyed up my creation. It was a dowel, though a little lopsided. I realized after trying it a few times how much practice Grandpa Samuel must have needed to turn out the elaborately tooled spindles he did; I was clearly not good at it.

Still, even though it didn't serve any purpose, there was something satisfying about it. The smell of the wood. The touch of it. The sound. And then taking my dowel and using the gouge, which peeled away curly ribbons of wood, widening the groove as it deepened. It was a sensory experience, which supported Isobel's theory that we are here in this world only to use our senses. To eat and drink and sweat and feel afraid and feel contented, and, ultimately, to love.

As Grandpa Samuel and I worked on the lathe that morning, I felt my sadness lifting. The focus and concentration demanded by the work gave me great relief, and I felt satisfied. I wanted to practice until my chair legs were as perfect as those turned by Grandpa Samuel, who had been tooling chair legs for years as part of an assembly line that had no other stations. I wondered if one day a man would show up with a truck to take away the spindles. "I'm ready for those ten thousand chair legs I ordered," he would say. And we would all be amazed that Grandpa Samuel had been working on his lathe for a reason.

Maybe that man would be God.

"Take it off the spindle," Grandpa Samuel said to me.

I removed the chair leg from the lathe.

"Feel it," he said.

The wood was warm and fragrant. I felt like Harry must have felt when he carved Ben's hand. The soul of the wood braiding with my spirit, with the spirits who lived in the Post-it notes, and the playing cards stashed in the walls. Riddell House breathed. It moved. It slunk along so slowly we didn't notice.

At lunchtime, I took Grandpa Samuel up the hill to the house and made sandwiches. Serena was at work, but there was plenty of roasted turkey in the refrigerator, and Serena had baked bread earlier, so it was nice and soft. My father had been in a closed-door session all morning with Richard in the library. I didn't know what they were talking about—check that—I knew *exactly* what they were talking about; I didn't know what they were saying. I finished making the sandwiches, got a bag of potato chips from the pantry, and a couple of Cokes from the icebox.

Grandpa Samuel's T-shirt had a red and blue logo on it, and it read:

WE DON'T HAVE TO CARE

WE'RE EXXON

AT EXXON WE'RE PART OF THE PROBLEM

He smiled at me and squinted his eyes. He had a big mouthful of food and he was chewing and chewing. He took a long drink of Coke.

"Tendons," he said.

He stopped chewing and got a strange look on his face. He reached into his mouth with his thumb and forefinger and fished about. He withdrew a piece of turkey and placed it on his plate.

"I don't like tendons," he said.

I didn't think Grandpa Samuel was crazy. I wasn't even sure he was demented. But I *knew* that he was very strange.

"Do you want me to check your turkey for tendons?" I asked. "I tried to get them all—"

He cut me off with a confident shake of his head.

"Good sandwich," he said, evidently pleased enough to continue eating.

As we were finishing up lunch, I heard the library door crack open, and soon Richard and my father came into the kitchen. Richard was unburdened; my father was carrying the big blue binder and some other folders, which he set on the table. Richard said hello briefly, nodded to my father, and then left. My father sat down at the table.

"That looks good," he said, eyeing our sandwiches.

"I don't like onions," Grandpa Samuel said.

"Can't you take them out if you don't like them?" my father asked him.

"I didn't put any in his," I interjected. "He's not complaining about something or needing to fix something. He's making a statement of fact. That's what he does. He's like a living Magic 8 Ball. You shake him up and turn him over and he'll say something. Sometimes it makes sense; sometimes it doesn't."

"Wow," my father said. "Where have *I* been?"

"Mount Sovern Academy!" Grandpa Samuel blurted out. "A *decent* education."

My father laughed and looked at me.

"Think about that for a second," he said. "There are ten thousand schools out there that provide a 'superlative' education, or an 'excellent' education, or a 'fabulous' education. My father sent me away to a school that provided a 'decent' education."

I did not indulge my father in his self-pity.

"Do you want me to make you a sandwich?" I asked.

"I'd love it if you did," he replied. "But I sense it may fuel resentment, so I can make my own."

"I'll do it."

So I made him a sandwich—with onions—while he shuffled through his papers and Grandpa chewed his tendons. When I returned to the table with a plate for my father—including a pickle spear—I saw that he had unrolled some drawings—a survey of some kind—and opened the binder to lay out an array of colorful brochures. He thanked me for the sandwich and took a bite, while admiring his display.

I picked up a brochure for a retirement community. Kensington

House. It sounded positively regal. It was located in Bothell, near the northern end of Lake Washington. The brochure was full of photos of old people smiling and laughing, playing bridge and croquet, visiting museums and attending concerts in parks. It looked pretty good. If I were old, I'd want to live there. They had a book club on Tuesday nights. They did yoga, and they had three restaurants plus a café on the grounds.

"I apologize for getting upset the last time we broached this topic," my father said to Grandpa Samuel.

"Topic?" Grandpa Samuel asked.

"The future of Riddell House," my father said.

Grandpa Samuel got a sour look on his face. He leaned back and stared at his plate and chewed the inside of his cheek. His eyes got cloudy, as if he'd turned off his mind.

"Or not," my father added.

I felt a twisting in my gut: a pang of guilt or inner conflict. Again, I was forced to confront my dilemma. Of course I wanted my father to succeed, to get some money, and then to fly to England with me so he, my mother, and I could live happily ever after as a family. But, at the same time, I didn't want my father to succeed by destroying what was left of Ben's legacy. I wanted to come through for Ben. As much as I wanted my father to succeed, so I wanted my father to fail. I wondered what would have happened if I'd gone with my mother to England for the summer and had never seen Riddell House. Oh, the whimsy of fate.

"Why don't you tell *me* about it?" I suggested helpfully after a moment.

"Forget it," my father groaned, disgusted.

"No," I persisted. "Seriously. Tell me about the plan. This Kensington House place looks pretty nice. Have you visited it?"

"No," my father grumbled, "I haven't."

"Maybe we should go check it out. See what it looks like in person. Look, Grandpa," I said, holding the brochure out for him. "Look at all these old people having a good time."

Grandpa Samuel raised an eyelid and peered at the brochure without moving, like a lizard basking on a rock in the sun; he couldn't be bothered to actually *move*.

"I don't like people," he said.

"Sure you do," I said cheerfully. "You just don't *know* many people."

"The people I do know, I don't like."

"You need to meet *these* people. These people are super nice. And once you get to know them . . . You didn't know me a couple of weeks ago and you like me, don't you?"

"The only one," he admitted reluctantly.

"So it's possible. Friday nights are movie nights. They show the classics. Movies you haven't seen in years."

"I don't like the movies," he croaked.

"Forget it," my father said, shaking his head. "Let him die and be buried in this house for all I care. This is the only thing I've ever asked him for. I never asked him for money or trust or love, and he certainly never offered any on his own."

My father gathered the folders and reached for the drawings, but I got to them first and rolled them out.

"What's this?" I asked. "Is that Riddell House?"

My father sighed, resigned himself to participating in the presentation, and pointed to the middle of the top drawing.

"*That's* Riddell House," he said. "There's the cottage. And see the wheelhouse down by the creek?"

"Fascinating," I said. "So this is like a— What do they call it?"

"It's a survey. And underneath is a topographical, so you can see the hills and the bluff."

I set the top drawing aside on the kitchen table and it started to curl up, so I motioned for my father to use sandwich plates to keep it flat. Then I studied the topographical map. It had a lot of curvy thin lines on it.

"The closer the lines are to each other, the faster the elevation change," my father explained. "Each line denotes a different elevation, see? Look here, by the bluff. The lines are so close together, it's almost one thick line. That's the cliff."

"Ah," I said, rubbing my chin, pretending I had never seen a topographical map before. "I see. And what's this other drawing?"

My father staked out the topographical map, and I held the third drawing open. Riddell House wasn't on it. Neither was the cottage. But the wheelhouse was.

"This is the proposed replat. The lots are all very big, as you can see. High-value real estate. Plenty of setback. The current drive would have to be moved, so this is a new road, and there has to be a turnaround at the end of it, here, for fire trucks. It's part of the code."

"So how many lots would there be?"

"Twenty lots," he said. "Ten acres each. It's the law of diminishing returns. If we try to pack more lots in, the value per acre will drop. The threshold seems to be twenty lots of ten acres."

"What about Observatory Hill?" I asked, pointing to a part on the map that had been cordoned off.

"That would be part of a reserve. The family graveyard would be left intact with a small fence around it. And there would be a plaque about the history of The North Estate. Two acres will be set aside for that."

"Wow," I said, trying to sound impressed. But I thought: *Two acres out of two hundred? Benjamin Riddell's legacy reduced to two acres?* "You guys thought of everything."

My father winked at me, which pissed me off. I was being forced to pitch a ridiculous proposal to Grandpa Samuel, and now I was a co-conspirator?

Everybody was talking about this sort of thing back in 1990. Even as a kid I knew about it. They called them McMansions. People with money—not the super rich, with their multiple homes and their private jets; just the regular rich people, who had a big house and maybe a time-share at a ski resort in Montana—wanted their space, and their extra bedrooms, and their walk-in closets, their four-car garages, and their hot tubs and saunas and wine cellars and lap pools and sprinkler systems and invisible dog fences, and they wanted their hardwood floors and their stainless-steel appliances and TVs in every room and alarm systems to keep others out. They wanted gates that opened with garage door clickers, and their house numbers on brass plaques. They wanted well-lit, even pathways so children and elders wouldn't trip and skin a knee or break a hip. And they didn't realize they were raising a generation of children who could only walk on level ground. The pathfinders of the world, henceforth, would be confined to the pre-paved paths.

But I remember very clearly, standing in the kitchen that afternoon, feeling a flash of rage against my father. I had half a mind to grill him on the impact those twenty soulless McMansions would have on the local environment: the sewage, the toxic fertilizer seeping into the water table, the emissions of dozens of gas-guzzling cars neatly tucked away in their multicar garages, to say nothing of the aesthetic decimation of the last few acres of old-growth forest in an urban setting.

But what good would that have done? I swallowed my lecture of righteousness and winked back at him. And I nearly gagged at my own wretchedness.

(Ben was teaching me, and I was learning. But was I learning quickly enough?)

One of the dark gray folders on the table had "Riddell House Inspection Report" printed across the front of it in silver letters. I picked it up and paged through it while my father busied himself with the drawings. The report was full of information and photos and a narrative analysis. It explained what the house was made of—no surprises there: it was all wood—but visual inspection of the exterior logs suggested that rot was likely present and the inspectors recommended bore testing, especially of the load-bearing logs. And there was stuff about drainage and the foundation and the systems and the

fire safety—or lack thereof. Basically, it was like living in a box of kindling. The fact that we hadn't burned to death already was shocking.

"It doesn't look good," I said, and then I casually passed the report to
Grandpa Samuel, who actually took it and looked through it.

"So it would take *a lot* to stay here, then," I said to my father. "I mean,
if you wanted to be safe."

"An awful lot," my father said.

"I mean, to bring it up to code—"

"Oh, I don't think you could bring it up to code," my father jumped in.
"That would be cost-prohibitive. And you don't have to do anything like
that; an existing house is grandfathered. I mean addressing the electrical
issues, and— But it would be smart to replumb the place. You've tasted
the water."

"It tastes like rust," I said.

"Galvanized pipes. They're so full of rust and gunk, the flow is re-
stricted. The water pressure on the third floor is practically nonexistent."

"But the water pressure down here is okay," I said.

"Right," my father agreed. "Because they've cranked up the pressure so it works on the top floor, but now it's around one twenty or one
thirty psi coming in from the meter, and if anything blows, it's serious
flood time. No. If anyone intended to live here for the long term—or
the short term, for that matter—he would be wise to think about the
plumbing and doing something about the rot in the timbers that hold
up the ground floor. Those are two crucial things just to keep the house
standing. It would be smart to install French drains at the corners to try
to direct some of the rainwater away from the foundation. And I don't
know when was the last time the timbers were treated for wood-eating
insects. There's evidence all over the basement—"

"Termites?"

"Wood beetles."

"Wood beetles," I echoed seriously, and then I turned to Grandpa
Samuel, who was deep into the report. "What do you think, Grandpa?"

He looked up, and for a second I thought he was crying. But his eyes always looked like that. They seeped and looked glassy. I figured it was an old person's thing. Or maybe I was wrong; maybe he was crying.

"I can't leave," he said quietly.

"Sure you can, Dad," my father said, sounding very gentle. I didn't think I'd ever heard my father address Grandpa Samuel as Dad before, except that very first day. My father slipped into a chair at the table. "Think of how easy it would be. Movers come and do all the work. There's a brochure right here on downsizing. Think of how comfortable we'd all be after. But most of all, think of Trevor."

My father reached out and pulled me toward him like we were making a commercial for the Church of the Latter-day Saints or something.

"Think of Trevor's college education. Think of him getting a good start in life. You know? He'll want to start a family of his own one day, and wouldn't it be nice for him to have a little nest egg that you could provide him? You've always said that Grandpa Abe didn't leave you with anything. Wouldn't you like to correct that? Wouldn't you like to provide for your grandson the way you wish your father had provided for you? You can fix the wrongdoing of Grandpa Abe. You can fix it right now! Wouldn't that feel good?"

"I can't leave," Grandpa Samuel said again.

"Why not?"

"Because she's still here."

My father recoiled slightly.

"She's not here, Dad."

"Yes, she is. She's here."

"She isn't here, Dad. She's dead."

"She dances for me at night."

"She really doesn't," my father said tightly, and I could see that the infinite kindness and patience he had been showcasing for us was not so infinite after all.

"Serena says she can't hear her, but I can. At night. I hear her dancing."

"That isn't her, Dad," my father said, his voice rising, his anger getting the best of him. "It's what Serena says: squirrels dancing on the roof. It's rain. It's woodpeckers pecking this place apart."

"Sometimes I hear music."

"Goddamn it, Dad!" my father barked. He stood so quickly, he knocked over his chair. "There is no music! There is no dancing! She's dead, Dad. She's been dead for a very long time. And she's not coming back, and her ghost isn't here, and she doesn't dance for you, and she doesn't play Billie Holiday records on the record player. She's dead!"

I was disturbed by my father's anger, because I knew—or I *believed*— that my father *did* believe it was Isobel. His anger meant Serena had gotten her hooks into him.

Grandpa Samuel looked down at the report and shook his head.

"No," he whispered.

My father gathered himself. He shook his head as if to clear it of cobwebs. And then he put his hands on the kitchen table and leaned over Grandpa Samuel.

"You still can't step up and be a man, can you? You can't do the right thing for your children and grandson. You have a chance to be a man, but you won't step up and do it."

My father raised himself to his full height, gathered his papers and documents. He slowly rolled his drawings. He moved to the kitchen door before looking back one last time.

"I don't particularly care," he said. "I have plenty of time. One day you'll die and this nightmare will be over. But I'd be concerned about Serena, if I were you. She's extremely anxious. If you drag this out with doctors and competency hearings and all that, I have a feeling she'll make your life very difficult. And when she wins—which she will, by the way—you can kiss Kensington House good-bye. Serena is not above revenge. As a matter of fact, she showed me the place she really wants to put you. It's next to the Taco Bell on Aurora Avenue. You know, behind the strip mall with the 7-Eleven and the paintball store? Apparently they've been moved up Medicare's rating scale from 'much below average' to 'below average.' Good luck with that one, Dad. I'm pretty sure Mom won't be dancing on the roof of that place."

He left.

Grandpa Samuel began rubbing his stumps hard, like he was trying to get something out.

I hated the idea of selling off Riddell House to make room for McMansions. I hated it because it wasn't what Ben wanted, and because Riddell House was so important to Grandpa Samuel.

But my father was *my father*! And I wanted him to like me. I wanted him to *love* me. And I wanted him to be happy with my mother and me, like we were happy before. Because we *were* happy once. I know it sounds sappy, but picking pumpkins on a brisk fall day, or following a creek deep into the Connecticut woods for hours and hours, or throwing rocks into an angry winter ocean . . . I remember these things. I remember looking at my parents and then knowing what love really was. I remember it so clearly! In their eyes! Between them! I saw an energy that was going back and forth between their eyes, and in that energetic stream the entire universe existed!

I sighed heavily, and Grandpa Samuel stared at me, waiting. Sad and lost.

He was waiting for me to tell him what to do.

"Let's go down to the barn," I said, and I touched his elbow. "We'll make some chair legs. So they're ready when the customer comes to collect them."

"Someone's coming to collect them?"

"He's coming," I said. "I'm pretty sure. One day, he'll come."

Grandpa Samuel nodded once and let me help him up. And then he let me lead him down to the barn.

29

A FIGHT OVERHEARD

I wrote in my journal until late. Just past eleven o'clock, I got up to use the bathroom and I heard voices from the kitchen. Serena and my father were talking; I moved quietly along the hallway to the servants' stairs; I eased my way down to the first floor and stopped inside the door. I perched on the bottom stair, and, from there, I could hear everything.

"It's like he has an instinct for it," I heard my father say. "He knows exactly what to say to drive me crazy."

"Patience, Brother," Serena said. "It's a matter of timing. Seeing the opening and taking it. You're letting your frustrations get the better of you."

"I don't care anymore," my father said. "Forget it. Let him stay here and rot. Who cares?"

"*I* care, Brother Jones. *I* care. You need to take some deep breaths and center yourself. You need to focus."

I heard some movement, a chair, someone sitting.

"I'm still skeptical of the legality of this scheme," my father said.

"It's not a scheme, it's a plan," Serena said sharply. "And of course it's legal. The lawyers explained it all clearly, didn't they? These are professionals, Jones. Really."

"I guess it doesn't seem like it *should* be legal."

"Why in heaven's name not? He'll get fair market value for the house. The money will be put in a trust for him. It will carry him through his years of decline and decrepitude until death finally claims him. We will also make our share—which we deserve! We deserve it! And Dickie's company will make its share on top of that. I mean, really, Brother Jones. It's a stunningly simple yet brilliant plan of *my* devising. I would think you would be celebrating me, not doubting me."

There was shuffling in the kitchen, then the sound of a heavy glass being set on the table.

"You're getting awfully friendly with that bottle," Serena said.

"I'm self-medicating. For stress."

"It's a rather all-purpose medication, I suppose. It heals any ailment, like castor oil."

"Just like that."

There was silence then. Shuffling around. I heard the refrigerator open and close, then another door. Then beeping and the sound of the microwave oven fan.

"I suppose I should have guessed that Dickie wasn't your type," my father said. "You just go and hang out in their offices?"

"I'm interning."

"You don't get paid?"

"I'm investing in my future. And I told you, I'm receiving 'good faith' money. It keeps us in carpaccio."

"I should have known that he was just part of your plan," my father said. "Obviously on a deal this sophisticated, you would need a real estate expert on your team. Why shouldn't you barter expertise in bed for expertise in the real estate market? You make a fine concubine."

"That's a bit harsh. I have needs, too, Brother Jones. My choosing

Dickie was simply killing two birds with one stone. But then, I'm the one who sees opportunities when they are presented to me, unlike you."

"I can't imagine spending more than five minutes alone with him."

"There's not a glimmer of romance between us?"

"Not a glimmer."

"Who *is* my type, then?" Serena asked.

"Someone smarter. Someone stronger."

"Someone like you?"

"More like me than like him," my father replied.

The microwave beeped and the door was opened.

"Do you want some of this?" Serena asked. "I can remove the tendons, if you like."

"And what's with the fucking tendon thing?"

"It gives him something to control."

"Really? Talk about setting your sights low. A victory over tendons!"

"I've waited for this so long," Serena said, her voice tired and dreamy.

Legs of a chair scraped the floor as she sat at the table.

"It's been hard for you, I'm sure," my father said.

"At first it wasn't hard, it was just a lot of work. Work isn't hard; it just is. But when your high school graduation date passed and I hadn't heard from you, that was hard. And as I waited for you to return to me and you didn't—weeks into months into years—that was hard. I won't deny it. I fell deeply into despair. But when I felt the worst, I conjured your image in my mind, and your final words to me: 'I will return for you.' And my faith was restored."

A long silence. I could picture my father and Serena so clearly: my father with his drink, Serena daintily eating her warmed turkey slices in small bites.

"What will you do with your share of the money, I wonder," Serena said eventually.

"I want my house back and I want my life back," my father said flatly.

"It was never *your* life," Serena pointed out. "You just lived it for a little while. The drudgery, the blandness."

"My life hasn't been entirely bland."

"No? Well, then, you've buried some of the excitement in your description. I would think teaching juvenile delinquents how to build wooden boats until you lost so much money you had to declare bankruptcy couldn't be considered electrifying stuff. On the other hand, if you had gone broke in an explosion of fabulous globe-trotting, shopping sprees at Harrods with an American Express Black Card, and relentless sex and drug orgies on your private yacht, I could see your need for understatement."

"Is that what excitement is?" my father asked.

"My point is that you've never reached for your true potential," Serena said with some urgency to her voice. "After Daddy sent you away, you snuffed out your own flame. You know what your potential was when you were young: you could have done anything! But instead of doing anything, you did nothing. Why?"

"I'm a victim of circumstance," he said.

"It's not a matter of circumstance," Serena snapped. "It's a matter of weakness. A matter of pathetic self-flagellation. You need to set yourself free, and how you do it is by getting rid of this place. Giving it a kick so it tumbles over the edge of the precipice and plummets toward its destiny. You can't care about what happens to Riddell House; you must turn your back on this place, like Orpheus leaving the shadows of hell: don't look back or you'll lose everything! When you finally let go, Brother Jones, you will be free to truly shine!"

I heard someone stand up. I heard water in the sink. I pictured Serena washing her plate.

"And what are you going to do with *your* share?" my father asked, which I thought robbed the moment of its poetry. Something inside me—a spark!—reignited for Serena when she spoke like that. Such drama. Such power.

"I'm going to travel the world," she said. "See things, go places. I'm going to be liberated from this hellhole, and I'm going to visit all the most fabulous places on earth, and maybe even some not so fabulous. You're welcome to join me if you like. We could be traveling partners, take a cruise around the world with a cabin on the lido deck, wear formal clothes to the late dinner seating, drink champagne under the stars of the Southern Hemisphere."

A cruise, I thought. *An around the world cruise! The brochure!*

"I have responsibilities," my father said.

"Do you mean Trevor?" she asked with a contemptuous laugh, and I was startled to hear my name being invoked by her. "You have to be a good father like *your* father was? Honestly, Jones, your naïveté can be charming, but it's tedious as well. Having a father who wanders through the house with dead eyes like you do, as if you're a zombie, is no better than—and, in fact, one might argue *worse* than—having no father at all! Your 'responsibility' can be given to your wife. I haven't heard the phone ring in the past few days. She hasn't been checking in very regularly, has she? How is my dear sister-in-law, Rachel? Is she coping without you? Absence makes the heart grow fonder? Or absence makes the heart realize there wasn't much there to begin with?"

"You're a bitch," my father said sharply.

"Am I?" Serena said, her voice cheery but strained. "A bitch? Or am I someone who speaks to you honestly, like no one has ever spoken to you in your life? Are you sure I'm evil? Or am I someone who has expectations for you, who sees your potential and wants you to reach it, who actually has a love for you that's strong enough for me to tell you the truth you need to hear: you've pissed away your life until now, Brother Jones, and I won't tolerate it. I won't let you indulge in your pathetic pantomime any longer. Snap out of it, Brother! I'm not a bitch. I'm your savior!"

Silence then, long and deadly. And then three quick steps, a scuffle over something.

"Put that fucking bottle away," Serena snapped, and a cupboard door slammed shut. "You're a fucking drunk like your father. It's a coward's way out, and you are surely a coward. Buck up, boy. It's time to stop cowering in the corner. It's time to step up and take responsibility for your actions. You can't hide from what you've done. You can outrun all the other boys on the track team and feel strong. You can feel sure. But you can't outrun yourself, can you? That's why you came home. That's why you came back to Riddell House. Because whenever you stop running you have to face yourself. And you know what you did."

I heard a slap. A hard slap—hand on face. I heard a gasp of surprise and a body collapse to the floor; it had to be Serena, because, after a moment, I heard heavy footsteps cross the room and pass in front of the door I was hiding behind. Those were my father's footsteps. The footsteps paused, then continued down the hallway and out the front door. Moments later, I heard the spray of gravel as the rental car pulled away from Riddell House.

When my father was gone finally, I cracked open the door an inch and looked out. Serena was pooled on the floor, sobbing, holding her face in her hands. She wore a pretty dress, beige with a pale green and pink floral print. Spring. And her auburn hair. And her tears. Though I thought better of it, I couldn't stop myself; I went to her, crouched over her, put my arm around her shoulder and felt her lean into me as she cried.

We stayed like that for a minute or more. I felt so awkward with the warm, quivering body of Serena pressed up against me. Her sobs slowed and then stopped. I went to the sink and filled a glass of water, which I brought to her. She sat back, pushed the hair from her face, and drank.

"You've been listening," she said with a laugh of regret. She sniffed loudly.

"Why did Dad hit you?"

"I pressed on a bruise that's still sensitive. It was a chance I took. I did it willingly, and I accept the consequences of my actions."

I saw the scarlet mark on her face from the slap. I went to the freezer and wrapped some ice cubes in a tea towel; I brought it to her. She allowed me to hold it against her cheek.

"What bruise did you press on?" I asked. "Why did he get so mad?"

"There are certain things best kept private between a brother and a sister."

"Like what things?"

She smiled at me gently. I felt strange being close to her when she was so vulnerable. I held her in my lap, for she hadn't moved from the spot where she had collapsed. I held her, and her face was on my shoulder and I pressed the ice to her cheek and she looked up at me sleepily, reached with one hand, and stroked my face.

"In another universe, we would have been good friends," she said. "You and I would have been very close. But I'm afraid this is the universe we're stuck with."

"I wish you would tell me."

"It's not for me to tell."

We stayed like that for quite a while, until the ice melted enough that water dripped down her cheek. Then I helped her up and walked her down the hallway to her room. She stopped me at the threshold and did not allow me inside.

"There is part of him inside you," she said. "Which is why you are so clever. But there is part of your mother, as well. Which is why you will survive this family. Of all of us, you will survive."

She leaned in and kissed my forehead. It was soft and loving and I felt my soul shudder with the understanding that Serena and I were very much alike, as she said. But we were also entirely different.

"'To sleep, perchance to dream,'" she said, and she smiled at my lack of reaction. "You didn't roll your eyes, which means you don't know the reference. You are still a boy and you have much to learn; I know you will learn it, and then you will be a man. Good night, my nephew, and thank you for your empathy. It means more to me than you can imagine."

She closed the door.

30

BEHOLD, THIS DREAMER!

We were more than a week into our stay—ten days by the calendar— and I had taught myself how to walk down the long dark hallways without making a sound. I had familiarized myself with all the stairways that were obvious, and some that were not, back stairs and front, servant stairs and front-of-house. I had found linen closets with hidden panels to store things; what was stored in these places over the decades, I didn't know. I understood Riddell House in a way I could only describe as fundamental. Sometimes, when I walked down the long corridor at night and ventured into the south wing, I felt as if I had *become* the house. The house told me when to turn, where to go next, what to discover. And when I stopped in a room during my nightly explorations, I always knew Ben was there with me, because I breathed with measured breaths and I didn't move a gram of body weight; I made no sound. I waited until Ben's shallow breath fell out of sync with mine, and I could hear us both breathing.

I didn't want anything from Ben but the truth. He was there when my grandmother died. He knew what happened between my father and his mother and father, and he seemed to be the only one who was willing to tell me anything.

I stood in a room that was entirely empty except for a bare mattress on a metal frame. The moon shone across the water and tickled the ceiling and walls with flecks of light. I heard Ben's breath, independent of my own, so I knew he was with me. He placed his hand on my shoulder and leaned toward me so I could feel his phantom weight, and he whispered my name.

"Tell me," I said, but he said nothing.

That night, I had another dream.

Caked with mud and dirt, shivering in the cold rain that has soaked into his bones, Ben stands in the meadow, gazing up at Riddell House, the symbol of all that is right and all that is wrong in the world. The place built to shelter him from suffering; the place that is the source of his pain. The only thing he sees is Harry, looking up at him from the ground, his eyes blazing red, and yet a peaceful look on his face, as if he had already reached a place where pain no longer existed.

Ben caused Harry's death. In his rage against his father, he broke Harry. He broke him so he couldn't save himself. The moment of Ben's greatest joy—confessing his true love for Harry to his fiancée, and her accepting the truth of it—forever bonded with the moment of Ben's greatest sorrow, the death of his soul mate. And now what does he do? And now where does he go?

Soaking wet and filthy, he enters Riddell House. Leaving muddy footprints on the rug, he goes to his father's study and sits at the desk. With a shaky hand he scrawls a note to his father, an attempt to explain. He must go. He must find Harry, even if it means leaving this world.

He leaves the note on the desk and walks down the hill to the barn. The evening is falling on the meadow, and a cold wind blows, causing him to shiver even more, if that's possible. He takes his equipment bag from the barn and trudges through the woods to the base of the tree. The tree.

With grim determination, he straps on his gaffs and slings his flip line around the trunk, like he's done a thousand times. He digs a spike into the bark until he feels the bite; he sets his weight on it and mounts the tree. He stabs his other spike into the trunk and he is ready. For the first time in his life, he doesn't ask the tree to protect him.

The climb is not fun for him; it is a chore. It is difficult. It is painful. He feels he is not climbing by himself but carrying the dead body of Harry with him, hanging from a rope tied to his waist. He feels the burden of Harry's soul. The guilt of Harry's death.

And so he climbs endlessly. He climbs so slowly, the tree seems to grow taller as he climbs; he may never reach the top. Fatigue racks his body, his core. He is cold and tired and hungry. He aches.

It's hours before he reaches a familiar place, and night has fully fallen. He finds the perch where a branch had broken off in a storm years ago. He pauses on the perch and looks out to the silhouette of the Olympic Mountains, a distinct black line against the horizon. His vista gives him some hope that nothing can diminish the beauty of this world. The wind is blowing strongly, and he trembles so violently, he nearly loses his grip. But he holds tight. No, he thinks. Not yet. For a moment, overwhelmed with fatigue from the previous night's events, he thinks he should return to the ground to meet Harry, because Harry has made some stew for him and is waiting in the cottage for his return. But Ben remembers that Harry is dead, and so he continues up, higher still, until he is holding on to a trunk that is so thin it is almost impossible. The resilient trunk sways under his weight and sways in the wind, and he sways with it. It is frightening to be so exposed, so naked, nearly three hundred feet in the air.

He looks out to the black, star-riddled sky, and sees the face of Harry before him, hanging in the air.

Such a simple thing, to feel a loved one is with you, even after death. And yet, so painful.

Ben reaches out. He is holding on to the tree with only his legs, which are wrapped around a trunk no thicker than his arm. He reaches out for something. But for what?

The sky. He reaches out and takes hold of the sky. He grabs on. And in that moment, a breeze comes that is strong enough to sweep him off the tree and take him away. He is still holding on to the sky; his fingers grasp the charcoal fabric of the atmosphere, and so he drifts in the air, weightless, buffeted by the wind.

And then he soars. He ascends into the stratosphere and beyond. He flies, and Harry is before him. They look at each other and laugh at their indifference to the laws of physics. Ben reaches for Harry, but Harry remains just beyond Ben's reach. Still, Ben is happy: they will leave this world forever.

But the breeze stops, and Ben sees the truth of it: he won't be able to follow Harry. Harry disappears into the ether, but the weight of Ben's guilt will not allow him to follow. His suffering is too heavy to let him escape. He reaches desperately, frantically for his soul mate, but he can't catch hold.

He falls. Slowly at first, he gains speed until he is plummeting to earth at a terrifying rate, his stomach in his throat, he cannot breathe, cannot suck a breath of air; he falls, but he is not afraid. He knows there is no more reason for him, and he is satisfied with that. Because he hears the earth call. The soil, the rocks, the clay. He hears it call to him, and he knows that the earth ultimately wins. It always does. We will, all of us, end our lives here. Even the birds.

It is not long, and it is not painful. At least, he doesn't remember the pain. And then, without a sense of time passing or of place changing, he can feel his toes and fingers grasp the moist earth, his belly pressing to the ground; he can smell the dirt, alive, ever shifting, changing, growing, dying, and he knows he is still a part of the earth.

All is darkness until he learns to see. All is silence until he learns to hear. All is still until he learns to move. And when finally he stands and looks around at the dark woods and hears the night trains sounding their horns as they rumble by—when he sees that he is alone—he knows one thing with terrible clarity: this is where he is destined to be, and this is where he will stay.

This is where he will stay.

I woke up from my dream feeling queasy and edgy and dark.

Ben had given me a dream, as I asked. But he hadn't given me the dream I wanted: the dream about my father. He had given me a dream about himself.

I understood that Ben felt guilty about Harry's death, and that's why he was stuck and waiting to fulfill his promise to Harry that their special place would be returned to nature. But what I wanted to know right then was why my father was so messed up. There was some connection that I couldn't quite fathom. I believed without a doubt that Ben had the answer and could give it to me. But he wouldn't do it, and I found that very frustrating. Why wouldn't he give me what I had asked for?

I tried to fall asleep, but I couldn't. Or maybe I didn't try very hard. Because the dream he gave me felt too real. The sting of the rain. The pain of the climb. The dread of the fall. I felt cold under my bedsheet though it was at least seventy-five degrees in my room. I felt the cold and the rain, and I felt the dirt under my fingernails from Harry's grave, and I felt the joy at seeing Harry's face. I felt the sense of resignation at the moment of Ben's realization: he wasn't going anywhere.

31

BAD AUNT

It was late afternoon the next day when I stepped out into the breeze-less courtyard behind the house. The sun felt good on my skin, and I lifted my face to the sky with my eyes closed to indulge in the warmth for a moment. When I broke my meditation and returned to the world, I caught sight of my father, very far away, on the other side of the orchard, pushing a wheelbarrow of refuse away from the fire pit and off into the woods. And then I noticed Serena near me, sitting on one of the marble benches in the formal garden, reading a book. She looked up as if on cue, and beckoned. How bizarre; she came from nowhere; perhaps *she* was a ghost.

She had an ashtray with her, and a pack of cigarettes, as well as the ever-present bottle of Jim Beam, which seemed to constantly refill itself. Maybe there was a secret pantry in the house with fifty bottles of Jim Beam, like the cupboard with fifty cans of tomato soup in the servants' kitchen. While I wanted to continue on my way, I knew I'd been caught, so I approached her. She set down her book spine up and adjusted herself on the bench.

"I want to have a look at you," she said. "How is your head?"

"Fine."

"Let me see it."

I went to her and knelt down before her patiently while she examined the yellowing bruise on my forehead. Her arms were elevated and my head was tipped down so I was face-to-face with her cleavage. I could smell her citrus scent.

"Are you looking at my breasts?" she asked.

I was shocked. They were in my field of vision, but I wasn't *looking* at them.

"Are you having dizzy spells?" she asked before I could answer.

"No."

"Hmm. Okay."

She released me and patted the bench next to her. "Won't you join me?" Could I refuse? I took a seat.

"I would offer you a cigarette or a drink, but you're too young for those things," she said. "You're still a boy; I wouldn't want to stunt your growth."

She took a deep drag from her cigarette and followed it with a sip of whiskey. The sun was glaring and bright, and I shielded my eyes to better see Serena. She looked older than usual.

"Welcome to our Grey Gardens," she said with a sweep of her arm.

"Why do you call it that?"

"I'm referring to a documentary from the seventies. It was about Jackie Kennedy's crazy relatives who used to be rich and then became poor. They lived in a mansion that was falling down around them, but they refused to leave."

"They should have sold it to a developer. Then they could have gotten rich again."

"You said it, Nephew."

She crushed out her cigarette, stood up, and gathered her things.

"Come with me," she said. "I have something to show you."

I followed her into the house and to Elijah's study, which was a dark room with a gigantic desk surrounded by hides of dead animals—heads intact—decorating the floor and walls. She set the bottle, glass, and cigarette paraphernalia on a side table near a club chair. A desk stood opposite a gaping fireplace with black irons and a mantel of petrified wood. The windows were small and the glass was tinted amber, so it was dim in the room even when the sun was out. Serena sat behind the desk in a massive leather chair and indicated that I should sit opposite her on one of the hard-back chairs.

"This is where all the business of Riddell Timber was conducted," she said, "after Elijah moved to The North Estate full-time. Before that, he worked out of his house downtown or at Riddell headquarters in Columbia City, just south of downtown."

"History," I said.

"Exactly. History. You've discovered some of it already, I know. But here's some more. When Elijah's wife, Sara, refused to move west with his second son, Abraham, Elijah disavowed them both. For many years they did not speak at all, and, in fact, Benjamin's funeral was the first time Elijah laid eyes on Abraham, his only living son. Abraham was eighteen at the time. He went on to graduate from college and work at a New York banking institution to learn the trade. When his mother died he returned to Elijah an orphan. Elijah took him in, but he never grew to trust Abraham. Ben's death had greatly changed Elijah, and, in Abraham, Elijah saw the things he disliked most about himself: a rapaciousness that bordered on reckless or even cruel. Elijah wondered if he had been so callous when he was a younger man. He had been."

"How do you know all this?" I asked.

"I listen, I pay attention, I piece things together. Elijah knew of Abraham's desire to develop The North Estate after Elijah's death, which is why he put the house into a trust."

"So Abraham couldn't develop the land, but his family, if he had one, could still live here."

"And be cared for, at least until the trust ran out of money. Abraham had little of his own money. Elijah left him with bits, but not enough to thrive. What little Abraham had, he squandered."

"That's why Abraham pushed you and Dad to develop the land," I said.

"Exactly. Grandpa Abe knew he would never have the land to develop; he wanted *us* to do it. It was on those summer afternoons, as I sat on Grandpa Abe's lap, playing with his beard or drawing him pictures, that he told me all of what I'm telling you now. About the trust Elijah created. How if Abraham left The North Estate, the land would immediately be turned over to the city. He could stay, but he would never gain control of the land."

"Ah," I said, understanding the mechanics. "Elijah trapped Abraham here."

"Indeed," Serena replied, satisfied that I had followed her logic. "Abraham grew to hate The North Estate; it became the symbol of his imprisonment. Due to his avaricious nature, Abraham stayed here to enjoy the benefits of the trust and the lifestyle it afforded, even as he frittered away his own holdings. You can imagine how terrible it would be to live a life in such conflict! Before he died, Grandpa Abe took me aside. He told me that most grandparents leave something to their grandchildren, but he wouldn't be able to do that. He said he couldn't leave me anything at all, except this house. He made me promise that, when he was dead, I would make Grandpa Samuel sell Riddell House so we could have the riches he wished he could give to us—to your father and me, both."

"Did he tell anyone else?" I asked. "Dad or Grandpa Samuel?"

"He said I was the only one strong enough to follow through. He said that Grandpa Samuel was weak and would be against it, and Brother Jones, he said, would side with Grandpa Samuel. He said it was up to me."

A red flag went up in my mind, but Serena's story was quite compelling.

"So Grandpa Abe mortgaged himself to the hilt. He borrowed. He stole. God knows what he did. Because he knew that, when he died, the trust would be dissolved, Grandpa Samuel would get the land and could develop it for *a lot* of money. And Abe knew that the assets in the trust couldn't be violated by his personal debt. So, it was a plan."

"But Grandpa Samuel didn't follow his part of the plan."

"When Grandpa Abe died, he was deeply in debt," Serena said. "The creditors and lawyers couldn't take the house because it wasn't his, you see, but they could take everything else. Grandpa Samuel was left with the house, the few assets that were still in the trust, and nothing else. On top of that, he was ousted from the lowly post he held at Riddell Industries, so he had no job either. You know, when a man can't provide for his family . . . Well, it's difficult on the male ego, that moment of admission."

Which was what my father had to do. I saw it. I knew it was hard on him.

"Do you know what 'emasculation' means?" Serena asked.

"It's when you're no longer a man."

"Hmm," she agreed, nodding. "Euphemistically. If you can imagine a man emasculated in front of his family. So everyone could see. So his children could watch, and his wife could watch as his manhood was taken from him. You can imagine, the level of . . ."

"Humiliation," I said.

"Your word, not mine. But it's a good word."

"Devastation."

"Another good word."

I remember that my father didn't cry when he told us we were losing our house, but he was close. My mother shook her head quickly and stood up to make some tea. That's what she did when she was upset. She made tea. They never really fought that much, even when things weren't going well between them. But they fought that night. The night my father told us there was no more hope that we could stay in the farmhouse,

my parents fought loudly. They were fighting about me. The next morning, at breakfast, my mom made me bacon and eggs over easy and toast,
even though she almost never made breakfast.

"Your grandfather in Seattle is ill," she said, setting down the plate.
"You'll need to visit him with Dad."

"What about you?" I asked.

She shook her head slightly and looked away.

"I'm not part of that equation," she said.

So typically my mother. So clinical.

Serena cleared her throat to get my attention.

"Mother and Daddy could have sold The North Estate for a lot of
money the day the trust was dissolved, but they didn't. I don't know why;
considering Daddy's condition, we may never know. Still, there were
enough assets left from the trust to keep us in shoes and rain jackets for
a time. Maybe that's why they didn't sell the house immediately; they
thought there was time. But the limousines were gone, as were the staff,
the groundskeepers, the pool, the tennis court, and the dream that the
funicular on the cliff would one day be repaired."

"You had a house, and money for food," I said. "I mean, you didn't
have nothing."

"But we could have had so much more!" she blurted out, seeming to
lose control for a moment, though she quickly regained it.

"It wasn't as horrible as it could have been," she said after a moment.
"But the stress of the ordeal broke Daddy. He began drinking heavily, as
I've already told you. He was frustrated and depressed. He would sit in
the barn by himself drinking. We hardly ever saw him. Mother grew ill.
Her illness worsened so quickly, and then she died. Daddy sent Brother
Jones away. And Daddy has continued to refuse to sell the property. And
now we are here."

Serena got up from her leather chair and walked to the back wall of
the study. Over an oaken credenza hung a dark oil painting in a gilded
frame; she removed it from the wall. Behind it was a safe.

"Why do they always hide safes behind paintings?" I asked.

"This was put here before it became clichéd to do so," she said. "A cliché is a cliché because it's true. You know that, Trevor."

She spun the safe dial this way and that, entering the combination, and then she turned the lever and opened the vault door. She reached in and removed an expandable file folder and a small booklet. She returned to the desk and set them down before me.

"These are the papers that explain in detail everything I just told you," she said, placing her hand on the file packet. "It includes the original will and the trust documents. All of it."

"Why are you showing them to me?"

"Because I trust you. If something were to happen to me, you must follow through and redeem your legacy. You must sell this land for as much as you can get, because it is your inheritance, and you deserve it."

"What about Ben and Elijah and what they wanted for the land?" I asked.

"They're dead," she said. "What good is a promise between dead men?"

I perked up at her apparent contradiction.

"But you believe in spirits," I said. "You talked about the ghost in the secret stairway. So if you believe in spirits, then promises between the dead people, and between the dead and the living, would be just as binding as promises between the living. Isn't that right?"

She stiffened.

"Dead people are removed from time," she said after a moment, "and therefore forget the urgency of temporal life. Unlike me. Who knows what might happen next?"

"What are you afraid will happen next?" I asked.

She fell silent and blinked at me several times—I like to think, appreciative of my rhetorical acumen. She sighed and tapped the file before her.

"Mother died of ALS," she said. "There is a genetic component to it. It's not common, but one can be tested for the gene, so one might know."

She stopped abruptly and raised her eyebrows.

"You have the gene?" I asked. "You've been tested?"

"Mother died when she was forty years old. That will likely be my fate as well."

"I didn't know."

"How could you? But you see the motivation for my actions and intentions. You understand why there is some urgency."

"Isn't there some kind of therapy?"

"There's no treatment. There's no cure. There is only death. But let's not dwell on such talk. I have instructed my attorney to draw up my will. It will name you as my sole heir. Everything I have, everything I own, will pass directly to you when I die. Not to your father or anyone else. To you."

"Thanks," I said, not quite fathoming the implications of her declaration.

"I want you to have the life I never had," she said, leaning back in her chair. "I want to give it to you. But I need something in return. We call that quid pro quo. Do you know what that means?"

I shook my head.

"It's Latin for 'if you scratch my back, I'll scratch yours.' Do you like getting your back scratched, Trevor?"

"Sure," I said hesitantly.

"So do I. What do you say to me scratching your back if you scratch mine?"

"It sounds kind of creepy, honestly," I said, picturing her and my father dancing to Billie Holiday.

She laughed and stood up. She took the folder, returned it to the safe, closed the door, and spun the dial. She returned the painting to the wall.

"Then I guess we're done here," she said, turning back to me. "You are dismissed."

I sat for a moment, unmoving. Promises to dead men. Lots of money. Parents falling back in love once the burden of their financial stress was lifted. My lack of life experience.

Serena didn't move, either, she just smiled at me. Finally, she cocked her head and raised an eyebrow.

"Is there anything else?" she asked.

"What do you want?"

"Oh," she said innocently, returning to the leather chair. "So you want to play. I was under the impression . . ."

"What do you want?" I asked again.

"I want to fulfill my destiny," she said. "I want to sell the house and land, as my grandfather instructed. And then I want to travel the world. My world has been so narrow; I want to broaden it before I die a horrible death. I've been a workhorse, tied to a grinding wheel, walking in circles my entire life; I want to be free of it so, when I walk, I find myself in a different land. Dickie has put together a very smart proposal, which will bring in many dollars. Your father was supposed to get Daddy to sign the power of attorney by now, but he has failed. I need you to do it."

"Why would Grandpa Samuel sign it for me if he won't sign it for you or Dad?"

"In our family, fathers hate and distrust their sons, but they adore and revere their grandsons. Your grandfather hates your father. He banished him from the family twenty-three long years ago, as you know. I've tried to soften the hatred over the years, but, apparently, it hasn't worked. So you need to get Grandpa Samuel to do it . . . for *you*."

"Does my father hate me?" I asked.

"I don't know," she said. "Does he?"

I wondered if he did. Or if he didn't outright hate me as a person, did he hate me as a concept? The fear that my father might hate me struck me as very real in that moment. Maybe he wanted to be rid of me; I was just a burden to him. I was trying to force him to stay with my mother when maybe that's not what he wanted at all.

"What's more important to you?" Serena asked after giving me plenty of time to worry about my relationship with my father. "Your aunt, who is sitting before you, and the few final years of her tragically shortened life? Or a ghost? A promise to a dead man."

"Why don't you sell things?" I asked in a final attempt to discover a logical reason to go against Serena's plan. "The furniture, the rare books, the silver service, the painting of Elijah. I bet someone would pay a lot of money for that; it's history."

"But that's not really the point, is it?" she asked coldly. "That's not the point at all."

"But it's a question," I said firmly.

Serena smiled tightly at me and leaned forward, her elbows on the desk.

"Check the music room," she said. "There's a rug with nothing on it. If you look closely, you'll see three indentations—wear marks. That's where the Bösendorfer stood, a valuable grand piano that was purchased by Elijah Riddell in 1903. I sold it so we could have little things like food and electricity and gas for the stove. Creature comforts. Grandpa threw such a fit, I cannot describe it to you. He refused to eat for six days. Were you here for that?"

"No," I admitted reluctantly.

"Then you'll have to trust me when I tell you I can't 'sell things' until we can get him out of the house. Do you understand?"

"Yes," I said.

"Good. Do we have an agreement?"

After a moment, I nodded, admitting to myself that the immediate needs of the living probably did outweigh the wishes of the dead, though not necessarily in every situation.

Serena opened a desk drawer and removed a thin folder. She stood up, circled around to the front of the desk, and handed the folder to me.

"This is a power of attorney document," she said, standing before my chair. "It needs to be signed by Grandpa Samuel. But it must be signed in the presence of a notary public."

She then handed me a business card.

"This is the number of a mobile notary service. They guarantee to be on-site within thirty minutes of your call. His passport is in the folder as well."

"Didn't Dad have that?" I asked.

"I told you," Serena replied. "He didn't get the job done, so he's been relieved of his duties."

She looked at me and smiled a bit.

"I think you can do the math on this, am I right?" she asked.

I looked from her to the folder and back.

"You'd have to promise to put him in the nice place," I said. "Kensington House. Not the bad place next to the Taco Bell."

She laughed.

"Whatever gave you the idea I would put him in a below-average facility?" she asked. "You've been reading too much Eugene O'Neill."

Eugene O'Neill? I knew he was a famous playwright, but that was all I knew.

"I've never read *any* Eugene O'Neill," I said.

"One day you will, and then you will know. Nevertheless, I give you my word that Kensington House will be Grandpa Samuel's new home. It's a graduated facility, so, as his condition deteriorates, they can accommodate his changing needs—as you know, his brain is like an Alka-Seltzer tablet in a glass of water: it is rapidly dissolving. I am touched that you're so concerned about his welfare, even though you hadn't met him until two weeks ago. You have a refreshing level of empathy and compassion that is quite uncommon."

She leaned forward and braced herself by placing her hand on my thigh; she kissed my cheek. Since I was sitting and she was standing, her cleavage was in my face again, and the scent of citrus oil filled my nose. I wondered if she really had the ALS gene, or if that was another of her tactics. Serena's brazen manipulations.

"Everyone loves a good back scratching," she whispered, and then she brushed my cheek lightly with her fingers. "Sorry," she said. "You are too cute to resist."

I felt nothing as she went off, except that I knew I was over her. My first crush, gone already. And then my thoughts turned to the task I had been given, and whether or not it was something I could—or should— attempt to accomplish. Sure, it would be better for the living people, Grandpa Samuel included. And maybe, if I did it, I could end the Riddell cycle of a father hating his son. Maybe my father wouldn't hate me if I delivered him his house.

32

BONFIRE OF THE MEMORIES

My father had prevailed over the blackberry bushes, which were not bushes at all but snarling ropes of vicious, razor-sharp thorns that engulfed anything they came up against, swallowing trees and structures alike, evidencing the forest's relentless desire to take back what was rightly hers. In a heroic display of his own relentless nature, my father had whipped back those vines—beaten them down with a machete, a pickax, and a shovel. He tore up the roots, and with a power washer from Aurora Rents, he blasted clean an outdoor cooking structure known as the fire pit. It was a matter of principle for him. The fire pit was a piece of his childhood that he refused to allow to be forgotten. The house could go to hell, as far as he was concerned. The fire pit was important to save.

And so, the day after I had gone to the dark side and pledged to help Serena, I helped the others carry bags of supplies down the hill and across the orchard. My father had already prepared a fire, which was truly a piece of architecture, and I was duly impressed. It was like a ceremonial funeral pyre or something. My father had never built fires when I was growing up. We never went camping, and we didn't have a fire pit at the farmhouse, so I wasn't sure I'd ever seen my father build a fire outside before. But this one was magnificent—the kindling sticks and the wedges of dried wood and the crumpled newspapers beneath, all bracing each other, leaning together to form a perfect cone of combustible material.

"The design of a fire is important, Trevor," Serena said to me as my father struck a match and lit a few corners of newspaper. "Air circulation is crucial. A fire needs to draw cold air in from the bottom to feed its insatiable hunger for fuel."

The fuel was extremely dry; it hadn't rained since I had been there, and there was no telling how long before that. So the crackling began and the flames leapt, and soon, as Serena said, the kindling created a chimney; cool air was sucked in from below and rushed up to the top and, like magic—we had a bonfire.

Stone benches encircled the fire pit, and we all took our places. Even Dickie was with us that evening, sitting next to Serena on a bench; Grandpa Samuel and I sat on another bench; my father sat by himself on the far side of the crescent. My father reached into the cooler, which rested on the bench next to him. He pulled out a beer and passed it to Dickie, and another for Serena. He looked at me.

"What do you want? We have Coke in here," he said of the cooler.

"I'll take a beer," I said.

My father looked at me hard, and then, much to my surprise, he twisted off the top of a beer and handed it over. I realized, then, that being an adult was just about bullshitting everyone around you. Just do things until someone stops you from doing those things, and then say, "Oh, that isn't allowed?" I took a swig and didn't like it. It was bitter, and not at all what I thought a beer would taste like. Bitter bread. I set the bottle down by my foot, and I must have made a funny face because my father didn't look at me, but he said, again, "We have Coke in here."

I sheepishly handed him the beer in exchange for a Coke, and I felt like a dumb kid, but my father didn't make a fuss about it, so neither did I.

The fire was raging and loud. We sat, our faces and hands and arms baked by the inferno, and our backs and necks left to cool. It was after nine, but still light out, because Seattle was practically South Alaska in terms of latitude. For a long time we were silent, staring into the flames.

"Mother loved a fire, Trevor," Serena said eventually. "We built fires every weekend night, winter or summer, as long as it wasn't raining, and sometimes even when it was raining, if it was only a drizzle."

"She liked a hot fire in the winter," Grandpa Samuel echoed.

"She did. She said fires were transformative. She told us fires provided light to lead souls through the darkness of our universe. Everything in this world begins with fire and will end with fire, and so it is *through* fire that we can find the answers to the riddles. Didn't she say that, Brother Jones?"

"She did," my father agreed.

"She was a very forgiving woman," Serena said. "Mother was very forgiving, Trevor. I believe I inherited that trait from her. Your father inherited her impulsiveness and passion. I inherited her generosity of spirit, her forgiveness."

She looked at my father significantly. He avoided her gaze for a moment, leaning forward with his elbows on his knees, but when she didn't continue speaking, he grew impatient and looked up at her and nodded as if to say he understood that he had been forgiven for his transgressions, whatever they were. I knew. She was talking about their fight in the kitchen.

"Daddy couldn't start a fire with a blowtorch, but Mother?" Serena said. "She was very good at building fires. She taught your father how to do it. Isn't this a magnificent fire, Dickie?"

"Indeed, my love."

"I remember . . ." Grandpa Samuel said.

"You don't remember much, Daddy," Serena said. "What is it you don't remember this time?"

Grandpa Samuel was silent for a bit, then he said: "I don't remember."

"No, you don't remember, and sometimes it's best that way. Sometimes it's best to start fresh. Every day, fresh. Living always in the present, unburdened by the pain of the past. Most of us drag around our misdeeds like giant dead birds tied to our necks; we condemn ourselves to telling every stranger we meet the story of our anguish and inadequacies, hoping that one day we will be forgiven, hoping that we will find a person who will look at us and pretend to ignore the ridiculous dead birds hanging from our sunburned and weather-beaten necks. And if we find that person, and if we don't hate him for not hating us, if we don't hold him in contempt for not treating us contemptuously, as we expect to be treated—nay, as we *demand* to be treated—well, that person will be something of a soul mate, I imagine. That's got to be in the definition somewhere, don't you agree, Trevor, my fellow bibliophile and reader of fine poetry? But not you, Daddy. Because you can't remember. Sometimes I envy you, Daddy. I really do."

"No. . . ."

"No, I suppose you're right; I will never envy you. Did you remember what it was you wanted to say?"

"No."

"Of course not. It's fine, Daddy. There are more terrible ways to die."

Silence again, and then Serena stood up and gathered the willow sticks that had been stripped down to green wood. She gathered the marshmallows.

"The fire is still too hot," my father said.

"Oh, poo," Serena said. "So we burn a few. It will take forever for the fire to burn down to embers."

"Fine."

He took a stick and poked the tip through a marshmallow, then another. He handed the stick to me, and I aimed it toward the fire.

"Tell us about your wedding day, Brother Jones," Serena said. "Sing to us, as we gather around the fire. Weave us a story from your memories."

"I don't think that's very interesting to anyone," my father grumbled.

"It is to *me*," she replied. "And I don't think anyone else minds."

"I really don't want to."

"It's important for you to reveal yourself to your son," Serena said significantly. She turned to Richard and instructed him to pass me the chocolate bars and the graham crackers. "And now tell us what it was like, Brother Jones. It was in England, we know that much. Tell us."

It was clear that my father felt uncomfortable, but it was also clear that he couldn't resist Serena's urging.

"It was in an old stone manor house," he said. "In an old, rolling country club."

"A magical place!" Serena said. "A place that will last forever."

"Frayed around the edges," my father clarified. "There were seams showing."

"Like *this* house."

"Not nearly as bad, but . . ."

"Tell us."

"The day started with rain showers, but then it got very beautiful, sunny and warm. Then it cooled off again."

"The service was outside?"

"No, in the chapel. The reception was outside, while it was clear. We ate dinner in the dining hall as the fog rolled in."

"Oh, the fog!"

"Drama," Richard observed.

"Yes, drama!" Serena exclaimed. "Magic!"

She nodded, satisfied, and passed napkins to me, since I was struggling with my melted chocolate and gooey marshmallow concoction.

"She wore a white dress," my father said without prompting. "I wore a suit; it was the first suit I ever owned. She was so beautiful. She had her hair put up, which I always liked because it showed off her smooth, sloping neck. Even still, when I see her from across the room and she has her hair up, I feel something. Happy. I don't know. Contented."

"I think we call that love, Jones," Serena said. "That feeling we can't quite describe but thirst to possess."

"Her family was . . . funny, you know. They're a very caustic family, and I hadn't met many of them before the wedding. It's all about dry British humor with them, like you'd see in a movie. But they love each other, you can tell. There's a connection between them that's deeper than all that."

"Like you had with Mother."

"Something like that, I guess," he said. "I liked being with her family."

My father stopped talking and stared into the fire, and I could have sworn I saw tears pooling in his eyes. I was moved by it.

"Where is she now?" Richard asked loudly, breaking the moment.

Serena glared at him.

"Your wife," Richard clarified in a more suitable tone. "I'm afraid I don't know her name."

"Rachel," my father answered.

"Yes, Rachel. Where is she now? Why isn't she here, sharing this seminal moment with us?"

"She's in England," Serena explained. "She and Jones are taking a bit of a break. There have been many changes recently, so it only seemed right to accommodate Rachel's request for space. Isn't that right, Jones?"

"Magic doesn't last forever," he said.

"You shouldn't be afraid," Serena said soothingly.

"I'm not, I don't think. Afraid of what?"

Serena stood up and circled around the far side of the fire, behind the flames, to the cooler, which she opened to remove a bottle of beer.

"It's okay to want things," she said, kneeling next to the cooler, in front of my father; she put her hand on his knee. "It's okay to change. We're always so afraid. We live our lives in fear, like we're children afraid of going to our first day of school. There is nothing to fear about the unknown. Tomorrow is *not* going to be the same as yesterday, so why do we *need* it to be?"

She twisted off the top and handed the bottle to my father.

"Hey, I thought you were getting that for me," Richard teased.

"Relax, dear," Serena said, taking another bottle from the cooler and circling back to him. "There's plenty for you."

She walked toward him and didn't stop until she was inches from his face. She reached down and pressed his head to her belly, and as she did so, she leaned back and took a long drink from the bottle. She took the bottle from her lips and looked at me deliberately as she released Richard's head; she handed him the beer. Still she didn't take her eyes off me, and I wondered if she was going to have sex with Richard right there by the fire and then murder him and eat his heart, or twist off his head and swallow it like a giant humanoid praying mantis.

She did neither. She took her seat and looked down her nose, somewhat satisfied.

"Trevor," she said softly, almost inaudibly.

And the heat from the fire engulfed us all.

"I remember!" Grandpa Samuel blurted out, startling everyone.

"What do you not remember now, Daddy?" Serena asked with an obvious roll of her eyes. "And please make it good."

"I remember a fire," he said.

"A fire. There were so many fires, how do you know which was which? How do you know you're remembering the fire you think you remember and not another one?"

Grandpa Samuel looked at her, baffled, and I wondered if he would succumb to her deliberate attempt to confuse him. I hoped he wouldn't.

"I *think* I remember," he ventured.

He said it feebly enough that Serena cast it aside and began collecting garbage and bottles. Richard and my father helped her, and, soon, they had collected all the things and placed them back in the bags.

"Are you coming?" Serena asked Grandpa Samuel and me.

We looked at each other, then we looked at Serena.

"We'll stay for a while," I said. "To watch the fire."

"Ah," Serena said, her face dawning with recognition. "An excellent idea. I see, Trevor, that you are more clever than I thought. Yes. Alone time, so you can attend to your mission. Be sure to scuttle the coals before you leave; we don't need to start a wildfire tonight."

She gathered the remaining bags and followed my father and Richard, who had already started back to the house. I picked up a long stick and poked at the fire. The darkness was nearly complete, though some of the spilled sun still clung to the mountains.

"When I was a boy," Grandpa Samuel said after a time.

I was relieved that he seemed to really remember something. I wanted to hear it.

"What happened when you were a boy?" I asked.

"My father took me to a logging site, up north, near Chuckanut," he said, and the embers glowed. "I was six years old, I think. He wanted me to see the world of men. I had only lived here at Riddell House. I had been raised by my mother and the nannies, alongside my sisters, as if I were another girl like them."

"You had sisters?" I asked.

"Two. Daisy and Alexandra."

"What happened to them?"

"I don't know. My mother left with them, and we never heard from them again. When my father died, the lawyers tried to find them; they never could."

"So they weren't there when your father took you to the logging site?"

"They were at home. They left after that. They left because of that."

"What happened at the logging site?"

"The hills had been clear-cut. My father left me with the other boys while he went to attend to things, and, at the end of the day, they lit fires. All over the mountain. They burned the stumps and branches and scraps of wood left behind; they piled them into giant piles and they lit the piles on fire. It was gray and cold and almost raining. It smelled of burning wood."

Grandpa Samuel fell silent in the glow; I smelled the smoke on myself.

"What else?" I prodded.

"The boys had hatchets. The older boys. They took out their hatchets and chopped on a chopping block. Small pieces of wood. They took turns holding the wood and chopping, always with the grain so a sliver curled off. I was fascinated by it. I'd seen loggers chop down trees, but these were boys like me, but bigger, and they were chopping things, too. So my father told one of them to show me how to do it. 'He's awfully little,' the boy said. 'And he's never held a hatchet before.' My father yelled at the boy until he was almost in tears—that's how my father was; he was mean. The boy stood behind me and held my hand with the hatchet in it. 'Never cut with a dull ax,' he said, and my father said, 'That's right!' The boy held my hand and guided it down so I cut a sliver of wood off the split of firewood. The boy was relieved and smiled like he had been spared his life."

Grandpa Samuel looked over at me and nodded.

"Was your father proud of you?" I asked.

"My father told the boy to let me do it myself. He made the boy step away from me; he wanted to see me do it. So I held the wood steady and I lifted the hatchet over my head. The boy was afraid, but I wasn't. 'Let it drop straight,' he said. 'It'll cut all right; it's sharp.' But I knew what my father wanted, so I did it."

He paused as if he'd run out of steam, his eyes fixed on the fire.

"What did your father want?" I asked.

"He wanted me to show them I was tough. That I was a man. The other boys made fun of me and called me names because I was raised with money and my mother let my hair grow long. They said I would never be a logger. I wasn't one of them."

"But you were rich and they weren't," I said. "You were never supposed to be a logger. That's the way the economic system works, isn't it?"

"My father told me you can always tell a real logger. A real logger is always missing a finger or two. I lifted the hatchet and brought it down."

I felt a quickening of my heart; I anticipated the end of the story already.

"I didn't mean to do it," he said, lifting his left hand into the air and looking at his missing fingers. "But there was nothing I could do to stop it; it had already happened."

My heart was beating so fast I couldn't breathe. He was telling me the truth.

"I didn't cry," he said. "I held out my hand to show him. To show them all. A real logger is always missing a finger or two. I was a real logger."

"You said you fell through a window," I protested weakly.

"My mother told me that. She took me to a window in the house and she broke it out with her fist and she said, 'Remember that sound. That's what it sounded like when you fell through the window.' She pointed at the glass lying on the hedge outside the window, and she said, 'Look at that glass. That's what it looked like.' She reached out her hand and sliced herself open on the jagged pane. She didn't cry out. She squeezed her hand and blood poured out of her wound and onto the rug. 'That's what your blood looked like when you lost your fingers,' she said. 'This is what you will tell people when they ask. This is what you will remember.'"

Neither of us spoke. We looked down at our hands, we looked into the fire. The sky was black then, and the orange of the embers illuminated our faces.

"When we got home, he handed me to her," Grandpa Samuel said. "'Call the doctor,' he told her. I was feverish and weak, but I remember it so clearly. 'You raise him now,' my father said to her. 'He's no good to me anymore.' He handed my mother a handkerchief with my fingers inside. 'These are no good to anyone, such as they are.' My mother wailed. She demanded to know what had happened. 'This is timberland,' my father said. 'Men lose fingers.' And he walked away."

I slid over a little bit on the bench, and then I slid over a little more until I was up against Grandpa Samuel. I reached for his hand, the left hand with the missing fingers, and I took it in my own.

"But you weren't a man," I said. "You were a little boy."

He shrugged, and I held his hand tightly as we watched the fire die.

33

QUID PRO QUO

I awoke to another day. The entire morning, I moped around the house feeling lost to the point of despair. The damage was so deep, the wound so profound, I couldn't imagine the world ever healing. I felt such sorrow for my grandfather, who, as a young boy, felt compelled to prove his mettle to his father by chopping off his own fingers on a chopping block. And then, to be so disregarded. *He's no good to me anymore.* Words that hurt him so much, he used them against his own son. "You're no good to me anymore," Grandpa Samuel said to my father before he sent him away.

That afternoon, I went down to the barn with Grandpa Samuel, still feeling upset. So much so that I reached out to him. I took his hand, so he looked down at me as we sat at the workbench.

"I love you, Grandpa," I said out of the blue, and, when I was a kid, I never said "love" if I wasn't forced to. But I felt love then, and I felt it so strongly—in my gut—that I had to say it out loud.

Grandpa Samuel looked over at me and smiled, his old-man eyes watery as always.

"I love you, Jones," he replied. But I didn't mind that he didn't know who I was.

We walked together back up to the house, which was still empty from the day. My father and Serena had gone to Seattle for business meetings and had not yet returned. I found a bag of pretzels, which Grandpa Samuel and I ate as we sat at the kitchen table and waited for the feeders to come and feed us. Such were our lives. I was fourteen and Grandpa Samuel was seventy-three. We both depended upon the kindness of our feeders. But the feeders did not come.

At half past six, the phone rang, startling us both. The image of my mother flashed into my head because she was the only one who had ever called. How quickly we are trained. Pavlov's dog.

"Pick it up," Grandpa Samuel prompted. So I did.

"Hello?" I asked hesitantly. "Riddell House."

"Trevor? It's Serena. How are things there?"

"Fine," I said, relieved at the familiarity of her voice.

"Listen, we got caught up," she said. "Meetings and meetings. So we're going to get some dinner downtown. Can you make something up for you and Grandpa Samuel?"

"Sure," I said. "But what?"

"Well, I don't know. Do you cook?"

"Some."

"There are eggs," she suggested. "Oh, you know what? In the freezer in the basement there are burritos. Grandpa loves those burritos. You can use the microwave to cook them."

"But there aren't any stairs," I said, remembering my last adventure in the basement. "The staircase is broken."

"What?" she asked. "Oh, you mean? . . . How on earth did you? . . . No, that door has been boarded up for years. Tell Grandpa to show you the way down. It's in the hallway behind the butler's pantry. The back stairs are fine. How on earth did you find the front stairs to the basement? It's a wonder you didn't kill yourself!"

"I just noticed the door," I said, lost in her barrage of words.

"But if you're not starving and you want to make it easy, order a pizza from Pizza Pete's. They're very close and they know us. There's a menu in the drawer next to the stove. Can you do that?"

"Sure."

"Grandpa knows where we keep the pizza money. Call them and order what you like. If you get a salad, get it without olives; Grandpa won't eat olives. And don't listen to him if he asks for a pizza with green peppers. They give him terrible gas. No green peppers."

"Got it."

"Can I depend on you?" Serena said after a moment.

"You can depend on me," I replied.

"Then your father and I might have a bit of a nice dinner to celebrate. Everything is in order, Trevor. We only need your piece of the puzzle, which I know you will deliver. Have you called the notary? Have you gotten Grandpa Samuel to acquiesce?"

"Not yet."

"Hmm. But you'll work on him now, won't you? You can't say I haven't allowed you ample opportunity. I've arranged for you to be alone with him for an extended period. I should think—"

"I'm working on it," I said.

"Good. And when you accomplish it? Well, that's when the fun will really begin, yes? If we don't make it home before ten, be a good boy and put Grandpa to bed, will you?"

"Yes, Aunt Serena."

"Don't call me Aunt Serena," she said. "I really detest it. Please call me simply Serena."

"Yes, Simply Serena."

"See you soon, Clever Trevor," she said. "I love you. More than that, I *respect* you. I consider you a peer, and that is the greatest respect one person can have for another."

I hung up and did as I was told; soon a teenager not much older than I brought food to our back door.

Grandpa Samuel picked at his pizza but seemed to get enough to eat. He leaned back in his chair looking contented and rested in a way I hadn't seen before.

"You look happy," I observed.

He smiled at me.

"I didn't take my pills," he said. "The pills give me an upset stomach, but I need to take them for my disease. Serena makes me take them before dinner, but I forgot and she's not here."

"Should you take them now?" I asked, slightly alarmed that I had been derelict in my duties; had Serena instructed me to dispense medicine? I didn't think so.

Grandpa Samuel leaned in. "They don't help," he whispered to me. "They keep me awake at night so I have to have the other medicine to help me sleep."

"But I feel bad," I said. "If you need your medicine, you should take your medicine. It's important."

Disappointment swept over his face, and he pouted.

"They're in the cupboard," he mumbled, pointing.

I rose from the table and opened the cupboard door. I removed the medicine bottle inside.

"How many do you take?" I asked, glancing at the label for instructions. It was an amber bottle with a safety cap, but the label was worn away.

"Two," he said. "Unless I've been bad today."

"You've been good," I confirmed, shaking two oblong tablets into my palm. I noticed writing on the tablets, stamped into the coating. I looked more closely. "I don't think this is the right bottle."

"Yes, it is."

"No," I said. "Is there another?"

"That's the one!" Grandpa Samuel blurted.

I felt a terrible sinking in my stomach. It wasn't medicine Serena had been giving Grandpa Samuel. Stamped on the tablets was the word NōDōz.

"How many pills did you say she gives you at night?"

"Two, I said. Before dinner. Unless I've been bad. Then she gives me more."

"And this medicine keeps you up at night, so she gives you the other medicine to help you sleep? The medicine we make with the milk?"

"That's right," he said. "I don't like it, but I'm sick, so I need to do it even if I don't like it."

It was almost beyond belief. Serena would jack him up on caffeine in order to sedate him with alcohol? The only reason to do such a thing was to drive him mad. Or to make him seem forgetful and incoherent, like he had Alzheimer's.

"You don't have to take the pills tonight," I said definitively, putting the bottle back in the cupboard.

"Serena will be mad."

"I'll lie. I'll tell her that you took them, okay? Sometimes it's good to have a break and get a good night's sleep. It won't hurt for you to miss one day."

I closed the cupboard and resumed my seat at the table. Grandpa Samuel smiled at me kindly and placed his good hand on mine.

"You'll always take care of me," he said.

"I will."

"Do you promise?"

"I promise, Grandpa."

"Then I want to give you Riddell House," he said.

"What?"

"I want to give it to you so you can take care of it. Call the man to come and sign the papers."

I swallowed hard. A wonderful gesture, but . . .

"You can't give it to me," I said. "I'm not an adult."

Grandpa Samuel furrowed his brow.

"Grandpa—"

"Elijah sent me a letter," he said. "I was going to sell the house, like my father wanted. But Elijah sent me a letter, and Isobel said I couldn't do it. She read the letter and said I couldn't. She made me promise."

"What letter?"

"The lawyers gave it to me. They said they couldn't take the house, but they could take everything else. And there was the letter, and Isobel made me promise."

He had a tired, perplexed look on his face, as if this were a dilemma that had haunted him for a long time.

"I can sign the papers," he said. "And then you can decide."

"I can't decide," I said. "I'm a minor. I'm not really a person. If you sign the papers, then Serena and Dad get to decide."

He thought for a bit.

"But you'll take care of me," he said confidently.

"I'll always take care of you, Grandpa. I told you that. But—"

"Then I'll sign the papers."

I remember feeling paralyzed by his words. Suddenly the fate of Riddell House had been thrust into my hands. What was I supposed to do? How could I make such a decision? I certainly didn't have the life experience to justify such power. And yet, there it was. I could choose my own fate. I could decide between my parents or my history. There was no guarantee that turning over the house would assure that my parents even stayed together, I knew, but it was right there, hanging like a ripe fruit on a vine. I remember briefly thinking about Ben's wishes to return the estate to the forest, but I thought more deliberately about Grandpa Samuel. A little boy and his missing fingers. An old man with a dark past and a dim future, eating tomato soup and saltine crackers in a crumbling mansion, being fed caffeine pills by his daughter. Didn't he deserve proper treatment as well? Kensington House, a warm place with a meal plan, social activities, proper medical care. Sure, he wanted to stay at Riddell House, but it didn't seem like the best place for him. And if Serena wanted to develop the land in order to pay for Kensington House, was that really so wrong?

"Call the man," Grandpa Samuel said again. "I want to sign the papers."

And so I did. I called the man. Thirty minutes later, the papers were notarized. The deed was done.

34

HOUSE OF STONES

Riddell House was old and decaying. Anyone could see it. Listing to one side as if sinking into the soft earth. Downspouts broken, misguided rainwater seeping into the timbers and around the window frames until they bulged outward, swollen with moisture. It was falling down without any help from me, so what did it matter? And shouldn't Serena be able to get something for it? Shouldn't we all be allowed some of the wealth we had missed out on?

Riddell House was not meant to live forever. If you look at some houses made of brick and stone, like in the country near Danbury, or when we used to drive up through New England in the fall to see the leaves turn and to buy apples at the roadside stands, paper bags full of small crunchy apples, tart and sweet at the same time to make my mouth pucker, and we would stop at the corn mazes so I could run around and be a kid while my mother and father watched, laughing, grinning, holding hands (I remembered when my parents used to *hold hands!*). If you look at the houses we'd see when we stopped on the side of the road and we'd get out of the car to gaze across fields and over stone fences, and my mother would recite the Robert Frost poem she liked so much about the phantoms who didn't like walls so they knocked them down when no one was looking, if you look at those houses you would see.

"How I would love to live in that house," she used to say—without discrimination, I thought. As long as the house was built of stones and had a roof of shake or slate, and painted window frames. If there was smoke coming out of the chimney, she would say it for sure. But even if there was no smoke, she would say: *How I would love to live in that house.*

"I would love to live in that house with you," my father would say. Every time.

"It reminds me of home," my mother would offer with a shrug, not really to anyone.

I was little, so I didn't understand why stone houses reminded her of our wooden farmhouse; stone houses weren't like our home at all. But she meant her *old* home. Where she grew up in England on a thumb of land that stuck out into the ocean, where they used stones to build their houses so they could endure the brutal winter storms. She had a longing even then; I should have known she would go back there even then.

If you look at those houses, you see people built them to *last.* They were solid. Immune to wolf attacks, wind and rain and fire. Nothing could take down those houses. In contrast, Riddell House looked almost compostable. Like it was meant to crumble after a time and feed the earth with its remains, worms crawling through its hollow core, seedlings sprouting on its rich bark; an old tree becoming a nursing log, feeding the children of eternity. Yes, humongous and titanic in its scale and scope. But at the same time fragile. A house of sticks.

And what was it that I really wanted? What were my goals? as Serena asked me before. I wanted a family. I wanted my parents to be my parents, and not anonymous roommates in a shared living environment; I wanted them to *care*. I wanted them to be happy together. I wanted them to be happy with me. I wanted permanence in a constantly changing world.

I wanted a house of stones.

All was dark. I lifted my head from the desk where it was resting, nested on my folded arms. I lifted my head because I heard the low rumble of a car's engine. I heard the crunching of tires on gravel. Doors closing with satisfying clunks. They were home. I took the folder from the desk and made my way down the hall. I hesitated before entering the kitchen. I could hear them rattling around the big room a little sloppily, as if slightly drunk; they shouldn't have been driving. They were setting a bad example for me.

"They must have gone to sleep," my father observed.

"Daddy has never been known as an early sleeper," Serena replied.

"The house is dark. Should I go check on them?"

"What does it matter? It's not as if there's anything to fear out here, with the possible exception of our man-eating raccoons."

"Man-eating raccoons?"

"They've been known to eat men," Serena said, and then she made a fake growly sound.

"Really?" my father asked. "I'm not sure I believe that."

"*Believe!*" Serena bellowed ominously, and they both giggled. Definitely drunk.

I cleared my throat and entered the room.

"How did your meetings go?" I asked.

Serena and my father glanced at each other with the surprised aspect of the guilty.

"Splendidly," Serena said cheerfully. "How was dinner with Grandpa Samuel? Did you get him to sleep all right?"

"Everything was fine," I said. "We had a visitor."

"A visitor?"

I hesitated for a moment, feeling strangely anxious. It wasn't too late. I could make something up quickly. A ghost visited us or something. I didn't have to give it to her.

And yet I did have to give it to her. If only to protect my grandfather. I handed Serena the folder. She took it and looked inside.

"My, my, my," she said, shaking her head in disbelief. "Well, it goes to show that if you need a man's job done, you'd best get a man to do it. Brother Jones, you should take lessons from your talented son."

She handed the folder to my father, who studied the power of attorney inside.

"Look at what Trevor has done for you, Brother Jones. He has delivered Riddell House to you. Tell him how pleased you are."

"I am pleased," my father said.

"Delighted?" Serena suggested.

"At least," my father agreed. "Delighted, at least."

Serena came to me and took my face in her hands. She planted a big kiss on my lips. Her breath smelled like wine.

"I hope you are suitably proud of your achievement," she said. "I hope you feel the monumental nature of your accomplishment."

She returned to my father's side, slipped her arm under his, and the two of them admired the power of attorney together proudly, as if it were their newly born child.

I wanted to cry. The idea that the development was within their grasp and was bringing my father and Serena closer together was completely antithetical to my own goal of reuniting my father and mother. The only shred of redemption I could find in the whole deal was that my grandfather would get proper medical attention, if he even needed it. Otherwise, it was just another broken promise to a dead person.

I muttered a good night and walked down the long hall to the foyer, up the front stairs. I could have sworn I heard a sorrowful sigh as I walked down the hallway to my room, but that was probably wishful thinking. I climbed into bed, turned off my reading light, lay back on my pillow, and waited. And I hoped. I hoped for the door to open in its ghostly fashion. I hoped for the spirit of Ben to enter my room and take a seat on the creaky rocker and let me know everything was okay. But Ben did not come.

35

A SEDUCTION

The following morning, the house was quiet as usual, but a different type of quiet. A quiet filled with dread. I imagined my father and Serena were at their lawyers' office now, hurriedly filing claims and forms and permit requests. Environmental impact statements. A grotesque scene played out in my mind: fat old men with stiff collars, laughing and slapping each other's backs, rollicking in the exploitation of The North Estate. Finally, the deathblow to the Riddell Empire would be struck. It was not enough to bring the memory of Elijah Riddell to his knees. No, Elijah Riddell had to be humiliated, violated. His great empire could not simply vanish, it had to be dragged through the muck and shit and piss of a thousand years. Flayed open and parted out. Twenty ten-acre lots for twenty ten-bedroom McMansions. Two tiny acres allowed to grow into a wild, untamed, unblemished forest. It was a travesty. A travesty of a mockery of a sham of a travesty.

I found coffee still in the coffee machine, and it wasn't quite cold, so I poured myself some and put it in the microwave. When it was hot, I added ice cream. I tasted it, but the ambrosia had turned sour. There was no more magic.

I looked in the refrigerator for some breakfast, and found the left-over sausage pizza from the previous night. It smelled okay, so I took a piece and ate it cold while standing at the counter, which was something my mother hated. "The human body needs to sit to digest properly," she once told me. I later discovered that wasn't true at all: the human body is designed to digest while crouched over the warm carcass of a recently killed wildebeest or antelope or something, not sitting at a table. It turns out human bodies were designed long before the first table was invented. But my mother didn't trifle with such details.

I put a second piece of pizza in the microwave. When it beeped, I made a plate and was heading for the porch to eat my pizza in the morning air, when I noticed a flash of light hit the wall in the front parlor, like the reflection of a mirror or a watch face catching the sun. Quietly, I slipped into the parlor to investigate, and I heard voices. Whisperings. Voices from the past? I saw the flash again. I looked out the front window. Serena and my father were sitting together on the porch swing. My father's watch flashed in the sun, which crept around the edge of the house. I didn't feel very cloak and dagger, so I didn't bother hiding—I sat on the couch and ate my pizza at the coffee table—but I ate very quietly so I might not be detected. I could hear their conversation clearly.

"Sometimes things change," I heard Serena say. "I read an article recently which quoted a marriage counselor who suggested marriage licenses should come up for renewal every seven years. It would avoid the messiness. And having to reevaluate one's relationship would become a natural thing. You know, people get locked into a permanent contract and they don't know how to get out. They cheat on one another, they act badly and they do it sloppily so they'll get caught. Why not just put it out there? That was a fun time we spent together; it's time to move on."

"That doesn't take children into account," my father replied.

"Children are resilient," Serena said with a pshaw. "They adapt. Look at me. My mother died when I was eleven. My father was basically an invalid, or at least an incompetent loser for most of his life. You were gone. I learned to adapt. I didn't melt into a puddle the first time a bucket of water was thrown on me. I made it part of my story; I survived. A real-life Lieutenant Ripley."

"From *Alien*?" my father asked. "Sigourney Weaver?"

"Yes, but, more significantly, from the sequel. The first was a better movie. The second was a better representation of a woman's ferocity when pushed to the breaking point."

"I didn't think you went to the movies."

"Why is that? Because I ride a bicycle? Really, Brother Jones, you must learn to be more creative in your thinking. I ride a bicycle, I chop wood, I churn butter by hand when I need to. I would milk cows if we had any. And not simply for the gratification of a job well done, to reap the bounty of my honest and clean effort, but also to keep myself fit, my arms and legs strong and supple. I don't need to lace on expensive running shoes and press the start button on a treadmill to get exercise when I have a grocery store I can ride my bicycle to. What does Rachel do to keep fit?"

"Rachel?" my father asked, seemingly startled by the question. "Nothing, really."

"Really? Yet she maintains her figure?"

"She's softened a bit over the years."

"Hmm," Serena wondered. "She's let herself go?"

"Is that the phrase?"

"It's *a* phrase," Serena said pointedly. "Is it *your* phrase?"

"No, it's not my phrase at all," my father said after a moment. " 'Softened' is my phrase. And she's quite attractive, thank you."

"Men are visually stimulated," Serena said. "That's simply a reality; it carries no judgment. Men are attracted to youth and vivacity. May

I be terribly bold and inquire into the level of intimacy you share with Rachel?"

There was a long pause, and I laughed to myself. Serena. She sure knew how to knock down a door without breaking the hinges.

"I don't believe that's any of your concern," my father replied.

"Your welfare and happiness are entirely my concern," Serena said. "Here, sit down in front of me and let me massage your shoulders; you're very tense. Let me work on you a bit."

To my dismay, my father did what she said. I heard the porch swing creak as he rose, and the floorboards groan as he sat down in front of Serena, and I heard him moan as she laid her hands upon him, and then, "Ah!" he complained.

"That's some knot," she said. "I'll work it out. Breathe for me."

And more silence, which I found disturbing because I knew the longer she had her hands on him, the deeper her hooks would be set.

"You have very strong thumbs," my father said, his voice dreamy.

"You're holding years of tension and anger in your muscles. It'll take some work to get it all out."

I stood up and went to the window to peek at them. My father was sitting on the porch with Serena behind him on the swing. She was leaning over and pressing the point of her elbow into his back. The image was so striking to me, even disregarding their sibling relationship. It just seemed the last thing on my father's mind was my mother, or even me. I felt so stupid for being duped into thinking the money from the sale of Riddell House would resolve my parents' issues.

"It hurts," my father said.

"Those are the toxins. Your body creates toxins when it's in stress, and then your muscles hold on to them. You need to have regular massages to clear yourself out. You're carrying decades of toxicity in your muscles. All the anguish you had to endure as a boy. All the anger. That's why you're so tight and inflexible. We'll have to go way back to get all the toxins. Back to when you used to run. Remember that? Your gait was perfect so you could run on the railroad tracks, your feet landing perfectly on the ties. You would run for miles following the parallel rails that extended off into infinity."

Serena's voice had taken on a melodic, hypnotic tone. She stopped with the elbow maneuver and began massaging my father's scalp. Jesus. Couldn't my father see that she was trying to seduce him?

"Oh, that feels good," my father said sleepily.

"I'm sure it does. We'll work back to that awful moment and clear you of the toxins and then we'll work forward, and then into the future. Think of what it would be like to live like Elijah lived, with money for things and servants and food prepared by chefs. That's what I see on our cruise. Nothing to do but relax and enjoy. Stroll around the deck with its weathered teak handrails. Swim in the saltwater pool. Nap in the sun and read books. Oh, the books we will read! Make port in an exotic land and hike up a mountain to a sacred temple. Pray with the people; pray to the gods! Feel the heat on our skin, the sun. Feel the sweat, slick on our arms and faces. Taste the fruit and the fish of the local village. Nothing has ever tasted as fresh. And then, returning to our ship, we will freshen ourselves and dress for a formal meal and, afterward, dance before an orchestra. Not a sad man with a Plexiglas piano and a drum machine. An orchestra! Dance so everyone sees how beautiful we are. How perfect."

It took me a minute before I realized: the image Serena had conjured of the cruise *included my father*.

She stopped speaking, but continued massaging my father. Continued *touching* him.

"How does that sound?" Serena asked.

"How does what sound?"

"Our circumnavigation of the globe, Brother Jones. Together."

I couldn't take any more. It was just too much. She'd been planning it all along. I turned quickly, exited the parlor, marched through the foyer, and out onto the porch.

"Very funny," my father said.

"Very *wonderful*," Serena corrected.

"What's very wonderful?" I asked, startling them both.

"Trevor!" Serena exclaimed, standing quickly.

"What were you guys talking about?"

"Nothing, just . . . the development," she replied. "How wonderful it will be when things are finally under way—of course, all thanks to *you*. Let me get you that glass of water you wanted, Brother Jones."

She hurried past me and into the house. I thought it strange that she was flustered; it was the first time I'd seen her so.

"What were you guys doing?" I asked my father when Serena had gone.

"Nothing," he said, standing up and dusting off the seat of his pants.

"It seemed like something."

"Serena was showing me something she'd read about. A detox massage thing. She read about it in *Cosmopolitan* magazine, I think."

"Oh, yeah," I said suspiciously. "I think I saw that issue at the grocery store."

My father nodded unsurely and stepped off the porch.

"I'm going to take a walk to the bluff," he said. "You want to come?"

"I'm good," I said.

He walked off. And, more significantly, Serena didn't reappear with the purportedly requested glass of water. The truth will out, indeed.

36

TRUTH OVER LOYALTY

I was hiding in my room reading one of Harry's journals, which I had disguised by making a dust jacket out of a brown paper bag. There was a knock, and my father said through the door, "I'm driving Serena to the grocery store. You want anything?"

I didn't.

When they had gone, I knew I had to act quickly. I had to take back the power of attorney. I rushed down to the study and rifled through any papers I could find. The folder wasn't among them. I didn't think she would have left it out for me to find. No. I figured it was either in the safe or in her room. The safe was impossible to search; Serena's bedroom wasn't.

Serena's room was nicer than Grandpa Samuel's, though it was in the same servants' quarters suite. Her room was much bigger than his, like someone had taken down a wall at some point to make one room out of two. She had a double bed, not a single like Grandpa Samuel. She had a dressing table and a large closet filled with dresses and skirts, some in subdued winter tones, some in light spring colors. So many, and they all looked new or lightly used; many were in garment bags, some still with tags. There were many, many boxes of shoes stacked upon each other, all with recent price tags on them, all the boxes seemingly unblemished. Her dresser was filled with soft, lacy undergarments. I lifted one from the drawer and held it up; it didn't look comfortable. I put it back and resumed my search.

She had books of all kinds. Paperback romance novels. Crime thrillers. Classics of literature. On her dresser were several framed photographs: one of her as a teenager, sitting on the bluff; one of her as a child, holding the hand of a teenage boy who must have been my father; another of a mother nursing a baby while a young boy looks on. I had never seen photographs of my father's family before. Oddly, I didn't find any evidence of manly things, no boxer shorts or running shoes or even a second toothbrush.

I wanted to conduct a thorough investigation of all the details of Serena's life, but I had a limited amount of time, so I had to focus. I went through the papers on her desk. Business stuff. Electric bills and such. Not what I needed. I checked under the bed. The upper shelf in the closet. Nothing.

Worried that they would be back soon, I decided to cut my search short. Serena must have tucked the power of attorney away in the safe, and that would prove nearly impossible to get at, unless Ben wanted to open it for me. Maybe. Before I left, I stood at the door and faced the center of the room. With all the mysteries of Riddell House, I found it hard to believe there wasn't a mystery in Serena's room. I wished for Ben to come help, but he was likely upset with me for betraying him; he didn't seem to be on his way.

And then I noticed something very subtle. A slight ripple beneath the rug on the floor, as if the rug pad had a wrinkle in it and was causing the slightest ridge. I lifted up the corner of the rug and saw that my suspicion was correct. The old mesh rubber rug pad was creased. I gave the corner of the pad a tug to remove the crease and detected a dark spot on the floor underneath the pad. I peeled back the corner of the pad more and saw the outline of a trapdoor with a small metal ring, lying flush with the floor. There was a secret in Serena's room after all.

Carefully, I rolled back the rug and the pad until they cleared the trapdoor. The door itself was two feet by three feet, I estimated, and it wasn't hinged; the entire platform came up when I lifted it. Inside the shallow space was a wooden box nearly the size of the void. I lifted it out and set it on the floor. I opened it and found immediate gratification. The folder with the power of attorney was right on top. I took it. Beneath were envelopes, letters rubber-banded together, and an old magazine.

It was an issue of *WoodenBoat* from November 1979, and pictured on the cover was my father. I had seen it before, and still thought my father looked silly with long hair. I also found brightly colored brochures— a stack of them—for various cruise lines. Bingo. My pulse quickened. Catalogs and itineraries. One of them was like the one I had found in my bedroom. It featured the grande dame of all cruises—around the world on the *Queen Elizabeth II*. To complete the journey would take nine months. Nine months at sea. Climbing mountains to hidden temples in exotic ports of call. Enjoying formal dinners onboard. Dancing before an orchestra.

I removed a thick envelope that seemed more official. I opened it. It was a letter addressed to Mr. and Mrs. Jones Riddell, Riddell House, The North Estate. "We at Cunard Line are delighted that you have reserved your around-the-world cruise with us. . . ."

Holy crap. Tickets. Serena wasn't kidding when she told my father how she wanted to spend her share of the money. She had already spent it! Her plan was already in motion.

I took out the rubber-banded packet of letters and flipped through them. They were all in identical envelopes made of fancy linen paper with return addresses embossed on the back flaps: Riddell House, The

North Estate, Seattle, WA. I pulled the first envelope from the bundle. It was addressed to Jones Riddell, though there was no address written beneath the name. It was not sealed. I removed the letter.

My Dearest Brother Jones,

As we danced together this evening, I felt an incredible swelling of joy inside me. It felt so *right* to be in your arms, as I have always imagined it would. Of course, I was nervous upon your arrival. Who wouldn't be nervous? I've waited for so long, and so much has passed without us knowing each other, what if my instincts were wrong?

They weren't, I now know, and I believe you know, too. You felt what I felt, your arms wrapped around me, your power and energy feeding my hungry soul.

Things will come together in the next few days. You will see my plan take shape. You needn't worry about a thing; I have accounted for everything. You simply must stand with me and allow it to happen. In a few short weeks, our destiny will be fulfilled.

I have put down a deposit with the cruise line, reserving our room. I had to borrow money from Dickie, but he has been very generous with cash now that he sees my plan is coming to fruition. We will fly to New York for a New Year's Eve sailing through New York Harbor, past the Statue of Liberty in all her glory, and then our journey will truly begin. I so look forward to spending the months with you, sailing all the oceans of the world, seeing such wonderful things. Merely the thought of you and me in our formal attire, dancing in the grand ballroom of the *Queen Elizabeth*, makes me quaver with delight.

I promise to clean up some of those old trunks in the barn for our trip. You know, those are valuable antiques and would fetch some money at auction, or so I've been told. Vintage steamer trunks crafted by Louis Vuitton? But we won't sell them; we will *use* them, and our voyage will be filled with romance and charm, like the olden days.

In the meantime, there are details to which I must attend, so I must end this letter more abruptly than I care to. Still, know that I love you with all of my heart, and feel assured that I am dedicated to you with all of my being.

I knew you would return for me.

Love,

Serena

I flipped through the bundle of letters again, this time looking more closely. All of them were addressed to my father.

I was utterly creeped out. Serena was crazier than I had thought. In addition to the obvious intention on her part to engage in an incestuous relationship with my father, there was also the question of her sanity. I didn't believe my father would go with Serena—I *couldn't* believe he would, although maybe I was wrong about that, too. But with her having invested some twenty years of fantasy time, writing letters, and taking imaginary cruises, I saw that something could go terribly wrong. Her plan the whole time had included my father. That's why selling off antiquities and rare pianos for cash didn't satisfy her. Getting by wasn't the point; getting Brother Jones was.

Worried that they would return and discover me, I returned the letter and the tickets to the box. Then I hesitated. I would need them as evidence; I had to tell my father about this. And yet, it was a dangerous game I was playing, for if Serena discovered things missing, she would surely come after me first. Still, I had to take the chance. I kept the tickets and the letter, and the power of attorney as well. I replaced the hatch lid and folded down the rug pad and the rug, trying to leave the same slight ripple that was there when I'd noticed it. I scanned the room to ensure I hadn't left anything amiss; all seemed to be in order. I turned out the light and left. As I walked back to the main halls of the house, I felt chilled. Not because I was cold. Because I was scared shitless of what was to come.

37

A SUDDEN LIGHT

Later that afternoon, my father and Serena still hadn't returned from the grocery store, which only added to my agitation. I could picture my father in Serena's clutches for an extended shopping trip, and I didn't like that image at all. I picked up the phone and dialed my grandparents' number in England. It was nearly midnight Greenwich time, and I knew my mother would yell at me, but I didn't care. She answered immediately, and I was glad of that; I didn't want to have to go through any middlemen. At the same time, I wasn't sure what exactly I wanted from my mother. Reassurance. A steady hand on the tiller, a phrase she always used when talking about her relationship with my father: "I'm the steady hand on his tiller," she would say. Maybe I just wanted a steady hand.

"Are you asleep?" I asked.

"I was reading," she replied. Her voice was soft. Hushed. I liked it when she was soft. "Everyone is asleep; I wanted to pick up before the ringer woke them."

"Sorry to call so late."

"Better that you call late my time than late your time. I'm sorry we haven't spoken in a few days. Your father says you've been very busy investigating something. *Delving.* Probing into the history of Riddell House. It's fascinating, isn't it?"

"You talked to him?" I asked.

"Of course. I've called a few times; you've always been away some-place. But that's your personality. Since you were a boy, you would never let an injustice go unchallenged."

I wondered about my personality. Was that the case?

"What injustice?" I asked.

"What happened to one of your forefathers. Your father told me. You're outraged that an uncle of some level of greatness committed sui-cide because he was homosexual."

"That's not right—"

"Of course, it's not right. But people were not as accepting in those days as they are now."

"No, I mean, that's not correct," I said, feeling flustered by the appar-ent conversations my parents had been having without my knowledge. "Ben didn't commit suicide, I don't think. I mean, I don't know. I didn't say that. I mean, he loved Harry. But he died of a broken heart. He didn't commit suicide."

"Your father mentioned an arranged marriage," she said after a mo-ment.

What could I say? My mother couldn't possibly understand the subtlety of Ben's life and death from her vantage point. Maybe he *did* commit suicide; I didn't know. But I certainly wouldn't have drawn that conclusion based on the evidence I had.

"I'm not sure exactly what happened," I said firmly. "And anyway, that's not why I called."

"I'm sorry, love. I won't make assumptions. Please tell me why you called."

"I don't know what to do."

"About what?"

"About the house."

"Didn't you already do it?" she asked. "Dad said you got your grand-father to sign over the house. Wasn't that the goal?"

"It was *someone's* goal."

"So you've done it, sweetness. You're all done."

Not by a long shot, I thought.

"What am I supposed to do about Ben?"

"Ben?" she asked, sounding confused.

"My forefather. My uncle of some level of greatness. The spirit of Riddell House. He gives me dreams. He showed me how he died. How Harry died. He showed me in a dream."

"A dream? So it was your imagination."

"No, I dreamed it. And I dreamed it again. And I dreamed it again."

"So therefore, it must have come from . . ."

"I've *seen* things, Mom," I said with great force. "*I've seen things! Tell* me I didn't see the *truth.*"

There was a long pause, in which I was convinced my mother was wondering if I'd completely lost it.

"I'm sure your father has told you some of this," she said eventually, because she had to say something. "I'm sure you conjured an old memory. There's a logical explanation. Did you eat something spicy before you went to bed?"

I sighed loudly and heavily, and I hoped it was heard by my mother, half a world away.

"So you still don't believe in Ben?" I asked. "After all I've told you. You don't believe he gives me dreams that let me see the past? You don't believe I've seen *him*, do you?"

"I believe in Ben like I believe in Jesus Christ," she replied. "He was a man. He lived some time ago. He was not the son of God."

I was ready to cry. I had called my mother for support, because she told me she would always be there to support me. She wasn't there.

"I have to go," I said.

"Where are you going, Trevor? Are you all right?"

I hesitated before I replied.

"Are you and Dad getting divorced?" I asked.

She hesitated.

"There's no easy answer to that question, I'm afraid," she said finally.

"I need to know. And I need to know *now.*"

"I don't know, Trevor. There's a lot of work to be done. A *lot.*"

"But if you get the work done."

"I believe, deep in my heart, that our love for each other is strong enough to survive this, yes. Dad has been very conciliatory of late. I believe the stress of losing everything took an awful toll on him, and, now that everything's gone, he's reassessing. I like to think that my forcing him to return to Riddell House with you is something that's helped him a great deal."

"You forced him?" I asked. "I thought he forced you to let him take *me.*"

She paused.

"There was no alternative. He had to go. He said he only would feel safe if he could take you. So in that sense, I suppose we agreed it was the only option available."

"I need to know one more thing," I said. "If Dad suddenly had money, would that change things?"

"No, Trevor," she replied without hesitation. "It's not about money. Really."

"So if he was still poor, you would take him back?"

"There's more work—"

"Assuming he does the work."

"You're growing up," she said. "You should learn this now—don't worry, I'll remind you again as needed: if money affects who you love, then it isn't really love."

"Thanks."

"For what?"

"I don't know," I said after a moment. Because I really didn't know. But I was thankful for something.

We hung up then. I retrieved the manila folder from under my mattress and brought it to the kitchen. There were some things I was in control of, and other things I wasn't. This particular thing, I was.

I removed the notarized power of attorney from the folder and held it over a cast-iron frying pan on the stove. I took a match from the blue and red box, struck it, and held it under the center of the paper, but I blew out the match before the paper caught fire. Destroying it wouldn't do anything; they would just get another somehow. No. I had to hide it. I had to keep it safe. If I could somehow turn my father, it might be a useful weapon to have; I still believed that I might be able to get my father to change his mind, stop the subdivision, and allow the property to return to wild forest. I believed my father could be redeemed. So I put the document in the one place I knew was safe from Serena's prying eyes—Elijah's secret room.

After I had hidden the envelope away in the secret room and descended the stairway to the dark vestibule above the linen closet, I heard something: a brush of fabric or something. Slight, but deliberate. In the dark chamber where I had first seen the specter of Ben, I pulled the ever-present box of matches from my pocket, took out a matchstick, and struck it. In the sudden burst of light, I saw someone. Two people, actually. A woman, and a boy nearly my age. They sat against the wall at the top of the stairs, whispering to each other.

They paid no attention to me at all, so I crept closer. The match burned down and I shook it out. I quickly lit another. They were still there. I crouched down before them.

She was not old. Not much older than Serena, probably, and she was so beautiful and kind looking. And the boy, with his dark eyes and his firm jaw. I knew immediately he was my father.

"I'm sick, Jonesy," she whispered to him. "And one day I will die. But I promise I will come back to visit you, like our friend comes to visit us."

"But then you'll be a ghost," my young father whispered to her in reply. "I don't want you to be stuck."

"I won't be stuck, sweetness. Spirits can visit, too. Whenever they like. I'll come back for you. I promise."

My match burned out. I lit another, and Isobel, my grandmother, who was still there with my father, looked up at me as if she could see me. And maybe she could.

She reached out and touched my cheek, which felt like a feather brushing against my skin.

"Faith," she said, and she blew out my match.

38

THE HAUNTING

I woke up with a start. Had I dreamed it? No.

It happened before I went to sleep. I had seen Isobel and my young father in the corridor above the linen closet. I'd felt dazed afterward, because seeing them brought everything into focus. My father *did* believe. He did have faith. Isobel had promised to visit him, but she never could because my father changed after he had been sent away by Grandpa Samuel. My father became dark and cynical, and then lost everything. He was forced to return to Riddell House having lost his faith.

But things were not as expected at Riddell House. Grandpa Samuel spoke of dancing footsteps, and my father heard them, too. So he went to the ballroom to look for his mother. He came back to Riddell House because he thought she might be here. Of course he did.

I felt sick to my stomach. Not the bad feeling I sometimes got when I knew I'd done something wrong, which would have made sense and which I would have accepted. I felt an intense nausea, like I had been poisoned. I didn't have to vomit, but I wished I did. I walked down the hall to the bathroom, almost staggering from my queasiness; I paused a couple of times to brace myself against the wall as I swooned with vertigo. Was it the leftover pizza I'd eaten for breakfast? Did I have food poisoning? Or was I being punished for having betrayed Ben?

I reached the bathroom and turned on the faucet. I splashed cold water on my face several times, then glanced in the mirror and was so startled I gasped: Ben stood behind me—only for a moment; then he was gone.

I whipped around, wrenching my neck and feeling a stabbing pain. No one was there. I turned back to the sink and felt my forehead. Did I have a fever? Was I seeing things?

Another wave of nausea swept over me, more intense than before. I closed the toilet seat and sat down until it passed. It must have been the pizza. I would never trust a sausage again. Another wave brought with it terrible cramping in my stomach. I doubled over and moaned. And that's when the lights went out. Not metaphorically. The lights actually went out, plunging me into darkness in the bathroom. A cool breeze brushed the back of my neck.

I stood and opened the bathroom door. The hallway was dark as well. The entire house was dark. It wasn't a blown fuse; it was a power outage. I laughed ruefully. People with their air conditioners; the power grid can only take so much. I made my way to the end of the hall and opened my father's door. The room was empty. I listened carefully and heard talking from downstairs. I descended the front staircase, hoping Serena had an Alka-Seltzer or Pepto-Bismol. As I reached the foyer, I noticed flickering lights. My father and Serena must have lit candles because of the blackout.

But there were too many of them. They were everywhere. And they weren't candles. I surveyed the room; the wall sconces—which I remembered as electric—were alit with flame. They had been transformed into old-fashioned kerosene lamps. I looked up to the atrium. The chandelier in the foyer, a beautiful and intricate tangle of vines and crystal, with leaves and berries cast of bronze, was glowing a golden yellow; it, too, was burning kerosene, not electricity, as I remembered, making me think I was in an elaborate dream, or maybe a re-creation of Riddell House from long ago, or a wax museum, or— And the voices. Not just two. Not my father and Serena. But many. I peered into the ladies' parlor; it was filled with women, at least a dozen of them, in long stylish dresses, sitting in clusters, holding cups of coffee or tea, and chatting, laughing, with several servants hovering at the ready. Who on earth were these people? The women were wearing elaborate jewels and their hair was piled high on their heads and they seemed so elegant. They were from a different time altogether.

I continued down the hallway and paused before the billiard room, inside of which I heard men's voices. I looked in and saw eight or nine men in black tuxedos. Their ties were undone and their collars unclasped or removed entirely. They were holding snifters of brandy and smoking cigars, joking and laughing boisterously. They were mostly older and heavyset and unhealthy looking. I leaned in to see who these people were and was amazed to see Elijah Riddell sitting on the sofa talking to another man! My great-great-grandfather. Alive and well. I wanted to go in and talk to him. Introduce myself. Meet the others, whoever they were. But then one of the men walked over to me. I thought he would say something, but he didn't. He simply closed the parlor doors in my face as if I weren't there.

I worked my way down to the dining room, which was a mess. Food still on the table; dirty place settings and half-filled wineglasses and half-empty platters. A pig carcass sat on a cart next to the table, an apple wedged in its mouth, but most of its flesh having been carved away. Glasses and glasses and glasses. Remnants of every kind of food one could imagine smeared across plates in a decadent display of gastro-snobbery. It would have turned my stomach if my stomach hadn't already been turned, and then I realized my nausea had passed and I felt better. I continued to the kitchen, which was busy with servants cleaning up after the dinner party while a strict-looking man in a tuxedo supervised their work. The staff was quite large, and all in uniform, working so diligently.

I slipped through the work area unnoticed and out the back door. I walked around the house to the formal garden. It was dark in the night, for while there was a half moon and stars, puffy clouds blew across the sky, periodically obscuring the celestial light. The only other light came from torches lining the garden path. In the darkness, I noticed a man standing before the fountain—which was flowing and not stagnant. The man's back was to me, but he seemed to sense my presence, for his shoulders relaxed as if he were expecting someone. The man was outfitted in a natty tuxedo, and he sipped a dark liquid from a snifter. But this man was obviously not one of them; he was young and trim and athletic. He turned to reveal his face. It was Ben.

"Did you introduce yourself to my father?" he asked me.

"I didn't want to disturb him," I replied, feeling more bewildered than afraid. "He was with company."

"A pity. I'm sure he would have been charmed to meet you. I wonder what he would have said upon meeting his progeny, generations removed. I wonder if it would have made him feel nostalgic."

"Who are those people inside?" I asked.

"Did you introduce yourself to Alice?"

"No—"

"I would have wagered you'd have taken the opportunity. She is an enchanting young woman, Alice Jordan."

"Am I dreaming?" I asked. "Are you really Ben?"

"I am Ben. And as for those people? Among them you will find our good friend James Moore. C. D. Stimson is there as well, along with his wife, the two of them ushering high culture into this primitive land. And their architect-friend, a Mr. Kirtland Cutter hailing from Spokane, who follows them around always clucking like a chicken. I'm sure the judge is still with them, drinking away; he never misses a free meal. And Mr. James Jerome Jordan himself. These are the *controllers*, Trevor. They don't actually create anything themselves, but they control the people who create things, and so they control the dissemination of those things. One does not make money by *creating* things, you know. One only makes money by exploitation. You've heard these ideas before, I'm sure.

"The people you saw in the house are forming Seattle into something that suits their vision. For them, the city sits like a mound of wet clay, and they have their hands stuffed inside up to their elbows. Did you hear some of their conversation? You must have listened in. I'm sure there was talk of the regrade project. Always a source of controversy. *Let's cut the trees and level the hills and call it progress!* And likely there was talk of water mains and sewers to carry their shit and piss into the sound. Pontifications on the merits of seawalls and infill. And Moore, gloating over that shell of a hotel which he fleeced from Denny after the Panic; Denny deserved better, for what he's done for this town. I've heard their discussion a thousand times: tedious at best. But I suppose you agree, for you have left them to join me outside. Would you like a brandy? I'll send for one straightaway; you look like you need a bracer. I'm afraid my glass is empty or I would offer it to you."

I felt flustered by Ben's rant, and I was sure I looked flustered as well.

"I'm dreaming this, right?" I asked again. "You're here because I ate a piece of sausage pizza before I went to bed?"

Ben smiled patiently at me and set his glass down on the rim of the fountain.

"Do I look like indigestion, Trevor?"

"But you're not real."

"I'm not *substantial*."

"I don't understand—"

"I think you *do* understand, Trevor, for you seem to have understood everything to this point. You've seen the signs; you've read the clues. And yet you struggle."

"Maybe I don't have the life experience to understand," I said.

Ben laughed, put his arm around my shoulder, and led me away from the fountain.

"You're fond of owning the narrative, aren't you?" he said. "An interesting personality trait. You like to think of yourself as an observer, but you crave to be in the thick of it, don't you?"

"How did you do it, then? Appear like this and have the others in the house appear? And if you can just do something like that, why didn't you do it sooner?"

"Would you have believed it sooner? No. You would have run and hidden under your bed. Perhaps you'd have gone mad. Perhaps you would have medicated yourself into a stupor. You would have fallen into line with convention: madmen and substance abusers see what you are seeing; 'normal' people do not. Isn't that right?"

"I guess," I replied with a shrug as we continued walking down the path.

"You guess?"

"I know. Yes. I know."

"So, then. I had to wait until you were ready."

I stopped and looked at Ben.

"I gave away your house," I said. "I'm sorry."

"I put you in a difficult situation," he said, "as I did with my father, long ago. It was unfair of me to put him in that position. He was double-bound, feeling an obligation to me and to my brother, equally. And to my brother's heirs, as well. My father did what he thought was best. To satisfy his conflicting promises, he devised a plan, the history of which you know."

"Serena told me."

"She's told you things that are true, as well as things that are not true," he said. "My father was very generous with Abraham; Abraham

was neither appreciative nor sound with his inheritance. Yes, Elijah donated much of his fortune, but he did not abandon his heirs, as Serena
would have you believe. But why hear it from me, when you can know
it for yourself?"

He handed me a letter, which I turned over in my hands. It was addressed: *To My Future Heir.* I began to open it, but he stopped me.

"Not now," he said.

I respected his request, so I folded the letter and slipped it into my
pocket.

"I thought you were the one," Ben said as we walked further up the
path. "Perhaps you're not. Either way. I will see this through."

"I don't understand. Do you choose to stay here, or are you stuck
here?"

"Good question," he replied with a laugh. "Perhaps I have chosen to
be stuck here. Because we all choose our fate, whether or not we admit
it. Do you see?"

"I think so."

"It's not so much how we act, but how we judge ourselves for our actions. I am responsible for Harry's death—"

"But it was an accident. At least what I saw."

"But not what *I* saw," he said. "I saw it differently. And until I can
absolve myself, I can't move on—I *will not* move on. When this area has
returned to the wild forest, it will be the symbol that I have done so."

"And then you and Harry can come back to visit together?"

Ben glanced quickly at me and smiled again, but this time it was with
sadness at the corners of his eyes.

"You've been reading his journals," he said. "You know him well.
Would that one day you feel the love for someone that I still feel for
Harry, and will feel for eternity."

"I got Grandpa Samuel to sign his name on a piece of paper," I said,
"and because of that, you'll be stuck here for hundreds of years. I'm so
stupid. It'll be the end of the world before this place is a forest again."

"Harry will wait for me. He understands. He knew intuitively that climbing a tree—and he and I climbed some of the tallest trees that ever existed, taller than trees are allowed to grow anymore—climbing a tree isn't about getting somewhere; it's about *being* somewhere. And if we're comfortable with that notion, then I suppose we have all the time in the world, don't we?"

We continued walking up the hill.

"Maybe it's not too late," I said hopefully. "Maybe I can still do it. I can still release you."

"Can you?"

"I think so. But if I make it work, I'll need a quid pro quo."

Ben laughed outright. "What is your quid pro quo, my great-grand-nephew?"

"I want the truth," I said firmly, though a bit unsteadily, because sometimes the idea of truth frightened me. "I want *all* of the truth. You've shown me so many things; I know you can do it. My father came back here to see Isobel. Will he ever see her? Why does he want to see her so badly? And why did Grandpa Samuel send him away?"

Ben sighed. He spoke to himself and ticked off something on his fingers. Maybe my information requests? I don't know. But soon, he faced me.

"I believed Samuel would be the one," he said. "He turned away from me. Then I believed it would be your father, but he loved his mother too much to see anything else. Then I believed it would be you. But you listened to Serena. You believed her. And she manipulated you. You know that, don't you?"

I did feel manipulated; I nodded.

"Money won't solve your problems, Trevor. You will be disappointed if you expect it to."

"You sound like my mother."

He laughed.

"Your mother understands certain things, but she doesn't understand everything. She doesn't understand what you and I understand, does she? That takes a certain amount of belief."

"How can I make her believe?"

"There's no answer to that question," he replied. "At least to nonbelievers. Belief has to come from within, not from without. If it's forced upon you by tradition, it never really means anything."

"So how does a person believe?" I asked.

"By seeing the beauty in everything. By seeing the potential in every moment. God created all things, Trevor. God loves all things. When you love all things as well, you will find your happiness."

I thought about his words as we walked further into the night, the gravel crunching under our footsteps as the clouds bounced off the moon.

"I found this place when I was scouting yards to harvest," he said. "It was unbearably beautiful, really. To stand on the bluff here, with nothing but the forest behind me, and the sound before me, and the mountains. When the sun was right, it was a shock to the senses. We were going to clear-cut the entire area, because it was the most efficient method. But my father had spoken of having an estate, and when I saw this place, I told him I would build him an estate here that would put his society friends to shame. However, I would do it only if he spared these trees. And I would do it under one condition: I required full control of all aspects of the estate. He agreed, because he wanted me near him so I would be close to Alice. Early on, I brought Harry up from the coast to be with me, and to help me manage the construction as well. The two of us rode our horses along the road through the city of Fremont and up through Phinney's place and past his zoo, and we came to the point over there. Much of the area had already been cut, but not The North Estate.

"We stopped our horses on the ridge, just where it crests when you enter the property. We surveyed the acreage from afar, and we admired the land for such a long time. I looked over at Harry, and saw tears in his eyes.

" 'I've never seen a place so special,' he said.

" 'It's for you, Harry,' I told him. 'It's for you and me. This is a place we will always have.'

" 'Promise me we will have it forever,' he said."

Benjamin stopped speaking, and we continued walking along the path for a time.

"Did you promise him?" I asked, wanting him to continue the story.

"I did," Ben said. "I promised him that this would be our place for eternity, and I would not rest until it were so. I promised him it would forever be the jewel he and I first saw together. So we built a house for my father that I knew would crumble with time. The house itself would feed the forest around it. And somehow—I'm not even sure I knew how—I felt my love for Harry would always be here."

We stopped walking, and I realized he had led me all the way to the top of Observatory Hill.

"I believe they've all gone home," Ben said, gesturing down the hill toward the house. "You can go back to bed now, if you like."

He had led me to his grave; we were standing at his tombstone.

"I want the truth about my father," I blurted out, afraid Ben might vanish.

"It's not for me to give," he said. "It's for your father to give."

"But he won't tell me. Why won't he tell me?"

"Some things are so painful, they tear a person's soul. It's too difficult to see."

"The tear is difficult to see?"

"No. The act of tearing is difficult to see. It's difficult to watch a soul being torn."

"I can handle it," I said with great resolve. "Show me what happened to my father. And then I'll deliver you the house so you can fulfill your promise to Harry."

Ben sighed with half a laugh.

"So we have a deal?" I pushed.

"I'll give you what you ask, because I can."

"And I'll return your land to the forest."

"I don't require a quid pro quo," Ben said. "Serena needs such things; I don't. You've allowed me to feel things I haven't felt in a very long time. The earth and the breeze and the smell of blossoms. I shield my eyes from the glow of the sun."

"I did that?"

"You won't see me anymore, Trevor. Nor will you hear from me. I'll give you what you have asked, and then I'll leave you alone to make your way in Riddell House. It's time for you to make your own decisions."

He held his hand to his brow as if to shade his eyes. I looked in the direction he looked and saw a bright star in the sky. When I turned back, Ben was gone.

I ran down the hill to the garden. The fountain was no longer running, though water dripped from its basin, as if it had recently been filled. I hurried around the rear of the house and fiddled with the fuse box; nothing seemed out of order. Still, the house was dark. Maybe it was a power outage after all. I went into the kitchen, which was empty of people, though, oddly, not empty of dirty plates. What a strange haunting, I thought. Almost as if Ben wasn't very good at the whole ghost thing. He could conjure the scene, but then he forgot to put everything away. I made my way down the dark hallway, which was silent except for the ticking of the grandfather clock, which echoed throughout the first floor. And, as in the kitchen, the rooms were devoid of people, but not of their detritus: snifters and cups and saucers, and even a lit cigar, which uncoiled a thin stream of smoke into the parlor. When I reached the foyer, I thought it odd that the clock was ticking: it hadn't run at all since I'd been there, and in its stoic silence somehow gave me the impression that it hadn't worked in years.

I heard mumbling coming from the study and looked inside. Two men occupied the room, one sitting and one standing. The sitting man was Elijah, I could tell by his hair. And the standing man—the man in the tuxedo from the kitchen—must have been Mr. Thomas.

"Master Ben's body has been laid out in the parlor, sir," Mr. Thomas said. "As you have requested."

"Stop the clock, Mr. Thomas. Remove the pendulum. It is important to mark the moment of my son's death, so others will know."

Mr. Thomas left the room and passed directly in front of me without taking notice. He proceeded down the hall, opened the door to the grandfather clock, stopped the pendulum from swinging, and lifted the weight from its hook. I approached the clock; the hands said six-fifteen.

"I'll try, Ben," I said out loud. "I don't know if I can do it, but I'll try."

Mr. Thomas closed the door to the grandfather clock and returned to the study to attend to Elijah.

"It is all we can hope for," he said as he passed me, and I wasn't sure if he had spoken those words in response to me or to Elijah. Or if Mr. Thomas had even spoken the words at all.

When I awoke from my dream in the middle of the night—or from Ben's haunting, I should say—I found a letter in my hand. The letter he had handed me. It was real.

I opened the yellowed envelope and removed the sheaf of paper that was inside. The handwriting was a neat, looping cursive. At the top of the page, the embossed name Elijah Riddell had been crossed out with a pen swipe. The date was March 5, 1916.

To My Future Heir,

If you are reading this letter, you are alive, and I congratulate you on your achievement. If you are reading this letter, your father—my son, Abraham Riddell—is dead, and for that, I express my deepest regret. Though Abraham and I didn't see eye to eye very often, I did care for him in my own way.

I also cared for my first son, Benjamin. It is because of a promise I made to him that I am writing to you now. The attorneys who have presented you with this letter will describe to you the details. My objective in leaving this letter for you is to express the *sentiment* properly.

When he was alive, I promised Benjamin that, when Riddell House was no longer useful, it would be returned to untamed and wild nature forever. It was to be his legacy. It was to be *my* legacy as well, I suppose. A small jewel preserved, which could one day be held up against the mountain of jewels I have destroyed in the name of progress. No matter the justification, a promise is a promise and I vowed to uphold it, while also providing for the rest of my family.

Abraham, your father, became fixated on developing The North Estate. I don't know why he held on to the idea so tightly, but he would not unclench his jaws. He threatened me. He cajoled me. He cursed me. He cited my refusal as proof that my love for him was not as pure as it was for Benjamin. His claim was not untrue—Abraham has always been a fool and a laggard and a squanderer of fortunes—but that is not why I have held fast to my promise.

When I was a younger man, I would have dismissed my obligation to the deceased, even if he were my son. "What good is a promise to a dead man?" I would have protested. I would have been happy to bequeath this property to my living son upon my death, as is custom. But something very special has happened in recent weeks that has changed my mind entirely. Benjamin, my deceased son, has returned to me.

Oh, do not be afraid! He is not a phantom or specter who instills fear! He is my son, as gentle as ever. He visits me in my study. He sits with me and comforts me. And, most of all, his presence has convinced me that I have nothing to fear from my imminent demise.

Now that I have seen him in his spirit form—and I am convinced it is him!—I can say only that I truly believe in the afterlife. And I believe that a promise to a dead man is as substantial as any promissory note one might sign in the flesh.

In order to prevent Abraham from breaking my promise by exploiting The North Estate for profit, I have formed a trust that will hold my estate after I die. The trust will be dissolved after Abraham's death. Should he have no heirs, the estate will immediately be turned over to the city and dedicated as parkland. Should he have heirs—*you* presumably—the estate will be yours. I welcome you to live here as long as you like, and your heirs as well. I ask only that you carry forward my promise: when you or your heirs leave this place, either by attrition or volition, I beg you to allow it to return to Nature, as my son Benjamin wanted.

I cannot compel you to do so, but I implore you to look into your soul and carry forth this most important mission.

I am not proud of everything I have done in my life. In fact, there is a great deal of which I am ashamed. I have tried to reconcile my offenses since Benjamin's death, for his death, while tragic, taught me a very important lesson: no man is beyond redemption as long as he acts in redeemable ways.

The North Estate is in your hands. I beg you to see to the redemption of our family.

My peace I give unto you,
Elijah Riddell

I lay in bed in the darkness. I wanted to read the letter over and over again to prove to myself that it was real. That Ben had actually given me a souvenir in a different dimension, and I had carried it with me here. The letter from Elijah to Grandpa Samuel. *To My Future Heir.* The letter that Grandpa Samuel had told me he'd received from the lawyers. I had it in my hands.

Had Ben taken it from Grandpa Samuel's room? And how did Ben give it to me? I hoped to puzzle it out, but I was overcome with grogginess, and I quickly fell into a dark sleep, as if someone had pulled a sack over my head. Immediately, I began to dream. . . .

*   *   *

I go downstairs to the ladies' parlor, but it isn't a parlor. It's been converted into a bedroom of sorts, with a large hospital bed in the center of the room. Next to the bed is a rolling medicine cabinet filled with bottles and towels and various other medical implements. The room smells of antiseptic and urine. Lying on the bed is a bedraggled figure, a corpse almost, sunken eyes, long hair scattered and thin. She labors to breathe with the help of a ventilator, which is held over her mouth and nose by an elastic band, forcing air into her lungs in a jerking motion.

"Did you ask Dad to do it?"

The question is asked by a young man, a teenager, who is perched on an ottoman with his head bowed.

The suffering woman blinks deliberately.

"He couldn't?"

She blinks again, holding her lids closed.

"I'm sorry," he says. "I'll take care of you."

They say the pain of Lou Gehrig's disease is exquisite, brilliant, absolute, and relentless. But we all learn to live with different levels of pain; with no alternative, we cope. What breaks the will is the isolation. Or so they say.

"You've gotten so light," he says softly to the woman as he adjusts her pillow. "When did you get so light?"

She says nothing because she no longer has a voice. She's so light, she's practically no longer there. So light, a breeze might sweep her away like a wisp of smoke.

The young man stands, and I see who it is: my father; a teenager. He goes to the woman—Isobel—and tucks her blanket around her. He leans down until his forehead touches hers and he holds there a moment before standing up.

"You have to tell me," he says. "Blink twice, so I can see it. Blink twice so I know."

She does. She blinks her eyes quite deliberately.

Young Jones stands erect and closes his eyes. He must be considering

whether or not he has heard her correctly. Whether or not she is asking
what she is asking. He must wonder if he has misunderstood everything
from the beginning, if the special connection he has with his mother, his
unique understanding of her condition and her needs and her desires, is
actually his desires, his needs, voiced through her. He must wonder.

He leaves the room, and I follow. We go to the library, step into the
room, and stop. Samuel is sitting against a bookshelf, books spilled on
the floor around him. His legs are splayed before him, and in his lap
is a wooden cigar box. He is cradling it, flapping the lid, lolling his
head against the hard wood of the shelf behind him. He is crying. He
is drunk.

"Give it to me," Jones demands.

"No!" Samuel cries.

"Give it to me!"

Jones snatches the box from Samuel, and Samuel cries out, reaching
for the box impotently.

"Don't take her from me!" he howls.

Jones stands over his father.

"It's time," he says. "If you won't do it, I will."

"It's not time! It's not time for her to go. I'm not ready!"

Jones looks at his father with contempt. He leaves the room with the
cigar box, and I follow. He takes the box to his mother's parlor room, sets
it on the bed, and opens the lid. He removes a needle, which he attaches
to a syringe. He holds it before his mother along with an ampoule of clear
medicine. He's asking her. . . . She blinks again, though even a blink seems
painful.

"Tell me this will send you to a better place," he says. "Tell me you will
be free to go places I can't even imagine. Tell me that, if I do this, I will see
you again somewhere when you are without this disease."

She closes her eyes tightly and nods her head ever so slightly, but
enough for Jones to see. Enough for him to be sure. He fills the syringe. He
tears open the alcohol swab and dabs it on her arm.

"Why did I do that?" he asks her with a rough laugh. "Why did I swab your arm? Are we worried about infection?"

His laugh obscures his tears.

"I love you, Mom," he says. "More than anything on earth."

His hand trembles, but he overcomes his hesitation. "My peace I give unto you," he says, and with resolve he slips the needle into her skin, pushes the plunger, and empties the syringe. He removes the needle, sets the syringe down on the table. He removes her mask and switches off the ventilator. He sits on the bed and hugs his mother. Within a minute, the pauses between her shortened breaths grow longer. Her muscles fall slack. And then—not long at all—with a final exhale, Isobel Jones Riddell is dead.

Jones gathers the medical paraphernalia and returns it to the box. He takes the box into the hall, and I follow him into the library. Samuel has passed out against the bookcase, slumped over on the floor. Jones places the cigar box behind the books. He picks up the remaining books from the floor and returns them to the shelf to obscure the cigar box. The last three volumes are the collected works of Eugene O'Neill.

When it is done, Jones stands over his unconscious father and grinds his teeth; I can see his jaw muscles bulge from across the room.

I hear a sob. I turn. Standing next to me in the doorway, an arm's length away, is eleven-year-old Serena. Young and pretty, with her auburn hair and her white nightgown and her bare feet.

Jones hears the sob as well and looks over. He crosses quickly to us, kneels before Serena, and hugs her tightly. She cries into his shoulder, and he rocks her back and forth until she settles down.

"Go up to bed," he says gently.

"Will I die, too?" Serena asks. "Will I die like Mother?"

"No," Jones says, shaking his head. "You won't die like Mom."

"But what if I get sick?"

"Then I'll save you."

"What if you can't save me?"

"I will save you," Jones says emphatically. "I promise. Whatever hap-

pens, I will be here to save you, Serena. I will always be here to save you. No one can stop that. Not even Dad."

"I love you, Jones."

"I love you, Serena. Go to sleep now. I have things to take care of. Things you don't understand. When I'm done, I'll come upstairs and tuck you in. Okay?"

She hesitates for a moment, then she asks: "Brother Jones? Do you really promise? Cross your heart?"

And he: "I promise, Sister Serena. To the very core of my being, I promise. And there is no deeper promise than that."

So she goes, because she has faith that Brother Jones will not let her down.

I opened my eyes. The light was seeping around the cracks in the curtains and the birds outside were chirping almost angrily; dawn was upon us.

I tucked Elijah's letter into my notebook, went downstairs to the library, and turned on one of the reading lights; it was dim in the room, though I could see well enough. I knew the spot I was looking for exactly. I had been there before, even if it had been in a dream. I found the collection of theatrical works. I removed the three thick volumes of Eugene O'Neill's plays, reached my hand behind the remaining books, and felt it. A cigar box.

I removed the box and took it to the oak reading table. Beneath the yellow light, afraid of what I might find, I opened it.

Inside, I found a syringe and a glass ampoule. I scrutinized the vial. The label said NEMBUTAL. The ampoule was empty.

Struck by a thought, I pinched my arm and felt the sting; I was awake.

I laughed regretfully. Who keeps such a secret for so long? Only my father.

I replaced the box and the books, tucking the secret away again for no one to find. I went upstairs, feeling more lonely than I ever had in my life. I wondered what to do next. What did my father and his torn soul need? What did *I* need?

I found myself outside my father's door. I silently opened it. He stirred and turned over in bed.

"What's going on?" he asked groggily.

"I'm afraid," I said.

"Of what?"

He strained to focus his blurry eyes.

"I had a bad dream."

He nodded and cleared his throat. And then he did something he hadn't done in years. In his half sleep, maybe, his walls were down and he reacted out of instinct. He lifted the sheet and held it open for me, like a tent. Like he would do when I had a nightmare when I was five. I didn't hesitate long. I slipped across the room and into the warm bed. My father closed the sheet over me and cuddled against me, protecting me, shielding me from all that was dangerous and toxic in the world.

"I'm sorry," I whispered, wiping my nose, the tears of a child pooling in my eyes. "I'm sorry you had to do it."

He moaned a bit; he was more asleep than not and didn't hear my words. But he felt them, probably. Hopefully.

"I'm sorry you had to do it," I repeated so softly I might have been the only person in the world to hear. But that didn't matter to me in that moment. It didn't matter at all.

39

DOUBLE JEOPARDY

I didn't have much time. Serena would soon discover the missing documents and things would change rapidly in Riddell House.

I chose a little-used bedroom on the second floor, in the south wing, which was a more remote, almost decommissioned part of the house: the room contained only a small dresser and a single bed with a bare mattress on a metal spring frame. On the bed, I laid out my evidence: the copy of *The Mountains of California* and the letter from Ben to Harry which I had discovered within, my father's wedding ring from the basement, Elijah's diary from the secret room, Harry's journals from the cottage, the letter from Elijah to his future heir, photocopies of the microfiche research I had done, the transcript I had made of the letter Samuel scribbled on Post-it notes when channeling Ben, and the incriminating box from behind the Eugene O'Neill plays. I also placed a key on the bed—the one that unlocked the footlocker. I knew it was dangerous to reveal such things, but I had to commit to the intervention if I had any hope of it working. I withheld the power of attorney, the tickets, and Serena's letter, however; I would resort to the howitzer only in the most dire of situations. I arranged all the things on the bed as a sort of twisted show-and-tell, and then I went in search of my father.

I'm sure I wasn't fully aware of the nuances of the Riddell legacy when I was fourteen; I was really going on instinct and intuition, trying to do right by Ben. Looking back now, I see clearly that the guilt of generations of Riddells was pressing down on my father with such force, it was suffocating him. And I suppose, while I might not have been able to define it this way when I was young, I did feel it in a way I couldn't quite explain: the oppressiveness of that guilt would spill over to me if I didn't take corrective action. Our family was buried under generations of rotten leaves and fallen trees and damp earth. It would be a difficult path to redemption, but the soil was light and fertile. There was a sense of potential in the earth above our heads. A feeling of hope: we could claw our way out, if we had the will. All we needed was a seed to sprout, and a sprout to inch its way to the air; then we would all survive.

I found him in his room, taking a nap. I woke him because it was important. I led my grumbling father down the hallway to the little bedroom, and, once there, I waved my hands before the display.

"What is all this?" he asked.

I told him everything. I showed him the first Post-it I'd found, on which Grandpa Samuel had inscribed "MUIR MTNS CA"; how my mother led me to John Muir, which led to the letter inside the book. I told him about the cottage and the journals and all of it. Everything. The hand, the wedding ring in the basement, the box with the syringe. And then I told him about the secret room and Elijah's diary. I explained that the trust papers were in the safe in Elijah's study, as well as Serena's will, which she was using to bribe me.

"What safe?" he asked.

"Behind the painting over the credenza," I said. "You know. Like in the movies."

He looked at me blankly. Obviously, this was news to him.

"Serena showed me," I continued. "She has the ALS gene."

His look turned sour.

"And look," I said, finally, removing the smoking gun from my pocket: Elijah's letter. "A letter from Elijah to a future heir. Ben gave it to me while I was sleeping, and when I woke up, I had it in my hand. Go on. Read it."

He did. He removed the letter and read it, and then he replaced the letter in the envelope.

"Why are you doing all this?" he asked, irritated.

"You can't sell the house to developers," I said. "I mean, it's in Elijah's letter. You can't make The North Estate into tract housing for rich people. We have to make things right."

"We?" he said, clipped.

"Ben is here. Remember what you said? Spirits can come and visit, but a ghost doesn't see the door. A ghost is stuck. Ben is stuck; we have to release him."

"By turning Riddell House into a park."

"Yes," I said, relieved that my father finally understood. "Exactly. When you put the hand back on the stairs, you said to me, 'Sometimes you have to set the universe right.' Remember? You need to set things right, Dad. Developing this land and sucking the money out of it is only going to extend the curse. We'll just have to do it over and over again until we get it right."

"You woke me up for this?" he asked, shaking his head and waving his hand over the evidence I had assembled.

He reached down and picked up his wedding ring. He slipped it on his finger.

"It was in the basement," I said again. "In a cubbyhole."

"A place a mouse would stash it. A mouse that was attracted to shiny objects."

"Or a spirit who steals things. And do you know what else? Serena gives Grandpa NōDōz."

"What are you talking about?"

"The Alzheimer's medication she gives him. It's not medication; it's NōDōz. When you guys were out and I was feeding Grandpa, he asked me to get it for him, and the pills in the container had NōDōz stamped on them."

"That's crazy," he said with a snort.

"No, *Serena* is crazy. Think about it. She jacks him up on caffeine before bedtime and then gives him 'medicine' to help him sleep. You know about the medicine?"

"I know about the medicine," he admitted. "But this is ridiculous and I simply refuse to believe it. You're suggesting that she's using a deliberate and systematic method of sleep deprivation in order to make him act erratically? Where did you come up with this idea?"

"Arthur Koestler," I said. "*Darkness at Noon*. Mom made me read it. Sleep deprivation is considered torture and is banned by the Geneva Conventions."

"Oh, give me a fucking break, Trevor!"

"I don't think Grandpa has Alzheimer's," I went on. "I think she's trying to drive him crazy and make him seem forgetful and disorientated all the time so we'll push to get him to sign the power of attorney, which she needs to develop the property. See? It's all part of her plan. I bet if you tried to get him declared incompetent, the doctors would say he isn't incompetent at all. That's why it's so important to Serena that you or I get the power of attorney. She needs the documentation. The paper trail. Add that to the fact that she wants to take you on an around-the-world tour and jump your bones—"

"What the *hell* are you talking about?" he demanded.

I hesitated. I wasn't sure anything productive would come from playing the cruise ticket card at the moment. It was a lot for my father to digest. Adding incest to the mix might not take us in the right direction.

"Meanwhile," I said.

He shrugged and scratched his elbow, thinking. He picked up the cigar box with the syringe and the empty ampoule. He opened it and looked inside. He winced and set it back down on the bed.

"You have no idea what you're doing. You have no idea how you're hurting me with this . . . this *oral report*. I have to go."

He started toward the door, and I knew he hadn't understood at all. He'd heard, but he'd nullified the evidence.

"This is all real," I blurted. "I found all of these things in the house! I'm not making it up."

"So you're not making it up!" he snapped. "So it's all true? You feel justified using truth as a bludgeon? You feel justified in beating me with this—the tools of my mother's death? Really? You've figured out the big mystery—I hate myself for what I've done—and you're going to trot that out like some sick fifth-grade science project? You think you have the right to judge me? You spend your time digging up evidence to convict me of a crime. Well, let me tell you, I've already been convicted of that crime. I've already been hanged for that crime. I'm still hanging! Every day I have to dig my fingers into the space between the rope and my neck to make some room so I can breathe. I will never be cut down. I will never be free of this noose. But you want to try me again, and convict me again, and hang me again. What can I say to that, Trevor? That's double jeopardy, and that's not allowed in the Geneva Conventions. So keep your judgment to yourself."

"That's not what this is about—"

"If you think we're changing our plans because of the deathbed wishes of a man who's been dead eight decades—a man who gave away everything he had and left his heirs with nothing—you've got another thing coming. That man raped the world. Elijah, your new idol. Elijah Riddell was a ruthless privateer, a timber baron, a vicious raider of businesses. He destroyed people's lives. He destroyed nature. You realize that, right? And to assuage his guilt, he wanted to give it all away before he died. He did it so God would forgive him. And now you've decided it's your mission to fulfill his destiny? Well, that's really sweet. But you know what, Son? I've got bills to pay. I've got mouths to feed, including yours. I need to put a roof over our heads. Now you have morally justifiable ideals to throw in my face? Ideals are nice, Trevor, when you're fourteen years old. But you can't eat them, you can't sleep on them, and they sure as hell don't keep you from getting wet in the rain. So do me a fucking favor and take your Hardy Boys crime-solving skills somewhere else."

His face red with fury, he reached for the doorknob.

"But I thought—"

"You thought what?"

"I thought you didn't care about the money. I thought you only wanted your house back. Your life back."

He looked back at me.

"What led you to believe that?" he asked angrily.

"I overheard . . . something . . ."

My father took his hand off the doorknob. He turned to face me.

"You were eavesdropping?"

"I couldn't help it," I said plaintively. He had no idea of the things I'd overheard. "You were in the kitchen."

He snorted and darkened his brow and clenched his fists. He moved swiftly across the room and stood over me. He didn't strike me, but he exuded the energy of a strike, so I felt as if I had already been hit.

"You are not to listen in on my private conversations," he said sternly. Murderously, I would have said, were I writing a novel. He waved his hand toward the bed. "You will put this shit back where you found it. And you will not speak of it again. You will do what Serena instructs you to do, and you will do it quickly and with great resolve. Do we understand each other?"

"Yes," I said, cowed.

"Do we understand each other!" he shouted like he was some psycho military drill sergeant.

"Yes, sir," I repeated louder. "We understand each other . . . *sir!*"

I added the extra "sir" because I didn't like him talking to me like that. I thought that deserved an ass-tag, so I ass-tagged my father with an extra "sir," and he noticed. Oh, man, did he notice. His lips got all tight and his eyes narrowed on me and he raised his hand to slap me. But he didn't. He hesitated. And that hesitation was enough to tell me that he and I both knew I was right. He had the resolve to threaten, but he didn't have the resolve to act. Not like the resolve he must have had to inject a lethal drug into his mother. That was the true measure of commitment.

He turned his open palm into a pointing finger and stuck it in my face. A waffle move if I'd ever seen one.

"No more words," he threatened.

He wheeled around and marched toward the door; I knew this was it. It was my play, and I had to make it.

"Dad," I said forcefully, so he stopped.

"I said no more—"

"She's already gotten the tickets. They're in your name. I'm pretty sure she got the money from Dickie as an advance against the development of the property. I can show you—"

He didn't turn around but held up his hand as if to say "Enough." I stopped speaking.

"I don't believe you," he said. "I don't believe anything you're saying. I don't believe it now, and I will never believe it."

And then he left the room.

In that instant, I knew my father was not my ally. And if he was not my ally, even blowing him up with a howitzer loaded with evidence wouldn't help.

I gathered my things. *Our* things. My family's things. I gathered them because I valued them, and I knew they were important, and I would not let them go easily, as I wouldn't let go of Elijah's promise to Ben.

As I wouldn't let go of Ben's promise to Harry.

40

BEN'S TREE

I had failed. My plan—which really wasn't much of a plan at all, consisting only of convincing my father to do the right thing—was a miserable disappointment. It didn't work. So that was it. Ben was gone, stuck forever in the netherworld because I couldn't help him. Worse. Because I couldn't change my father's mind, I had become Ben's jailer. He had been doing pretty well hanging out with Grandpa Samuel until I came around.

I felt like an idiot.

I wished I could talk to Ben. Or at least see him again. I felt trapped by Riddell House. No friends. No strangers. No one.

I wandered the hallways hoping to see or hear a sign. A creak or a door moving or *something*. In the kitchen, I ran into Serena, who was cheerfully baking corn bread for dinner as if she were in a movie or a television show about the perfect housewife. Her hair lovely; her makeup divine. She was wearing a light dress, open at the neck and tight around the waist, as was her style. Her toenails had changed color:

they were painted orange, which I thought an odd choice. Still, it indicated she had spent time on herself that afternoon, which I saw as a
positive sign; she hadn't noticed the missing power of attorney or cruise
tickets yet.

That's right! I still had the power of attorney. I could destroy it. That
would foil their plans.

Alas, it would only delay their plans, I knew. For Serena wouldn't
stop until she succeeded, and I knew the only one who could convince
her to give up the development plan was Brother Jones. Without my
father, I had nothing. I might as well give back the power of attorney.

Serena quizzed me on my demeanor. To avoid real conversation, I
tossed her a bone about my chat with my mother and my mother's proc-
lamation that divorce might or might not be on the horizon, leaving the
conclusion totally ambiguous. Serena greedily snatched up that bit of
information and began to salivate, drooling all over the floor.

"When change is on his horse," she sang to me, "it is important for us
to accept it, rather than struggle against the ineluctability of fate."

So I left. I went outside and I knew I had to escape. I had to get out
as quickly as possible. Freight-hop, maybe, although leaping onto a train
traveling fifty-five miles per hour didn't seem like a smooth move. Running for it on foot seemed equally foolhardy.

And then I saw Ben's tree.

Ben's tree.

I ran down the hill to the barn. I climbed up into the loft, and found
the canvas bag behind the footlocker. I opened it. Gaffs and ropes and
gloves. Old and worn. Rusty metal. Cracked leather. But still, not entirely
unusable. I dug deeper. A length of chain—a flip line—better than rope.
When I'd first found the equipment, I didn't know what it was for. Now
I knew. It was tree-climbing equipment.

I took up the bag and ran off into the woods. Down through the cool
ravine, where I heard a train sounding its horn, through the thickest
parts of the woods, where the ground was spongy and like a trampoline

that I danced across. I knew where to go without thinking, as if someone were guiding me.

I arrived at the base of the thick tree and sized it up. I placed my hands on the trunk and addressed the tree. I said what Harry and Ben used to say to the trees they climbed: "I would like to climb you now. I thank you for your protection." I'd seen it in my dream.

I strapped on the gaffs—heavy metal spikes with thick leather straps that dug into my knees. I dragged the chain around the base of the tree and pulled on the gloves. I had never climbed a tree before. Not with spikes and a flip line, at least. But I had climbed it in my dream, so I knew what to do. I snaked the chain up the tree, and when it was above my shoulders, I kicked a gaff into the bark. I put weight on the spike, but it slipped free and my foot skidded to earth, scraping the inside of my knee. I winced at the pain, but I tried again. I gained purchase with one gaff, then tried the other, then was stuck. I tried to whip the chain up the tree, but when I did, my center of gravity changed, a gaff pulled free, and I skidded back to earth. Another scrape.

Again. After two successful gaffs, I lost purchase, and, though I tried to hold on to the tree with my arms, I skidded down, shredding my forearms on the rough bark. I tried again, and again, and again. For more than an hour I tried to get at least a few feet off the ground. Ten feet above the forest floor would have been a victory. But I couldn't do it.

Exhausted, frustrated, and bloody, I stopped. My thighs and knees were bruised. The gaffs had worn the flesh from my ankles and calves. My arm muscles were spent, and a bark rash ran from armpit to wrist on both arms. Still, I was determined to conquer the great tree.

"How do I do it?" I asked the tree. "How do I climb you? You let Harry and Ben climb you, but you won't let me? Why won't you let me climb you?"

The tree said nothing.

"I am a Riddell," I said to the tree. "I can save you. If you let me climb you, I promise I will save you so that you can live forever. You will be part of the immortal forest."

The tree did not answer.

"Ben," I said. "Help me."

But he did not help. Or did he? For I had a thought in that moment of Harry's journal, and of his observation that we focus on the contradiction and the separateness between and within ourselves, not on the union. And I thought that perhaps my believing that I had to conquer the tree to climb it wasn't the point at all. The point was for me to *join* the tree and be one with it. So I focused on the tree with that thought deeply in mind, and, after a moment, I felt something shift. The energy, or the wind? I didn't know. But I knew with some great assurance that I should take two fistfuls of slack out of the chain. I knew I should set my weight by pushing my hips into the trunk, that I should arch my back and keep my wrists above my shoulders and take smaller steps and kick harder into the bark and set the gaff with my weight firmly before shifting onto it.

And so I did. And so I climbed. With sheer determination and grit, I climbed. Two steps, then four, then eight. Whether it was my will or the tree's acceptance of me, or Ben's boost, I didn't know. Because I didn't think about it. I thought only about climbing: my gaffs in the bark, my hips into the trunk, my back straining to hold me.

When I had reached the lowest branch, I pulled myself onto it and sat for a moment. The ground was very far below me, seventy feet or more. A fall from this height would surely mean death. And yet, it wasn't enough.

"I want to get to the top," I said out loud. "I want to see."

I removed my gaffs, my sneakers and socks, because that was how they climbed in my dream and that was how I would climb. Up I went, and up higher still, into the belly of the tree. Into the place where the tree held me close and my climb was easy, where the tree coaxed me even higher. I didn't look down. I didn't question the wisdom of my journey or how long I had been climbing. I simply climbed. Higher. Until I reached the point that the branches grew thin and the trunk tapered. Until I knew I was near the top.

"How high will I go?" I asked the tree.

The tree didn't answer, so higher I went, to the very top. To the place from which Ben had departed. I knew it because I had seen it in my dream.

The world spread out before me in all directions, and I clung to the swaying spar of tree as the wind circled us and pushed us about. The mountains and the water and the city sparkled in the distance. The houses and the people below. I could see the breeze sweep through the branches of the trees around me, the ripples of light reflecting off the leaves and needles. From the tallest of trees on a hill so high, I felt I could see the whole world. I could see all of humanity. It was terrifying, but I was not afraid. It was thrilling, but I was calm. Because everything was in its proper place for that moment. I could feel it—the rightness of my world! I would not fall, because the tree was holding me; the tree would not break, because I was holding it. In the quiet at the top of the tree, I heard the music of the breeze as it drifted past my ears. In a mash of dizzying colors and movement, I found a clarity of sight. In that moment I knew why Ben and Harry had climbed trees to the very top; I knew what they felt; I *felt* what they felt.

I've tried to explain these things to my mother over the years; she will not be convinced. Maybe it was her upbringing, or maybe her personality. Or maybe just her obstinacy. I don't know. But I've tried to tell her what she may never come to believe: at that moment in Ben's tree, when I was fourteen years old, my life changed entirely. Before that, I wanted to believe; after that moment, I *knew*.

Oh, my faith has flagged at times. It's easy to fall back into the same routines and paint over the sublime with coat after coat of indifference. But now, in this moment of my telling this story to you, my faith is full. And I promise you something: when you have touched the face of God, you can never unlearn what you have learned. You can never unsee what you have seen.

As I clung to the top of that tree, a feeling welled up inside me so powerfully that I let go of the tree and reached out to the sky. I reached out and tried to grab the blue. I wanted to be carried away into the ether. I wanted to be all of everything.

But the sky wouldn't have me. The sky refused to fall low enough for me. And I heard a call from below. My name. Someone calling my name. From the top of the tree, I could see the meadow before Riddell House, where a small figure—my father—stood by the kitchen door calling for me.

I called back, but he couldn't hear.

Quickly, gingerly—almost possessed—I descended the tree to the lowest branch. I strapped on my gaffs and used the chain to descend the trunk as if I'd done it a hundred times. I bagged the equipment and ran through the woods and across the meadow to my dinner.

41

THE DUMBWAITER

I went in the front door instead of the back and called to the kitchen that I wanted to change my shirt before dinner. My arms were caked with dirt and dried blood from my climb, and my hands were black with pitch. I ran upstairs and washed as best I could; I masked my wounds with a long-sleeve T-shirt.

Downstairs, dinner was already on the table. In addition to the usual vegetables, bread, and lemonade, my father had grilled kabobs, which meant he was completely under Serena's spell.

"Where did you get off to?" Serena asked me offhandedly.

"Just hiking around."

She glanced at me suspiciously and passed the peas to my father, who served himself some and passed them along. When we had all been served and had begun eating, my father stood up abruptly.

"We forgot Dad's medicine," he said.

Serena immediately grew tense and sat rigidly in her seat.

"I'll get it—" she said.

She started to rise, but my father waved her off and moved quickly to the cupboard. Oh, no, I thought. This isn't the best way to handle it. Really it isn't. He retrieved the medicine bottle and scrutinized the label. He opened the lid.

"I can do it, Brother Jones," Serena said. "Really."

"I'll do it. He gets two? Or three?"

"Two," Serena admitted.

She watched tensely as my father shook two pills into his palm. I'm sure she was wondering, as was I, how it would play out. He looked at them closely, and then he looked at Serena deliberately. The room became still. Very still.

"It's effective, this medicine?" my father asked archly.

After a pause, Serena broke their stare and poured lemonade into Grandpa Samuel's glass.

"You would be surprised how effective," she said as if she had just dodged a bullet.

He nodded and replaced the pill container in the cupboard. He returned to the table and set the pills in front of Grandpa Samuel. He resumed his seat, and I wondered why he didn't say something! What was the point? Not only of corroborating the truth but of doing it so obviously in front of Serena? I didn't get it at all. Grandpa Samuel swallowed his pills with lemonade.

"It's good to see you so concerned about Daddy's well-being, Brother Jones," Serena said, flashing her smug cat eyes at my father.

"It's important that we all work together on this," my father said. "Alzheimer's is difficult for everyone involved."

"It certainly is," Serena agreed.

And then we ate dinner.

I was baffled by my father's behavior. I already knew he and I weren't on the same team, but I thought his complicity in Serena's scheme was

born out of willful ignorance. A collaboration by benign neglect. I didn't
realize my father would actually take part in the scheming and manipulations. I thought that was all Serena's doing. Nevertheless, I had hidden
the power of attorney, which I equated with stealing the distributor cap
of an old car, like they do in the movies. It slows the guy down for a
while, but it never stops him completely.

As I headed to my room, I was struck by a different thought. It occurred
to me that each time I had seen Serena give Grandpa Samuel his Alzheimer's medication, a visit from the dancing ghost of Isobel had followed
in the night. The thought was so provocative, I stopped still in the hallway.
Pills. Restlessness. "Medicine." Dancing. While I pondered the connection,
I noticed a shadow. I heard a creak. Was it Ben, unable to resist giving me
a clue? I walked down the hall to find the door to a small pantry space ajar.
Had my uncle of some level of greatness returned to me? I pushed the door
open to reveal a small, empty, white room with a counter against one wall.
On the counter was a wicker clothes hamper. I pushed the hamper aside,
revealing a hatch door. I opened the hatch and found the shaft.

The dumbwaiter shaft.

I hopped up on the counter, ducked inside the shaft, and climbed the
ladder to the top. The hatch on the third floor opened into the closet in
the ballroom. Just like that. Fascinating.

I closed up the hatches and slipped from the house unnoticed to visit
Grandpa Samuel in the barn. I scavenged a hammer and some small
nails from his workbench and returned to the house. I was going on a
hunch. Instinct. Alzheimer's meds equaled Isobel visit. And Isobel always magically vanished when she was noticed. I could do the math, as
Serena liked to say . . .

I tacked the hatch door shut in the ballroom closet, being careful
to make as little noise as possible, and then I returned the hammer and
remaining nails to the barn, at which point I spent the evening keeping
my grandfather company by reading to him from Harry's journals as he
worked on his chair legs, time we both enjoyed.

42

REDEMPTION

Later that night, I was lying on my bed, trying unsuccessfully to write my impressions of my journey to the top of the tree—it was so clear and so vivid, yet the words would not come to describe it; I was distracted by the trap I had set with the dumbwaiter, and I wondered if it might actually work—when my father knocked and let himself in. He perched at the end of my bed, his elbows on his knees, looking through his hands at the floor; he said nothing. I put aside my journal; I didn't believe my father had come into my room looking for something, but to offer something instead.

We sat silently for quite a while before he spoke.

"Grandpa Samuel was supposed to do it," he said. "The doctor who gave us the medication said that Grandpa Samuel should give her the injection in case something went wrong. If there were an investigation and someone were held responsible, he said, it would be better for it to be him. Because I still had my whole life ahead of me. People didn't do things like that twenty-three years ago—assisted suicide, or whatever they call it; I'd call it euthanasia. People went to prison for it. They still do."

My father laughed. He cleared his throat and fidgeted about a bit. He stood and walked across the room to my desk.

"Fathers are supposed to do that for their sons," he said. "I would do it for you."

"You would go to prison for me?"

"If something risky had to be done and I were in a position to protect you by doing it? Absolutely. Yes, I would."

"But your father didn't."

"No, my father didn't."

"Is that why you gave him the NōDōz at dinner tonight?" I asked.

My father was stung by the comment.

"I wanted to know for sure," he said. "I needed to see."

"But you didn't have to give the pills to him. You could have called Serena on it."

"And then what would have happened?"

"I don't know," I admitted.

"It's better that she think I'm complicit in the deal. Until I can figure out what to do."

He stopped talking and we sat in silence for another minute. Finally, I opened the drawer in my bedside table and removed Serena's letter and the cruise tickets, in their neat little envelopes. I held them in the air.

"What are those?"

"Evidence," I said. "You said you didn't believe I had any evidence. Here it is. Cruise tickets. Check the names, if you want."

He took them from me, opened one of the Cunard envelopes, and read the contents.

"And this?" he asked of Serena's letter.

"Read it."

He did. When he finished, he dropped the letter and the tickets on the bed and shook his head sadly.

"What on earth made her think I would go on an around-the-world cruise with her?"

"Don't you get it?" I said. "That's what this whole thing is about. There are serious rare books in that library. Like hard-core, really rare books. She could sell them and have a boatload of money. But she doesn't want the money."

"What does she want?"

"Come on, Dad. Don't be dense. She wants *you*."

He laughed.

"That's crazy!"

"'Signs point to yes,'" I agreed, quoting a Magic 8 Ball.

"You know," my father said, "when I was a kid I loved magic. I loved the idea of escaping from something. I loved Harry Houdini. I mean, I *worshipped* him. There was a magic shop down in the Public Market, and I would hang out there just to *feel* the magic. I taught myself how to pick locks, even, and I would have my mother lock me in an armoire with a chain around it and I would try to escape. I read everything I could about Houdini. When I think about the tragedy of his death, it still makes me sad. He wasn't just a magician and escape artist, he was a showman, and so he had to put on a show, even though it killed him."

He stopped, and then he sat down at the desk chair, lost in thought.

"Why are you telling me this?" I asked.

"Houdini was famous for exposing fake mediums and clairvoyants. He claimed to do it in the pursuit of truth and justice. But I'm not sure that was his motive. I think he really *believed* in the afterlife. He wanted to see his mother and his father again. And so he made it his mission to debunk the fakes in order to find the authentic. He didn't do it because he *didn't* believe, he did it because he *did* believe. My mother believed, too. And she promised me she would come back to see me after she died, if she could. If it were possible."

"I know."

He looked at me curiously, but didn't question my comment.

"My father sent me away a week after she was buried," he continued, "so how do I know she hasn't been waiting for me here the whole time? I mean, she dances for Grandpa Samuel, doesn't she? I've heard it, haven't *you*? She's *here*, isn't she?"

"I'll tell you what I know," I said after a moment. "But only if you tell me that you believe in this stuff. Did you see Ben at the top of the stairs? Or was it the power of suggestion, like you said before?"

He looked at me for more than a minute. I think he was trying to discern whether or not I really knew anything at all.

"I saw him," he finally admitted.

"So you know?"

"Yes, Trevor, I know. Now tell me what you know."

I told him. I told him everything I had seen, from the beginning to the end, the same as I had in the upstairs bedroom, but this time he listened differently. And then I told him about seeing Isobel in the dark at the top of the stairs.

He said nothing for a long time, then he asked if he could see the matches I had. I took the matchbox out of my pocket and tossed it to him. He turned it over in his hands.

"It was a game," he said. "It was a trick. That's what they told me, anyway. I was about your age when I started to doubt her. I went down to the magic shop in the Market and asked the guys working there if there were really spirits. If magic was really magic. No, they said. There are no spirits; there is no magic. None of it is real. Houdini debunked all the mediums, and then he debunked himself by never returning to his wife. They convinced me that my mother was playing a trick on me, and that tricks were for children."

"So what happened?"

"I told her I didn't believe."

"And then?"

"And then she died," he said.

"But that had nothing to do with—"

"Everything has everything to do with everything," he said. "That's the message. Everything has everything to do with everything. No thing, no person, is not a part of the everything. How do I know that she didn't make herself sick and die just so she could return and show me the truth?"

"I don't think someone would do that," I said. "I don't think if someone really loved someone, she would do something like that."

"I'm very confused right now," he said, tapping the matchbox against his thumb. "My head hurts. I don't know what's going to happen with me and Mom, with me and you, with Grandpa and Serena . . . I don't know what's going to happen to *me*. If I brought you here for a reason—even if I didn't know it consciously—then *this* is the reason. What do I do now?"

"You should do what Ben wants you to do," I said without hesitation. "You should return Riddell House to the forest."

"What about Serena?"

"You're going to have to stand up to her and tell her you're not developing the estate."

"Should I tell her we'll sell the books for money?" he asked, truly confused.

"She doesn't want money."

"Should I tell her we'll sell the books *and* I'll go with her on the cruise?"

"Is that what you want to do?" I asked, surprised by the question.

"I *raised* her," he said, pleading for my understanding. "My mother was terminally ill and my father was a hopeless drunk. I did everything, Trevor. I cooked, I cleaned, I helped with her homework. I washed her clothes. I read books to her. I went to the parent-teacher conferences and talked to the teachers about her performance in school. You don't understand how life was around here. I mean, I have to offer her *something*."

"You have to give her what you can," I said. "But even if you give her everything, she might not be satisfied."

GARTH STEIN

He sighed because he knew my answer was true. He stood up and walked to the door, placed his hand on the doorknob, and looked over at me.

"I've been speaking with Mom," he said. "On the phone. I feel like I'm in high school again; I look forward to her phone calls."

"Really?"

"Yeah, and I think it's all going to work out, you know? I know this has been tough on you, and I appreciate the faith you've shown in me. But we're making headway and I have a good feeling."

"Really?" I asked again, wondering if it was true or if they were fooling themselves, and if they were fooling me along with them. If we all wanted to be fooled, because in a fool's world, everything works out in the end.

"Yeah. I mean, no promises—"

"Sure."

"But, I mean . . . a status report . . . yeah. 'Signs point to yes.'"

I could see how my father struggled to arrange the facts and conversations and ideas in his head to make them add up, and how there was more hope than conviction in the look on his face. Still, I appreciated his effort.

"Anyway, thanks for the talk," he said after a moment. "Apparently, your mother raised you well while I was away."

"You were never away," I said.

"I was away," he corrected me. "I was around, but I wasn't really . . . engaged. After all, I am my father's son."

"You're being a little hard on yourself, Dad."

"Yeah? Well. I probably deserve it. I apologize for my transgressions, Trevor. I hope that one day you can forgive me."

"It's okay," I said. "I mean, you're my father. Isn't that the way it works?"

We looked at each other for a moment, long enough to know that the apology was offered and accepted, and then my father held up the matches.

"Do you mind if I keep these?"

"Go ahead," I said. "There's a drawer full of them in the kitchen."

"You should go to sleep."

He left, and I turned out my light, but I couldn't fall asleep; as always, the history of Riddell House kept me awake.

After a few minutes I got up and headed for the south wing. I was pretty sure I knew where my father had gone, and when I reached the linen closet and saw that the door was open, I knew I was right. The false wall was ajar. I pried it open and looked up the spiral staircase into the darkness. I heard a scratching sound, saw an orange glow at the top of the stairs. The glow lasted a dozen seconds, then went out. A few seconds later, another scratch, another glow. And again. And again. My father hoping to see his mother.

I didn't interfere with his quest. I didn't know why she wouldn't appear for him as she had appeared for me. Maybe it wasn't really her I had seen; maybe Ben sent me a message in her likeness. There were so many theories, I had no way of knowing. But I knew that nothing I could say to my father would stop him, and nothing I could do would satisfy his need to make contact with Isobel. So I left him there with his matches and I returned to my room. I took Elijah's diary from the sock drawer where I kept it, and I began to read.

3 March 1916

My dead son came to me this evening. He sat with me. We spoke. He left moments ago.

For these many years I've waited. I've kept my faith. I've always believed he would return and I would see him again. So I was not surprised when he appeared. Instead, I was overwhelmed with a feeling of contentment and satisfaction.

In my room, the sun in the window, a glass of port by my side, I was making an accounting of what I have done: a ledger sheet that showed lives I have destroyed and forests I have ravaged, against donations of money and land I have made, institutions and cities I have helped, as well as individual grants to those less fortunate than me. Ben taught me that what I have carved from the earth is not for me to keep, but for me to return to the earth. I was making my accounting as the afternoon sun flickered through the needles of the trees and upon my ceiling, and I looked up to the window, which looked out upon Ben's tree, and he was there in the room with me.

"Ben," I whispered. "Such a sight for a dying man. You have come for me. Does it mean I am forgiven? Does it mean I am not beyond redemption?"

Ben knelt beside my chair and I reached for him. I touched him.

"Have I redeemed myself, Ben?"

"You have."

"I have prayed for it to be so."

"It is not in prayer, but in deeds that we find absolution," he said to me.

"Do you accept my compromise?" I asked him, referring to the trust I had put into place to allow Abraham and his heirs to continue living at Riddell House. "I didn't want to break my promise to you—"

"You have kept your promise to me."

"But the estate. The park—"

"The promise is mine, Father. It's a promise I made to Harry, and the obligation belongs to me. You were just holding my promise until it was time."

"Time for what?"

"Time for you to be released," Ben said.

"Am I released?"

"You are," he said. "I will stay now, until I fulfill my promise to Harry."

He left me then, but I didn't feel alone.

I must go downstairs now to rest. I will sleep better than I have slept in my entire life, for I know that I have lived my life rightly. I have made mistakes and I have hurt people, I do not deny that fact.

But I have corrected those mistakes vigorously once I understood the error of my ways.

I must go downstairs to find Thomas, my faithful friend. He will help me to bed, for I am tired and require a nap.

The cook is braising a rabbit for us tonight, which I love very much, and look forward to eating.

Elijah Riddell died a hero. I read his death notice in the *Seattle Post-Intelligencer*, March 12, 1916. The banner headline was A CITY, A NATION, MOURNS DEATH OF ICON. Front page, above the fold.

The same man who had been skewered by the press twenty years earlier for all the cynical, shark-like deals he made. The man vilified for destroying entire forests, ruthlessly shutting down towns and schools, and treating his workers and their families with no mercy at all. By the time he died, he had redeemed himself to some degree, at least.

Enough to be forgiven by his son.

43

THE TRUTH WILL OUT

At 3:02 A.M., I heard voices. It was not unusual. Nothing was unusual in Riddell House.

I went downstairs to investigate and found Grandpa Samuel with a glass of medicine. Sitting across from him at the table was my father, also with a glass of medicine. They were talking about boats or wood or something. They were talking about the house or Isobel or Serena. They were talking about the wind that came from the southwest, from the Pacific Ocean, raced through the mouth of the Columbia River and around the Olympics, bringing in the rain. They were talking about trees.

"Are we being too loud?" my father asked when he saw me in my pajamas, standing sleepily in the doorway rubbing my eyes.

"I couldn't sleep," I lied.

"Join the club," he said jovially, indicating a seat.

I wondered if I should join them. I wasn't sure it was right. But then I saw the liquor jiggling in the bottle and realized they were in full swing and wouldn't mind my company. I grabbed a Coke from the fridge, took a glass from the cupboard, and sat at the table. My father topped off Grandpa Samuel's glass.

"Maybe a little less milk this time," Grandpa Samuel said.

"Good idea," my father agreed.

And then we toasted. The three of us. Grandpa Samuel, who seemed to be carrying on his own conversation in his head, nodded vehemently.

"I should have been the one to do it," he said.

"But you didn't do it, Dad," my father said. "And it had to be done. So *I* did it."

"You should have let *me* do it," Grandpa Samuel protested.

"But you *didn't* do it."

"No."

"So *I* did it. It had to be done."

"It had to be done," Grandpa Samuel agreed after a sip of his medicine.

They drank again, and refilled, and I knew they were rocked.

"So why did you send me away, then?" my father asked his father. "You at least owe me an explanation. Why?"

"I couldn't do it."

"Then why did you send me away?"

Grandpa Samuel nodded his drunken nod, but didn't reply.

I knew what they were talking about, and I remembered Serena's talk about emasculation. That was why Grandpa Samuel sent my father away. You can't take away someone's manhood like that.

"You banished me," my father said. "You told me you never wanted to see me again. Why?"

Grandpa Samuel ruminated. Ideas swimming in his head.

"Ben is nervous," he said.

My father shook his head in confusion and looked at me.

"Ben is here?" I asked.

"Ben is always here."

"What about Isobel?" my father asked. "Is she always here?"

Grandpa Samuel was silent for a moment, then he spoke: "When she dances, she's here."

"But not usually?"

"Not usually," he said. "But Ben . . . he's nervous."

"Why?" I asked.

Grandpa Samuel looked at me with milky eyes. His seeping eyes and his sagging face and the whiskers that bristled on his cheeks and eyebrow hairs that were so long, and his long white hair, and his T-shirt that Serena had put out for him, his twisted black T-shirt that said: FUCK MEAT.

Fuck meat.

It was like a haiku. So simple and yet so complex. Ezra Pound might have translated it from the Chinese.

"It made me sick to look at him," Grandpa Samuel said to me. "She wanted me to do it, but I couldn't, so she asked Jones. After he'd done it, I couldn't look at him without feeling sick."

"Dad, I'm right here. You can talk to me."

"I knew I would poison him if he stayed. He would be infected by my sickness. I didn't want him to live his life hating me for hating him."

"Dad," my father tried to interrupt, frustrated that Grandpa Samuel was speaking only to me and not to him. "Say it to *me!*"

"I failed my son," Grandpa Samuel said to me. "I failed Isobel. I failed my father."

Grandpa Samuel fell silent, as did we all. After a moment, he reached for the bottle of medicine, but my father stopped him and took the bottle himself.

"No more medicine for you," my father said. "We're going to get you off this medicine."

My father stood up and put the bottle away in the cupboard.

"We'll find you a doctor and get your diagnosis sorted out and figure out what you really need."

He closed the cupboard, and, as he passed Grandpa Samuel, the old man reached out and grabbed his son's wrist, stopping him. They met eyes.

"Will you forgive me, Son? I didn't mean to hurt you. I meant to protect you. I was wrong in what I did. I beg you. Please forgive me."

My father still wore a hard look on his face; he was not disposed to forgive anything. But he looked at me, his own son, and I nodded significantly.

"I forgive you," my father said.

And that was all it took. Grandpa Samuel burst into a sobbing bout that was truly impressive. Slobbering and snot and waterworks. The whole deal. My father touched the back of Grandpa Samuel's head. Father leaned into son and they embraced, more or less. A quasi, rigid embrace, and I knew there had been some kind of closure between them, though the wound was so deep, the scar of it would always show.

I left them there in the kitchen; they didn't need me anymore. I went upstairs to my room, and, from the second-floor landing, I could hear a faint shuffling sound coming from the ballroom. Isobel . . .

Quietly, so quietly, I slunk up the stairs to the second floor, and down the hallway to my room. I grabbed my flashlight and then I slipped up the stairs to the third floor. On the landing, in the antechamber of the ballroom, I paused. The double doors to the ballroom were closed, but I clearly heard footsteps and music coming from inside. I reached for the doorknob. I turned it gently so it made nary a click. I pushed the door open and peered through the crack. And there she was.

How elegant. How lovely. A young woman with her hair up, wearing a long brown dress that billowed and fluttered as she spun on her bare feet. My grandmother. And though it was dark in the room save the moonlight trickling in the windows, though it was hard to see, I was almost sure I recognized those feet. I never had thought of myself as a foot fetishist, but perhaps I had some of that in me, because I *knew* those feet. And I was pretty sure the toenails were painted orange.

"Serena," I whispered so softly, almost inaudibly, but loud enough for the dancing woman to hear. She looked to the door, then fluttered across the room toward the stage. I rushed into the room and flipped on the light switches. They didn't work.

The ghost floated around the room and then vanished. I clicked on my flashlight and scanned the dance floor. She was gone. I crossed to the phonograph and clicked it off. And then I heard other sounds. Scratching sounds. I went to the closet with the dumbwaiter shaft and listened closely. I heard grunting, followed by pounding, followed by a scratching, clawing sound. I didn't dare open the door.

I ran down the stairs to the first floor, past my father and grandfather, through the kitchen, and outside to the fuse box. As I guessed, the same glass fuse was unscrewed; I tightened it. I returned to the kitchen.

"Dad," I said. "You need to come now."

He rose from his chair immediately.

"What's wrong?"

Grandpa Samuel also started to get up.

"Wait here, Grandpa," I said.

"Wait here," my father agreed. "We'll be right back."

I led my father up to the ballroom; the light switch worked.

"What's going on?" he asked.

"Isobel," I said. "She was here and she ran into the closet. I trapped her."

We went to the closet door and opened it. The closet was empty.

"How do you trap a ghost?" my father asked.

"She's not a ghost," I said. "She's Serena."

I shone my flashlight into the back of the closet, where the hatch was located.

"That's a dumbwaiter shaft," I explained to my father. "It goes all the way down to the basement, and it stops on the second floor; maybe there's a hatch on the first floor, too, but I haven't found it. I took the shaft down to the basement when I hit my head. I figured Serena was behind the dancing footsteps, so after dinner, I nailed the door shut.

When I came up just now to investigate, I saw her run in here. I heard her trying to pry the hatch open. It *has* to be Serena."

My father grabbed my flashlight and stepped into the closet. He shone the light against the back wall as he knelt in front of the hatch and looked closely.

"There's blood on the wall," he said.

He felt the wall with his hand, found something, and pulled it away.

"A fingernail," he said.

He held it up for me to see; it was a fingernail, torn from the quick of a finger. It belonged to Serena.

We found her in the bathroom of the servant's wing, a box of Band-Aids spilled open on the counter before her amid scraps of paper wrappers and discarded backing strips. She was meticulously applying Band-Aids to her fingertips, pulling them so tight.

My father and I stood in the doorway for a long time before she noticed, such was her level of concentration. When she looked up, we could see makeup streaked on her face from tears, and blood on her forehead and cheeks from pushing hair from her face with the backs of her bloodied hands.

"They'll take forever to grow back," she said with a sad laugh.

"How long have you been pretending to be Mom?" my father demanded.

Serena sniffed and laughed. "Forever," she said, pushing past us and moving into the common area. "Forever and for always."

My father hovered behind her, but Serena wouldn't meet his eyes. She paused by the kitchen table, setting a hand down to steady herself. She smoothed her dress, straightened her hair, corrected her posture, all in an effort to compose herself. She looked straight at my father and said: "I'm ready to take your questions."

"Why did you do it?" my father asked, still fixed on her.

"To please Daddy," she replied. "Why else?"

"Why did you need to please *Daddy*?"

"When you left, he was distraught. Mother had died; you had killed her . . ."

I glanced at my father; it was slight, but I saw the nick from Serena's blade.

"She was gone," Serena continued. "And then you were gone. And Daddy was distraught, because he had only me, and I wasn't good for anything, was I? I was eleven years old: a child. It was only Daddy and me and Riddell House with its creaks and leaks and the history of its pain painted into the walls. You can feel it, can't you, Trevor? It's in the walls. It's in the foundation."

She looked at me, and I nodded.

"I can feel it."

"And one night I danced," she said, crossing over to the couch and sitting down expansively, entirely in control of her narrative. "I could really use a fucking cigarette right now. Trevor, be a dear and fetch Aunt Serena's cigarettes, won't you?"

She indicated a cupboard door, and I looked inside. A pack of Marlboros, an ashtray, and a lighter. I brought them to her. She took a cigarette, lit it, and inhaled deeply.

"Don't be corrupted by my negative influence," she said to me, exhaling smoke into the air. "Smoking will kill you. I could really use a fucking drink right now."

"Serena," my father said sternly. "Why did you need to dance to please Daddy?"

"One night I was thinking of you, Brother Jones. I remembered what it was like to dance with you, when Mother was so sick that to move her hand or scratch her nose was agony for her. And you and Daddy would carry her up the stairs to the ballroom. I knew how painful it was for her, but she wanted to see us dance. And we danced, didn't we, Brother Jones? We danced. 'It was a time,' as Daddy would say. And one night, when the house was empty because you and Mother had left, I went up to the ballroom to dance with you, even though you weren't here. I was eleven years old, and I played records and danced because I couldn't sleep for the loneliness. The following morning Daddy said to me: 'Did you hear the footsteps last night?' He said: 'Isobel is dancing for me.' And he was so happy. He was so happy that she had come to dance for him that I did it again and again, and I kept doing it. Don't you see, Brother Jones? It wasn't a lie; it was a different truth."

An uncomfortable silence settled upon us.

"I thought—" my father began, but stopped himself.

"There are many truths, Brother Jones," she said. "There are an infinite number of universes, all existing side by side, or so the scientists say. All existing concurrently. But we have only *this* universe in which to live; we can't have the other universes. Of all the glorious universes we could possibly have, *this* is the universe we're stuck with."

My father tried to digest her words. He wanted to understand. But he didn't seem able.

"I believed," he said. "I *believed*."

"And what's wrong with believing?" Serena asked him. Serena pleaded with him. "Brother Jones, I want to know. What's wrong with hoping? What's wrong with wanting something so badly you can't stand it? What's wrong with wanting something so much, you'll do anything to get it?"

"I don't know," my father said after a moment. He dropped down on the couch across from his sister. He closed his eyes, lifted his face to the heavens, and reached his arms out for the sky. "I don't know."

"There's nothing wrong with believing," she said. She got up from her couch. She moved over to stand before him, and she looked down on his raised face, his eyes still closed; she hovered over him. "And we can *still* believe. I have tickets. I have a stateroom reserved for us. On the *Queen Elizabeth II*. A voyage around the world! Think of it. I've never left here. I've hardly been off The North Estate. Brother Jones, you and I will sail *around the world*!"

She lowered herself and knelt beside him on the couch, next to him, up against him.

"Sail around the world," he repeated from his rapturous pose.

She held her face over his, then she kissed him. He accepted her kiss for a moment, but then he snapped to, like coming out of a hypnotic trance. He grabbed her wrists, sat up, and shook his head.

"What are you doing?" he demanded.

"It's all right, Brother Jones," she soothed.

"You were kissing me. Why were you kissing me?"

"I wasn't—"

He stood up, and, as he did, he twisted Serena's wrists in a way that made her gasp in pain.

"You're hurting me—"

"What were you *doing*?" he shouted at her. "Don't do that again! Don't you ever touch me like that again!"

"Please let go!" she cried. "You're hurting me!"

He stopped, as if he suddenly realized his physicality was overpowering her. As if he suddenly saw how large he was and how small she was, how frail she was, how broken. He released her.

"You told Trevor you have the ALS gene," he said darkly. "It's not genetic."

"It *can* be—"

"In the rarest of cases, which this isn't. You don't have ALS. You won't get ALS. You told Trevor that to manipulate him. Everything you've done since we've been here has been done to manipulate one of us. You lie as easily as you tell the truth—*more* easily!"

"I feel a pain in my nerves—"

"I'm not going with you on a cruise," my father said forcefully. "I'm going to England to be with Trevor and Rachel."

"That's not true! Trevor said that you—"

"It is true. I love my wife, and I'll go to her if she'll have me. It doesn't matter if Dad wanted to send me away or not, or if Mom wanted me to put her out of her misery or not, or whether I came back to you or not. Because you told me, Sister Serena. You just said it: this is the universe we're stuck with."

"Brother Jones!" she wailed.

"I am not going on a cruise with you," he repeated forcefully. "We are not dancing on the *Queen Elizabeth II* together. We are not visiting exotic lands."

He started to leave.

"Brother Jones!" she cried out to him. "I'm the one who stayed behind! I'm the one who feeds him every day, who washes his filthy underwear, cleans his vomit when he gets sick, picks up after him like I'm his slave. When I tried to leave, he *promised* me this house. He *promised* it to me so he could keep me here and keep me his slave. And he lied! Give me the house, Jones. You have the power; you can make him do it. Give me this house, Brother, so I can destroy it. Give it to me so I can smash it down and grind it into the earth with the heels of my boots. So I can scrape the ground clean of its filth. So I can chop up the land into teeny tiny pieces and sell it to ignorant people with their ignorant dreams. So I can escape this godforsaken place and run away as far as possible before those stupid dreamers wake up and realize how toxic the soil is here. How corrosive it is to the human soul!"

"It can't be," my father said. "It isn't right. We have to set the universe right."

"It *is* right!"

"We can sell the things. The silver settings and the china. We can sell the rare books. You can have the money from all of it; I don't want any. Then you can go around the world on your cruise. You can see the world that you so desperately want to see."

"How can I leave here? Who will take care of Daddy?"

"I'll come back and stay with him," my father said. "Or I'll bring him to England for a while. What does it matter? That's a problem that's easy to solve. And when he finally dies, we'll do what Elijah and Ben wanted us to do with the land. We'll do what's right. In the meantime, you'll get your money and you'll get to travel."

"I don't want money!" Serena said. "I don't want to travel!"

"But you bought cruise tickets—"

"With you!" Serena cried. "I want to travel *with you!* I want to see the world *with you!*"

My father stared at her for a long time. It felt like minutes, but it couldn't have been; it was time counted in breaths.

"I'm afraid that's not possible," he said finally. "I'm sorry, Serena, but that's not happening."

Something swept across her face. Fatigue or resignation or the realization that the endgame was not going to tip in her favor; that it was time to lay down her king and accept her defeat.

"You should get some sleep," my father said. "We all should get some sleep."

She didn't respond, so my father shrugged and glanced at me. He tipped his head toward the door and we retreated.

"If you leave me now," Serena said, sounding so weary from the night's events—from her life's events—that my father and I stopped. "If you leave me now," she repeated, "I will hurt myself. I will hurt myself until I die. And I will suffer, Brother Jones. I will make it take a very long time. I will make it horrible, so when you find me, you will know I have suffered. You will not have prevented my suffering like you did with Mother. You will feel my agony when you see my dead body. If you leave me now, Brother Jones, I will gouge my suffering into your soul so you will carry the scar forever, and you will never be free of me."

"Serena, don't say that."

"It is the truth, Brother Jones," she said, looking at him clearly. "I promise you."

My father closed his eyes and nodded to himself, as if to agree that he knew she would do it. She would do exactly that.

"Go on," he said to me. "Put Grandpa to bed in my room tonight. He doesn't need to see Serena like this. It's nearly four; both of you go to sleep. I'll stay here with Serena and make sure she's safe."

I nodded as my father joined Serena on the couch. He put his arm around her shoulders, and she folded into him as he stroked her hair.

"Is there anything else I can do?" I asked.

"No," my father said. "Do what I've told you. She'll be fine once she falls asleep; we can get her help tomorrow."

So I left them there on the couch and I did what I was told: I helped my grandfather get to bed, and then I fell asleep myself; the sky was already transforming into the palest shade of blue a person could possibly imagine.

44

THE LAST DANCE

A knocking on my door jarred me awake. It was just past 5:00 A.M., so I had gotten less than an hour of sleep. I felt nauseous and drugged with fatigue. It was already light outside, since Seattle was practically in the Arctic Circle and the sun never set. And still the knocking at my door continued.

I rousted myself from the bed and opened the door. Grandpa Samuel stood in the hallway looking disheveled. He was wearing his old-man pajamas and slippers, and his hair was out of an Albert Einstein poster. He smelled slightly of a campfire. I wondered briefly if I should be concerned about his personal hygiene.

"Go back to sleep, Grandpa," I said.

"Isobel is dancing again!" he whispered loudly at me.

But how could that be?

I listened. It was true. Footsteps and music. What was Serena thinking?

I led Grandpa Samuel upstairs to the ballroom, and there she was—

Serena—dancing in great, graceful circles around the room in the thin morning twilight.

I started to say something, I began to intervene, but Grandpa Samuel put his hand on my elbow to stop me. He held his finger to his lips and whispered, "It was a time."

So beautiful. She really was everything from every dream a man has had about a beautiful woman dancing. Perfect. And so we watched and we watched. I pulled over folding chairs so we could sit and watch her mesmerizing dancing as the room brightened. It was as if time had stopped altogether. And yet there was time, for the music played, the song ended, another song began. And when the record side ended, she turned it over and started dancing again. She knew we were watching her. She enjoyed being watched. She was wearing a different dress. Dark and velvety and heavy. It seemed too hot for the summer weather. She reached for the needle of the phonograph, placed it on the record, and began to dance again. I saw beads of perspiration on her brow, and it occurred to me how hot it was in the ballroom. I was sweating as well. And I noticed the smell of a campfire coming off Grandpa Samuel, so I leaned over and sniffed near his hair.

"Are those the same clothes you wore at the campfire the other night?" I whispered.

"What?"

"You smell like a campfire."

"It was a time," he said proudly, turning his attention back to Serena.

I felt uncomfortably hot, so I got up and crossed the dance floor, giving Serena a wide berth. I opened one of the windows facing the meadow. Cool air immediately rushed at me, and it felt good on my face. I opened another, and a third.

"Clever Trevor," Serena said, dancing toward me.

I looked up and was surprised by how close she was.

"That will only make it end sooner," she said.

"But it's hot in here."

"Yes," she agreed, "it is hot. Sit down and let me dance for you."

She led me back to my chair, and I sat. She resumed her dance. For several songs, Grandpa Samuel and I watched her. But I was fidgety. I couldn't help feeling that something was terribly wrong with the whole situation. And the smell. I sniffed again.

"I smell something burning," I said to Grandpa Samuel. "Are you sure you didn't light a fire at the fire pit or something?"

He shook his head, still smiling.

I got up and wandered over to the doors to the ballroom. The smell was more distinct. Something *was* burning. I reached for the doorknob; Serena stopped dancing abruptly.

"Oh, Trevor," she said impatiently. "You're really doing everything wrong. If you want the moment to continue, you can't do these things. You know the principles of building a campfire. You can't say I haven't educated you."

I looked back at her.

"What did you do?" I asked.

And then I understood. I knew what she had done.

"Fire," I croaked, but my throat was too dry to make a sound.

"Fire!" Serena cried mockingly. "Fire!"

"Where's my dad?" I asked.

I opened the ballroom doors, and a blast of hot air knocked me backward, like the wash of a jet engine. The vestibule was filled with dark smoke. I could hear the snapping and popping of dry wood being consumed by the roaring flames beneath me. I heard a pounding on the stairs growing louder and louder, and then my father appeared through the smoke. He pushed me inside the ballroom and shut the door.

He was covered with soot and char. He pressed his palms into his eyes.

"I can't see!" he cried.

He pulled his hands away and blinked hard, seeming to get his bearings.

"It's insane down there," he shouted. "The whole place is on fire. We have to get out of here."

I thought about possible routes; which stairs were the safest? Ah! The shaft. The dumbwaiter. I ran to the closet and opened the doors.

"If she didn't start it in the basement," I said, "this will get us down there, and then we can get out the cellar doors in the butcher shop."

"But you nailed it shut."

"I used brads. We can bust it open."

So that's what we did. My father kicked at the hatch door until he splintered it and could tear it away from the shaft.

"Come on," he called to Serena and Grandpa Samuel. "Let's go!"

Grandpa Samuel obediently responded; Serena moved back to the ballroom doors.

"Grandpa first," my father said, pushing Grandpa Samuel toward the shaft. "Go down as fast as you can, Dad, then wait for Trevor."

He helped Grandpa climb through the opening. Grandpa Samuel started down the ladder. When he had cleared the rungs, I climbed in after him.

"Where's Serena?" I asked.

My father noticed her by the doors and called out to her: "Serena! Let's go!"

She hesitated a moment, then opened the ballroom doors and ran off down the corridor into the burning house.

"What the hell?" my father yelled. "Serena! Where are you going? We have to get out of here!"

Time stopped for a moment as my father glanced after Serena.

"Dad! Come on!"

"Follow Grandpa down," my father commanded. "I'll be right behind you. We have to get out of the house and into the meadow. Go, quick!"

I went down, and he followed me. Down, into the hot bowels of the house. We could hear the fire raging around us. Quickly we descended until we emerged in the basement, which was warm and moist and dark. Grandpa stood waiting for us, quaking with fear. My father moved quickly to the cellar doors—he knew this place, for sure. He pushed the heavy metal doors open—the ones I couldn't get open by myself—and cool air rushed in. I helped Grandpa Samuel up the steps, and then I followed. My father stayed behind in the house.

"Come on," I called into the basement.

"She's my sister," he said, partially hidden in the shadows. "I promised her I would save her."

"Dad—"

"I have to try. Don't you understand? I raised her."

"Dad, she doesn't want to survive this."

"I have to—"

"We've come this far! We can't go any farther!"

"She's my sister," he repeated. "I love you, Trevor, but please understand that I have to try. If I don't find her right away, I'll come back. I'll meet you in the meadow."

"You can't go back in there!" I screamed, frustrated that he wouldn't come out of the shadows, and yet also afraid to go in after him. "You'll die!"

"One quick look," he said hurriedly, stepping back into the darkness. "Then I'll meet you in the meadow."

And he was gone.

I didn't know what to do. Chase him down? Grab him by the ankles as he climbed the ladder in the chute? Pull on him until he fell on top of me, then hit him on the head and drag him out of the basement? I couldn't do that. And even if I could, he would have found a way around me. Because he was committed to something—a promise he had made—and he wasn't going to stop until he had fulfilled it, as Ben wasn't going to stop until his promise had been fulfilled.

I took Grandpa Samuel by the elbow and guided him to the meadow until we were far enough away to feel safe.

"Where's Jones?" he asked me.

"He went after Serena."

"He came to save her. That's why he came home."

"He came home to see Isobel again," I said.

From the meadow, the house was alive with orange flames licking up the sides of the broken windowpanes. I could hear the shattering of glass and small explosions of things bursting from the heat. Quickly the fire spread. From room to room to room. From the first floor to the second to the third. I scanned the area for my father and Serena, hoping to see them running from the burning house, but they were not to be seen. I prayed to someone—I prayed to Ben—that somehow my father and Serena would be saved. But I felt no cool breeze on my neck. I felt only the blazing heat as Riddell House burned.

45

SAILING AWAY

Oh, Mom. How many times had you told me the story of how you fell in love with Dad? When you told it, something about you changed. Your face would relax, and your voice would soften, almost like you were feeling the emotions all over again. I liked it when you told it to me, because it made me love you. It made me love you and Dad.

But the night Riddell House burned, you weren't there. So I had to tell the story to myself.

You were studying at Harvard—"reading," I would say, if I wanted to sound like a Brit—working toward your Ph.D. in comparative literature. You were so smart, speaking French and Spanish in addition to English. Studying your Dickens until you knew everything there was to know about Pip and his motivations. You were quite proud of yourself, young and saucy with the perfect accent that drove men crazy, flouncing about Cambridge with the world at your feet. You'd made something of yourself despite your upbringing, all those brothers and sisters fighting for the handful of biscuits you had to share with your weak tea. Your father read electric meters for a living, which didn't amount to much. Your mother altered women's clothing. You read books constantly, for which friends and relatives alike mocked you. "You'll never amount to anything, reading all those books," they said. "You need to learn to type!" You knew that reading would get you everywhere. It would take you around the world! And so it did.

Scholarships to the best schools. Accolades and awards. They were all shocked, weren't they? Their crooked British grins slapped from their crooked British faces. When you came home from Oxford for the holidays, your mum sat you at the head of the table. She had you tell stories of your travels to your brother and sisters, and she made them listen to you with a silence as stony as the walls of your simple farmhouse. You smoked cigarettes and decried the narrow-mindedness of the university regents, who kept their men's and women's colleges separate. You teased the boys from school who used to tease you. You blew on their necks and nibbled their ears until they were reduced to quivering puddles in your hands, and then you dropped them to the packed earth and left them there to evaporate; you left them wondering when you had become so smart and so beautiful and so cruel.

You took the scholarship offer at Harvard. You taught Cervantes and Robbe-Grillet to freshmen. You labored over your dissertation. And then you realized it was all for nothing. One day, reading yet another of thousands upon thousands of blue book essays you'd graded over the years, you had an epiphany: if you had to read another essay that compared and contrasted the significance of honor and society in *Tristan* and *King Lear*, you would pluck out your own eyes! ("Out, vile jelly!")

That summer, you took a waitressing job in Newport, Rhode Island. Your best friend's family were members of a yacht club, and her father got you a job in the cocktail room so you would get bigger tips. Men with thick fingers patted your tight bottom, which was safely tucked into tight white polyester slacks. Your petite figure looked good in your regulation navy-and-white skintight polo shirt, and your long neck was such a temptation with a yellow kerchief knotted around it. Your dark hair was bobbed and you had your English accent and you did quite well for yourself, didn't you? Until it all came apart at the seams.

He was swarthy and wind kissed, and his eyes shot beams of light at you when he turned them on beneath his long lashes and dark brow. He was wearing open-toed leather sandals, which was not allowed on the deck. He was wearing trim shorts that exposed his muscular legs. Again, not allowed. His arms were filled with an understated power—not thick and bulky, but with every muscle vibrating beneath smooth, tanned skin. They all gathered around him. You didn't know why—was he somebody famous? Why would the members allow such a flouting of the rules? They pulled up chairs, the metal feet scraping the deck, ten of them, twelve. Then more came, and they pulled tables together to accommodate their numbers—strictly against the rules. You went to the bar over and over again to retrieve gins with tonic. How many runs did you deliver? And pretzels and peanuts and cocktail mixes, members arguing over who would buy him his next drink. Each time you placed a cold drink before him, he smiled at you with his eyes until you had been reduced to a puddle yourself. You were captivated, entranced. You had to have him, as did all the others, the board members and committee members and senior members in good standing.

"Who is he?" you asked one of your co-workers as she gazed at him from a distance.

"They call him Jones," she said.

"What does he do?" you asked.

"Me, if I have anything to say about it," your co-worker said.

She had no idea who she was up against.

It was an accident, you say when you tell the story. There are no accidents, Dad, the onetime superstud says. You came around the corner with your tray of drinks and ran right smack into him, soaking him in gin. The chairman of the board swiftly and severely reprimanded you, but Jones cut him off.

"Please don't do that," he said. "It was my fault; I was looking down. I hope I didn't injure the young lady. Please. There should be no crying over spilled gin."

Someone laughed at his joke, and the tension was defused. The chairman gave you the key to his office and told Jones where the guest clothes were, the ones he kept in case someone showed up without the proper attire, or tripped and fell off the dock, as sometimes happened. As you unlocked the door to let him inside, he placed his hand on your shoulder.

"I would like to take you sailing," he said.

"I would love to go sailing with you, Mr. Jones," you replied.

"Sunset, then?"

You had to scramble to get someone to cover the rest of your shift. You waited for him on the dock, and he led you to an exquisite wooden sailboat. You'd never seen something so beautiful. He gave you a thick sweater because you had worn a light dress to impress him with your girlishness. He warned you it would get cold on the water. And you sailed with him out onto Narragansett Bay as the falling sun set the sky ablaze.

"Is this your boat?" you asked him.

"No," he replied. "I built it. The owner let me take it out as a favor."

"No offense intended, Mr. Jones, but I don't know what it is you do. Build boats? Are you famous?"

"I have a bit of a reputation," he said, modestly omitting that his rapidly spreading reputation was in having a unique and special touch with the creation of wooden sailboats, such that the fabulously wealthy patroness Greta von Tiehl, granddaughter of the founder of the yacht club at which you worked, had commissioned one of his hulls. Which was what the fuss was about.

He turned the boat in to the wind and let the sails luff, and they made a loud clapping sound. He sat down next to you and touched your face with his rough fingers, but the roughness felt good to you; it felt like home.

"Are you enjoying our sail?" he asked.

"I am enjoying it, Mr. Jones," you replied. "But I wish I knew your given name. You've only been introduced as Mr. Jones."

"You know my given name already," he said. "You know everything about me already."

He kissed you, and you kissed him, and the sail clapped as if in applause.

And you, my dear mother, were in love.

46

AFTER THE FALL

I don't know how long Grandpa and I stood there watching. Five minutes. Thirty minutes. An hour. I don't know, because I was numb. In the distance, I could hear sirens. A neighbor must have seen the smoke and flames; a neighbor must have called. The sirens were getting closer. I heard a loud boom, something exploding. Part of the roof collapsed, shooting sparks high into the air. Some of those sparks settled on and ignited other parts of the shake roof. More fire. A hot summer: no rain, and a wooden firetrap of a house. It wasn't long until a wall collapsed, and then more fell in on itself. The fire trucks arrived, but the firefighters seemed baffled by the rage of flames with which they were confronted; they had no tools to fight such an inferno. Forest-fire helicopters would have been of little use; thimbles of water thrown on a volcano by tiny men with tiny buckets.

I watched the firefighters as they mounted an attempt, despite the odds. They were going to try, because trying was what they were supposed to do. But they all knew already. Everyone knew. Riddell House was gone; there was nothing left to save.

Brother Jones did not escape Riddell House that morning. Nor did Sister Serena.

For a few days after the fire, I imagined that my father and Serena had escaped together. Maybe they had used a secret back staircase to exit the house. Maybe they ran away, escaped down the creek to the railroad tracks, and hopped a freighter bound for a distant land. Maybe they were dancing this very minute to old records they found at the local Goodwill in whatever town had accepted them as strangers. Maybe they would live happily ever after.

But I wasn't allowed to cling to that fantasy for long; their remains were discovered. The investigators from the city identified them by their teeth. Even Serena, as untraveled as she was, had dental records; thus was the evidence. Thus was the proof.

Because the earth calls. The soil, the rocks, the clay. It calls to us to remind us, to make sure we remember. The earth will ultimately win. It always does. We will, all of us, end our lives here. Even the birds.

FINAL REUNION

"What happened after that?" Beth, my younger daughter, asks me when I've finished my story.

She's sitting in the tall grass of the meadow of The North Estate Park, where we've come as a family to scatter the ashes of my grandfather— her great-grandfather—Samuel Riddell, who has recently passed away. Though we have spent many years in England and, later, in Connecticut, my grandfather's final wish was to have his ashes scattered at The North Estate.

Beth, who just turned eleven years old, looks positively like an angel, all long blond hair and tanned skin, and a white, willowy dress. All blue eyes and freckles and a bit of mischief in her smile.

"Did Grandma Rachel come to collect you?" Belle, my older daughter, asks. Belle is less girlish, and more like my wife, I think. A bit more forceful, a bit more tenacious; feminine, to be sure, but with an edge.

"She stayed in England," I say. "She sent her brother to collect me, though I'm sure I could have handled it. She didn't want to confront certain things, I think."

"Is that why she walked away when you started telling the story?"

"I don't know," I say. "Probably. I stopped trying to figure out my mother a long time ago."

"Where is she?" Belle asks.

"She went that way," Sophie, my wife, answers, pointing to the edge of the woods.

"If you follow the steps down into the ravine, the creek will take you out to the sound," I explain to them. "But if you follow the path out to the bluff, there's a gazebo that has an amazing view. If it's still there."

"You answered Belle's question, but you didn't answer mine," Beth complains.

"I'm sorry, honey. What was your question?"

"What happened after that? What did you do after the fire?"

"We did what Ben wanted," I said. "That's why this is all a city park now, with the parking lot and the signs and the plaque that says THE NORTH ESTATE. And then Grandpa and I got on an airplane and flew to England to live with my mother. And then I grew up. And then I fell in love with your mother, and we had babies—you two. And we've been living happily ever after ever since."

I pull Sophie to me so our hips bump, and I kiss her with theatrical passion so the girls think I'm kidding, but I really do mean it. I mean every bit of it. I love her so much I can hardly stand to look at her. (Sometimes I'm amazed that I can feel such feelings, but I know they exist inside of me, whether or not I am able to communicate them to those I love.)

"Gross," Belle says, an appropriate reaction from an adolescent girl.

"What about Ben?" Beth asks, unfazed. "Is he still here?"

"No," I say. "Grandpa and I set him free."

"How are you so sure?" Belle asks defiantly.

"Because I saw him go. It took them a long time to put out the fire, and what was left of the house was very hot for many days. That's why it was so difficult to find my father's and Serena's remains. But the evening after the fire, as the sun was setting, I went back to the house—as close as I could get—"

"Where did you sleep, if the house burned down?" Belle asks.

"They wanted us to go to a motel, but Grandpa Samuel refused to leave. He insisted on staying in the cottage. Neighbors brought us camping equipment—lanterns and a butane stove and sleeping bags—and food. We camped inside the cottage; it wasn't that bad. Anyway, that evening I was so tired, I wanted to sleep for a week. But my father and Serena were still missing, so I couldn't sleep. I snuck out of the cottage and went back up to the house to—I don't know why I went, actually—to feel what it was that I had lost? As I stood there, looking at the smoldering remains of a once-magnificent house, I felt a breeze on my neck—"

"There's always a breeze when he arrives," Belle whispers to Beth.

"When *who* arrives?" Beth whispers back.

"When *Ben* arrives. Duh."

"That's right," I say. "There's always a breeze when Ben arrives. I looked behind me, and he was standing next to me like I'm standing next to you."

"What did you say to him?" Beth asks.

"I told him he could go. The house was gone, and Grandpa had agreed to turn the land over to the city, and so there was no reason for him to stay any longer."

"But your dad died," Beth points out. "And Serena, too. Weren't you sad?"

"I was very sad—"

I stop, surprised by the upwelling of emotions I feel at this moment. I have rationalized my father's and Serena's deaths for so long, they have become the stuff of legend in my mind. Their deaths were necessary, I've always told myself, to free me, and to free future generations of Riddells from the burden Elijah carried. It made so much sense to me, I thought I was beyond the emotion of it. But standing on the bluff and talking to my daughters about it catches me off guard, and I have to take a moment to gather myself.

"My father promised to save Serena," I say, finally. "He had to try. He couldn't *not* try."

I pause and rub my chin, wondering if my daughters can understand what I can't fully understand. Sophie puts her hand on my shoulder and squeezes.

"What did Ben do?" Beth asks.

"He nodded to me. He knew the debt had been settled and he could go off to find Harry, or do whatever was coming next for him. He walked across the meadow to the edge of the woods. I saw him disappear into the woods right over there. See that tall tree? That's his tree."

"That's Ben's tree?" Belle asks.

"You *climbed* it," Beth says reverentially, which makes me smile. "To the very top!"

"And then I watched Ben climb that tree to the very top," I tell them. "He held on up there, swaying in the breeze, for quite a while. Then he reached up with his hands and he took hold of the sky. A gust of wind came and swept him from the top of the tree, and off he flew."

They follow my finger as I point in the direction I saw Ben depart.

"He didn't fall?" Belle asks.

"No. He didn't fall. He flew off into the sky until he was so small I couldn't see him anymore; then he was gone."

None of us speaks for a long time. Minutes, maybe. We look at the grass, we look at the trees. We look at Puget Sound and the Olympics. We wander a few feet from each other, but we still remain a unit; we stay close. We look at the sky, and at the path of Ben's flight. In a sense, we celebrate Ben's liberation with our silence. I like to think so, anyway.

"We should visit the graves," I say after a time. "Up on Observatory Hill. My father and Serena and Ben and Harry are there, with my grandmother and great-grandfather, and great-great-grandfather, too. And then we can go down to the beach."

"The *beach*," Beth cries emphatically. "Finally!"

"I'll take them to Observatory Hill," Sophie offers. "You should go find your mother. You can meet us at the beach."

"When are we going to scatter Grandpa Samuel's ashes?" Beth asks.

"In a bit," Sophie says. "After we see the gravestones."

She gives me a kiss on the cheek.

"Go," she says. "Find your mother and look after her."

The three of them head off across the meadow. I watch as they cross over the footprint of where Riddell House stood twenty-three years ago. No evidence of Riddell House exists, but I can still see it. It's still there for me.

I make my way down the path until I emerge from the brush and see the gazebo. She's there, as I knew she would be; she's not the beach type. But I'm curious to see that someone is with her.

She's sitting with a man. He reaches for her hand, and she offers hers so that their fingertips just barely touch.

I'm curious for a moment, but not really. I know that man. And I know that gesture. I remember it from a motel next to a highway in New Haven.

My mother, after all this time, has been reunited with my father.

I almost laugh, but I don't because I don't want to give myself away. I watch them together, talking and laughing and talking more. And then she leans her head into his shoulder. And then she lifts her face and he kisses her. They are complete. They are together.

I don't want to disturb them, but I want to speak with my father as well. I want to tell him that I understand his promise to Serena, and his promise to himself, and his promise to the dead, and that his leaving me was not an act of abandonment, but an act of love. I want to tell him that I know. But I don't interrupt them, because I've already told these things to my father. I've felt his presence at different times and different places in my life. I know he's been with me to see things and hear things, to share things with me and my family.

But my mother has been so alone—and so angry—because she has never found reason to believe. I see now that everything is different. I know, because I see her with him. And if I see her with him, then she must see him, too. Which means she believes.

And my thoughts are so loud that I disturb the moment, I ruffle the energy of the universe. For everything has everything to do with everything. My father turns and looks over his shoulder at me. He smiles and nods, and then he fades into the air. He dissipates like smoke and is gone; my mother is alone in the gazebo.

I approach. She hears me and turns. She's wearing her sunglasses, and she has such a peaceful smile on her face; she seems somehow more contented than I've seen her since I was a child.

She is still my mother, with her sharp features and taut skin and dark, curly hair. The way she'll talk and talk around things until you throw up your hands and say, it's fine, I give up, you win. But she isn't the same mother I remember from so long ago in Connecticut. She's not the mother who took me fishing when I was a kid because my father was obsessed with building his wooden boats so he didn't have time for me, or the mother who loved the first apples of fall when we would go on our drives upstate—the snap and explosion in your mouth of that first, tart bite—or the mother who would cry and be unable to finish reading me *The Giving Tree*, because she was so overcome with sadness at the image of the old man sitting on the stump. That mother died in the fire with my father.

But I don't know. As Serena would say: There's so much we don't know, how can we pretend to know anything at all? Serena, with her forever blue toes.

I sit down next to my mother in the gazebo. She looks over at me, takes a quick breath, and purses her lips. Through her sunglasses, I see tears welling in her eyes.

"I know," I say.

"You know what?" she asks with forced nonchalance. "What do you know?"

"I saw him with you."

She shakes her head quickly. The tears in her eyes bulge, and then flow down her cheeks from behind her dark glasses.

"I can't believe it," she says, and she leans against my shoulder, which catches me by surprise, because she has never leaned on me before.

"It's impossible, isn't it?" she asks. "He was here, wasn't he? Didn't you see him?"

"I saw him."

"So you are my witness."

I put my arm around her, and she folds into me, and I like the feeling of being able to comfort my mother. It's not something I've felt before.

"He said he knew that one day you would bring me back here," she says after a time.

"I would have brought you sooner, but you—"

"But I refused," she says. "I was afraid. I didn't know he's been waiting here for me all along."

"No, Mom, he hasn't been waiting. He's always been with you. You just haven't been able to see him."

"It's The North Estate, then, isn't it?" she asks, sitting up straight and composing herself. "I was sitting here, and I felt a breeze. It was cool and pleasing. This place is so beautiful and I could feel the magic of it, and then I heard someone say my name and I turned, and he was there. He sat with me, like you're sitting with me. We talked, and he held my hand. Then he kissed me and told me that he will always love me and I should never be afraid."

I rub my neck, thinking of my father and my mother together again. What I had always wanted. I finally did it; I'd accomplished my goal. Although not very conventionally, I suppose.

"The last thing he said was, 'My peace I give unto you,'" she says. "I must have looked confused, because he told me you would know the significance of those words."

My peace I give unto you. My mother sees my reaction, and it's her turn to reach out to me. She holds me and rocks me back and forth like a mother should. All of the emotions about my family, my father, but also the generations before him, Elijah and Ben and Harry. Isobel and Serena. My grandfather and his fingers. Everything spills out of me until I feel purged.

"Those words are from the book by John Muir that Ben wanted me to see," I say when I am ready to speak again. "*The Mountains of California*. I tried to tell you about Ben's messages when I was fourteen, but you wouldn't believe me. Those are the words Dad said to his mother moments before he euthanized her. I saw it in a dream. Those same words are on Benjamin Riddell's tombstone, who died in 1904. *My peace I give unto you*."

"I'm sorry," she says. "I thought you were making up stories—going a little crazy in this house with your imagination and nothing to keep you occupied. I didn't know *how* to believe you. I'm so sorry."

"None of that matters because you believe me now."

And so we sit silently for a time, as the minutes stretch out against Puget Sound. We indulge in the Zen of Grandpa Samuel. Until my mother finally breaks the moment.

"Your story," she says. "I didn't think I could stand to hear it."

"I know."

"I apologize for walking away like that. I shouldn't have."

I allow her admission to pass in silence.

"I'm ready now," she continues with a resolve in her voice I haven't heard since my childhood. "I'd like to hear your story now."

I consider her request. She has never wanted to hear the story of that summer. Whenever I've started to tell it, she's shut me down or walked away. But now?

"I just finished telling it to the girls," I say. "And it's pretty long and involved. There is no short version."

"Tell it to me anyway."

"I have to find them. We have to scatter Grandpa Samuel's ashes. And we need to get some lunch—they're going to be hungry soon."

"Look," she says, pointing. "Look out there to the beach. You can see the children from here. And Sophie is with them; she's so lovely; she is the hand on your tiller, Trevor, and it is a steady hand she uses to guide you. Your father and I are very proud. They're having fun down there, can't you see? We have time. Tell me your story, won't you? I believe I am meant to hear it here, in this place."

I am conflicted, as always, by my mother. In some ways, I suppose I've blamed her for my father's death: she didn't come with us that summer, and so she failed to protect us. A childish reaction, but an honest one. But I also feel that what happened that summer was part of my journey, as it was part of hers. As it was part of my father's. I remember Ben's words to me, written on dozens of Post-it notes, telling me that we *are* connected, despite our need to disbelieve, our need to doubt. And I understand, finally, that I've been trying to tell my mother this story since it happened. All I've wanted was for her to know it, and for us to feel our connection again. This is why I came back here with my family, with my grandfather's cremated remains, with my mother's agnosticism. To see one more time if my mother could believe me. And I remember the single word that Isobel said to me when I saw her in the flash of a match struck at the top of a dark stair.

"Faith," Isobel said.

And so I will tell my mother the story she wishes to hear, because I have that. I have faith.

"It was a long time ago," I begin. "Before technology changed the world—"

A train blows its horn in the distance, interrupting me. The train is saluting my great-great-grandfather Elijah Riddell, and so, in a way it is saluting me. I have fulfilled the wishes of Elijah and his son Ben; I have moved on from my past, as others in my family have been unable to do. I am always looking to my future.

I catch sight of the long freighter snaking along the tracks several points down. The trains will forever salute Elijah Riddell.

"Tell me the story, Trevor. Please."

"A man brought his son to see The North Estate for the first time," I continue, and I reach for my mother's hand. "The boy stood on the dusty gravel drive and looked across the meadow, and what he saw was stunning—a mansion larger than anything he had seen in his life, and it was made entirely of trees, as if it were still growing out of the forest from which it was taken. . . ."

ACKNOWLEDGMENTS

David Braun, Lisa Eeckhoudt, Kassie Eveshevski, Laurie Frankel, Joe Fugere, Gary Grenell, Derek Humphry, Molly Jaffa, Brian Juenemann, Jonathan Karp, David Katzenberg, Jeff Kleinman, Tim Kovar, David Massengill, Jim Minorchio, Kevin O'Brien, Robert Pace, Sandy and Stephen Perlbinder, Alan Rinzler, Jenn Risko, Bob Rogers, Marysue Rucci, Howie Sanders, Jennie Shortridge, Yolanda Stein, Deon Stonehouse, Dawn Stuart, Trish Todd, Melissa White, the Center for Wooden Boats, Folio Literary Management, HistoryLink.org, Seattle7Writers, Shoreline Historical Society, the wonderful people at Simon & Schuster, my team at Terra Communications, Tree Climbing Planet . . .

My fearless sons, Caleb, Eamon, and Dashiell, who are destined to change the world for the better . . .

And my brilliant and beautiful partner in life, without whose editorial input, criticism, ideas, passion, and unrelenting encouragement, this book would have remained forever hidden away in a secret room of my soul . . .

Drella

ABOUT THE AUTHOR

Garth Stein is the author of three novels: *Raven Stole the Moon, How Evan Broke His Head and Other Secrets,* and the *New York Times* and international bestseller *The Art of Racing in the Rain.* He also conceived The Novel: Live!, a writing marathon to support literacy, which spawned the novel *Hotel Angeline: A Novel in 36 Voices.* Before turning to writing full-time, Garth worked variously as a documentary filmmaker, a playwright, a teacher, and as a stage manager on Theatre at Sea cruises for The Theatre Guild.

Garth is cofounder of Seattle7Writers, a nonprofit collective of sixty-five Pacific Northwest authors dedicated to fostering a passion for the written word and strengthening ties between readers, writers, librarians, and booksellers. He lives in Seattle with his family.